SAVAGE TRACKER

MAFIA WARS - BOOK FIVE

MAGGIE COLE

PULSE PRESS

PROLOGUE

Selena Christian

YOUNG AND DUMB IS ONE OF MY MOST HATED PHRASES. IT feels carefree and implies it's okay to make mistakes, since you have all the time in the world to turn around and fix them. For me, young and dumb can't be my reality. I'm not stupid. No matter what names my ex-husband, Jack Christian, berated me with, I never completely believed him when he screamed at me. He would say I was an idiot or declare I was thick as pig shit. He did it so many times, it should have affected my self-esteem, but for some reason, I wouldn't give him that. Buying into the notion that I somehow became stupid seemed to be another thing he wanted to take from me. He stripped me bare of everything I had, but my belief in my brain was one thing I refused to sign over to him.

Looking back, I ignored every warning my family gave me regarding my ex-husband. So maybe I do fit the phrase, but

1

when I think of my situation, I can't help gravitating toward different ones. What comes to mind is blinded by love, or even young and naive.

When you're barely twenty, living at home with your parents, and waitressing on a small Greek island, the promises of a fairy-tale life from a man like Jack are hard to resist. In my case, it was impossible.

One look at Jack and I wasn't sure what to do with the flutters in my stomach. There wasn't any doubt he was older, more worldly, and held ridiculous amounts of power. He appeared to have money, but it wasn't something I cared too much about at twenty. Sure, the gifts he bestowed on me for the three weeks he was in town, I accepted with excitement. Everything about him, and us, was a whirlwind of adrenaline and new feelings I never had before. Every breath he took held confidence I hadn't witnessed in a man before. He could charm anyone with his smile alone. Add in his American accent and dominating presence, and I didn't stand a chance. At the time, I didn't even understand what his powerful aura meant. It made me feel danger and safety all at once. He said he would protect me and never let anyone hurt me. I was his and would always be. If I hadn't been so innocent, I would have understood the balance that needs to exist between a woman and a man when one party has the virility Jack does. Unfortunately, I knew nothing about what happens when you devote your life to a controlling man who doesn't put anyone's needs but his own first.

He made a vow to me. If I moved to the United States and married him, he would give me an incredible life. We would have it all—together. I could barely breathe, contemplating the thought of him leaving and never seeing him again. It was too much to bear. So, against my parents' wishes, I let him sweep me off my feet and away to another continent.

My father was so angry, he wouldn't allow my mother or siblings to come to the wedding. Jack was only a few years younger than my father. My mother begged me not to move and claimed, "You're throwing your life away if you marry him."

Nothing was farther from the truth as far as I was concerned. Jack *was* a life. He represented passion, excitement, and adventure. His world was something I never saw before and probably never would without him. And dating him was unlike any Greek boy I had ever met. He wasn't my first sexual encounter, but I could have been a virgin. Everything with Jack was like experiencing it for the first time but without the awkwardness. He knew what to do, how to do it, and my body submitted to him in ways I didn't know were possible. When he commanded me, I liked it. I assumed it was because he was a real man and knew what he wanted. I never understood why tingles lit up my nerves the first time he made me kneel in front of him. Or how pride swept through me when he taught me how to open up the back of my throat to take all of him in my mouth. If anyone else had bossed me around, it would have offended me. Not with Jack. I couldn't get enough and would have willingly knelt on the floor all night if it made him happy, when we first met.

We got married in the United States since Jack said it was easier to get me a green card if we married there instead of Greece. We had a huge wedding. All of Jack's business associates filled a six-hundred-person ballroom. I knew no one except Sister Amaltheia, a nun from the Greek Orthodox church. Jack allowed me to attend the first six months we were married. I wasn't super religious, but it helped me when I felt homesick. The members almost all spoke Greek. I would go to mass then the luncheon, but Jack soon stopped me from going. He claimed it was cutting into our weekends, and when he wasn't working, my time was his. I was his wife, his property, and he never let me forget it.

Our life was nothing like the world he promised me. We married within weeks of arriving in the United States. The day I vowed to love, cherish, and obey him was bittersweet. It pained me my family wasn't here, but I was determined to have the fairy-tale life Jack promised me.

It didn't take long before Jack's charming, loving demeanor changed. I soon found myself in a foreign country with no money, no family, and a husband who was a monster. The real Jack wasn't kind, funny, or loving. The real Jack was physically violent, into punishments that included mind games, and knew how to rip my heart out. He could continue to tear it to shreds even when I thought he couldn't destroy it anymore. He didn't use safe words. He controlled everything in my life, right down to allowing me to use the bathroom. And after the first few months of marriage, I never again felt safe.

When Sister Amaltheia had me meet with Kora Kilborn, my divorce attorney, it gave me the courage to divorce him. I still didn't have money and couldn't move out though. Somehow, Kora convinced his attorney to have him stay out of my side of the house, or it was going to hurt his company going public. I'm not sure how she did it. Some nights, he would scream at me through the locked doors while I sat on the other side, shaking. I would call Kora, and I assumed she called his attorney. Jack's phone would ring, and I'd hear him bark out, "Larry."

It was a miracle when Sergey Ivanov swept me away from Jack and gave me a safe place to stay. It was more than I could ever ask for, and when the divorce went through, I bought the condo from him.

I've never had anything that's mine. The amount of money I got from the divorce is more than I know what to do with. Besides buying the condo, Kora wanted me to keep a body-guard with me when I go out, in case Jack still wanted to come after me. I wasn't sure how to even arrange anything like that, but Kora called and said Sergey had men in his employment who could be my bodyguards if I wanted to hire them. Of course I said yes, thankful I had it taken care of and could breathe again.

My condo is perfect. It's brand new, luxurious, and in down-town Chicago. My building overlooks the river. I'm on a lower floor, but there is also a rooftop. It overlooks all of Chicago and Lake Michigan. It's one of my favorite spots to hang out. Plus, I keep hoping maybe I can meet some new people.

Over the last ten years, I've gotten used to loneliness. When I escaped Jack, I promised myself I'd never let another man control me. But lately, I can't stop the urges I feel to fall into my old role. Several times, I've had to erase my search history, stopping myself from going through with the crazy ideas in my head. They started as seeds, but they've germi-nated and keep growing.

I'm trying to kill off every vivid dream and urge I have to fall back into anything I had with Jack. Ninety percent of what we had, I shiver in fear thinking about. Yet, the other ten is clawing at me. It's digging into my loneliness, and I'm not sure how much longer I can last. I wonder if I gave in to my desires if I could scratch my itch and then move on with my life.

It's wishful thinking. Stepping into the past can only harm me. How can it not? But all I keep thinking about is how much I need it.

I've tried to distract myself. I've joined my new friends' weekly yoga and brunch routine. I found a few places to volunteer. I even ordered the faucet I wanted to replace. It's the one I wanted instead of what Jack insisted we buy.

When I ordered the faucet, I never knew it would be the catalyst for so many things. The moment it arrives, delivered by the sexiest man I've ever laid eyes on, I feel the earth shift under my feet. The icy-blue, piercing eyes, wavy dark hair, and tattoos covering his neck, arms, and hand scream he's more dangerous than Jack could ever be. His charming smile and dimple barely peeking out on his cheek make his threatening aura seem nonexistent. It's extreme opposites and makes him the most intriguing person I've ever met.

Don't be a fool again. My intrigue with Jack only got me in trouble.

He speaks, a thick Russian accent rolling out of his mouth, and my knees go weak. "I'm Obrecht. This was delivered to my penthouse by accident. Are you remodeling?" His eyebrows lift, and his eyes linger on me.

God help me.

There's nowhere to hide. It's like I have a sixth sense for it. His expression is dominant. It's full of everything I'm craving. I hold the door handle tighter, stopping myself from dropping to my knees and waiting for him to give me a command.

"No." My voice squeaks, and I clear my throat. "No, only the faucet."

Amusement twinkles in his eyes. "Do you have a plumber coming?"

I shake my head, forcing myself to maintain eye contact with him instead of staring at his feet. I admit, "I thought I would call Sergey and ask who he recommends."

His lips twitch. "He'll recommend an Ivanov."

"Oh. Okay." I stare at him, not moving.

"I'm an Ivanov." His lips curve more, and my heart skips a beat.

I tilt my head. In a teasing tone, I reply, "So you live in the penthouse but are the plumber?" It comes out, and my face heats when I realize my voice sounds flirty.

"Nope. Just for you." He winks, making my cheeks blaze with fire.

I'm not supposed to let anyone inside. Jack isn't a man who loses well. Kora has warned me not to let my guard down. "Let me see your ID, please."

He puts his arm around the box and reaches into his pocket. He hands me his wallet. "ID's in there."

Holy mother of all accents.

"Do you always let strange women go through your wallet?" I ask.

His eyes trail over me. "No. Once again, only you."

I breathe through my pounding pulse and open his wallet.

His license reads Obrecht Ivanov, has the penthouse address, and his birth date shows he's forty-five. His picture is just as panty-melting gorgeous as the man in front of me.

Who on earth takes panty-melting photos for their ID?

How is he forty-five? I wouldn't have thought over forty.

I glance at him and open the door wider. "Come on in. I'm Selena. Sorry to be rude."

"Being cautious isn't rude. Don't ever apologize for it," he firmly states.

"Are you Sergey's brother?"

He snorts. "Cousin."

"Oh." I stare at him, and there's a moment of awkward silence. I reach for the box, but he doesn't let me take it.

"I've got it. Is it for your kitchen?"

"Yes."

"Okay. It shouldn't take me too long." He walks past me into the kitchen.

My eyes follow him. My pulse increases as I stare at the way the fabric of his T-shirt stretches perfectly over his taut flesh. And I've never really checked out a man's ass before. If Jack had caught me looking at any man, he would have punished me. I've seemed to have forgotten all my previous rules. I can't tear my gaze off every part of him, including the tattoos on his arms and neck.

He spins and catches me ogling him. My cheeks heat again as he says, "Do you enjoy living here?"

I snap out of it and join him in the kitchen. By the time the faucet is on, I'm in trouble. The air is electric. Every urge I've tried to kill resurfaces like a ripple in the water. It expands until I feel as if I'm about to burst at the seams.

When he leaves, disappointment hits me. The loneliness I've struggled with annihilates me. For hours, I stare at the faucet thinking about him and what it would be like to kneel in front of him.

That's part of Jack's world. I'm out of it. I cannot go back.

Every time I go anywhere over the next week, I look for Obrecht. When Monday night comes, I can't handle it anymore. I pull out my laptop and look at the clubs I know Jack never goes to.

Just this once. I'll get the urge out of me. Then everything will be okay again.

No one will know me.

The lingerie I bought when I went on a shopping spree for my new post-divorce wardrobe stares at me in the closet. I slowly put it on. The membership I applied for online to get into the club deals with code words. I memorize them all. I give my bodyguard instructions to stay in the car and not escort me inside. He argues with me, and I remind him I'm the client.

"You will get me fired," he says in his thick Russian accent.

I point to the door of the club. I hate being rude, but he can't come in, and I can't chicken out. I need this. "Do not go in there. If you do, there will be consequences."

That's the thing about "if." It represents scenarios that aren't real. The consequences I imagined weren't anything like what happened from leaving him outside.

Every single promise I made to myself to get rid of my itch once and for all becomes impossible to keep. Obrecht Ivanov is part of my "if." He's the equivalent of being on a deserted island and having a lifeline. Once you grab hold, it's impossible to let go until someone makes you.

But I should never have forgotten Jack's threats. For the first time, I wonder if I've become stupid. The dumbest thing I ever did was believe I could escape the wrath of Jack Christian. I should have known how deep his ties with the devil are and that he can reach me anywhere. Maybe I allowed myself to live in a fantasy world because I knew Jack would never stand for another man having me. If I had admitted it to myself, I'd have to let Obrecht go. Seeing each other was a dangerous game. I told him about Jack, but he didn't flinch. He wasn't scared, nor was he willing to let me go. All it did was make him fight harder to claim me.

Once you freely give yourself to someone when you never thought you would, in ways you never imagined you could, unleashing yourself from them is impossible. When someone else comes along and grabs hold of your leash, the thing you cherished suddenly becomes a nightmare.

Obrecht Ivanov

HUNDREDS OF MEN AND WOMEN HAVE BEEN THE SOURCE OF MY focus over the years for various reasons. Some I needed to find so my cousins, brother, and I could destroy. Others were more of a safety precaution. I followed their every move to know for sure what side they were on. If I had to take a guess, I'd say half are still alive, and the others we deemed enemies. Those men, we didn't hesitate to torture for information and kill. The planet is a better place without them walking around. The third category are the few who I've kept my eye on to make sure they were safe.

Sergey's latest request fits into the last bucket, and it's having effects on me I don't like. From the moment I saw her golden legs stretched across a lounger, an uncomfortable feeling hit my chest. I didn't even see her face. I only saw those long, sun-kissed legs. And they aren't legs full of bone. They're a perfect sculpture of flesh and bones with a tad of meat on them.

Jesus Christ. How did I miss seeing her?

I ignored the feeling and left the rooftop. I was covered in sweat and didn't need to be late. Then I stepped out of the shower and got a text.

Sergey: *Can you do me a favor?*

Me: *What's that?*

Sergey: *The woman on the roof...can you keep your eye on her?*

My heart beats faster. The vision of those perfect legs enters my mind again.

Me: *Want to tell me why?*

Sergey: *She's about to settle a divorce, and her ex isn't going to be happy.*

Please tell me her ex isn't who Sergey had Adrian digging up dirt on.

Now I get to be a babysitter.

At least she lives in my building, and it'll make it easier.

He wouldn't ask if it weren't important to him.

Me: *This guy knows where she's at?*

Sergey: *No. I'll send you his picture. If you see him hanging around, let me know.*

Me: *Done.*

He sends me a picture of Jack Christian from his company website, and my anger bubbles. It's the same bastard Adrian's had numerous trackers follow. Adrian and I spent the previous night in an underground private club, documenting proof of Jack and his friend, Judge Peterson, engaging in all kinds of debauchery. I took a quick nap when I got home, went for a workout on the roof, and didn't know anyone was in the corner loungers.

And now all I can imagine is how angry this douchebag is for losing possession of those sexy legs.

Me: *Looks like a prick.*

Sergey: *Yep.*

Me: *What did he do to her?*

Sergey: *I don't know all the details, but he hurt her.*

One thing an Ivanov doesn't handle well is men hurting women. There's always a rage stewing in my gut. Most of the time, I keep it under wraps. The times I get to engage in it are a sweet release for me. I'd be more than happy to show Jack Christian my wrath.

Me: *Then I kind of hope he tries to come near her on my watch.*

Sergey: *Thanks. Message me if you see him.*

Me: *Will do.*

I didn't ask Sergey any more questions. I didn't need to. Tracking is a world I've submerged myself in. I took care of my pending business and spent the rest of the night digging into everything I could find on Jack Christian and his wife, Selena.

From the outside, he looks like the typical, highly successful entrepreneur with a trophy wife. Selena is about twenty years younger than him. She's beyond gorgeous with an exotic flair. Before I read anything about her, I guessed she is Mediterranean. Her Greek olive skin is flawless and her brownish-green eyes have an innocence about them. But I'm not ignorant. She can't be that innocent if she was married to Jack. He surely put her through hell before she escaped. Her long, dark, wavy hair is thick and hangs a few inches past her breasts, which are so perfect, I wonder if they are real or fake. Her nose is long and straight, perfectly positioned on her oval-shaped face. Her pouty lips are always smiling. To the public, she looks happy, yet I see the sadness in her eyes. It's a skill I have, almost as if I can read people's emotions.

For several weeks, I watch her, keeping my distance so she doesn't see me. The urge to meet her gets so pressing when I speak to our security team in the building, and a package arrives for her, I act in haste. I sign and tell them I'll deliver it.

It's uncalculated, impatient, and stupid on my part. For several hours, I play the role of her friendly neighbor, helping her switch out her faucet. She doesn't seem bothered and isn't questioning how long I'm taking to do it. Of course, the constant breaks to talk to her aren't helping me finish.

Selena's eyes travel to my feet again. It's like the universe has to play with me. I've been restraining myself from commanding her to kneel from the time she opened the door.

Who am I kidding? I've wanted her to kneel since I looked at those legs.

Besides the time spent under her kitchen sink, every look she gives me is restricting the room in my pants.

She's not a bottom. She's just flustered.

I wish she'd stop blushing every time I look at her.

She looks like she's in her early twenties, not thirty.

How was she with that monster?

What did he do to her?

Is she biting on that plump little lip of hers to mess with me?

I groan inside. Even after several hours, I'm still not used to her intoxicating scent of lavender and something else I can't put my finger on. It has a woodsy flair. "All done," I proclaim and begin to break down the boxes.

"Thank you. I-I can do that," she says with her angelic voice. It's another thing driving me crazy. She sounds so young, and it's the icing on the cake. She stands next to me and picks up the faucet box.

There's an aura of energy around her.

Few people have it.

Annika had it.

The thought of the woman I spent years loving, the one I bought an engagement ring for with the notion of spending the rest of my life with, makes my stomach clench. It happened years ago when I was in my twenties. It's why I don't date. If someone could penetrate my life so thoroughly without me having any clue who they really were, then something is wrong with my radar.

After Annika, I became a tracker. I wanted to know how to dig up every bit of information on someone I could so no one ever could trick me again. Annika was a Petrov, placed to mess with me because I am an Ivanov, which made the betrayal even worse. I already hated the Petrovs based on what they did to my cousins and aunt. It happened right before my sister Natalia was kidnapped, raped in one of the Petrov whorehouses for over a year, then left on our doorstep, dead. Extreme guilt eats me daily. I didn't have the ability to see who Annika was or find Natalia the year she was missing. If I had had the skills back then that I have now, Natalia would still be alive. Annika would never have been part of mine or my family's life. And to this day, I always wonder if Annika had anything to do with Natalia's kidnapping.

As good as I am at tracking now, I still don't trust myself around women. So, my sexual needs are taken care of at specific, exclusive clubs where I have a membership. Members can only engage with those they bring into the club or other members tested for STDs every month. If you bring a guest, only you can engage with them. You can't return to the club until you submit new documentation after several weeks pass. Members and guests wear wristbands, so it's clear who is who. In the club, I can get what I want, when I want it, and don't have to deal with all the relationship issues or risk of betrayal. One thing I've learned about humans is we all have weaknesses. Those are things I'm used to exploiting to get whatever information I need. I won't allow anyone else to fool me ever again. I'm the one in control, and it's going to stay that way. The ramifications are too horrible to allow myself to fall into any more traps.

Selena tries to open the other end of the box, but it's glued. Her nail breaks, and she winces. "Ouch!"

"Let me see." I pick up her hand. The middle of her nail has a line going through it. A large piece of her acrylic is on the counter, and I squeeze her finger, trying to apply some pressure to it to take away the sting.

She slowly glances up at me, her doe eyes shifting from brown into a slight green color. Her long lashes frame them. Her mouth forms a tiny O, and her cheeks flush.

Kneel, I say in my head and reprimand myself.

I need to get out of here.

How was she with Jack Christian?

She was only twenty when he married her. The thought of her ten years younger and being swept away from her family, under his exclusive control, makes my stomach churn. From all the information I've gathered, Selena's family is no longer in the picture. It's not unusual for a man like Jack to break off all ties to their wife's family and friends. From what I can tell from the several weeks I've observed Selena, she doesn't have many people in her life. I added another one of our guys to watch her when I can't, and so far, she hasn't left the building very much. The few times she left, she had one of our guys with her. She only went to Kora's office. Last week, she went to get her nails done. All her groceries are delivered, and she stays between the roof and her unit.

I don't move, continuing to keep my hand wrapped around her finger. She's barefoot, and although she's tall, the top of her head comes to my chin. "Does that feel better?"

"Yes," she breathily says, and my dick twitches.

"Guess you'll need a nail appointment. I'm only good for applying pressure," I tease and wink.

She blurts out, "I'm sure you're good at other things." Her face turns crimson when I cockily raise my eyebrows. She quickly looks down, and I groan inside again.

Kneel, my dorogaya.

I need to get out of here.

I release her finger. "I'll handle the boxes." I step out of her aura and focus on the cardboard. When I finish, I put it under my arm. "I'll take this to the recycle bin."

"Umm, okay. Thank you. This was..." She glances at my feet again before straightening up and looking me in the eye. She smiles. "It was very kind of you and nice to meet you. Is cash okay?"

"Cash?"

"To pay you for installing the faucet?"

I snort. "No payment. I'm happy to help. If you need anything else done, give me a shout. Why don't I leave you my number?" My pulse hammers in my throat, and I wonder if she can see it.

She tries to bite back her smile. "Sure."

I take my phone out of my pocket. I already have her number, but she doesn't know that.

She rattles it off. I pretend to put it in. Then I text her.

Me: *It's Obrecht.*

"There. Now you can get a hold of me if you need anything."

"Thanks. What other services do you provide?" she teases.

Everything you need.

Not helping matters.

She's fifteen years younger, is freshly divorced, and there's no way she's into what I am.

Plus, she's my neighbor. I don't need her getting the wrong idea and thinking I'm available for a relationship. A woman like her surely is going to want a commitment with whomever she sees.

I shrug and walk to the door. I need to get out of here and cool off before I say something I regret. "Seriously. If you need anything, I'm only an elevator ride away."

"Thank you. You don't know how much I hated that faucet."

"Hmm. I'm not a faucet connoisseur, but what was wrong with it?"

Her face darkens. She takes a deep breath. "This may sound stupid, but this condo is the first thing I've ever owned. It's different than where I used to live, which is why I love it. But that other faucet, well, it...umm...it was the same as the one in my other house. I don't want any memories of that place." She turns away as if ashamed of her past, blinking hard.

I stare at her until she turns back. When her eyes meet mine, there's so much pain in them.

What did that bastard do to her?

"You have good taste. The new one looks great, much better than the old one."

"Yeah?"

"Yes."

She hesitates then says, "Thank you again. You've made my day."

Against my better judgment, I scan her body. When I get back to her face, she's holding her breath. There's a fire in her eyes.

Kneel.

Time to go.

"Have a good day, Selena."

"You, too, Obrecht."

I spend the rest of the day trying to turn off my thoughts about her, but I can't stop wondering what she would sound like saying, "Yes, sir."

2

Selena

IT'S INCREDIBLE HOW A FAUCET CAN BRING YOU SO MUCH happiness. Of course, the memory of Obrecht's T-shirt halfway up his ripped torso, lying on the floor with his head inside my cabinet, doesn't hurt. I drink my coffee, staring at the silver metal and thinking about the tattooed stars he had running down his perfectly sculpted V, past the waistband of his pants.

For the last three days, all I can think about is him and the way his dominant eyes trailed over my body. It's not helping the loneliness I feel most of the day or the aching need growing bigger and bigger each passing second.

Jack controlled every part of my life, including my body. I don't want to have these thoughts. I should return to the way things were before him, but I was young and not very experienced. I'm not sure what I'm supposed to return to. In many ways, I feel as if all I've ever known is Jack. The two boyfriends I had before him are faint memories.

Instead of just researching sex clubs, now I imagine Obrecht going to one with me and being my Master. It's driving me insane. I even dreamed about it last night.

I need to get out of my house and find something to keep me busy so I can get my mind out of this rabbit hole I can't seem to escape. Now that my divorce is over, I want to start living again. I'm not sure what it looks like, but my life is a blank slate, ready to have color on it.

It's only been a few weeks since my divorce. The day after, Kora's office informed me she had a family tragedy take place and won't be working for a while. Her assistant informed me they were sending a car and a bodyguard to have me sign more forms. After I hung up with her, Sergey called and told me what happened. Then he repeated what Kora told me a few days ago. He said the driver and bodyguard are his, and he thought it would be best if I continued to use them. He offered to do it for free, but I insisted on paying him, since I now have more money than I'll ever spend.

Jack never shared anything with me regarding our assets. He was so sure I was his property and would never be able to leave him. We didn't even have a prenup. When Kora dug up his assets, I was in shock. I had no idea how wealthy Jack was or what I was entitled to get from our divorce. All I wanted was my freedom and not to be homeless on the streets or deported back to Greece.

And that's another issue. Jack always used my lack of citizenship as a threat. If I go back to Greece, I would have nowhere to go. My family disowned me. I'm not the first family member that's happened to, either, so I'm fully aware once my father cuts you out, that's it. There is no changing my situation. They gave me the ultimatum to leave Jack and come home, or that was it. I was already trapped. Jack knew my every move. I had no money or access to it. He even recorded my phone calls. I was Jack's wife in public and his property at home.

The sun shines through the window, warming my skin. The river has a few kayakers on it, and several pedestrians are walking as runners pass them on the pavement. I shower and get ready for the day. My nail is still not fixed, and I catch it while shampooing my hair and wince.

I need to fix it.

It's still not super safe to go places.

Why did I get them in the first place?

Jack required me to have my nails perfect at all times. During the divorce, they grew out, and I eventually peeled the remainder off. My natural nails never felt as nice as when I had my acrylics. Kora told me what time Jack would be in her office signing the divorce papers, so I went to get them as a mini celebration.

Now, I'm regretting it. I shouldn't have done anything that required maintenance. It means I needed to go out in public, and it's still something I'm a tad anxious about even though I have a bodyguard. Plus, it feels strange having someone follow me.

I finish getting ready, grab the envelope stuffed with statements on accounts and other assets I now own, and my laptop. While I love my condo, the best thing about it is the rooftop. During the day, most residents are working, so it's usually empty. It's beautifully designed and overlooks Lake Michigan and the city. An artificial turf, playground equipment, and a decked-out gathering area fill the space. I avoid my usual spot, which is in the corner with loungers. Instead, I sit at the table in front of the gas fireplace and spread out my papers. I take a handful of glass rocks in the centerpiece and put them on each form so nothing blows away. It's not a breezy day, but I don't want to take any chances.

One of my goals is to understand what is on each of these pages. I don't want to be left in the dark anymore, but after trying to decipher things, I wonder if I'm attempting to do something impossible.

Did Jack only keep our finances away from me because I don't understand a word on these statements?

Is this something I need special skills to understand?

Am I expecting too much from my uneducated self?

"Ugh," I groan in frustration and put my hands over my face.

A deep, Russian accent hits my ears. It's as if life gets injected in me. "What's wrong, Selena?"

I put my hand over my forehead to shield my eyes from the sun and look up. Pure male sweat glistens all over Obrecht's rock-hard upper body. I gape at him, counting not six but eight muscles on his abdomen. My eyes drift to the bulge growing in his pants, and I glance at his feet.

Please tell me to kneel.

Snap out of it!

I quickly glance at his cocky smirk.

Oh jeez!

"Something wrong?" he repeats.

"I..." I clear my throat then motion to the papers. Heat rises in my cheeks. "I've lost my eggs and baskets! Do you need a degree to read these things? Maybe I'm not smart enough to understand what's on them?"

Amusement crosses his expression. "You've lost your eggs and baskets?"

"Oh, sorry! It's Greek. It means I'm completely lost and confused."

He sits next to me, and when the scent of his sweat flares in my nostrils, I lean closer and inhale it deeper. My lower body pulses so fast and hard, I squirm in my seat. He points to a statement. "May I?"

Should I let him see what I have?

He owns the penthouse. He's got money, so what do I need to worry about?

"Help yourself. I was about to throw it in the firepit."

He chuckles and picks up the form. After a few minutes, he scooches closer and puts the paper in front of me. He turns his head so it's right next to mine, stares at my eyes, then mouth, then back to my eyes.

How are his eyes so blue? Are they even blue? It's like looking through glass with only a hint of a blue tint.

"There are some things on here you should sell."

"Sell?" I reply, feeling panic creep in my chest.

He nods. "Yes." He points to several symbols that mean nothing to me. "This, this, and this."

"I don't know what those letters are," I admit.

"Do you want me to explain it to you?"

I glance around the roof. No one is up here. "Do you have time?"

"Sure. Once you get it down, it'll be easy."

"Okay. Thank you. I…um…" I gaze at the sparkling water on Lake Michigan. I don't know what is too much information to spill about my life and what isn't. The guy already changed my faucet, and now I'm having him teach me how to read financial statements. He's going to think I'm utterly incapable of doing anything.

"Haven't ever seen these before?"

Shame, fear, and anxiety fill my chest. I turn and blurt out, "My ex-husband didn't show me any of this. Maybe it's because it's too complicated? I should probably pay someone to just take care of this for me." I start to stack the papers.

"Stop," he commands.

It's deep and dominant, and my core stirs. Flutters take off so fast, I get dizzy. I immediately stop and bow my head, waiting for further instructions.

Tell me to kneel. Oh God, please tell me to kneel.

My lips begin trembling. The spot between my thighs gets damp.

Neither of us moves. It feels like forever as I sit there, papers midair, head lowered, body quivering for him to give me another command.

He finally puts his hand over mine, and a soft whimper escapes me. More heat rises to my cheeks, and I continue focusing on the table.

"Look at me, Selena."

I obey, and my heart pounds harder. His eyes swirl with power, control, and danger. Jack had all those things, but Obrecht has something else, and it confuses me.

Kindness fills them. It chokes me up.

"Breathe," he commands, and I immediately take a few deep ones. In a calm, soothing voice, he continues, "Good. Now, why don't you let me organize this for you and then we can go through them. You don't have to manage any of this if you don't want to, but you do need to know how to read them. If you don't, you won't know whether to fire or keep a manager —if you go that route," he says.

"O-okay."

He points to the papers in the far corner. "Hand me those."

I do as he asks.

He smiles. In a teasing tone, he says, "Glad you know how to follow orders, dorogaya."

"Dorogaya?" I ask.

"Dear. Darling. It also can mean expensive."

My insides spin, doing the happy dance. "Well, I'd rather be expensive than cheap, right?" I flirt and bat my eyes.

What am I doing?

His lips twitch. "I wouldn't put you and cheap in the same sentence." He studies me another moment then redirects my gaze to a stack of papers. He points to each one. "Each of these piles represents a different asset. Retirement accounts, non-retirement accounts with investments, liquid bank account reserves, real estate, and privately held businesses."

My anxiety grows. "Am I supposed to already be over-whelmed?"

"Yep." He chuckles then leans into me and lowers his voice. "Since you're smart, don't get used to it. You'll be reading these like a pro soon."

"Really?"

"Without a doubt." He spends two hours explaining how to read the statements and giving me his advice on what he would do if it were his money.

"Is this what you do for a living?" I ask.

"No." He puts all my statements back into the envelope.

"Well, I don't discriminate. Can I hire you?" I tease but am also serious.

His smile is so Mr. Nice Guy, I'm confused again by how he can be when he has so many qualities I fell for in Jack. "I'm here to help if you need it, Selena."

"How do you know all this if it isn't your work?" I ask.

He shrugs. "I guess you could say it's a hobby. I keep up on it. It's always kind of interested me."

"Wow. Well, it's impressive." I reach up to his neck and trace over one of his tattoos. Jack didn't have any tattoos, neither did any of the boys I dated before him. Obrecht is covered in them. "Is this a snake?"

"Yeah."

I lean behind him and at the face of the snake. It's fiercely opening its mouth and sticking out its tongue. It makes it feel like it's ready to bite you. "Why is the face on your back?"

"Snakes are everywhere. It's a reminder for me to never turn my back."

A chill goes down my spine. It's how I feel about Jack.

He picks up my hand. "How's your nail doing?"

Heat courses my face. "Still broken." I feel embarrassed I haven't fixed it. If I had let this go this long with Jack, I would have been severely punished.

He tilts his head and runs his finger over the jagged edge. "Looks dangerous."

"I'm going today to fix it," I blurt out.

His phone buzzes, and he releases my hand. He glances at it then back at me. "I need to shower and get ready for work."

I rise. "Me, too. Thank you again."

"Not a problem."

He puts his hand on my back and guides me to the elevator. I almost sink against him but refrain. There is an elevator for the penthouse and one for the rest of the building. He makes sure I'm in mine before getting on his. When the door shuts, I exhale and stare at my nail. I decide I need to stop being a scaredy-cat and get it fixed. When I call to schedule the appointment, the lady asks, "Is there any other service you would like today?"

I glance at the website where I got the phone number off of and reply, "Yes. Can I get a massage, pedicure, facial, and wax?"

"Mmm..." The line goes silent for a moment. "Does it matter the order?"

"Nope. I've never spent the day at a spa before, so I don't know the difference," I admit.

"Aww. You're going to love it!"

"I'm sure I will."

"Great. You're all set. Please arrive at least fifteen minutes early to fill out paperwork." She goes through the other amenities then I hang up and leave.

Over the next few days, I decide it's time to start painting my canvas. I go on a shopping spree, picking out all the clothes I used to want to wear but was never allowed. I book a hair and makeup appointment and get a cut. I have the stylist turn my black hair a blondish-brown. I buy all new makeup to go with my new look and have the girl show me how to apply it.

Every night, the ache in my loins grows bigger. I study one of the clubs I never went to with Jack and decide to be a big girl and take the plunge. I apply for a membership. It's not hard. All I have to do is fill out the form and pay the fee.

I add condoms to my next grocery order. Jack made me get the shot. He didn't want kids. It wasn't something we discussed before we got married, but I'm fortunate he didn't want them. Our house wasn't somewhere I would have felt safe with my children, and I'm glad I don't have to still deal with Jack. I continued getting the shot. Maybe some part of me knew I would eventually need the protection.

I don't want to think about what could happen to me, but this urge I have to be touched is spiraling out of control.

I'll just be a responsible person, and everything will be fine. Only one time and then I can get rid of this itch.

Pending flashes across the screen, along with a smaller print that reads, "We will email your membership within 24-72 hours of approving your application."

When my head hits the pillow, nervous anticipation fills me. I go back and forth in my head, wondering if I dare to go. I finally fall asleep, wondering about Obrecht. There's so much that's confusing me. The more I try to figure it out, the worse my obsession gets.

I thought he might be a Dominant, but he could never be my Master. They aren't nice. They don't do selfless acts for their slaves. The kindness residing in his eyes doesn't exist in any Dominant I've ever met.

How can I crave him when I'm so desperate to submit?

It doesn't make any sense. All I know is I can't stop thinking about submitting. Even though he can't give me what I need, my obsession with him won't go away.

31

3

Obrecht

EVERYTHING ABOUT SELENA MAKES ME UNCOMFORTABLE. SHE'S breathtakingly beautiful, innocent at times, and complies with all my demands instantly. My gut wants to tell her to kneel and see what she does, but my brain tells me she's an abused woman who had to do whatever her husband said for fear of her life.

She can't possibly want or need what I'm aching to do with her. The obedience I'm seeing has to be a residual effect of her abusive husband. I'm not sure the details of her and Jack's relationship, but I'm sure she was at his beck and call, ready to comply with every demand he wanted. In some ways, her behavior reminds me of what the BDSM community would determine as a bad Master/slave relationship. What that almost always equals is a slave who didn't give their consent to be one or a Master who abused one who did.

Either way, the way she bows her head and stays frozen at times, waiting for me to give her the next order, tells me I need to handle her with care.

It also makes me hate myself. Her submission heats the blood in my veins so hot, it bubbles whenever I'm around her. I can't stop envisioning her kneeling before me, naked, in some sexy outfit, or even in what she's wearing now.

She's a smart woman. There's no way she would ever want to be in any submissive position ever again. And I'm an expert at reading people's emotions. When she bows her head, I see a whirlwind on her face. Confusion and pain laced with hope and lust.

It's a residual effect, I reprimand myself for the millionth time. It's early in the morning. I woke up and couldn't fall back asleep. My stomach growls. I finally give up and decide to go to a cafe down the block. I can catch up on the latest in the stock market and have some breakfast.

I step off my elevator at the same time Selena appears. I haven't seen her in a few days, and my heart hammers in my chest. She's lightened her hair, has on makeup, and looks as if she's about to walk the runway. She's wearing jeans and a form-fitting T-shirt, but her face is photo-worthy stunning.

"Wow," I say before I can stop myself.

"Morning. What's wow?" She smiles.

I swallow hard. My mouth goes dry. "Isn't it too early in the morning to look that nice?"

Her face blushes. My balls remind me how blue they are, and I try to stop my wandering eyes from continuing to check her out like a dirty old man.

33

"Thank you. I...umm..." She scrunches her forehead and bites her lip.

"You lightened your hair?" I ask.

She reaches up and twists a chunk of it around her finger, and I about shoot my wad in my pants. The number of times I've dreamed of tugging on those locks is too many to count. She meets my eyes. "Yes."

"It looks great on you."

"Thanks."

I continue to tease her. "Are you going to a magazine shoot at five in the morning?"

"No. I-I couldn't sleep, so I thought I would go for a walk."

Matvey, one of our bodyguards, steps next to us and nods to me. "Obrecht. Ms. Christian, do you need an escort somewhere?"

She nervously glances between us then explains, "I know it looks weird, but my ex isn't very nice. Kora and Sergey thought—"

I put my fingers over her lips and instantly regret it. They're the softest pair of lips I've ever touched. "I deal with Ivanov security. I know why he's here."

Her hot breath exhales on my fingers, but then she furrows her eyebrows again. "So, you know everything about my ex?"

About how he's the biggest dickhead on earth, and I still haven't decided what to do to him yet or when for hurting you?

34

"No. I know you hired Ivanov security to assist you, but that's it. I don't know what happens in anyone's marriage."

It's a half-truth. I know way more about her, but I'm not going to admit it.

Her lashes flutter, and I'm unsure whether my answer made her more or less worried and embarrassed. I glance at Matvey. "Give us a minute."

"Sure, boss." He goes back to his position with the security team that runs the building.

I shouldn't do it. My impulse control is nonexistent like it always is around her. "Did you eat breakfast?"

"No."

"I'm going to the cafe down the street. Want to forgo Matvey and have breakfast with me?"

Her lips turn into a tiny smile I can't seem to get enough of. A buzzing grows in my nerves. She glances at Matvey then nervously asks, "Will it be safe? Sergey said I shouldn't go anywhere without one of the guys."

"I'll make sure you're safe." I'll also have my guys inconspicuously following us in case her ex tries to take me out to get to her, but she doesn't need to worry more.

She bites on her lip for a brief moment. "Okay. I'd love to go."

Score!

What am I doing?

It's just breakfast.

I need to stay away from her. I spent all night concluding that observing her from afar was better for both of us. Instead, I give Matvey a knowing look, then guide her out of the building and down the street. As we walk, I keep my hand on her back. I tell myself I'm just protecting her, but all I want to do is lower my hand into her jeans and palm her heart-shaped ass, then stick my tongue down her throat until she moans.

The cafe is close to our building. We don't say much until we're seated in a booth. I intentionally have them seat us in the back of the restaurant, where I can see everyone coming and going and the street even though my guys are outside.

"Coffee?" the waitress asks, holding a pot in her hand.

Selena and I flip our cups, and she fills them. "Do you know what you want?"

I don't need to look at the menu, but Selena glances at it, then back at the waitress, with a stressed look on her face.

"Can you give us a minute, please?" I ask.

"I can just pick something," she anxiously blurts out.

I reach across the table and put my hand on hers. It's another thing I shouldn't do, but my body doesn't seem to be able not to touch her. "Take your time." I nod for the server to go.

"I'll be back soon," she chirps.

"I'm sorry. It won't take long. I—"

I squeeze the top of her hand. "Take your time, dorogaya."

She stares at the menu, and tears brew in her eyes. Her lips quiver, and a wet drop plops on the menu. She quickly wipes her face.

What did that bastard do to her?

"Look at me," I demand.

She immediately locks eyes with mine.

"There's no rush. If there was, I would tell you we were on a time constraint."

"I-I'm sorry. I don't know what's happening right now." She turns her face less than an inch then freezes, as if waiting for me to permit her to look away and fighting the urge not to move.

I reach across the table and swipe under her eyes. She softly gasps, and her pert breasts rise. I glance quickly at them then back at her face. "Tell me what's going on, and don't worry about what you assume I'll think."

She swallows hard.

I gently prod her. "It's okay, my dorogaya. Tell me."

"I...um...my ex used to get upset if I wasted his time."

Asshole. Like any time spent with her is wasted.

"So, you had to know what you were going to order without looking at the menu?"

"Yes. But...um..." She takes another deep breath. "I'm not picky, but I had a strict weight I had to stay at. He didn't want me to waste his money by not eating, so I always had to eat everything on my plate. He always ordered me a side salad with no dressing or an egg if it was breakfast."

My timeline to deal with Jack just got shorter. I maintain my calm composure and ask, "And what would happen if you didn't eat everything?"

More color drains from her face. "I would get punished."

"And what did that look like?"

The waitress comes back. "Are you ready?"

I don't budge my eyes from Selena's. "No. I'll let you know when we are," I tell the server then wait for Selena to answer my question.

"Do I have to answer this? May I have permission not to answer right now?" she whispers.

My dick pulses against my zipper, and I officially hate myself. We aren't in a relationship of any sort. I'm not her Master, Dom, or even boyfriend. She has no reason in this circumstance to ask me for permission.

It's clear to me Selena is still traumatized from whatever it is Jack made her do. I also know what she needs to hear to relax. "Yes, you may answer at another time."

She releases the breath she was holding and smiles. "Thank you."

"You're welcome. Now what kind of breakfast food do you like? And please don't say you're ordering an egg."

Her lips twitch. "Do you have something against eggs?"

"Nope. But if you lost any weight, you'd be one of those boney girls."

She raises her eyebrows. "Boney girls?"

"Yep. No curves, nothing to hold on to, all bones, and nothing exciting to look at, like right now."

Her face flushes. "I need to lose weight right now. I've gained fifteen pounds since I left Jack. I... I haven't been as conscious about my diet."

"You must have needed it, then. All I see when I look at you is a gorgeous, curvy, Greek woman."

What am I doing?

Telling the truth.

I need to shut up.

Her lips twitch, and golden flames erupt in her eyes. "Your accent is sexy."

"Mine? I don't have an accent," I attempt to say in a serious tone and as American as I can.

She laughs. "Your non-accent needs some work."

"I know. It's horrible, isn't it?"

She winces. "I say stick with your current Russian-American voice."

"Ouch." I pretend to stab my heart. "You still have your Greek accent."

Pride and sadness both cross her face. "I used to pretend I was American when I was little. I learned English in school and had the English version of the movie *Dirty Dancing*. My friends and I would always practice. It came in handy when I moved."

"I can put Patrick Swayze's moves to shame."

She bursts out laughing. "No, you can't."

"Oh, but I can."

"Seriously?"

"Yep. Maksim decided we all needed to learn to dance for Sergey's eighteenth birthday. We each had to pick out a type of dance and learn it. It took about a year."

Amusement fills her face. "Wow. What dance did you pick?"

"What do you think I chose?"

"Mmm... Cha Cha?"

"Boris picked that."

"Merengue?"

"Nope. That was Maksim's."

"I give up. What did you choose?"

I lean closer. "Mine was the tango."

"Interesting."

"Sergey's was way more fun."

"Why, what was it?"

"Hip-hop."

She laughs again, and it's like striking a match. If I could listen to her laugh all day, I would. "Are you telling the truth?"

"Yep. I have mad skills," I claim. "Of course, they come out in full force after several shots of vodka."

Her eyes widen. "Well, of course."

I take a sip of coffee. "So, you knew how to sound American before you came here, but why did you say it came in handy? You don't like your accent?"

"No. Not exactly." She nervously shifts in her seat.

"Are you going to tell me?"

She hesitates for so long, I think she's going to tell me she wants another pass. But she finally says, "Jack said his wife wasn't going to sound like a poor foreigner. He said I needed to sound American when we were around anyone. I-I worked really hard to obey him, but it was one of the easier things I had to do."

My stomach clenches and I fist my hand under the table. What she just told me is loaded in so many ways. And I don't want to think about what she had to do that was harder.

Stay calm. Don't freak her out.

I'm going to kill her bastard ex.

I take a deep breath. "So, you always wanted to come to America?"

She shrugs. "It always seemed so exciting compared to my little town of Pelion. It's a beautiful place, but when you're a child, you can't appreciate it."

"You ever go back?"

Her face darkens. "No. My family disowned me. There's nothing to go back for."

I blurt out, "Because of him?"

She nods.

"I'm sorry to hear that. I'm sure it wasn't easy on you." I take a sip of coffee but only to try and avoid her seeing any rage fuming from me.

She doesn't say anything.

I point to the menu. "Let's decide what we're eating before the server comes back." We spend a few minutes looking at the menu. When Selena looks up, I ask, "Do you know what you want?"

"Yes."

You better not order an egg, baby girl.

I motion to the server to come back, and she does. With a big smile, she asks, "And what can I get for you?"

"Selena?" I nod.

"Can I have the number six but no onions, please?"

I scan the menu to six, which is a Denver omelet.

"Sure. Wheat, rye, or white toast?"

"Rye, please."

"And you, sir?"

"Number two with wheat, please."

"Very well." The server leaves.

Selena takes a sip of coffee then asks, "Are you always up this early?"

"It depends. Not usually."

"You're in security, then?"

I'm unsure why I don't just say yes and leave it at that, but I reply, "Yes, but I mostly track."

Surprise fills her face. "Oh? What does track mean?"

What am I doing? I don't tell anyone this.

My pulse increases when I realize the predicament I'm now in. *What is it about this woman that makes me lose my head all the time?*

"When our security is worried about someone, I'm the person to dig in and find information on them. Sometimes, I go find them."

"Like a hunter?"

"I guess that's a good way to think of it."

She taps her cup. "Is it dangerous? It sounds dangerous."

I shrug. "It's not for the faint of heart."

"How did you get into something like that?"

My chest tightens. I finally reply, "It's a long story."

She tilts her head. Sympathy fills her expression. "You don't want to talk about it, do you? It's something painful?"

"Why do you ask that?"

She reaches across the table and puts her hand on my cheek. It creates lightning in my veins. She strokes her thumb under my eye. "I saw it here." She lowers her hand and traces my jaw. "And this clenched, as if you were about to grind all your molars out."

"You read people well," I tell her and feel an immediate loss when she removes her hand from my cheek.

"I'll tell you a secret if you want to know."

I lean closer and tease, "Well, don't keep me in the dark."

She licks her lips. My dick officially feels suffocated as she says, "I have these dreams."

"Sexy dreams?" I wiggle my eyebrows.

Her face turns as bright red as the booth we're sitting in. "I'm not talking about those ones," she blurts out then her face turns a dark crimson.

Come to daddy.

I'm such a pervert.

"But you're admitting you have porno-style dreams?"

She laughs. "Did I ever use those words?"

"Just need a yes or no, my dorogaya."

She covers her face in her hands.

No fucking way.

Jesus. This woman.

"Tell me more about these secret sexy dreams," I say then take a sip of my coffee.

She composes herself then says, "As I was saying, I have these dreams, and it's like I can see what's going to happen."

"So, you can predict the future?"

She tilts her head. "Are you making fun of me?"

"Nope. My mother has a sixth sense, too. She always knew when we were about to get into trouble," I admit. "So, how often do you have these dreams?"

"Maybe once or twice a year. I'll dream something, and it'll come true. Before I met Jack, I dreamed I was going to meet this bad man. He was faceless, and of course, I didn't put two and two together it was him. But I also dreamed I was moving to the United States. And the night before Sergey showed up outside the courthouse, I dreamed of the condo. I was there, drinking coffee and staring at my new faucet, which has happened pretty much every morning since you installed it."

"And you think about me since I delivered it, right?" I tease and wink.

Her face flares with heat again. "It was very kind of you."

The server refills our coffee. "Breakfast is coming out soon."

"Thank you," Selena says to her with a smile, and I nod.

"You have a gift. Do you ever dream things that aren't true?" I ask.

She puts both hands around her mug. "Oh, yeah. All the time. But my dreams are usually pretty vivid. I was—" She stares at her coffee.

I want to know whatever it is she doesn't want to say. So, in my most demanding voice, I firmly order, "Tell me whatever you were going to say. You can look at me, or you don't have to."

I officially just became a complete asshole by putting her in this position. If she was involved in what I think she was, she'll tell me.

She stays focused on her coffee but instantly replies, "I was always scared of sleeping. Jack said I talked in my sleep at times. One time he woke me up, and I don't know what I said, but I got punished for it."

I try again. "How did he punish you?"

"Please. I don't want to discuss it. If you make me—"

"You don't have to," I assure her, unable to handle the scared look on her face.

"Thank you, Mast—" She freezes, and mortification consumes her face. Her forehead wrinkles, and she gapes at her coffee.

She almost called me Master.

There is no more wondering what type of relationship she had with Jack. He was her Master, and she was his slave.

How much more damage did he do that I can't even see?

One thing I know for sure, Jack and Selena weren't in a healthy, consenting Master-slave relationship. I'm not a fan of the Master-slave concept, but I know for some people it works. But only in consenting situations.

The server brings our food over. "Is there anything else I can get for you?"

"Selena?" I ask, staring at her as she continues to gape at her coffee.

Her long lashes lift, and she pins her conflicted orbs on mine, then barely whispers, "No."

I turn to the server. "Thank you. We're good." When I turn back to Selena, she's staring at her plate.

I need to bring her back to me.

I reach across the table and tilt her chin up so she has to look at me. "Only eat what you want, okay?"

She takes a deep breath and smiles, "Okay. Thank you."

"What are you doing today?"

She shrugs. "I don't know. I think I might check out college programs."

"Really? What kind?"

"I don't know. I just feel like I need to do something with myself. I-I feel kind of antsy lately. Too much free time."

I spend the rest of breakfast keeping things light and trying to avoid any hard topics. When I drop her off at her apartment, she seems like her normal self.

It doesn't fool me though. Her scars run deep. I still have no idea what he did to torment her.

One way or another, I'm going to find out. Then, I'm going after Jack Christian. Anything he did to her, I'll make sure he experiences before I take every ounce of oxygen he has out of his lungs.

4

MC

Selena

I'M MORTIFIED THE REST OF THE DAY. I CAN'T STOP THINKING about my breakfast with Obrecht and how I almost called him Master.

Jack made me call him that. He told me when I was allowed to call him Jack and when I wasn't. If we were alone, I had to call him Master. It didn't matter if we were in the bedroom or not. I learned early on in our marriage what happened when I didn't call him the appropriate term.

Why am I so screwed up?

Obrecht isn't Jack. He's dominant but continues to show me his kindness, so he can't be a Dom or Master.

But he directs me at times as if he is.

All men must do that, and I couldn't see it, since I was with Jack for so long.

Obrecht must not know what to think of me.

This is happening because all I can think about is him and submitting. I need to take care of this itch and move on with my life.

My laptop dings during dinner. I open it up and take a bite of my salmon then freeze. The subject line of the email says, "Membership approved."

I stare at the screen, chew my piece of fish, then swallow it. My hand shakes as I take a sip of my Pinot Noir and debate about opening it. I shut my laptop and tell myself I'm not going through with it.

It doesn't last long. My curiosity wins by the time I'm halfway through dinner, and I open the laptop back up. I click on the email.

Dear Ms. Christian,

Welcome to Club Everything. Your entry ID is 7289. Your password is *DALMATION*. This password will expire in twenty-four hours.

Just a few friendly reminders. All guests and member activities must be consensual. Anyone not acting in accordance with our policies will be banned.

Please remember the social lounge is a sex-free zone. No kissing or touching beyond that is allowed. The buffet starts at 8 p.m. each night.

Theme parties are on our website and updated each month.

If you have any questions, please don't hesitate to contact us.

SINCERELY,

The Management

I RE-READ THE EMAIL, FEELING SLIGHTLY NAUSEOUS.

I'm definitely not going to feel sexy scarfing down a buffet.

I don't understand the buffet part. Jack and I never went to a club with food, only drinks. The last thing I'm looking to do is eat at a sex club.

It's not as high-end as I'm used to.

Jack won't be at this one. Don't be a snob. There's a reason I need to do this. Once I get this out of my system, maybe then I can act normal around Obrecht.

I can't finish my dinner. I scrape my plate, do the dishes, and refill my wineglass. It's a nice night, so I turn on the indie music station and sit on my balcony.

Can I do this?

I've spent ten years in sex clubs.

Yeah, kneeling all night while watching Jack screw other women.

Or submitting to Jack in front of everyone in the club.

My confusion continues to spin. I hated everything about the sex club nights. It was Jack's way of punishing me and showing all of his friends he was my Master, and I was his slave. Lucky for me, Jack wasn't ever going to share me. So, I never had to partake in his orgies or do anything with his friends. No one was allowed to touch me, except him.

Not a bone in my body has changed. Every moment in the clubs with Jack, I detested. It's why I can't understand what is causing me to go to one willingly.

I must be more messed up than I thought.

That's it. I'm staying home.

I replay my breakfast with Obrecht and cringe. The hottest man on the planet is in front of me, and all I can do is tear up, tell him my weight issues, and almost call him Master.

He was still sweet to me.

It's why I have to take care of this itch. He's not going to give me much more attention if I don't pull it together.

Obrecht's face, with his piercing, icy-blue eyes, rock-hard body, and Russian accent coming out of his plump lips, makes me shudder. I wish I could go up to his penthouse and kneel in front of him and wait for his command, but I know my signals are mixed right now. I'm not reading anything right. I'm so far down the rabbit hole of needing to submit and wanting him, I can't think straight.

He's not a Dom or Master.

But he commands himself like one.

He can't be. He's nice and treats me with respect.

I stop myself from having a third glass of wine. It's another thing I started since divorcing Jack. He never let me consume alcohol. I don't drink every night, but when I do, one glass is usually my limit. I've already exceeded my norm, and my tolerance isn't very high.

I leave the balcony and close and lock the door. I rinse my glass in the sink then grab a bottle of water to hydrate myself.

Halfway through the bottle, I stop pacing and glance at the wall clock. *Nine p.m.*

I'll just take a shower and go to bed.

Instead of sticking to the plan, I shower, then do my hair and makeup. My phone reads 10:10 p.m.

My stomach flutters, and I go into the closet. It's like being in a trance and unable to stop yourself. I keep telling myself I'm not going, but then I talk myself into it.

The drawer I designated for my lingerie only has a few outfits in it. I pull the four out and take them to my bed. I get another bottle of water from the kitchen then come back and stare at the outfits.

Jack always made me roam the clubs naked. He knew it embarrassed me. Plus, he wanted everyone, man and woman, to see what he owned and to know only he could have me. One thing I'm not willing to do is expose myself like that. I always wanted to wear sexy lingerie like many of the other girls wore. At least then I'd have some coverage.

What look do I want?

White and innocent?

Black leather?

Gold and glittery?

Red and devilish?

I finally decide on the gold set with the bling all over it. The bottom doesn't have any fabric. Rhinestones cover gold strands and hang in one-inch rows over my booty. There's a two-inch strip for the front of my body with rows put together so close, it covers my slit but nothing else.

The bra is a similar design. A longer strip wraps from the bottom of my bra around my stomach and attaches to the front of the bottom.

I stare at myself in the mirror. It may not be much more than being naked, but to me, it feels like an entire wardrobe.

This is for me, not Jack. That is the difference.

I'm asking for trouble.

I need this.

Since I don't have a huge selection of dresses, it doesn't take long to choose. I remove from the hanger the only black club dress I bought and slide it over my body. I pair it with the new gold stilettos I bought and open my jewelry box.

Adrenaline rushes through me, and I put my hand on the vanity to keep me balanced. After several moments pass, I lift the gold collar I bought. It looks like an expensive piece of jewelry, but it'll symbolize I'm looking for a new Dom without the leash.

I redo my hair and put half of it up so it's still down, but it's out of my face.

Stay away from the Masters. Find the Doms, and you can get rid of this itch, then never do this again.

When 11:30 hits, I leave my condo. Matvey rises when I step off the elevator. His eyes almost pop open. He's quickly at my side. "Ma'am. Where are we going?"

"I'm going out. I'll have you drop me off and stay outside the building," I direct him, knowing he can't come into the club, nor do I want him to know what I do inside.

He argues with me about safety the entire way to the club, but I'm not budging. When we pull up to the address, he cocks his eyebrows at me. "Ma'am, you cannot go in there on your own."

"I can and I will," I insist.

"You will get me fired," he says in his thick Russian accent.

I point to the door of the club. I hate being rude, but he can't come in, and I can't chicken out. I need this. I use the language Jack always did when he wanted to get his own way. "Do not go in there. If you do, there will be consequences." I walk away from him and into the building.

The lobby has black walls and a reception desk in the middle of the room. A woman wearing a red lingerie set with devil horns smiles at me. "Are you a new member?"

"Yes." My stomach flips, but I give her my number and tell her the password. She reviews the rules with me then motions for me to go through the door and into the lounge.

I step through, and my nervous butterflies increase. The walls are still black. There's a bar with a bartender. He's wearing a cock cage and nothing else. Booths and tables with chairs fill the room. Candles sit in the middle of all the tables. A few people are eating from the buffet, and my stomach does more somersaults.

I feel as if the entire room is watching me. Most women wear lingerie. A few are naked. Two are wearing a dress.

I debate about what to do or where to sit. I've already had my limit of alcohol.

Several men eye me up. I go to a two-top table and sit. A waitress comes over, and I order a club soda with a lime.

I get through half my drink, watching people go through the next door. More come into the lounge, and I realize it's full.

It's time to make this happen.

I can do this.

Then why do I feel like I'm going to puke?

Find someone who looks like Obrecht. I laugh out loud at the thought. There's no way anyone else on earth looks like him or even comes close. I rise.

I'm not sure why or where I plan on going, but as soon as I do, a man leans into my ear. "What are you looking for, sugar? Whatever it is, I'm sure I can deliver."

I spin and swallow hard. He gazes over me, and I struggle to keep my eyes on him. I read the club rules. I have to consent and create my terms outside of the playrooms. I can't do it once I'm back there, or I can get kicked out of the club.

"Umm... I...umm..."

He puts his hand on my cheek, and I suddenly freak out. I spin away from him, right into Obrecht's chest. He tilts my head up and studies my face with his icy-blue flames.

My insides quiver.

"Man, I was here first," the other guy says.

Obrecht doesn't take his eyes off me. "No. I was, but it doesn't matter. She's mine, aren't you?"

Obrecht's. Yes. I want to be yours. Please make me kneel.

I open my mouth to ask him, but no words come out.

If ever a man could look into my eyes and straight to my soul, it must be him. I can't tear my orbs from his.

The other man argues. "No, I came over—"

"Kneel, my dorogaya," he booms, and my pussy clenches.

I drop to the floor, my butt on my ankles, my shoulders straight and head lowered.

"Fuck off. You know the rules," Obrecht growls to the man, and I see his feet move away from us.

My entire body feels as if it's on fire. Obrecht takes my hands, pulls me up, then leads me through the door and down a hallway. He opens another door, locks it, then moves me to the middle of the room. It's dark. The corners of the walls are neon pink, but nothing else is registering right now.

I just need to submit.

"Kneel," he demands, and sweet relief fills me.

Obrecht crouches in front of me and takes my chin in his hand. He puts his face an inch from mine. "This is not the club for you, my dorogaya. You can get hurt here. Let me take you home."

My lips quiver, and a tear falls down my cheek. I'm not permitted to speak unless he tells me to if I'm kneeling for him.

He wipes my tear with his thumb. "Why are you crying, baby girl?"

So many thoughts race through my mind, and all of them have to do with him. All I manage to say is, "Please. I need it."

His face hardens. I think he's going to make me go home. Instead, he says, "What do you need?"

My voice shakes. "To submit. I don't know why, but I do. Please."

He strokes my cheek then drags his finger over my lips.

"Will you be my Master? Please," I beg, surprising even myself when it comes out so freely.

He shakes his head. "No. You do not need a Master. You are not meant to be anyone's slave."

"But, I-I feel so lost," I admit, and more tears fall. "I need to submit."

"Shh." He strokes the side of my head.

"Please," I whisper.

He studies me then freezes. "Okay. I will be your top."

"Top? I don't understand. Do you mean my Dom?"

"Similar, except you are free to do what you want after we leave here, Selena. You are not tied to me in any way, understand?"

"Is that not a Dom? I-I don't understand," I repeat.

He takes a deep breath. "You want to submit to me?"

"Please, Ma—"

He puts his fingers over my lips. "I am not your Master."

"What do I call you?" I ask.

He strokes my cheek. "You can call me sir."

"Yes, sir." More relief floods my body. I don't know why calling him sir makes me relax or feel better, but it does.

"What are your hard limits, Selena?"

I tilt my head. "I-I... why are you asking me this?"

"So I don't do something you don't want to do."

"But it isn't my choice."

Obrecht scoops me up and carries me to a couch. He sits down and straddles me on his lap.

I gasp as my almost-bare pussy rests against his hard erection.

"You like what you do to me, baby girl?"

"Yes, sir."

"Good. If you want me to do this, I want you to understand that everything is your choice. Nothing happens unless you want it to. If I do something you don't like, you use our safe word. What should it be?"

"Safe word? I... I've never had one."

His jaw clenches again. "We aren't doing this without one. Pick a word."

"Umm...can you pick, please?"

He smiles. "Sure. Let's say faucet. And if you want me to stop at any time, you say faucet. Now tell me you understand."

"I understand, sir. I will say faucet if I want you to stop."

"Good. What do you need? Is it pain?"

I shake my head hard. "No. I don't like the pain. I kind of like some ass slapping, but nothing too hard."

"Good, my dorogaya. I'm not really into pain, so that's good."

"You aren't?"

"No."

"Wh-what are you into, then?"

"No attachments. Controlling another person, including when they can and can't come. Some mind games. Bondage at times. Toys. Penetration anywhere in your body I want, with whatever I want. Is that what you need?" He stares at me and licks his lips.

Everything he says turns me on. "Please, sir."

"Kneel," he commands.

I slide off his lap and onto the floor. He scoots to the edge of the couch so I'm between his legs. He roughly grabs my chin and pushes it up so his face hangs an inch above mine. "Before we get started, you owe me a promise."

"Sir?"

He keeps his firm hold on me, but his index finger grazes my cheekbone. "You're never stepping foot in this club again. If you want a club, I will tell you where to go, understand?"

"I'm-I'm sorry, sir. I—"

"I want to hear you promise me," he insists.

"I promise."

He licks my lips with the tip of his tongue. I moan, wanting to open my mouth but knowing he hasn't permitted me.

His Russian accent becomes thicker. "How much do you think of me, my dorogaya?"

"All the time, sir." It comes out raspy and desperate, but it's what I am. So needy for him and what he can make me do.

"The first time you saw me, you wanted to kneel?"

"Yes, sir."

"Have you touched yourself while thinking of me?"

My cheeks burn. "Yes."

"Yes, what?"

"Yes, sir."

His lips curl, and my flutters take off again. He releases my chin, sits back on the couch, and points in front of us. "Strip. Then crawl to me like the sexy baby girl you are."

5

Obrecht

SELENA'S FLUSHED CHEEKS, WARM BROWN EYES GLOWING WITH the hint of green, and long, silky hair flowing around her are enough to send me over the edge. The pounding of my blood between my ears almost drowns out the music blaring into the room. It's only another reminder of why this place is nowhere my dorogaya should be. This club is not exclusive. It appears to be for those who want that comfort. The online membership application is a joke. Anyone can get in by paying the fee at the door and answering the questions, which is only basic information.

Name.

Address.

Phone.

Email.

Do you agree to our rules?

Do you have any STDs?

No proof of anything and pay the fee. It took me two minutes to get through the door. All it does is anger me. The people coming here aren't protected. Anyone could have hurt Selena, especially with no hard limits or safe words.

What she's looking for, they don't specialize in at this club.

She could have seriously gotten injured by someone who hasn't been trained.

Like that man who freaked her out.

The swirling concoction of rage and lust mix with the need to protect her. I'm not angry at Selena. I'm pissed that this place exists, and it doesn't keep its members safe. I'm enraged at the man trying to put his hands on my dorogaya and still claim her for the night when it was clear she was fearful of him and not interested. Every ounce of my blood boils that she doesn't know her hard limits and has never used a safe word. Bile rises in my throat, thinking about what those two things meant for her.

Yet, here she is, desperately seeking out submission. All I can do is continue to kick myself. I knew all day she was fragile. When I dropped her off, she tried to put on a good show, but I could see the struggle on her face of wanting to ask me something. She kept staring at my feet, and I convinced myself it was better for her if I put some distance between us. I assumed I triggered her in some way. Hell, I felt like she triggered me, but then again, I only need to be around her for a second before my dominant side is crying out to make her submit to me. I left her at her front door and told Matvey to keep a close eye on her. He was going home to rest, and Vlad came to take his place. I had the same conversation with him and reminded them both I was to get notified wherever she went.

I cringe thinking about what could have happened to her if I had been out of town or at the garage where my cousins, brother, and I take men to torture and kill them. Those stints typically last for days, and no one's phones are on. It takes too much focus to make sure you aren't killing the guy too soon and are stretching his life out as much as possible to get the information you need.

When Matvey texted me, I was debating about going to see her. All I got was a text with the address. I immediately pulled it up on my phone, and my gut flipped.

It took two seconds to know exactly what this club was like, and not one part of me liked it.

I shoved the thoughts of her with anyone, man or woman, out of my mind, vowing if anyone hurt her, I'd kill them on sight and damn the consequences.

The next text I received from Matvey sent my vexation into overdrive.

Matvey: *She refuses to let me go inside with her.*

I was already in my car, a street away. I called him and cursed him for the brief twenty seconds before I was barreling out of my vehicle before my driver parked. And I'll have to deal with Matvey later because it was more important that I got inside.

I watched her for several minutes. She was trying to be brave but wasn't sure what to do. Every head in the room turned to focus on her. It didn't surprise me. She's stunningly beautiful, looks barely twenty-one, and has an innocence about her. She finally sat down, and I was about to approach her when that dickhead did.

It wasn't a question about her choosing me. She *will* leave with me. No one is touching her in this place, or there will be a bloodbath.

She's mine.

Only tonight.

Forever.

I don't do long term or forever.

Focus, asshole. Give her what she needs, have a conversation with her tomorrow about safety, and go back to the friendship zone.

"Strip. Then crawl to me like the sexy baby girl you are," I command her, quickly slipping into my role.

Her eyes widen, and her breath hitches. She rises from between my legs and steps several feet back. Her head drops, and she reaches for her dress.

"Look at me," I growl, and she picks her head up. "Eyes on mine."

Jesus, she obeys so well.

My cock is so swollen it hurts, and I'm tempted to free it from my pants, but then I'd miss watching her strip show.

My beautiful dorogaya's hands shake as she slowly lifts the hem of her dress to her waist.

"Stop."

She freezes.

I take a few controlled breaths. The last few inches of her golden legs I've obsessed over come into view. A thin strip of blingy gold barely covers her slit. I curl my finger in the air for her to come closer.

She steps forward until she's next to my knees, dress bunched on her stomach, hands still trembling, and a drop of her juice glistening on her thigh as it oozes toward her feet.

The air fills with the sweet scent of her sex. I sniff hard then drag my finger over the drop of juice until it's near her barely-there panties. She shakes so hard she whimpers, her eyes growing heavy.

I hold my finger in the air. "Suck."

She wraps her lips around my finger, and my dick tries to break through the fabric of my pants. I lean forward, wrap my arm around her ass, and feel skin and more jeweled material. I weave my fingers through the different strips then kiss around the thin strap covering her pussy, slipping my tongue under the barrier but only once.

She tastes like a chocolate-covered pretzel, sweet and salty, so tempting, I have to restrain myself from ripping her flimsy panties off and eating her out.

Not yet.

She lets out a ragged moan and increases the suction on my finger. I remove my hands and mouth from her and knead her ass. "Spin, baby girl."

She turns, displaying her perfect, heart-shaped ass. I slide my finger under her dress and up her spine, and she shivers.

"Look at me."

She turns her head and meets my eye.

I drag my finger down and trace the curve of her cheeks. The thought of her fifteen pounds lighter pisses me off again. "This is perfection, baby girl. Do you understand?"

Her tiny smile erupts. In her breathy voice, she replies, "Yes, sir."

I kiss both her ass cheeks then sit back on the couch. "Step forward and continue."

She looks at the wall, takes one step, then pulls her dress off. She holds it in her hands with her head bowed. Her long, wavy hair flows below the back of her jeweled bra.

I stroke my cock through my pants, still resisting to free it, staring at her and her magnificence. A new creepy song comes on with people screaming, and I glance around the room.

"Go flip the switch by the door so the music turns off. Then spin so I can see the front of you."

She takes a step, but I stop her.

"Crawl with your perfect little ass in the air."

She drops to all fours and crawls. Her shoulders and head low to the ground, and her sparkled skin raised in the air.

She's the perfect little sub.

Bottom.

She's only a bottom. I don't have subs.

She gets to the door and reaches up for the switch. The music dies, and the room goes silent. She bows her head again and faces me.

"Eyes on me," I direct her again.

Her fiery orbs meet mine.

"Take off your bra."

She reaches behind her and unclasps it then slides it off both shoulders.

Are her breasts real or fake? I can't tell whether she's naked or clothed. I'm guessing they aren't real. They're perfect in proportion, and her nipples grow harder the more I study her.

I pat my thigh, and she drops to the ground and crawls to me. My testosterone flares again at how perfect she is at allowing me to command her. She shimmies across the floor, eyes locked on mine, silence in the air, except for our breath. She stops between my legs and kneels on her ankles.

I stroke her head, and she leans into my hand, closing her eyes briefly.

She's craving to be touched. I can see and feel how badly she needs it. I hold her hot cheeks with both my hands. I lean into her so my mouth is inches from hers. Her warm breath hitches then merges with mine.

"Do you like kneeling for me?"

"Yes, sir."

I slide my hand down her torso, fondling her breasts, and almost come unglued.

They're real. How is this possible?

I rotate my hand on each one while she whimpers. I continue down her body and slide my fingers under the strip of material covering her sex, teasing her clit with a few strokes.

She moans, never taking her eyes off me. The sound echoes in the room.

I remove my hand and drag her juices up her stomach and over her cleavage, until I get to her gold necklace. It's another thing she should have never worn into this place, and tomorrow we're going to talk about it.

For now, I lace my fingers under it. She swallows hard, and her throat pushes against my knuckles. Her pulse beats into my pinky. "When did you come last?"

Her cheeks turn a deeper crimson. "Last night, sir, thinking about you."

Jesus.

"You may answer without calling me sir each time," I tell her.

She stares at me as if she's not sure about it then bites her bottom lip.

"Do you have a question, my dorogaya?"

Her forehead creases. "Do you want me to call you Master?"

You're never calling anyone Master again.

"No. You will never call anyone Master again," I reiterate. Tomorrow we will discuss this in detail, but for now, I need her to feel comfortable. "Just answer my questions. If you want to call me, sir, you can, but you don't have to every time."

She releases a breath. "Okay. Am I doing okay? Do I please you?"

I groan inside, my dick pulses, and I wonder how she can think anything different. I brush my lips against hers as I speak. "You're perfect. Now unbuckle my belt."

Fear crosses her expression. She flinches but then reaches for my pants.

I grab her wrist. "What just scared you?"

She hesitates.

"Is there something you don't want to do, Selena?"

She fights tears. "When you use the belt on me, can you not hit my face with it? I promise I'll do whatever you want."

Jesus fucking Christ, I'm going to kill that bastard ex-husband of hers.

Why is she putting herself in this position?

I softly clarify, "I meant unbuckle my belt and unzip my pants so your pretty little mouth can suck my aching dick."

Embarrassment and more anxiety fill her expression. "Oh. I'm sorry. I—"

I put my finger over her lips. "Shh, baby girl. There's nothing bad you can say. You can tell me everything. But I won't be hurting you, minus a few slaps on your ass with my hand from time to time, understand?"

She exhales shakily, and relief fills her face. "Yes. Thank you. Can I please touch you now?"

I release her wrist and lean back. "You may touch me however you want right now."

She smiles, and my heart skips a beat. I keep one hand on her back, caressing her soft skin. I tease her nipple with my other hand. She skillfully unbuckles my pants then surprises me by putting my zipper in her teeth and releasing it. I lift my hips, and she pulls my pants to my ankles.

My erection springs out, pointing to the ceiling, and her hot breath hits it, sending tingles through my body. She works my cock with her tongue, licking it until I'm breathing hard.

"Suck it," I demand, no longer able to let her play how she wants. I fist her hair and watch her take my head in her mouth, sliding her tongue over the ridges while she adds suction before deep throating me with expertise.

Her mouth and moans become too much for me. I'm going to come, so I command, "Stop."

She looks up at me in confusion.

"Rise and take off your panties." I reach behind my head and pull off my shirt while she does what I ask. "Straddle me. I want your skin and lips on mine, and that wet pussy of yours clenching my cock."

She obeys, and I hold her chin in front of mine. I've seen all her medical records. I know she's clean and gets the shot. I have records of every place she's been. My usual stance is not to have sex with anyone unprotected, but she isn't just anyone. "I'm sliding in your tight little cunt without a condom." I wait for her to say the safe word, but she doesn't.

We're going to talk about this tomorrow, too.

"Do you have anything to say about that?" I ask her one more time, waiting for her to say faucet, but knowing if it were any other man in here, he'd already be in her without asking, since she never set the boundary at the start.

"Please," is all she whispers, as if in agony.

"Then kiss me like a good girl and show me how you take me."

She scoots her knees forward until they hit the back of the couch. Her clit throbs against my shaft. She presses her lips to mine, opening her mouth on contact, as if drinking in every part of me she can.

A fierce wave of adrenaline rolls through me, starting in my toes and working its way up my body as her tongue hungrily flicks through my mouth. Her breasts push against my chest, a glorious combination of soft and hard.

I circle my arms around her, firmly grasping her hips but holding myself back from shoving her on me.

She lifts them; the heat from her pussy sheaths my dick as she inches over me. "Oh God," she whispers against my lips.

A low rumble builds in my chest. The relief from all these weeks watching her, knowing she would submit and wanting it so much my head wouldn't stop spinning, overpowers me. I demand, "Take it all."

She sinks lower, working my shaft with her wet heat while kissing me in the same rhythm.

"More. Take it all now, or I'll make you," I growl.

"Make me. Please," she begs.

I groan and shove her so hard on me, she arches her back, and her head tilts to the ceiling.

"Thank you, sir. Oh God! Thank you," she cries out, her walls clenching my cock so hard, I hold her down against my legs.

"Look at me."

She brings her face to mine.

I slide my thumb over her swollen clit and rub it. Her insides spasm harder on me, and her breath shortens. "There's no coming until I permit you, understand?"

She scrunches her forehead.

"Speak freely," I order her.

"Please. I need it."

"Yes. You do. After you answer my questions, you'll be rewarded, understand?"

She closes her eyes. "Yes...oh..."

"Keep your eyes open. And when you come, you don't say sir. You say my name."

She obeys.

"Why did you come here?" I ask.

"I told you."

"Tell me again." I take my hand on her hip and create a new rhythm for her to maintain. She falls into it easily and is soon lazily grinding her body on me.

"I needed to submit."

"Why, my dorogaya?"

"I-I don't know."

I take my hand off her hip and slide it through her hair so I firmly hold her head next to mine. "You do. Tell me."

"I don't."

"You do." I increase the pressure on her clit. "Tell me, and I'll let you come."

"I don't know," she repeats.

"Yes, you do. Now tell me," I sternly demand.

Her eyes fill with tears. "I don't. I-I think I'm really screwed up."

Here comes the truth.

"Why do you think that?"

She blinks, and a tear falls. Her hips never stop moving, and I keep my thumb positioned on her in the same manner, playing with her bundle of nerves as her body begins to quiver.

"I hate these places."

"Then, why are you here?"

"I don't know," she cries out.

"You do. Tell me."

"I did. I needed to submit. I don't know why."

"You're lying." I increase the intensity of my thumb.

Her face contorts. I know she's stopping herself from coming. She learned how from years of being punished if she came when she wasn't supposed to. Guilt washes over me for using this against her, but the other part of me loves every minute of it. It's the only way to find out why she's here and what she really needs. I don't doubt she's a submissive, but there's something else driving her to come to this place. It's my job as the dominant party to make sure I give it to her. These mind games get me off, too.

"I'm not," she claims.

I grab her hip, thrust her harder on me, and rotate between pinching her clit and circling it ferociously.

"Please...oh God!"

"I'm not God, baby girl. What's my name?"

"Obrecht! Please!"

"No. Not yet. You tell me why you came here."

More tears fall out of her eyes as her body trembles harder. "To submit."

"Tell me the truth!" I demand. "Or I'm stopping."

"I am," she whispers.

"You aren't. Tell me now. Why did you come here?"

She finally caves, crying out, "I needed to feel someone. I'm so lonely! I'm so tired of being alone. And all I think about is submitting to you!" Tears drip all over as she sobs.

I release her hip and fist her hair. "Good, baby girl. Thank you for telling me the truth." I kiss her tears then slide my tongue in her mouth, giving her everything I've been holding back from her.

She moans in my mouth then cries out, "Please, Obrecht."

"Come, my dorogaya." I continue kissing her and roll my thumb faster on her.

Her lips and breath never leave mine. In a raspy voice, she cries out my name, and her eyes roll back.

As the tremors ignite, her body clutches me tighter. I take both my hands and thrust into her harder. Sweat pops out on our skin. Heat burns through my body. My balls tighten, and she cries out my name again. Her body goes limp against mine. Her juices drench my legs as her body convulses.

I wrap my arms around her then release my seed deep inside her, growling in Russian, "You're mine, my little baby girl. And he's going to pay for what he did to you."

Neither of us move. When I finally pull out of the curve of her neck, I tug her hair so she has to look at me. "We're going home now. You will never come back here. This is not a place for you. Do you understand?"

Her eyes fill with tears again. "Yes."

I swipe my thumb over her tears. "Tomorrow, we are talking about this."

She opens her mouth then closes it.

"Speak freely," I repeat.

Her lips quiver, and more tears fall. "Can we stay longer? I don't want to go home and be by myself."

I shouldn't say it. It's sending the wrong signal and setting her up to get attached.

"No. We aren't staying here, but I will stay with you tonight."

Her eyes widen. "You will?"

"Yes. Whatever you need, my dorogaya, I will give you."

6

Selena

NOT MUCH IS REGISTERING AS WE LEAVE THE CLUB. OBRECHT dresses me then himself. He picks me up and carries me through the club. His palm firmly holds my face to his chest, as if he doesn't want me to look at anyone. Or maybe he doesn't want anyone to see me.

I'm not sure which it is, but I close my eyes, inhaling his scent and listening to his heartbeat, feeling safe for the first time in what seems like forever. The air prickles my skin when we step outside. His car is waiting on the curb, and he holds me the entire way to our building. When the driver parks the vehicle, he murmurs, "We're home, my dorogaya."

Every time he calls me his dorogaya, or baby girl, a warmth seeps through my body. It makes me feel special, as if I'm his and no one else's.

He slides out of the car with me in his arms and carries me in the same manner as before. He sets me down and kisses my head. "Let's get these clothes off you. We need to shower."

"Wh-where are we?" I assumed he would take me to my place, but I don't know where we are. The room is dark. A gas fireplace creates a soft glow. It spans the entire wall across from the bed and curves onto the adjoining one, stopping at a doorway. The Chicago skyline blinks against a glass wall surrounded by blackness, which I assume is Lake Michigan.

"My bedroom." He strips me then himself, and leads me to the bathroom. He flips a switch, and another fireplace turns on.

"Wow," I whisper. The bathroom is as beautiful as the bedroom, in clean whites, blues, and grays.

He scoops me up and sets me on the counter. "Stay here, baby girl." His fingers climb up my thigh, torso, and neck until they rest on my cheek. Even with me sitting on the counter, he towers over me. He tilts my head, and he studies my face for a moment. I hold my breath and he admits, "You scared me tonight."

"I'm sorry."

"I know you are." He gives me a chaste kiss on the lips then retreats and turns on the shower.

I scan every inch of his hard flesh. The flutters in my stomach spark back to life. The face of the snake on his neck stares at me. The only other tattoo he has on that side of his body is on the right shoulder. It says Natalia, and I instantly feel a flare of jealousy.

He reaches into the shower to check the water then comes back to me. He helps me off the counter and leads me into the oversized stall.

I drop to my knees and bow my head. Water pours over me, but I don't dare move to shield myself.

He slides his hands under my armpits and yanks me up. I'm not sure how to interpret his expression. In a stern yet gentle voice, he says, "No, Selena."

I'm confused again. I've not done the right thing, and my chest tightens. I bow my head again. "I'm sorry, sir. I'm..." More tears fall. I wish I could stop them. I'm not sure what's happening or why I keep crying. I don't understand what I've done wrong.

He pulls me into his chest, embracing me and kissing my head. "Let me take care of you, baby girl."

He's going to take care of me?

No. This isn't right. I'm his submissive, or bottom, or whatever he wants to call it.

Is he testing me?

"Please. I-I only want to please you, sir."

A rumble rolls through his chest, and he sniffs hard. He tightens his arms. "If you want to please me, you will let me take care of you."

"I-I'm so confused," I admit.

"Yes. We will talk tomorrow, and everything will become clear for you."

"It will?"

He tilts my head, and his icy-blue eyes pierce into mine. "Yes, my dorogaya. I promise. Do you trust me?"

"Yes," I say, without even contemplating it.

He smiles, and little lines pop out around his eyes. "That makes me happy."

"It does?"

"Yes. Now be a good girl and let me take care of you." He kisses me on the lips then spends several minutes diligently washing every part of my body. I do everything he says, which only consists of a few things like spin or pick up your foot. When he gives me that command, he's on his knees, which baffles me more.

Obrecht remains kneeling on the tile, looks up at me, and asks, "What are you thinking?"

"I'm confused," I repeat.

"Yes. Tell me why."

I swallow hard. I don't want to talk about it. "May I have permission not to answer right now?"

He shakes his head. "No. You are to tell me right now."

My insides quiver. Obrecht takes his hands and moves them up and down my thighs, never taking his gaze off mine. "Tell me."

"J-Jack never got on his knees, and he didn't wash me in the shower. I'm not sure what to do."

"Exactly what you're doing. What did he do to you in the shower?" Obrecht asks.

"I-I had to wash him and do all the things he wanted. S-sometimes I got punished in the shower. He'd turn the cold water on, and I'd have to kneel for hours. Some..." I close my eyes then open them again. "Sometimes, he'd make me stare at the ceiling under the faucet or spray water on my face. If I choked or shivered too much, he would bring his leather belt into the shower."

Obrecht's face turns dark, and I think I'm in trouble.

"I'm sorry. Please don't be mad at me!"

He keeps rubbing his palms on my thighs. "I'm not mad at you. You've done nothing wrong. You've been a very good girl. Do you want your reward?"

"My reward?" I ask, once again perplexed by everything that is happening right now.

"Yes." He moves me until my back is against the wall and my legs are over his shoulders. His face tilts up at me. "Come as much as you want, baby girl."

My confusion only deepens. Jack never went down on me, even before we were married. I was the one to give him oral sex. The limited sexual experience I had before Jack was nothing like Obrecht Ivanov.

His mouth and fingers are a tornado sweeping through every inch of my pussy, flicking me, sucking me, sliding his tongue and fingers in and out of my sex. Right before my first orgasm, he takes his other hand and slips a finger past the hard ridge of my forbidden zone.

The room echoes with my cries and the water pounding down on the tile as he inches more in me, grunting as I writhe against him.

"Obrecht," I keep screaming as he continues to manipulate my body. It's as if he has a needle and is injecting me with straight adrenaline. I start to come down, and he shoots me up again. He doesn't stop until I can no longer hold myself up and my body is trembling above his.

He steadies me against the wall, rises, then kisses me. His warm body presses against mine, a contrast to the cold tile. While kissing me, he turns the water off and grabs a towel. He steps back and dries me off first before himself, which only adds to my list of questions.

He tosses his towel on the floor then picks me up and carries me to his bed. After I'm under the covers, he slides in next to me and pulls me into him so my head is on his chest. "You okay, my dorogaya?"

"Yes. Just trying to understand things."

He slides down and turns on his side so his face is next to mine. "Are you scared right now?"

"No. I-I feel safe with you. And warm."

He smiles and strokes my cheek. "I won't hurt you. I'll only protect you. Do you understand?"

My stomach tightens. I want to believe him. He's done nothing for me to think anything different, but I've never had that.

"I see doubt on your face," he gently states.

Tears consume me again. Before tonight, I thought I was doing good. But I guess that's what happens when you only consider Pandora's box instead of opening the lid and jumping in with both feet. "Am I really screwed up? Do you think you can fix me?"

His eyes widen. He slides his thumb over my trembling lips. "You don't need anyone to fix you. You're confused, baby girl, and it's okay. Tomorrow we'll talk, and things will be clearer."

I grip the gold collar still around my neck and admit things I've not told anyone. "Sometimes, I feel like I haven't escaped him. I wonder how it's possible. He always said slaves don't leave their Masters until they die. If he owns me, how am I still not his property? Am I really free, or am I just passing the time until he finds me and takes what is his?"

Obrecht's icy-blue eyes darken. His face hardens. "He doesn't own you. He never has."

"I have dreams he's trying to kill me. And..." I take a deep breath. "I don't know if it's a flashback of all the times I thought he was or if it's a premonition of what's to come."

Obrecht's voice turns so cold, a shiver runs down my spine. "If anyone is dying, it's him." He pulls me closer and kisses me. "Close your eyes and try to sleep, my dorogaya. Morning will be here soon."

Like always, I obey. I shut my eyes, but for once, I don't feel alone or scared. I sink deeper into the cocoon of Obrecht's warm, safe body.

When I wake up, the sun is shining into the room. I turn over, but Obrecht is nowhere. One of his T-shirts is folded, sitting on the bed. I put it on then walk out of the bedroom. I freeze in the doorway when I see him standing near the window, his hand in his hair, and aggressively speaking Russian into the phone. I drop to my knees, sit straight with my ass on my heels, and bow my head while he continues to have his conversation. His words come out fast. If I didn't know him, his voice would scare me. I'm unsure how much time passes, but he finally barks something else out, then it goes quiet. I don't dare look up or even attempt to sneak a peek at him. If he wants me to be his bottom, then I want to be a perfect one for him, whatever that means.

The air suddenly seems to shift. It feels as if too much time has passed in silence. I finally see his feet in front of me. He crouches down. "Look at me, Selena."

I obey, fixing my eyes on his icy-blue orbs.

He strokes my cheek. "No more kneeling."

My chest tightens.

I've done something wrong. He no longer wants me.

The events of the previous night come flying back to me. *He wasn't happy I went to the club.*

I didn't understand a lot and questioned him.

I must have been so dirty he had to wash me.

"I'm sorry. I'll do better for you," I whisper. "Please give me another chance."

He smiles, but there's sympathy in his eyes. I hate it. I don't want him to look at me with pity. My cheeks flare with heat. His gaze never leaves mine. "You haven't done anything wrong, baby girl. Come have breakfast, and let's talk."

My stomach flips, but I remember him telling me several times last night we would talk today.

He guides me over to the table, where food is laid out, but my stomach won't stop pitching. All I can think is I screwed up, and now I'm going to lose him.

7

Obrecht

"I don't give a fuck what Liam wants," I bark out in Russian.

"We have enough issues right now, don't you think?" Adrian replies.

I stare at the crashing waves of Lake Michigan. It's a sunny day, but nothing inside me feels happy. Jack Christian will pay for what he did to Selena. If it's the last thing I do on this Earth, I'm going to make him regret ever setting eyes on her.

Adrian lowers his voice. "I'm right. You're the one who always says when I'm spinning, I need to walk away. You're spinning right now—"

"He waterboarded her," I growl.

"He will pay, brother. But you need to keep your cool. I need your head in the game right now. If we don't sort out the issue with Dasha, every Ivanov is in danger."

I want to remind my brother it's his ex-wife and to deal with it himself, but I know I can't. And he's right. The issues his ex put us in with the Polish mob are nothing to dismiss. I order, "Put a tracker on him."

"We don't need to."

"Are you kidding me?" I bark.

"Easy! Liam has Finn on him."

"Fine! You call—" I freeze. Selena is kneeling in my bedroom doorway with her head bowed. She has on the blue T-shirt I left out for her to wear.

Jesus, help me.

It was a top-bottom arrangement. She's not understanding.

One more time, then I'll explain it to her.

No. She deserves better and is already struggling with all this.

"Call Liam and make sure he still has Finn on him. If anything changes, we're to know before it happens. And you make sure Liam knows this is nonnegotiable." I hang up and stare at my dorogaya.

I hate myself right now. The longer I stare at her, the harder my dick becomes. I fight my urges to fall back into our roles from last night. Selena needs to be educated so she can make choices.

We can't do this right now.

87

She thinks it's normal all the time.

That's what he made her do.

This is torture. Why does she have to be so sexy?

She's so young. I'm officially a dirty old man.

I approach her slowly. I crouch down in front of her. "Look at me, Selena."

She obeys, like the good girl she is, her eyes wide and so eager to make me happy. I ignore my throbbing erection and the urges raging through me. I stroke her cheek. "No more kneeling."

She inhales sharply. Her voice shakes as she whispers, "I'm sorry. I'll do better for you. Please give me another chance."

My heart pounds harder. I keep my focus on her eyes, trying to read her. "You haven't done anything wrong, baby girl. Come have breakfast, and let's talk."

I take her hands and pull her up with me then lead her to the table. I pull a chair out. Her head is down again, and I realize she's waiting for me to permit her. "Please, sit and don't bow your head."

She obeys, and I move her hair over her shoulder, then put my hands on them and rub her. I lean down to her ear. "Do you remember how things were when we went over your finances?"

She turns to see me. "What do you mean?"

"You weren't kneeling or looking anywhere but at me or the papers. I didn't have any power over you. Do you remember?"

"Yes."

"Good." I pull the chair out next to her and sit. "Can we switch over to that?"

Her lip quivers. She looks away for a moment. She asks, "You regret last night, don't you?"

I turn her chin toward me. "Not at all. Do you?"

"No. But-but you don't want me anymore?"

Oh, baby girl, if you only knew how much I want you.

"This is not about desire, Selena. We need to talk where you're in full power of your actions right now. That's all."

"Easy for you to say. You're not the one with the issues," she blurts out.

I snort. "I have my own shit to deal with, don't be fooled."

"Highly doubt it."

I drag my finger down her neck and around her collar. I shouldn't touch it. I hate what she thinks it means. She should know what it really means to be collared, not what she experienced. "Listen, baby girl, once I explain some things, a lot of these issues won't be issues."

"What about the things that are?"

I don't know.

"Let's take it one step at a time, okay?" I confidently suggest.

"Okay."

I loop my finger under her collar and pull her closer to my face. She shudders, and I almost groan out loud. She stares at my lips and swallows hard.

Fuuuck. I want to tell her to kneel and spend the day ordering her around in bed, but I can't. This is too important.

"I'm going to test you on this when we get done, so I need you to pay attention, okay?"

She furrows her eyebrows. Anxiety fills her voice. "Really?"

I grin. "Nope. But I want you to ask me questions so you understand it and remember that what Jack did to you was wrong. You were with him for a long time. If it takes a while to process this, it's okay." What I'm about to explain to her is complex and can take a bit to understand.

She blinks hard but bravely replies, "Okay, Obrecht."

I peck her on the lips and lean back, trying to distance myself slightly to reduce the fire burning in my belly. The urge to splay my hand on her spine, bend her over the table, and lift that T-shirt right above her ass is building. "Let's talk about the club."

Her face turns red.

"That was not the club for you," I state.

"I'm sorry."

"Yes, but let's talk about why it wasn't."

She turns in her chair toward me. "I chose it because Jack wouldn't be there. At least, we never went there."

"Okay. That was smart reasoning. However, a safe club has STD tests for its members, rules about guests, a *real* application process, and costs thousands, not a few hundred dollars."

She wrinkles her nose. "I didn't really understand the buffet."

"Oh, I know, right? Gross. That should have been your first clue," I tease but am also serious.

"I figured I just had to overlook it."

"No. Don't ever overlook your gut feeling. First, STD testing is more than checking a box if you have one or not. Legitimate tests are required, and it flows into guests. The application is several pages long, not what's on your driver's license."

"They didn't ask for a license number," Selena smirks.

"I'm glad you're having fun with this," I remark.

Her face falls. "Sorry. I'm just embarrassed."

"Don't be, but learn from this."

She nods. "I am."

I lean forward and pick up her hands. I shouldn't touch her but she's too hard to resist. Now that I've had her, the restraint I'd displayed before last night is shattered. "You always have to state your boundaries before you go into any session. Hard limits, safe words, and anything else they should know about your wants and needs."

She bites on her lip.

"No one should ever do anything to you that you don't want them to do. Understand?"

Pain fills her face. "Okay."

"And if someone does something to cross your boundary or just something you don't like, you say the safe word, and they should stop immediately," I inform her.

"Can I keep it as faucet?" she asks.

"Yes. You need to tell any partner what it is before you go into a session, okay?"

"Yes, but why are you calling it a session?"

There are so many things to discuss with her. Every question seems to lead to more. I debate where to go next and finally say, "The club we were at last night is a sex club. What you're looking for is a BDSM club."

My dorogaya's face contorts. "BDSM?"

"Bondage and discipline. Dominance and submission. Sadism and masochism."

She inhales deeply. She swallows hard. "Sadism? Masochism? I don't like pain."

Pride swells through me. I kiss her hand. "Good, baby girl. If you don't like pain, then you don't let anyone hurt you."

She releases a breath. "And it's okay? To say I don't want it?"

"Yes. Always. You negotiate before a session and always have your hard limits and safe word included. The club we were at last night, they aren't trained. You could have gotten severely injured in a session."

Her face reddens more. "I still don't understand what a session is."

"What we did at the club last night would be called a session. I was your top, and you were my bottom."

She shakes her head. "I don't understand why there are all these names."

"It's important to know who you're playing with and what they are and what they expect you to be. Otherwise, you can get hurt and both people won't get what they need," I warn. I pick up the pen. "Are you visual?"

"Yes. I suppose so. Umm... I thought with Jack I was a slave, but I thought I wanted to be a submissive, and then you say I'm a bottom."

"Ah. Let's look at this on levels, with no one being better than the other, okay?" I draw one line down and two across so there are six boxes. In one column, I put S-type and the other D-type. I slide my hand over the S-type column. "You're going to be one of these three on this side. I'm on the other."

"D for dominant?" she asks.

"Yes."

"I didn't know you were dominant," she claims with a straight face then breaks out in a smile.

"Funny."

Her grin widens, lighting up the room. "Okay, I'm following you so far."

In the boxes under the S-type column, I put bottom, sub, slave. Under the D-type column, I write top, Dom, Master. "What you were in with Jack is not how a Master-slave relationship should go."

"No?"

I hold her cheek and put my thumb on her jaw. I do it more to help me keep my cool than anything else. "Did Jack ask you to be his slave?"

"Ask?"

"Yes. Did he ask and you agreed?" I repeat.

"I agreed to marry him."

"That doesn't mean you agreed to be his slave."

"He said it did."

My rage grows again. I count to ten to stay calm. Everything I am wants to go directly to Jack's house and kill him with my hands. "A Master-slave relationship should always be between two parties consenting before the relationship begins. Forced slavery isn't healthy."

"But you're not a Master?"

"No, and I will never be."

"Why not?" she asks.

"It's not what I want. I don't want someone kneeling for me all day long or not able to speak up and make decisions. I don't want what happens in the bedroom twenty-four seven."

She looks away, and I realize she thinks it's a reflection on her, since she spent ten years as a slave.

"Look at me, baby girl," I say.

She obeys.

"You didn't choose what you had. I like commanding my women in the bedroom and discussing things freely outside of that. I want them to think and make their own choices for themselves when we're not in a session. Do you understand?"

"No."

"Right now, you aren't asking me to speak or what to think. On the roof, in your condo, at breakfast...those were all times when you weren't acting as a submissive. And as much as I got off controlling you in the club, I like the other side of you, too." I tuck her hair behind her ear. "Don't you like both parts?"

She tilts her head. The expression on her face almost kills me, and she replies quietly, "I don't know, should I?"

Oh, baby girl.

"Why wouldn't you?"

"I feel like something is wrong with me. I-I shouldn't want to do that after leaving Jack. Submitting is bad and wrong, isn't it?"

I rise quickly, fist her hair, and tug her head back. I dip down in front of her face. Her nipples press into my T-shirt. It's another thing driving me nuts, so I pinch one, then circle it.

She gasps, staring into my eyes.

"You think there's something wrong with submitting to me?" I growl.

"No," she breathes with fire in her eyes.

I walk my fingers down her torso, under her T-shirt, and onto her mound. "If I touch that pretty little pussy of yours right now, is it going to be wet and pulsing?"

She swallows hard. "Yes."

My fingers itch to slide lower, but I refrain. "Then doesn't submitting feel good, baby girl?"

"Yes," she whispers.

I lean closer to her mouth. "I loved every moment of making your body react to mine. There's nothing wrong or bad with submission if it's what you need and it's done safely."

"Safely?" she repeats.

I release her hair and sit back down. "Yes. A good Dominant will make sure you don't go past your limits. Their job is to give you what you need. You need to submit, but you need more than just that. A good Dominant will make sure you get it all and aftercare as well."

"Aftercare?"

"Yes. When you finish a session, your top or Dom should take care of you."

She ponders for a moment. "Is that why you washed me? You do that with everyone after?"

My heart pounds faster. "No. I don't ever do that."

More confusion fills her face. "But you did it with me?"

"Yes."

"Why don't you usually do it?"

"No one ever comes home with me." My chest tightens. I'm breaking all my rules with Selena. Now she knows it, too. But I couldn't have left her last night, even if she didn't tell me she didn't want to be alone. She pushes me with her question, and as uncomfortable as it makes me feel to discuss this, I'm so proud of her. Every question she asks me is necessary. It's beyond important that she understands what she wants and how to get it.

She asks, "Why not?"

"I'm a top."

"And I was your bottom last night?"

"Yes."

"I'm so confused."

I tap my fingers on the table then redirect her to the chart I drew. "Look at it this way. A top and bottom negotiate a session. They both get what they need, have some aftercare, and they go their separate ways, free to do whatever they want. The power is given only during the session. Are you following me?" I don't tell her a top can be an S-type or a bottom can be a D-type at times or about switches. There's so much in the BDSM world, and I need her to grasp the basics first.

She bites on her lip and nods. "I think so."

"Great." I point to the middle row. "A sub and Dom are typically in some sort of committed relationship. The power exchange is long term. It could mean every weekend or when they are together or Tuesday nights. It's not all the time though."

She examines the paper. "If you were my Dom, I could come upstairs every weekend and kneel but not during the week?" She raises her eyebrow in a hopeful way.

Fuck. I'm so tempted to tell her yes and ask her if that's what she wants. The visual of Selena kneeling before me all weekend, allowing me to command her for days in a row sets my blood pounding straight to my dick.

She can't know what she wants. She's not educated on her choices.

I don't do long term.

I force myself to not give in. "*If* that were our arrangement, but it isn't."

Her face falls.

"If you ever get into that type of relationship, it's consensual. Both people agree. Do you understand?"

She sighs heavily then nods. Her face falls further. "And what is the Master-slave relationship like? If the one I was in was wrong?"

I choose my words carefully. "This is the one I have the toughest time with, my dorogaya. I don't believe we should always be in our Dominant and submissive roles. One person always in charge in all aspects of life isn't something I agree with, but it exists. But even slaves who consent to be in that type of relationship shouldn't be abused how you were."

She hugs her chest and puts her feet on the bottom of her seat so her knees are above the table. She tugs at the bottom of the T-shirt.

"You were very brave to get out of your situation," I tell her and mean it.

She stares at the paper. "I couldn't have done it without Sister Amaltheia, Kora, and Sergey." She turns to me. "Do you know what Sergey did to get Jack to divorce me?"

My pulse increases. I don't want to lie to her, but I'm not sure why I tell her more than necessary. "Yes. My brother Adrian and I were part of it."

Her eyes widen. "You were?"

"Yes."

"How?"

I stroke her cheek. "If I could tell you, I still wouldn't. You shouldn't even know I was there."

"Where?"

Way to dig the hole deeper. I need to shut up.

I stay quiet.

She studies me for several moments. It's as if I can see the wheels turning in her head. Her eyes light up. "You saw him at a sex club and got dirt on him, didn't you?"

I try not to react, but I can't help it. "What makes you ask me that?"

"You go to sex clubs. He goes to sex clubs. I got more than I was legally entitled to."

I tug her onto my lap. She turns to me, and I kiss her, moving my tongue in and out of her mouth until she moans. I end the kiss and tap her head. "You're smart, baby girl. This is why I don't want you ever being anyone's slave. Do you understand?"

"Yes."

"But let me be clear about something. I would never participate in any club your ex goes to. I don't have sex with prostitutes, nor do I force women to do anything they don't want to."

She cups my cheek. "Then, why were you there?"

"We went there to get dirt on him. That doesn't mean we partook in the activities." My gut flips, wondering if she believes me. It's true. I detest prostitution. I know some women do it willingly, but many are forced into it, and all it does is make me think of Natalia's final year of life.

She opens her mouth, shuts it, then says, "Some nights, I didn't have to partake."

Every organ in my body seems to awaken. Part of me doesn't want to know. The thought of her going through what she did breaks my heart. The other side of me wants every last detail for when I have my day with Jack. I tighten my arm around her. "What did you do when you went to the club with Jack?"

"Only one of two things." Pain fills her eyes.

"Will you tell me? Please?"

She traces my lips with her finger. "I like touching you."

"I like touching you, too," I tell her. It's the understatement of the year. My soul feels like it's alive when my skin makes contact with hers.

Darkness fills her expression. "He would have me kneel naked all night and watch him while he screwed other women. Sometimes it was on these circle things that stopped my blood flow. If I moved, I paid the consequences. He would snort coke, and it kept him awake longer. Before we got to the club, he would take Viagra so he could go all night. When it wore off, he'd pop another one. Sometimes, my body hurt so bad, I wished I would die."

I pull her head to my chest and caress her hair. "I'm glad you didn't die. He won't ever do that to you again, I promise."

She looks up and doesn't look too sure. I'm about to reassure her when she reveals, "Other nights, he would still take the coke and Viagra, but I was the one whom he had sex with. Everyone would watch. If I cried or came, there would be consequences. If I didn't come when he wanted me to, there were consequences as well." Her eyes well with tears, and one escapes the corner of her eye. A sarcastic laugh comes out of her mouth. "Usually, he decided anything I did wasn't good enough. I always had consequences. Sometimes, I would pay for days for whatever I did at the club."

"What were the consequences, Selena?" I try to maintain my cool, but all I can think about is finding Jack today and taking him to the garage, then making sure his ashes are on the bottom of Lake Michigan.

She squishes her face and looks up at the ceiling. "I umm..." She releases a shaky breath.

"Take your time, baby girl. Breathe."

She follows my command. I continue stroking her hair. She curls into me like a kitten on my lap, and I wrap my arms tighter around her.

"There were so many things over the years. Starvation, dehydration, cold showers, hot showers, belts, whips, chains. Just...too many things." Her hot tears slide under my T-shirt and down my chest. "I should be grateful nothing left a long-term mark."

I count to ten again. "And did he force you to be with other people?" Everything she's telling me is making my stomach flip, but when I ask her, Natalia's face pops into my mind again. I sniff hard, trying to control my rage over what happened to Natalia and Selena.

Natalia's rapist and killers are dead.

I can still kill Jack.

I will kill Jack.

She shakes her head. "No. He liked to make it very clear I was his. He thought it bothered me to watch him screw other women. After the first year of marriage, I didn't care anymore. I stopped crying about his infidelity." She laughs again. "Isn't that absurd? Within the first few months of marriage, it was apparent what my role was, and I still cried after every session at the club where he would be with other women. I still assumed he loved me. How pathetic is that?"

I lift her face. Her brown eyes have sad swirls of green in them, and it pains me further. "There isn't a bone in your body that's pathetic, my dorogaya. You survived. Sometimes, the bravest thing is surviving."

"Instead of killing yourself?" she whispers.

My heart stops beating. "Do you think about killing yourself, baby girl?"

She shakes her head. "Not anymore. I used to want to, but Jack had cameras all over the house. I couldn't even pee without him watching me. I was so scared I would try it and not die, and then I would have worse consequences."

"I'm sorry you went through that. I'm so happy you didn't hurt yourself or worse."

She opens her mouth then shuts it and turns to the window. She twists her fingers in her lap so tight, her knuckles turn white.

I softly ask, "What do you want to ask me?"

She doesn't look at me. Her voice shakes. Hurt is in it. "You said a top and bottom have their session and go their separate ways. Is that what we'll be doing?"

I should tell her yes. It's what happens. It's the entire point of not being a Dom or Master. You get what you need, there's no emotional attachment, and you move on. Sure, you can play again, but it somehow doesn't seem right in this situation. If she goes to another club on her own, she might get hurt. She isn't ready to be out there by herself.

The thought of anyone else touching my dorogaya makes me feel ill. But I know myself. I don't do relationships.

Tell her yes.

I'm going to confuse her if I don't tell her yes.

No matter how hard I try, I can't seem to tell Selena yes. "Tops and bottoms can negotiate new sessions together. When the session ends, the control ends. Do you understand what I'm saying?"

The fire glows hotter in her eyes. She straightens up in my lap, straddles me, and puts her arms around my shoulders. Her lips are inches from mine, tempting me. She drags her nails on my neck, back and forth, and I hold in my groan. "Does that mean we could negotiate a session again? This doesn't have to be the end for us?"

Before I can stop myself, I say, "No, baby girl. This isn't the end of us."

8

Selena

RELIEF RUSHES THROUGH EVERY CELL IN MY BODY. HIS erection grows harder against my naked sex. I don't want anyone else touching me. I want *him*.

He said no attachments.

Too late. I was already attached before last night.

But he's not attached to me.

I need to respect his boundaries.

He just said we aren't over.

"When can we have another session?" I intensify the pressure of my nails on his neck.

His chest rises and falls faster. He clenches his jaw. "We need to set some rules, Selena."

"Sir, I prefer you to call me baby girl or your dorogaya." It's a bold move on my part. In the past, I never would have spoken up, but Obrecht keeps telling me to.

His cock twitches, which makes me smile.

"You've got a naughty streak in you, don't you?" he mumbles.

"Do you want that, sir? Me to be your naughty baby girl?"

He sniffs hard. His hands slip under my T-shirt. They're warm and large, and it feels as if both of them cover my entire back. I shiver from the tingles racing up and down my spine, as if ready to electrocute me somehow.

There's a rumble in his chest. His hot breath merges with mine. "It's important to me you understand what you want, baby girl."

"Yes. Thank you. I want you, sir," I admit, my heart hammering in my chest.

He studies me. The tension in the air builds. His icy-blue orbs fill with heat. After several minutes, he finally speaks. "I'll be your mentor. Then you'll know how to protect yourself but still get what you need."

I need you.

"What does that mean, sir?"

He swallows hard and licks his lip. "I'll teach you what you need to know and help you learn to negotiate so no one can take advantage of you or misunderstand you."

"Does this involve more sessions with you?"

"Yes."

"As my top?"

The corners of his mouth curve up. "Yes. Very good, baby girl."

"I will submit to you as a bottom?"

"Yes. You will submit. When the session ends, you will not continue to submit until you negotiate another session. Is it clear?" he asks, moving his thumb up and down my spine.

"Yes, sir," I breathe. "Can we start now?"

He continues studying me. It feels like forever. He opens his mouth to speak, and his phone rings. I almost groan out loud over the inconvenience. When he tears his eyes away from mine, he picks up his phone and sighs. "I have to take this." He answers in Russian, and within seconds, his hand stops moving. His eyes turn to slits. He says something back and hangs up. "I'm sorry, Selena. I have to go. Something has come up with work that can't wait."

"Oh. Sure. Sorry." I jump off his lap.

He rises and spins me into him.

I stare at his chest, breathing hard, suddenly embarrassed. It's a workday morning. He has a life. I'm the uneducated girl who begged him not to leave me last night after he rescued me from a dingy sex club.

He tilts my chin and pins his steel gaze on me. "Why are you sorry?"

"I don't mean to overstay my welcome. Thank you for taking care of me last night."

"Did I say you overstayed your welcome?"

I shake my head. "No, but—"

He dips down and kisses me. He possessively palms my head and ass, holding me tight to his warm flesh. It calms my nerves but creates a new pulsing all over my body. My body submits to his. If I were butter, I'd be melted and slathered all over him.

He murmurs, "That's better. Tonight. I will text you when I'm back. We will negotiate before we do anything."

"Okay," I agree, my excitement racing through my veins.

He holds his face next to mine. "No coming, baby girl."

Wait. What? I tilt my head. "Never?"

His lips twitch. "I meant before tonight. Don't go downstairs and play with that hot little pussy of yours."

My cheeks heat up. He has me so turned on, it's probably what I would have done. But how did he know?

He cocks an eyebrow. He bunches my T-shirt to my waist then strokes his finger over my slit.

I immediately widen my legs.

"Don't move," he commands.

I freeze, whimpering.

"What are your plans today?" he asks, as if he doesn't have his hand between my thighs and it's just a normal conversation between two people.

My brain can barely function with his hand on me and the thought of tonight. "Umm... I don't know. What day is it?"

He smirks. "Tuesday."

I rack my brain and cringe. "Nothing?" It's the boring reality of my world.

"Good."

Confused, I repeat, "Good?"

He reaches into his wallet and pulls out a wad of one-hundred-dollar bills. He removes his finger from my body, picks up my hand, and wraps my fingers around the cash.

"I have money," I say.

The corners of his lips twitch. "Yes, I know. This is for me."

I stay quiet, still not sure what the money's for.

"I'm sending you on a field trip. Vlad will escort you. You are not to ever ditch your bodyguard again, though, unless you are with me. Do you understand?" Anger settles on his face.

"I'm sorry. I shouldn't have—"

"No, you shouldn't have. You're going to get a punishment tonight for it."

My chest tightens with anxiety.

He must see it because he sternly says, "I'm not going to physically harm you with my punishments, Selena."

I exhale and smile. "Thank you, sir."

"Vlad will stay with you today. Forget about him and focus on your homework."

"What's my homework?" I ask.

"I liked the outfit you wore last night. You have good taste. Buy something that's only for me. I want to see your sexy ass in it. Something you'll never wear for anyone else. Understand?"

"I don't have anyone else."

His expression is a mix of approval and also struggle. I don't understand it until he says, "Yes, but after I train you, there will be other tops for you."

Or, you can just become my Dom.

I ignore the last comment and refocus. "Okay."

"You also are to choose three other items. Something you're curious about, something you know you like, and something you're afraid of." He releases my fist with the money and returns to touching me. His finger slides through my slit.

"Oh God," I mumble.

He leans into my ear. "I told you last night, baby girl. I'm not God."

Mmm, I pretty much think you're a sex god, Russian stud.

"Yes, sir."

His tongue swipes on my lobe, and I shudder. "Obrecht?"

"Hmm?" he replies, moving his lips down my neck.

"What time?"

He tilts his head up and cups my cheek. "I'm not sure. I have issues I need to sort out. I don't want you waiting around, but it could be earlier or later. Are you okay with that?"

I nod. "Yes. I understand."

His face brightens. "I'm looking forward to seeing what you choose."

"Umm, is there anything I shouldn't get?"

"No, my dorogaya. You get whatever you want. There are no wrong choices." He shimmies his finger through me and teases my clit quickly, pulls his hand away, and holds it in front of me. "Now give me a pretty visual for my day. Lick."

My stomach flutters. I start on the bottom of his finger, slowly licking my way to the top, then repeating it.

He groans, his orbs simmering.

"Can I suck you, sir?" I ask in my most innocent voice.

"Yes, you may."

I take his finger to the back of my throat and flick my tongue across it while moaning, pretending it's his cock.

He pulls away, fists my hair, and tilts my head up. "Be a good girl today. No coming or ditching Vlad. Got it?"

"Yes, sir."

He slides the finger that was in my mouth on my ass and pushes through my cheeks, so he touches my entrance. "Do you remember what I said I liked?"

"Yes."

"What did I say, baby girl?"

I intentionally leave out the no-attachments part. I recite, "Controlling another person, including when they can and can't come. Some mind games. Bondage at times. Toys. Penetration anywhere in my body you want, with whatever you want."

His chest presses into mine. The beating of his heart thumps into my shoulder. "You told me it's what you needed last night. Is that still what you need? Or is any of that no longer on the table?"

Jack did all those things to me. I always hated most of it. Even when I came, I detested myself for letting my body feel anything. He was rough, and it often hurt. But I want Obrecht, and I want him to keep wanting me. Last night was so different. I didn't feel any pain from anything he did, which wouldn't have been the case with Jack, so I'm not going to deny him anything he needs.

"Yes. I need it. The less you can make it hurt, the better," I add, since he told me also to speak up.

His face darkens. "Nothing I do to you is going to hurt, baby girl. All I'm going to do is make you feel really good. I promise."

I bite on my smile. More heat rushes to my face. "Thank you, sir."

"You've been very brave this morning. Since you just spoke up, I'm going to reward you."

"Oh?" My adrenaline bubbles in my veins. His last reward in the shower was pretty phenomenal.

"Vlad will take you."

"You're not going to give it to me now?" I ask, hoping I misheard.

An arrogant expression fills his face. "No, baby girl. All day, I want you wet, ready, and thinking of me."

"I already am wet, ready, and thinking of you all day," I blurt out then my face burns with heat.

He groans. "You just made me so fucking hard, baby girl."

"Yeah?"

"Yeah."

"Can I take care of you, sir?" I lick my lips, hoping he'll allow me.

His dick pulses against my stomach. "No. You can think all day about how much you want it."

"Another thing I already do," I point out then bite my lip.

He slaps my ass, and I jump. He rubs the sting and gives me a chaste kiss on the lips then releases me. "I have to get ready for work. Let me walk you to your place."

"I can go myself."

"No, you won't." He gathers my belongings from the night prior. I follow him into the kitchen and freeze.

God, I hate that faucet.

He puts his body behind mine and leans down to my ear. "You okay, baby girl?"

Get a grip. I take a deep breath and force a smile. "Yes."

He slowly releases me and escorts me to the elevator. When we get to my floor, he sticks his head out, glances both ways, then quickly escorts me to my unit. I step inside and spin. "Do you want to come in?"

"I have to go. Get ready, and I'll tell Vlad where to take you. I'll see you tonight."

Something in me has shifted, and I'm not sure who this girl is anymore. I reach for his arms. "Can you come in for just a quick second? It won't take long."

His face falls. "Sure. What's wrong?" He steps inside and closes the door.

I retreat two steps, slowly remove his T-shirt, then shake out my hair. I fold up his shirt and hold it out. I innocently say, "Thanks for the T-shirt. I'm going to shower now."

His eyes are flames licking my skin as he slowly reaches for his shirt and takes it from me.

"Have a good day." I smile and turn. I stroll across the family room, swinging my hips slightly. When I get to my bedroom door, I put my hand on the frame and glance back.

He hasn't moved. His one hand clenches the T-shirt, and the other is at the side of his thigh, balled into a fist.

"Actually, can I keep the shirt?" I ask.

"You can earn it back."

"Oh?" My flutters expand in my belly, and I'm glad I'm holding on to the wall to steady my weakening knees.

He curls his finger in the air, motioning me to come back.

I drop to my knees and crawl to him, with my ass in the air and my head lifted so I can see him. When I get to his feet, I kneel on the back of my heels and straighten my shoulders. I bow my head.

I hated crawling on the floor for Jack. I couldn't stand kneeling or bowing my head. Something about doing it for Obrecht feels different than when I had to for Jack. I wonder again how messed up I am for voluntarily doing this.

Obrecht crouches in front of me and tilts my chin. The heat from his body radiates into mine. My pussy pulses and I can feel juice rolling down my inner thigh. "Make sure you don't hide your ass with whatever you get."

"I won't, sir."

He studies my face. Whenever he does it, I always wonder what he's thinking. I don't know what he sees in me when he stares like that, but it always sends heat straight to my core. His eyes are the most beautiful set of orbs I've ever seen. They're intense, dangerous, and morph between ice and flames. I love every moment of him focusing on me.

"Enjoy your day. Lock the door." He holds out his hand, and I take it. He pulls me up, and as soon as I'm on my feet, he fists my hair. It's another thing I don't understand. Jack pulled my hair, but it would result in neck pain whether he did it during sex or to drag me around. Every tug from Obrecht is a delicious surge of tingles.

"Is there something I can do for you, sir?" I bat my eyes.

He kisses me but doesn't touch me anywhere else or let it last long. It's still enough to leave me panting for more. "Have a good day, my dorogaya." His cocky smile molds onto his lips. He releases me and leaves.

I lock the door and lean against it a few moments then get ready for the day. When I step into the lobby, Vlad is waiting.

"Ms. Christian, are you ready?" he says in his thick, Russian accent.

I need to change my last name.

"Yes. Can you please call me Selena?"

"Sure."

"Thank you."

He guides me to the car, and when I get inside, there's a note.

DOROGAYA,

WHEN YOU GET TO THE LOCKER ROOM, SEND ME A PICTURE OF your legs.

OBRECHT

LOCKER ROOM? WHAT'S HE TALKING ABOUT?

I take my phone out of my purse, hike up the skirt of my dress, and snap a photo of my hand on my inner thigh. I text him the picture.

Me: *Is this what you want when I get to the locker room?*

Several minutes pass.

Obrecht: *If you touch that sweet pussy of yours, I'm going to know.*

Me: *What if I touch it thinking of you?*

Obrecht: *Don't make me punish you all night.*

My chest tightens again at the thought of him punishing me.

He told me it won't hurt. He's not Jack.

Me: *What if my panties are so wet, I have to take them off for the day?*

Obrecht: *You keep your panties on when I'm not with you, baby girl.*

More flutters consume me. I slip my hand between the side of my panties and hip, as if I might be removing them, and take another photo. It shows the part of my panties that are slightly darker from this conversation. I send it to him.

Me: *What if I'm so hot I need to?*

So much time passes, I think he might not have seen it.

Obrecht: *When you get to the locker room, lay your panties flat on the bench and send me a photo. When you get home, do the same thing. Front and back.*

Me: *Yes, sir.*

The car stops, and I glance out the window. There are several shops.

Me: *We're at stop one. Gotta go.*

Obrecht: *Take a new photo of the exact shot you just sent me when you get back in the car.*

117

Me: *Yes, sir.*

I'm not sure why he wants the same picture with a different timestamp, but whatever floats his boat. I put my phone in my purse as Vlad opens the door. "Ready, Selena?"

"Yes. Umm...how does this work? Are you going to stand over me?" I don't know where Obrecht is sending me, but I know enough about it that I don't want Vlad breathing down my neck.

"No, ma'am. I'll stay back but keep you within my view."

"Great. Thank you."

He nods, leads me into a store, then glances around. He steps to the side near the door and motions for me to shop.

I've never been inside a place like this. It has everything from what I assume are more vanilla toys to hardcore ones that I know too well from experience hurt.

My chest tightens, and my heart beats super fast. I try to stop the panic. I don't like any toys. Even the most basic ones, Jack used to hurt me.

A sales lady with pale white skin, jet black hair, and dark-red lipstick approaches me. My heart races faster. In a friendly voice, she says, "Hi! I'm April. Is this your first time here?"

Something in her voice soothes me. I straighten up and smile. "Yes."

"Do you know what you're looking for?"

Heat fills my cheeks. "No. Umm...my—"

What is Obrecht to me?

She raises her eyebrow. "Top, bottom, sub, Dom, slave, Master, girlfriend, boyfriend?"

I laugh. "Top."

"I like to bottom, too," she says and winks. "Why did your top send you here?"

Something about April makes me feel like I can tell her all my secrets. I don't hesitate. "I need an outfit—one that accentuates my ass. And I have to buy something I'm curious about, something I know I like, and something I'm afraid of."

She wiggles her eyebrows. "That sounds hot. Who's your top? Can he be my daddy for the night?"

The heat on my cheeks gets hotter. *No, he cannot,* I almost say but then realize I'm thinking like an over-possessive, jealous woman when she's joking.

She doesn't wait for me to answer and takes hold of my arm. "Let's go find your outfit first. I think I know the perfect one. You'll look super hot in it."

I let April lead me around the store, which helps calm me when I'm looking at all the toys and other items. When I finish, I thank her and get in the car.

I take out my phone, snap another photo, and compare it to the other one. The damp part of my panties is slightly larger, but that's the only difference. I send it to Obrecht.

A few minutes pass.

Obrecht: *Put your phone on FaceTime and call me. Slide your panties to the slide, and V your pussy with your second and fourth fingers. Take your middle finger and stroke yourself, but don't you dare come, baby girl.*

I glance around the small backseat. No one is with me, so it's unnecessary. I take a deep breath, and another text pops up.

Obrecht: *I better hear you moan.*

I glance around the car again.

Obrecht: *Hit the lock buttons on the car door for the divider window and your door.*

Is he reading my mind?

Does he have a camera in here?

I scan the inside of the car again then hit the buttons. I lift my skirt, press the FaceTime button, and he answers.

"I have two minutes, my dorogaya." The blue sky surrounds him and the phone seems to be moving.

"Are you walking outside right now?" I ask.

"Yes." He turns his ear so I can see the earphones. "Now stop wasting time. I've given you orders."

"Yes, sir," I reply, lower my phone, and do what he texted me. My fingers slip under my panties, I V myself, then press my middle finger to my swollen bundle of nerves. The moment I make contact, I let out a ragged breath.

"Pinch it hard," he commands.

I obey. "Oh God!"

"I keep telling you I'm not God, baby girl. Now swirl."

I do everything he tells me, going faster, then slower, until I'm begging him to let me come.

"Please."

"Stop. Let me see your face."

I reposition the phone so we're looking at each other. His jaw clenches. "Enjoy the rest of your day, dorogaya. Don't forget what you need to send me." He hangs up while I'm still panting.

I immediately get a text.

Obrecht: *Get your hand out of your pussy, baby girl. No more touching yourself.*

I look down and realize my hand is still in the same spot. I remove it, and the car stops.

Obrecht: *Suck your finger clean. Video it and send it to me.*

Me: *We're parked.*

Obrecht: *Vlad won't get out until you unlock the divider. Now send me my video.*

I do what he says, spending several minutes sucking on my finger, hoping I look sexy. When I finish, I watch the video, then send it off.

Me: *This is what I'd like to do to you tonight, sir.*

I hit the button to unlock the divider. The car door lock pops next. I don't know if Vlad or the driver did it. Vlad opens the door and escorts me inside a building. When we get to the fifth floor, he holds the door open and motions for me to go through.

There are two chairs and a table with some magazines. A woman with spiked blonde hair sits behind a desk. The wall behind her reads *Hands*. She says, "Hi. You must be Selena?"

"Yes."

"Great. I'm Marilyn. Let me take you back." She escorts me into a private locker room and opens a locker up. "Your robe and sandals are here. Just put them inside or in the baskets when your service is over."

"Great. This might sound bad, but the person who said to come here didn't tell me what this is." I wince, realizing how bizarre it sounds.

Her grin widens. "Yes, Mr. Ivanov said he was surprising you. Before you leave, I'll give you all the details on your membership."

"My membership?"

"Yes. Mr. Ivanov bought you the top tier."

I stand stunned, not sure what he bought me, but my heart also skips a beat.

"I'm afraid that we can't give you a full tour today, but we were able to arrange the service Mr. Ivanov wanted you to have."

"And what is that?"

She beams. "You'll love it. It's a full body massage with two of our therapists. They'll stretch you and each massage you at the same time. Ever had four hands on you at once?"

"No."

"Trust me. You won't ever want a normal massage again. And you'll be so limber when they finish, your body will go into any position you want it to. Any other questions?"

I shake my head, speechless.

"Great. I'll let you get ready." She leaves, and I stare at the robe, trying to process everything.

My phone vibrates.

Obrecht: *Where are my pictures?*

I snap one of my legs and another one of my panties on the bench. Then I turn my thong and take one of the back. I send them off.

Obrecht: *Good girl. Enjoy your service, baby girl.*

For the next two hours, I'm stretched and rubbed. By the time I get back to the locker room, I'm relaxed but hornier than ever. Marilyn was right. I've only had one massage before, but four hands are a different experience.

When I get back in the car, I turn on my phone.

Obrecht: *Did you think of me during your massage?*

Me: *Yes.*

It's not a lie. He's all I thought about.

Obrecht: *Did you think of my mouth all over you?*

Me: *Yes.*

Obrecht: *If I flicked my tongue on your pussy right now, would you be ready to come for me?*

Me: *Yes.*

Obrecht: *V your pussy and send me a photo. And don't forget to take one of your panties when you get home.*

I return to our building and go inside my condo. I do everything he requested. After an hour of no reply, I get antsy and text him again.

Me: *Will we be at your place or mine?*

There's no reply so I pace in my condo, dying to see him. I finally get another text.

Obrecht: *My elevator code is 684538. Memorize it. Don't shower. Bring whatever you purchased with you, get dressed, and wait for me to come home.*

Me: *You aren't back yet?*

Obrecht: *No. Have a glass of wine if you want. I put a bottle of Pinot Noir out.*

Me: *How do you know I drink that?*

Obrecht: *I know a lot of things about you, baby girl. Now get your sexy ass up to my place.*

I gather my things and go into his penthouse. I set my items on the kitchen counter. When I glance at the sink, I freeze.

The old faucet is gone. An identical one to mine is in its place.

9

Obrecht

ALL DAY, I'VE BEEN PUTTING OUT FIRES. ADRIAN'S EX-WIFE, Dasha, created issues with the Polish mob and they only seem to get worse. One of our trackers, Makar, is in a coma. He was following her and is in stable condition, but still not capable of speaking or writing. So we don't have any idea what happened. Dasha's disappeared, and the other trackers we assigned to her can't seem to locate her.

My tracker, Gavriil, is missing. I assigned him to follow Ludis Petrov, Zamir's son, who runs their territory between Michigan and the East Coast. No one has seen or heard from him in two days. His phone goes straight to voicemail. It's not the first time he's gone off the grid. It happens when you're on the job. But my gut is telling me something is off.

I don't like anything happening to my guys, but my trackers are dwindling fast. Our guys are highly skilled, trained by me, and aren't easy to replace.

The only highlight in my day is my dorogaya, who's surprised me with her naughty side. The voice in my head keeps telling me to stop while I'm ahead. There's so much I need to do to help her. Part of me wonders if giving her what she needs and teaching her how to be safe are the right moves. My conscience is telling me I'm a greedy bastard for getting the benefits from it. The devil in me won't let me stop. The more I'm around her, the more I'm drawn to her. It's like trying to expect a fly to get out of the honey jar. It just isn't possible.

Between all the craziness of the day, I can't seem to locate Carla. She's a member of the same club as me. She's also a therapist who's helped many people in the BDSM community who've been through trauma. Selena only went to two meetings with the therapist Kora recommended. The woman she went to specializes in domestic abuse. On the outside, it should be a perfect fit. Knowing what I do about Selena, she needs someone who understands the BDSM world. Selena may not be into pain the way many people in the BDSM community are, but she's a submissive. She was in an abusive Master-slave relationship, and a typical therapist won't understand it.

I need to find Carla.

I'm leaving the third place I've gone to track her down, but she's nowhere. She hasn't returned my call or text, either.

Selena should be out of her massage now.

I text her.

Me: *Did you think of me during your massage?*

My phone rings, and it's Carla. I answer it. "You might be the hardest person on earth to track down."

She laughs. "I just got off a plane."

"Hope you were somewhere good."

"I was. I went to Jamaica. The new club they opened is good. You should check it out," she says.

"Maybe I will. Hey, I'm on limited time, and I wanted to ask you for a big favor."

"Sure. What do you need?"

My chest tightens. "I have a friend...well, I'm kind of topping her right now."

"Kind of? You know there's no 'kind of,'" she states.

"Right. Okay. So, I'm topping her. She just got out of a non-consensual Master-slave relationship. I should also mention I promised her I'd mentor her so she can learn to be safe."

"She's lucky to have you."

No, I'm the lucky one.

I'm going to hell for so many reasons.

"She was severely abused. I don't know all the details, but what she told me was enough. She only lasted two sessions with one of the top domestic abuse therapists in Chicago."

"Tetter or Cascade?" Carla asks.

"Cascade," I reply.

"Well, Cascade would be the better option for this, but she still wouldn't understand," Carla admits.

"Right. I hoped you'd meet with her? I'm not sure how to help her how you can," I admit.

There's a brief pause. "Sure. You know I'll help anyone who needs it in our community. Did she say why she stopped seeing Cascade?"

Guilt eats me. I rarely feel guilty about anything I do. I'm unsure why my conscience is involved in this, especially when Carla can help her. "She isn't aware I know she was going." The line is quiet for so long, I wonder if she hung up. "Carla? You still there?"

"Therapy is a personal thing. Does she want help?"

I quickly reply, "Yes. Of course she does."

"Are you sure?"

For a split second, I question it, then adamantly say, "Yes."

Carla groans. "You've gotta be kidding me!" She sighs. "I have to run. My suitcase just showed up open on the baggage claim."

"Ouch."

"Have her text or call me, and we'll set something up."

"Great! Thank you! Good luck with your suitcase."

"Not the suitcase I'm worried about," she grumbles and hangs up.

I glance at my phone.

Selena: *Yes.*

My dick goes back to feeling like it's sixteen again.

Me: *Did you think of my mouth all over you?*

Selena: *Yes.*

Me: *If I flicked my tongue on your pussy right now, would you be ready to come for me?*

Selena: *Yes.*

Me: *V your pussy and send me a photo. And don't forget to take one of your panties when you get home.*

One photo after another comes over, and I stare at them, salivating. *She's such an excellent little dorogaya.*

I compare the picture of her panties from the locker room and home. The damp spot is larger.

Fuuuck. I need to get home.

I roll the divider down and say, "Home." I roll it back up, pull up the video she sent me, and watch it like a boy who just discovered porn until another message pops up on the screen.

Maksim: *Need to meet ASAP.*

What now?

Me: *On my way.*

I redirect my driver, studying every picture she sent me and our messages. All the things I want to do to her are spinning in my head. When I get to Maksim's, he drops another bomb on me. "Darragh and Liam are on their way over."

The hairs on my arms rise. "Why?"

"Something about needing to tie up loose ends?"

"What the fuck does that mean?" I bark.

Maksim comes closer. His eyes pierce into mine. "Did you take a job from Liam?"

I scoff. "You think I'd work for the O'Malleys? Is this an actual question?"

"Boris said you got information on a judge for Liam?" Maksim raises his eyebrows in disapproval.

I point at him. "Your brother needed info on Jack Christian. The only way to get it was to help Liam. Without him, Adrian and I were never getting in. Don't be accusing me of shit—"

"We're supposed to be the wise ones," Maksim claims.

"Do you think for one minute I wanted to do any favors for Liam?"

Maksim sighs. "No. But I'm getting sick of finding out about shit after the fact. You and Adrian should have told me. It doesn't help when Darragh comes to me to discuss something, and I know nothing about it."

I relax a tad. "I'm sorry. You're right. I wasn't thinking straight."

"All of us need to get back on the same page. The Rossi's body count isn't as high as we need it to be right now. We can't let them gain too much power."

We started a war between the two most prominent crime families, the Petrovs and Rossis. We're trying to have them kill each other off, and it requires us to step in from time to time to keep things balanced. Plus, the Polish mob Dasha got us involved in allied with Rossi, and it muddied the waters.

"Call the come to Jesus meeting, and I'll support you," I tell Maksim.

He pats me on the back. "Good. I don't know why we seem to be unglued right now."

"That's an easy answer."

He puts his hands in the air. "Please, fill me in."

"All your women are causing issues. Before all these women, we didn't have this problem. We always knew what everyone was doing," I claim.

The doorbell rings, signaling Liam and Darragh are coming up the elevator.

Maksim's eyes turn to slits. "We had issues before our women came into our lives."

"Yeah, but it's making things more difficult, isn't it?"

Maksim shrugs. "Maybe so, but I'd rather die than live a day without my krasotka."

"I'm just pointing out—"

"Are you ever going to get over Annika?" Maksim asks, which takes me by surprise. Until I recently told Sergey, no one knew the real story, except Adrian and Maksim.

"I am over Annika," I claim.

"No, you aren't. You're still letting her affect your life."

I snort. "No, I'm not."

"You are."

"Have you been speaking with my mother?"

He chuckles. "Actually, Aspen and I spent the day with your mom on Monday. She met Aspen's dad while she was volunteering at the home. They hit it off. She was playing cards with him when we got there and didn't know it was Aspen's dad."

"How's Aspen's dad doing?" He has dementia, and Maksim moved him from a Medicaid facility downstate to a high-end, private one in Chicago.

He smiles. "He has more good days than bad. The new medicine they have him on is working better."

"That's good. I'm glad my mom found another card buddy. It'll keep her away from the bridal magazines."

"Bridal magazines! Who's getting married now?" Liam's voice booms through the room.

I groan internally. I have a love-hate relationship with Liam. Right now, he's the cause of me not spending the next week killing Jack Christian in the slowest, most torturous death I've ever orchestrated.

"No one. You better have a good reason for asking me not to kill that bastard," I bark.

Liam scowls. "Hey, it's nice to see you, too, Obrecht."

"You're pushing your luck with me," I warn Liam.

He crosses his arms. "I don't like it any more than you do. If you think I give a fuck about letting that prick live, you're wrong. But until his company goes public, you can't touch Jack."

"What does that have to do with anything? Selena already got her money from him. The preliminary numbers on his company going public are average. It's not even an awesome investment."

Darragh snorts and then sits in the chair while going into a coughing fit. He takes out a handkerchief that already has splotches of red. I have a momentary guilt trip for not saying hi to the poor bastard. He's got lung cancer and is dying.

"Dad, you want some water?" Liam asks.

"I'll get it," Maksim says and goes into the kitchen.

I feel even worse seeing Liam's pained expression. He got early parole after serving fifteen years in prison. His old man is dying, and he's about to run the O'Malley clan.

He'll probably run them into the ground.

That won't be good for the Ivanovs.

Maksim hands Darragh a bottle of water, but he waves him off. He takes off his tweed cap and points at me. "No one makes a move on Jack Christian or Judge Peterson until I say so."

"You aren't our boss."

Maksim steps next to me, and we both cross our arms. He pins his steel gaze on Darragh. "What's going on, Darragh? If you want the Ivanovs to respect your wishes against a man we want dead, you need to give us a good enough reason to."

"His company has to go public. Once it does, then you've got free rein."

"You don't give us orders," I remind him.

Darragh rises off the couch. It takes him a moment, but he steps in front of me. His eyes turn to slits. "Does our alliance mean nothing to you?"

I don't answer. I never asked for an O'Malley-Ivanov alliance. Boris couldn't stay away from Nora. There wasn't a choice once she got pregnant. The Ivanov blood mixed with the O'Malley's, and the next thing I knew, we were starting a war between the Petrovs and Rossis.

"He didn't say that," Maksim replies for me, which is probably best since I'm about to lose my normal ability to keep my mouth shut.

Darragh points to me. "After his company goes public."

"Every day that bastard lives is another day he can come after Selena," I seethe.

"We're watching him," Liam states.

"Why?" Maksim asks.

"It's O'Malley business. The public launch is right around the corner."

So much rage swirls in my blood. "It's not for months! Selena shouldn't have to live in fear any longer."

"Put a bodyguard on her," Darragh states.

"She already has our guys on her. Doesn't mean that sick bastard should live."

"No, but we've got Finn on Jack. He knows his every move."

"Apparently not, since Adrian and I needed to get the dirt on your guys for you," I belt out.

Darragh points in my face again. "You better watch your mouth, son."

"I'm not your son," I seethe. "But it was your son who needed us to do your work for you."

"For real?" Liam asks. Betrayal is all over his face. "It's interesting how you see things. What I remember is you and your brother not able to get any information on Jack until I gave you the in."

It was a low blow, but I can't seem to think straight, knowing Jack's walking around while Selena worries about her safety. I hate Liam is right.

He pulls out an envelope from his coat pocket and slaps it on the table. "I thought you might want this. I'll meet you in the car, Dad."

My gut drops. I'm not sure what's in the envelope.

"No, I'll go with you, son." Darragh addresses Maksim. "Get your family in order, Maksim. I keep telling you this. If any of you cross us, the Rossi-Petrov war won't be what you have to worry about."

"Is that a threat?" I seethe.

A sad expression fills Darragh's face. "No. It's the truth. All of Chicago might as well burn to the ground. If the Rossis or

Petrovs win because our families didn't work together, this city doesn't stand a chance. The war your family started, the one we're helping you keep balanced out, will change everything if one of them rises to the top and takes the other out. The shift in power will rattle every business, politician, and industry in this town."

"Killian was with us when we started that war. Careful who you blame, Darragh," Maksim reminds him.

"You made me a promise, Maksim. I expect all the Ivanovs to keep it."

Maksim scowls. "We've done nothing but keep our word in the alliance."

Darragh nods. "Let's keep it that way. Jack Christian doesn't get touched until his company goes public." He shakes his head and leaves with Liam.

When the elevator shuts, Maksim glares at me. "There a reason you're trying to piss Darragh off?"

"Don't get me started."

"Got something you want to say?"

"No," I grumble and pick up the envelope Liam dropped on the table.

Maksim sighs. "What's the deal with you and this Selena woman?"

"She lives in my building. We're friends," I say in a nonchalant voice, but my insides are on fire. Her ex needs to die. I rip into the envelope.

"For someone telling me women are causing issues in everyone's life, it sure seems like this woman is creating some in yours," Maksim states.

I don't answer him, and my gut flips. I mutter, "Jesus."

"What is it?"

The color drains from Maksim's face when I show him the photos. Timestamps of the last few days are on the pictures. Gavriil, my tracker I had following Ludis, is drinking with him and Mack Bailey. In several, they're sharing a girl I know is one of Petrov's whorehouse girls. My stomach twists tighter. The girl wouldn't have voluntarily gone there. All of the Petrov girls are kidnapped and broken in. Gavriil is paying Ludis money for her in another photo.

My guy. He's my guy.

Over a decade, he's been with us.

An Ivanov would never take advantage of any woman in a Petrov whorehouse. It can only mean he's on their side and not ours.

"Traitor," Maksim snarls.

"How did Liam get this?"

"We'd know if you hadn't pissed him off."

"Fuck!"

Aspen walks into the penthouse. "Am I interrupting?"

Maksim gives me a final scowl then spins. He walks over to her and kisses her. "No, my krasotka. Obrecht was just leaving to meet up with Liam. Weren't you?" He glares at me.

Shit. I stuff the photos back into the envelope. "Yeah." I kiss Aspen on the cheek.

"How do you like your new place?" she asks which leads to a full-blown conversation. A half hour later, I'm on the way out and pick up my phone. I call Liam. He doesn't answer and I call back. I get a text.

Liam: *Give me a minute.*

I wait for fifteen more minutes, stewing in my car, then call back.

"You'll have to wait. I'm busy now," he growls.

"Doing what? We need to talk."

"Oh! Oh! Please!" a woman's voice cries out in the background.

"That's it, little lamb," he says in a muffled voice. He replies to me, "Important stuff. You can wait. I'll call you when I'm free." He hangs up.

I punch the seat. "Damn it!"

I sit in my car, staring at the pictures, wondering how I could not have seen Gavriil for what he is.

He's a Petrov.

I put the pictures away when my phone rings. It's a telemarketer, so I send it to voicemail. I also realize I missed a text.

Selena: *Will we be at your place or mine?*

It's getting dark, and I'm getting more and more frustrated. I don't want her waiting around for me while Liam fucks whomever he's screwing.

God, I hope it isn't Hailee.

Was it her?

Not my business. I need to focus on my dorogaya.

I send Vlad a text.

Me: *Did the faucet get changed out?*

I saw Selena's body tense when she saw it this morning, so I had it replaced with the one she liked. I don't want her having any flashbacks because of my faucet. Plus, ever since she told me why she switched hers, mine has been bugging me.

Vlad: *Yes.*

At least something got done right today. I send Selena another text.

Me: *My elevator code is 684538. Memorize it. Don't shower. Bring whatever you purchased with you, get dressed, and wait for me to come home.*

Selena: *You aren't back yet?*

Me: *No. Have a glass of wine if you want. I put a bottle of Pinot Noir out.*

Selena: *How do you know I drink that?*

Me: *I know a lot of things about you, baby girl. Now get your sexy ass up to my place.*

Liam makes me wait over an hour, which only makes me angrier. When his car finally pulls up to mine, we roll down the windows.

"How did you get it?" I ask.

"I have eyes everywhere. You seem to forget I'm on your side."

"I don't have time for games, Liam. How long have you known about this?"

He scowls. "I'm getting tired of this. Did you see the date on the pictures?"

"Yeah."

"There's your answer. If you think I'd learn about a traitor in your house, when Nora's now an Ivanov, and not tell you, you think way less of me than I thought."

I hate how Liam keeps sticking it to me. "Where is he?"

Liam tilts his head. "You don't listen very well."

A chill runs down my spine. "Goddammit. We would have tracked him down and gotten every last piece of information out of him before killing him."

"Once again, you underestimate the O'Malleys."

"What did you find out?" I bark.

Liam's lips twitch. "A lot." He looks at his watch. "Too much to tell you tonight. I've got dinner plans. Maybe tomorrow we can talk."

"Liam—"

"Before I go. The next time you try to throw me under the bus with my father, or anyone else, we're going to have bigger problems than this."

I fall to my last resort. "Liam, he did horrible things to her. He waterboarded her for years, for Christ's sake."

He clenches his jaw. "After his company goes public, I'll deliver him on a silver platter to you. No one will touch him but you. But this event has to take place."

"Why?"

"We'll talk tomorrow." He rolls up the window, and I clench my fists.

I sit in the car for an hour, trying to calm down. I text Selena.

Me: *I'm on my way home. I'm sorry it took me longer than I thought.*

Selena: *It's okay. Have you eaten? I made you dinner in case you didn't. I hope it's okay I used what you had?*

I stare at the text. The last time a woman made me dinner, it was Annika. I swallow the lump forming in my throat.

Me: *Yeah, baby girl. It's okay. You don't have to ask to use anything in my place.*

Selena: *So...you'll be home soon?*

Me: *Five minutes.*

When I get inside the penthouse, something smells delicious. It's dark other than the glow of the city, fireplace, and candles that Selena lit. But the most beautiful sight I've ever seen is in front of the window.

She's kneeling, facing the city, head bowed, ass on her heels. She's wearing her new outfit and an apron. Her sexy ass is bare, except for a delicate piece of black lace over her hips and a black bow. It crisscrosses up her back and disappears under the apron over her chest. She's a magnificent piece of art with the city sparkling all around her.

She's mine.

For tonight.

She shouldn't be kneeling. We haven't negotiated.

"Stand up, baby girl, and grab your ankles."

I'm such a selfish bastard.

She rises, slowly moves her hands over her legs until she's holding her ankles. I step behind her and take a deep breath. I palm her ass cheeks.

"Did you enjoy your spa treatment?"

"Yes, sir."

"Why did you choose this outfit?" I drag my finger in a circle on her ass cheek then drop to my knees, inhaling the smell of her arousal. I rub my hands over her thighs.

She whimpers. "I wanted to be your gift, sir."

Fuck. My heart races faster.

"You did good, baby girl. You didn't shower, did you?"

"No, sir."

"Good. I've been waiting to see what you smell like after you've thought about me all day." I sniff hard and flick my tongue on her sex and groan. My chocolate-covered pretzel is tastier than ever.

"Obrecht!" she cries out.

I rise. "Stand up, baby girl."

She rises, and I spin her into me. Her face is flushed, and the green in her eyes swirls into the browns. Her lips are trembling.

I trace my finger over her mouth. "Why are you shaking, my dorogaya?"

"I don't know."

I fist her hair and tug her head back then lean my face over hers. "Are you scared of me?"

"No."

"I'm sorry I'm late and made you wait," I tell her again, even though I texted her earlier. It's true. I regret every minute not standing here with my gift.

My gift. Good God.

I study her face, trying to remember we haven't negotiated yet.

She needs to learn, or she'll get hurt.

No one else but me is touching her.

I'm a top, not a Dom.

She sweetly smiles, making my dick twitch. "It's okay. I'm-I'm glad you're home safe."

"You don't have to worry about me."

A tiny smile forms on her face. Those plump, pouty, goddamn lips I want all over me part, and she says, "I do. I was."

My chest tightens again. "What did you make for dinner? It smells good."

"Mediterranean fish."

I trace the middle of her neck with my finger, and she shudders. "Sounds good. Let's go eat and negotiate. I have a lot of things I want to do with you tonight."

She inhales deeply and opens her mouth then shuts it.

"Speak freely, baby girl."

"Thank you for switching the faucet out." She glances at my lips, eyes, then back to my lips.

"You're welcome. If there's anything else you don't like, tell me, and I'll fix it."

She furrows her eyebrows. "Really?"

"Yes. Is there something else you've seen you don't like?"

She shakes her head. Her eyes glisten. "No. I just...thank you."

I dip down and kiss her, but I only give her a little. I pull back and slap her ass. It's harder than the one I gave her earlier today. She jumps, and I rub her cheek. "That's for kneeling before we negotiated. You don't do that until you've set your boundaries, understand?"

"Okay, I'm sorry."

"Do you know why you don't kneel before you negotiate?"

"No."

I tug her head back farther, keeping my eyes glued to hers. "You hold the power, my dorogaya. If you kneel before negotiating, you've given it away. Don't do that."

"But I want you to have all the power."

Jesus. I hold my groan inside.

It's wrong. She can't allow me to have it all.

"No, baby girl. And don't tempt me to take it."

10

Selena

"WHY NOT?" I WHISPER, LOOKING UP AT OBRECHT. I'VE officially become more screwed up than I thought. It feels so good to have him order me around and be in charge. Something about letting him do whatever he wants with me, whenever he wants, digs into me.

His hot breath mingles with mine. Flames sear his orbs. "Come sit down."

"I need to get dinner out of the oven."

Obrecht gives me a chaste kiss and releases my hair. His palm stays on my ass. He guides me to the kitchen. "Do you need help?"

His question startles me. *He wants to help me with dinner? How is this possible?*

My job is to serve him. How will I please him if I don't?

"I have it. But thank you. Please go sit down. I want to please you, sir."

He studies me again with his intense stare. My flutters mix with worry.

"Did I do something wrong?" I fret.

"No, baby girl. I love that you want to please me, but you already do. I don't want you worrying about it."

"But you asked to help me," I state.

He arches an eyebrow. "Yes. Is something wrong with me asking you if you need help?"

I slide the oven mitt on and pick up the other one. "It's not your role to cook or help me."

"You are not my slave, Selena. You are my little dorogaya. I'm thrilled and very grateful you made dinner, but it is not your job. I do not expect it now and will not in the future. It is something nice you did for me, but I will never take it for granted."

I stare at the counter, wondering why everything has to be so confusing. If I didn't have dinner ready when Jack came home, even when he arrived home early with no warning, there were consequences to pay. Obrecht makes it sound so simple, but it all makes my chest tighten with anxiety.

He cups my cheeks. "You know what is going to make me happy?"

"No. What?"

He kisses my lips until I'm trembling in his arms. "Well, that makes me happy."

I can't help but beam from his praise, like he's Santa Claus telling me I've been good all year and deserve presents.

"Now I'm going to watch you remove the food from the oven in this sexy little outfit you got for me. Then I'm going to pour us a glass of wine and enjoy this dinner you made us."

"Us? Glass?" Once again, I'm confused.

"Do you not want a glass?"

"Umm..."

His face falls. "Tell me why you look so distraught, baby girl."

The strange feeling I have whenever I am about to tell Obrecht something I seem to have wrong fills my belly. "If I'm your bottom, don't you want me to use the bowls?"

His jaw clenches. The fire in his eyes turns to ice. "The bowls?"

"Umm... I was only allowed to have water. But I had to keep my hands behind my back and lap it from the bowl when Jack allowed me. He kept it on the other side of my food bowl. I was usually only allowed to drink after he finished eating." I point to the table. "I set them next to your chair."

Obrecht turns his head to the table, and his hands ball into fists. Red creeps up his neck and into his face.

Oh no. I said something wrong.

He's mad at me now.

I shouldn't have questioned the wine.

He beelines to the bowls, picks them up, then stares at the table. Time seems to stand still as I watch him take at least a dozen deep breaths. The more he doesn't speak or move, the more anxious I become.

He finally comes into the kitchen, puts the bowls in the cabinet, and takes out a plate, silverware, and another wineglass. He returns to the table and puts it next to his seat.

It only perplexes me more.

He tilts my chin. "You aren't an animal, baby girl. You don't deserve anything less than what I have. We will eat together, just like we did at breakfast. Nothing changes whether we are in public or private while eating, do you understand?"

I blink hard, not wanting to spend the evening crying like I did the previous night, but my emotions roll through my chest. I'm not sure what they mean or what to do with them. "I'm sorry I got it wrong."

"Don't be sorry. This isn't your fault. And you will never kneel on the floor next to anyone during a meal or lap up water or food with your hands behind your back ever again. Is this crystal clear?" he sternly says.

"Yes, sir."

He closes his eyes briefly. "No more sirs right now, Selena. We are not in a session. I should not be allowing you to call me sir when we aren't. I am Obrecht. You are Selena. My hot, sexy dorogaya. You are beautiful and smart. No one should make you feel anything less."

I glance at his chest, my insides quivering, feeling very stupid all of a sudden. *Why can't I get this right?*

The oven beeps. Obrecht steps back, and I remove the tray from it and set it on the stove. I arrange the food on a platter and spin.

Obrecht pins his gaze on me. The corners of his mouth curve up. "I think you're spoiling me."

"How?"

He steps forward, reaches behind me, and pulls the apron string. "Sending me naughty pictures. Cooking for me. Choosing the perfect outfit then making me wait to see the rest of it." He pecks me on the lips and lifts the apron over my head. He picks up the tray and steps back. His eyes travel the length of my body. "Out of all the dinners I've had, this is my favorite."

"We haven't eaten yet."

"I know. Whatever the food tastes like is a bonus." His orbs dart to the bow on my chest then back to mine. "I'm looking forward to unwrapping my entire gift."

Heat bursts into my cheeks. The things he says to me always make my heart stutter. He seems so sincere. He never says anything mean to me. Every word that comes out of his mouth is so different from what I'm accustomed to hearing.

He motions for me to go first. "Please."

It's another thing I don't understand. Jack always went first, and I had to follow him. He would never have carried a food platter or had me sit at the table when we were home. Mentally, I know Jack didn't treat me right, but it isn't easy to wrap my mind around.

When I get in front of the table, I wait for Obrecht to choose his seat. He surprises me again and pulls out a chair. "Have a seat, my dorogaya."

I cautiously sit as straight as I can. It feels like my chest is squeezing my heart. I watch Obrecht put fish, vegetables, and some orzo on my plate, then his. He sits then fills our wine-glasses.

I observe his every move. I'm a fish out of water, not sure what to do next.

He turns in his chair and kneads my shoulder with one hand. "What's going on in that pretty head of yours?"

"I'm-I'm not sure what to do," I admit.

He smiles. "Sure, you are. And I know you are because you ate breakfast with me at the restaurant."

"But that wasn't in your home."

"Right. And now I get to be in my house, with the sexiest woman on earth next to me, eating a dinner she made us, and drinking a glass of wine. Did I mention she's wrapped in a bow and making me harder than ever?"

I bite on my smile.

He hesitates then asks, "Will you feel different if you put your clothes on?"

I take a moment to ponder his question then shake my head. "No."

He grins. "Thank God. I might have cried if I had to cover you up."

A tiny laugh escapes me.

He kisses my cheek. "Relax. Enjoy dinner with me."

I take a deep breath. "Okay."

He holds his glass out. I pick mine up. "To a fabulous meal, our upcoming negotiations, and the sexiest woman I've ever had sitting at this table. Nostrovia."

"Nostrovia," I repeat, clink his glass, and we both take a sip of wine.

He takes a bite of the fish. "Mmm. This is delicious, baby girl."

I sigh in relief, not realizing I was holding my breath.

"Eat," he commands and nods to my plate.

I obey.

We eat in silence for a few minutes until he says, "Tell me about your day."

"You already know about it."

"No. I only know pieces. Fill in the blanks for me."

I take a sip of wine. "The store you sent me to had a nice girl named April. She helped me with everything."

"Yeah, she's great." He takes another bite of fish.

"You know her?"

He nods while chewing, swallows, and says, "She's a bottom at the club I attend."

My jealousy flares. I sit up straighter. "You've topped her?"

"No."

Curiosity replaces the green-eyed monster in me. "Why not?"

"She's into things I'm not."

"Like what?"

He wipes his mouth, takes a drink of wine, then turns to me. "I don't enjoy hurting women, even if it's what they want."

BDSM. Bondage and discipline. Dominance and submission. Sadism and masochism. "So you aren't a sadist?"

He hesitates, opens his mouth, then stops.

"Did I ask the wrong question?"

"No. I'm a sadist but not during sex or with women, the way you think," he admits.

"How? I don't understand."

"I don't inflict physical pain. Mine is mental control. And it fuels me to hurt men who have it coming to them. So yeah, I'm a sadist."

"What do you do to them?"

A tornado of emotions swirls in his expression. Is it rage? Disgust? Loathing? I can't figure it out, but it's intense and sends a shiver down my spine. He taps his fingers on his wine goblet. "I won't show mercy with a man who hurts a woman. I get great pleasure out of every second I make him pay. It's why you don't need to worry about ever going back to Jack. Very shortly, I will have my day with him."

The chill digs into my spine deeper. I reach for his arm. "Please don't do anything that harms you."

Confidence replaces the tornado. "You don't ever have to worry about me. I know what I'm doing, but it's best if you never repeat this conversation we're having. I shouldn't speak about any of this."

"Then why are you?" I blurt out.

His voice drops. "I'm not sure. The only answer I have is I trust you."

"I trust you, too," I reply.

He drags his finger down my cheek. "I'm happy to hear that. What did you buy at the store?"

My stomach flips. "Can I show you?"

"Yes."

I get up and walk to the counter. The air in my lungs gets thicker. I pick up the bag and return to the table. My hands shake as I remove the black face hood, the leather neck-wrist restraint, and a long, thick, black kinetic anal plug.

Obrecht's face doesn't show any signs of approval or disapproval. He picks up the black face hood. It goes over your entire head, and there's only a hole for your mouth. I cringe and look down at the table.

"This is something you're afraid of?"

"Yes."

He rubs my back. "Tell me why."

My chest tightens so much, I get slightly dizzy. Flashbacks of Jack putting a similar one over my head and keeping me in it for days, maybe even weeks for all I know, causes bile to crawl up my throat.

Obrecht tugs me onto his lap and circles his arms around me. He positions my cheek on his chest and strokes my hair. In a low voice, he says, "He used to use this on you?"

"Yes."

"Okay, baby girl. When we finish, we're going to cut it up and light it on fire, okay?"

I glance up at him. "You aren't going to make me wear it?"

"No. And you should never let anyone put this on you again. This is a hard limit for you. What does the thought of me putting a blindfold over your eyes do to you?"

I inhale a sharp breath, my stomach flips, and I squeeze my eyes shut.

"This means your hard limit is nothing over your eyes. You make it very clear, understand?"

"How?"

"You say my hard limit is nothing over my eyes."

"That's it?" I ask, surprised I don't have to explain things.

"Yes."

I trace the snake on his neck. "Do you want to cover my eyes?"

"No."

"Why not?"

"You don't like it or want it. It doesn't give me pleasure to instill fear in you or do anything you're not okay with." He kisses the top of my head then picks up the leather neck-wrist restraint. Two handcuffs connect to a long black strap. On the other end is a circular part to go around your neck and get adjusted. He strokes the leather and asks, "Is this something you like or are curious about?"

My heart beats faster. I could lie, but I don't want to. I swallow the big lump in my throat. "There wasn't anything in the store I like. I-I got that because you said you like bondage, and I think I might like it if it was with you. But he never used that on me," I add.

Obrecht freezes.

Maybe I shouldn't have admitted it.

He puts it on the table then kisses my forehead again. "Were you tied up in the past?"

"Sometimes."

"Do you have any good memories of it?"

I blink hard. A tear rolls down my cheek. "No. I have no good memories of anything. But I want to try it with you."

His arms tighten around me, and his chest pushes against me. "We will try bondage to see if you like it. If you don't, you say the safe word, and we'll stop. Do you understand?"

But what if he's enjoying it and I'm not?

"Selena, it's important to me we never keep doing something you aren't enjoying. And if you can't tell me, it worries me you won't tell someone else to stop. Promise me you will use the safe word if you don't like something."

"I promise," I reply.

He takes a sip of wine then picks up the anal plug. "This is something you're also curious about?"

"Yes. Are you mad I got two things I'm curious about and didn't do the assignment correctly?" April told me to get two things I was curious about and said my top wouldn't be upset, but now I'm not sure.

"I'm so happy you got two things and told me the truth. You get an A-plus on your homework, baby girl."

"I do?"

"Yes. Now, please tell me if you have used something like this before?"

I shake my head. "Jack just...um...." I bury my face in Obrecht's chest.

He sniffs hard. A few minutes pass, and he quietly asks, "What did he do?"

I don't leave the safety of his warm flesh and avoid his question. "April said it was to prep you for anal sex or to use during sex. She said she likes it, and it shouldn't hurt."

"No, it should not hurt. It should never, ever hurt. If it does, you're with the wrong guy. He's a dickhead who doesn't know what he's doing or is intentionally trying to hurt you. Either one is not someone you should be with," Obrecht snarls.

My pulse pounds harder everywhere—my veins, my throat, between my ears. I admit, "It always hurt with Jack."

"He's going to pay," Obrecht says so quietly, I almost think he didn't say it.

I leave the cocoon of his arms and straddle him then cup his cheeks. "I don't want to talk about him anymore. I want to forget him. Let's negotiate."

Obrecht's hardened face doesn't change. "Forgetting isn't always easy, Selena. I don't want to make things worse for you."

"You aren't. You couldn't," I insist.

He doesn't appear convinced.

"Look, you're the one with the normal, everything's perfect life. I'm the one with all the baggage. If I say it's possible to forget, then you should trust me since I'm the one who would know."

Obrecht's face fills with so much sadness, my heart almost breaks. He replies, "My life isn't perfect. I have plenty of baggage."

"Someone hurt you?" I gently ask.

His jaw clenches, and he shakes his head. "Not like they hurt you."

I stroke the side of his head. "It wasn't physical?"

"No."

"Sometimes mental pain is worse than physical pain," I state.

"What do you think is mentally worse than physical pain?" he asks.

"Love and betrayal." It flows out of me so fast and hits me in the face. I never really thought about it, but it's what I hate about Jack so much. I loved him. I gave him every ounce of trust I had. He betrayed me in too many ways to count. It hurt every time he did something new to try and destroy me.

Obrecht quietly says, "Yeah, that hurts pretty bad, baby girl."

Someone hurt him. The realization shocks me. He's so strong, dangerous, and fierce. I assumed he was untouchable, but it's clear he's not. His Natalia tattoo flashes in my mind, and I cup his cheek. "Natalia betrayed you?"

His eyes widen, and the color drains from his face. "What do you know about Natalia?"

"Nothing. I saw your tattoo and just put two and two together."

He turns away from me, staring out into the night sky, but I don't miss the pain emanating from him. I want to help him. To find out what happened and figure out how to make it all go away, so he doesn't feel this. I'm not sure how or what to do. If I could take it from him and add it into my pot of painful memories, I would.

He finally says, "Natalia was my sister. She was kidnapped, raped for a year in a whorehouse, and murdered. They threw her body on our doorstep."

I freeze and swallow hard. The pain looks so fresh on him. "When did this happen?"

He faces me. "About fifteen years ago. It's in the past."

159

Maybe I shouldn't ask him, but I want to know more about who would do such a horrible thing. "Who are they?"

His face hardens. Hatred fills his expression. "The Petrovs."

"I'm sorry. Should I know who they are?"

He puts his hands on my hips. "No, my dorogaya. They're the Russian mob, and I don't ever want you to know anything about them."

"You were friends with them? That's how you know about betrayal?" I ask.

He closes his eyes briefly. "No. That was someone else."

"A woman?" I ask. Jealousy rises in me again that he loved someone else. It mixes with hatred for whoever this woman is who had the gift of his heart and didn't cherish it.

"Yeah. It also happened a long time ago, but I know how betrayal from someone you love tears you in the gut," he admits.

"At least physical pain stops eventually," I point out.

His warm palms move to my ass. "Nothing I went through is close to what you experienced. I don't want you to ever take what happened to you and act like it is the same."

"Is love not love? Is betrayal not betrayal?" I ask.

He sternly replies, "It's not the same, my dorogaya."

"Why?"

"I never lost my freedom."

I'm not sure why his statement sits and stews in my mind. I know what a slave is. I understand Jack took my freedom and made me his. But I would willingly give Obrecht my freedom if it meant I would always be his. Jack was a bad Master. He was evil and cruel beyond measure. Everything about Obrecht is warm and feels safe, even though I could tell he was a dangerous man before he confirmed it.

He wouldn't ever hurt me.

That's what I thought about Jack.

I shudder.

"Are you cold?" Obrecht asks and rubs my back.

How screwed up am I? What am I doing?

I can't go back to what I used to do with Jack.

But he isn't doing what Jack did to me.

Obrecht studies me, but I'm not sure what to say. I glance down and see my breasts, with the bow neatly tied up around them, and my thoughts ping back and forth over whether this is right or wrong and what is wrong with me that I want anything resembling what Jack and I had.

My chest tightens, my heart pounds so fast, pains shoot through it. A quivering in my gut gets so rough, my entire body shakes. Goose bumps break out on my skin as sweat pops out.

"I have to go," I whisper and put my hand over my heart as another stinging sensation shoots through it.

Obrecht holds my face in his hands. "What's wrong, baby girl?"

I stare at his eyes, but they become blurry from my tears. Suddenly, I can't breathe. I can't see. I can't hear anything he says. The only things I hear are my thoughts and Jack's voice.

"I'll take care of you, Selena. You'll always be mine. Forever."

Then, he's screaming at me.

"You're thick as pig shit."

"Get in your cage."

"Kneel and don't move, or there will be consequences!"

"Bow your head! How dare you look at me!"

It cyclones over and over until I cover my ears, wanting it to stop but not sure how to make it.

11

M

Obrecht

"PLEASE STOP." SELENA'S WHISPERING THROUGH TEARS. SHE'S covering her ears and curled in my lap, rocking in a ball. Her body is clammy and trembling. It's approaching the thirty-minute mark since she went into her episode.

"Shh, baby girl," I keep saying to calm her, but nothing works. Every second that passes scares me more. I'm not sure what to do.

"Stop! Please!" she screams out, and her shaking gets worse. Her lips turn purple, and her body is covered in sweat but seems to get colder. I pick her up and carry her into the bedroom then put her under the covers. I take off my clothes and get in bed with her. I pull her to me, hoping my body heat can help her get warm.

She attempts to push me away, but I hold her tighter so she can't escape.

"You're safe, my dorogaya. Shhh." I put my leg over hers and kiss her cheeks. "No one is going to hurt you."

It seems to last forever until she's only softly whimpering. Her tears lessen, and she falls asleep. When I only hear sniffles and the sound of her breathing, I reach for my phone I put on the table and call Carla.

"Calling to see if my clothes survived baggage claim?" she answers in a chirpy voice.

"Did they?"

"Only half."

"Sorry to hear that," I say.

"Yeah, you should have seen the looks I got when everyone saw what did stay in my bag. Obrecht, what's going on?" she asks, her voice turning into concern. "I don't normally get two calls from you in one day. I'm open to booty calls, but unless you decided to become a sub, I'm going to have to pass."

I glance at my dorogaya, and she takes a shaky breath. I kiss her on the head and stroke her hair.

At least she isn't trembling anymore.

"Something just happened. I'm not sure what," I admit.

Her voice falls. "With your bottom?"

"Yes."

"I'm listening."

My mouth goes dry. "We were having dinner and talking. She seemed to go into some kind of episodic trance. She was crying, shaking, and sweating. Her body was freezing. I couldn't pull her out of it. She kept saying to please stop, but I wasn't doing anything." My gut twists as I tell Carla.

"Where are you now?"

"I put her in my bed to warm her up. She's asleep. Also, at the start, she was clutching her heart. I thought she might be having a heart attack, but then she just kept crying to stop." The visual of Selena distressed makes me tighten my arm around her.

"Sounds like a panic attack. What were you discussing before this happened? And be specific," Carla adds.

I rack my brain. It seemed to happen so fast. "We were talking about our day. I sent her to see April and had her pick three items."

"Is that when she went into her panic attack?"

"No. We started talking about things in my life and mental versus physical pain. I mentioned something about not comparing painful things in my life to what she's gone through and..." I attempt to recall exactly what I said. "Oh. She asked why, and I told her I had never lost my freedom."

"Hmmm." The line goes silent.

My heart hammers hard against my chest. "What does that mean?"

"My assumption is the freedom comment triggered something."

"What?"

"I can't be sure without speaking with her. Did she say anything else?"

"N—" Selena's voice enters my head, and I tell Carla, "She said she had to go."

"Hmmm."

"You're hmms aren't doing much for me," I state.

"Sorry. Honestly, I can't say much until I speak with her."

"Do you think she needs to go to the hospital?"

"I would hold off. See how she is when she wakes up in the morning. If you need me to come over, I can," Carla says.

"Would you?"

"Sure. But you should ask her first if it's okay. See how she feels when she wakes up, then ask her if she's open to talking with me," Carla directs.

"She'll be open to it. What else should I do tonight?" I ask.

Carla clears her throat. "Go to sleep. If she wakes up, talk to her."

"That's it?"

"Yep. Rest will be good for both of you. Call me in the morning."

"Okay. Thanks. Goodnight."

"Night."

I hang up, put the phone on the table, and scoot farther down in the bed. Selena stirs but doesn't wake up. She looks like a sad angel sleeping with her tear-stained cheeks.

I stare at her for hours, giving her butterfly kisses from time to time, wondering what's going on in her head. I replay the evening over and over, pissed at so many things. The rage I have toward Jack is at a level I can't even comprehend. Liam and Darragh's warning not to touch him until his company goes public flashes in my mind. I vow to make Liam tell me tomorrow why it's so important. All I want to do is kill Jack.

Images of my dorogaya kneeling next to him while he eats, then lapping up water and getting fed like a dog, make me feel sick.

She was willing to do it to be with me.

My baby girl is so confused.

I stroke her ass, and my thumb hits the bow of her panties. *My gift. She wanted to give herself to me as a gift.* Guilt tears at me because I love it. Every moment staring at her, talking to her, and just being with her, I love. I'm not used to wanting someone like this, and everything about my craving for her seems wrong when I watch my dorogaya sleeping with a pained look on her beautiful face.

I thought helping her understand her boundaries and how to get what she needs safely was the right thing to do, but now I'm unsure. Maybe I'm harming her more, and everything I've done is too much for her.

After a lot of debate, I decide I'll have Carla come over in the morning and tell her we can't be together sexually anymore. I'll be here for her as a friend, but I won't add to her pain or

MAGGIE COLE

confuse her more. She doesn't need to be triggered, and I did something to harm her. Self-hatred swirls through me. She's been through enough pain and should never have to go through any again.

I eventually fall asleep, adamant I'll do only what's best for her and hoping when she wakes up, she's not in a panic anymore. Like everything in life, intentions and reality can be total opposites. When I wake up, Selena is stroking the side of my head. Her eyes have green fire mixed into the brown. Her pouty lips are inches from mine.

"Hey, baby girl. Are you okay?" I quietly ask. Unable to stop myself, I brush my thumb over her lips. My body reacts. Blood pumps harder through my veins. My erection grows.

"I'm sorry. I don't know what happened," she whispers. There's so much confusion in her voice. It pains me further.

"Shh. Everything is okay. We'll talk in the morning. Get some more rest."

Her eyes dart to my lips. "I ruined our night, didn't I?"

"No."

She bites her bottom lip, and my dick twitches against her leg. She glances down then back to my eyes.

Jesus. I need to control myself.

"Have you had panic attacks before?" I ask, trying to focus on her and not the indecent thoughts roaming through my head.

"I-I think I had them when I was with Jack a few times. I never knew what to call them. I-I'd get punished for them.

168

D-do you want to punish me for ruining our night?" She holds her breath.

I hold her face. "No, baby girl. You should never receive a punishment for having a panic attack. You haven't done anything wrong."

She takes a few shaky breaths. "Okay. Can we negotiate now?"

My body betrays me again, pulsing against her and becoming so hard, I have to take a brief moment to find my bearings. "I don't think it's what you need right now. Close your eyes and go back to sleep. We'll talk in the morning."

Her lips quiver, and her eyes tear up. "You don't want me anymore?" So much betrayal and hurt fill her face, it pains me.

"I always want you. It's not about my feelings for you," I try to reassure her.

"If you want me, you'll take me. If I didn't do anything wrong, you wouldn't stop us from being together."

I hold in another groan. I shouldn't do it, but I give her a quick kiss and admit, "All I ever want is to take you, baby girl."

"Then let's negotiate."

Her tempting offer is hard to resist, but I try. "No. You need to sleep. Tomorrow we will talk."

"I did sleep." She rolls on top of me, pushing her knees on each side of my hips. Her wet heat hits my cock, and a low rumble fills my chest. "Do you not want your gift?"

You have no idea.

"It's not that, baby girl."

"Am I too damaged for you?"

"No. You aren't damaged, my dorogaya." My hand slips over her perfectly smooth ass cheeks. All the cravings I have about how I want to take her, boil in my veins.

Her lips brush against mine as she speaks. "All day, I've been wet for you, sir. I want you to use your gift. Please." She rubs her sex on my cock and whimpers.

It's not right.

I need to help her.

"Please. Don't throw me out," she whispers.

My heart tears. The things she believes about how I see her are a piece of glass shredding me. "I'd never toss you aside, baby girl. It's not possible."

"Then let's negotiate. I'll do whatever you want. I just want you to have me," she admits.

Fuuuck.

She swallows hard and arches her ass into my hand. "Do you want my ass? I'll give it to you."

So much.

She's not ready for it.

"I do but not tonight." There's no way I'm ever taking her that way unless she's prepared and can enjoy it. Part of me wonders if it will trigger more bad memories for her.

"Tell me what you want me to agree to. Please, sir." Her voice is desperate, but her eyes are what do it for me. They're a combination of need and fear, not of me, but of me rejecting her. It makes me lose all reasoning not to have her.

"No more sir tonight," I sternly tell her.

"No?" Confusion then rejection fills her face. Her voice shakes. "Please."

"I'm Obrecht. You're Selena. We're past the point of negotiations, baby girl."

"Why? What do I need to do so you'll have me? Please."

Jesus, she begs so well.

I'm going to hell for this.

"You can't sit on my cock with your hot pussy dripping all over me and negotiate. This is past the point of negotiations. We're at the stage where you need to say stop if I do something you don't like. Understand?"

She furrows her eyebrows. "Stop. Not faucet?"

"You can say either, baby girl, and I'll stop. I always will, understand?"

She nods. "Yes."

I fist her hair, slide my tongue in her mouth, and circle every delicious corner of her mouth. She flicks back, hungry, urgent, moaning, and grinding her body on top of mine. I end the kiss and command, "Sit up so I can unwrap my gift."

Her body relaxes, as if in relief. It only makes me harder. One last guilty thought about how she just had a panic attack, and this might not be the best thing for her circles my mind, but my selfishness wins. She sits in a straddled position and bows her head.

"Don't bow your head, baby girl. I want to see you."

She raises her face. Her cheeks flush, and I reach for them and glide my fingers over her jaw. She shudders, and the bow on her chest rises and falls faster. "What did you think when you saw yourself in this?"

"I-I hoped you would like it, and I chose the right outfit." She bites her lower lip.

"I don't like it. I love it. But did you see how sexy you are? Did you touch yourself?"

"No. You said I wasn't allowed."

"But you would have? If I allowed you to?"

Her cheeks burn. "Yes. I can't stop thinking about you. Can I touch you? Please?"

It's a question that surprises me. I'm curious where she wants to touch me. "Yes."

She reaches behind her and strokes my balls then cups them, squeezing them gently.

I groan.

"I-I kept thinking how much I want to please you. And..." She bites on her lip again, continuing to massage my balls.

"And what, baby girl?"

Her eyes peek through her long lashes. "I wanted to know what I could do to be better than your other bottoms."

My heart stammers in my chest. Before I can think about what I'm saying, I reply, "You are better. Every sexy part of you is better, but this," I put one hand on her head, "and this," I put my other hand over her heart, "puts you in front of everyone else."

Her eyes widen. "Really?"

My chest tightens. "Yes, baby girl. And if you have any doubts, you're in my bed where no one else has been."

"No one?"

"No. I told you this the other night."

"I just thought it's because you only moved in recently."

"No. You're special. Don't forget it."

She beams, and the feeling I can't seem to escape around her flares in me.

I'm in dangerous territory. I feel it but can't seem to get out of it. I'm in over my head. It's why I should stop all this right now. I move my hands to her thighs, trying to steady myself, debating how to handle whatever this is that's happening between us.

She takes my hand and moves it to her soaked, barely-there panties. She closes her eyes and sighs. "When I saw the neck-wrist restraint, I started to spiral."

My gut sinks in disappointment. I'm not going to do anything if it's already triggering her. When I saw it, all I could think of was how sexy she'd look in it and the many ways I would utilize it. "We won't use it."

"No. Please. I-I kept thinking of how you might have me wear it. Or how you would touch me if I were in it."

My cock pulses. "It wasn't bad thoughts?"

"No. Do you...umm...do you think you would like me in it?"

"Baby girl, there's nothing you could put on I wouldn't like." I stroke my finger over her panties, holding myself back from ripping them off her.

She gasps.

"Feel good, my dorogaya?" I push through her folds and onto her clit, the damp material between us, slowly rubbing her.

"So good," she breathes. Her eyes close, and her mouth forms a small O until her raspy voice asks, "Do you want me to go get it?"

Yes.

She isn't ready.

Let's see how she handles her hands behind her back.

"No. I don't want you to leave my bed. Right now, I want to unwrap my present. And I want your hands on me when I do." I grab her hips and move her forward so my cock is against her ass.

She immediately begins stroking my shaft with one hand and keeps her other on my balls.

How is this woman so perfect?

Her hands feel so different from anyone else who has ever touched me. They're soft yet firm. Every stroke she makes is with precision.

I pull the ribbon, collapsing the satin bow over her chest. I'm not sure if I love her ass or breasts more. I want to explore every curve of her body. I slide my finger around her fullness, watching her nipple get harder without me touching it.

The scent of her arousal flares in my nostrils. Her skin flushes with heat. Pre-cum oozes out of my cock, and she runs her nails over my shaft, then returns to shimmying her hand over it. I drag my finger through her cleavage and down her stomach, stopping on her mound.

I need to stop her, or I'm going to blow my wad.

Normally, I need a lot more than a handjob, but everything about her crashes through anything typical.

In a quick move, I flip her on her back and cage my body over hers. She gasps in surprise. I take her sweet lips with mine, fucking her with my tongue while my finger slips into her panties. I play with her clit until she's writhing under me and about to come, whimpering in my mouth.

"I didn't permit you to come, baby girl," I growl, knowing she's beyond the point of needing it after today but unable to not exert my control over her. And the knowledge that she's capable of not going over the edge from her years of practice burns in my mind. It makes me an official asshole, but I crave the ability to make her submit fully to me in all ways.

"Please, oh God! Please!" she cries out.

"I'm not God, baby girl! Don't beg him. He's not going to give you what you need. Now put your hands under your head."

I don't slow down the intensity or give her a break. I add more to it by dipping to her chest and taking each breast in my mouth, sucking hard on her nipples, and rolling my tongue on them.

"Obrecht! Please!"

She's not calling for God anymore. Good.

Her obedience almost makes me want to let her come.

Almost.

She can wait longer.

I slip down her dewy torso and slide three fingers in her at once and devour her with my mouth. It's not slow or teasing. It should send her into a straight-out orgasm the moment my lips touch her, but my little dorogaya isn't just anyone. She takes it all while begging me until her voice is hoarse. Her thighs shake against my cheeks. Sweat coats her skin.

Her final pleas are so emotional, I cave. "Please, Obrecht. I can't—"

"You can do anything you want, my dorogaya," I bark against her and return to feasting on her.

She begins to cry, and the sadist in me is finally happy.

"Come, baby girl," I demand.

She releases so hard, she soaks my bed while moaning, "Thank you. Oh God! Thank you!"

We're going to have to work on this God thing.

I let her have her moment, and when she starts to fall, I flip her over and order, "Hands under the pillow. Face turned on it so I can see you."

She never hesitates.

The satin bow on her ass only makes me harder. I yank her hips up, move her thong to the side, and thrust into her in one motion. Her eyes widen, and her mouth opens as she gasps.

"Who am I?" I bark, thrusting into her quickly.

"Obrecht!"

"Am I God?"

"No!"

"Don't call for him, don't thank him, don't think of him when I'm touching you. Understand?"

"Yes, sir," she replies.

Fuuuck! I love it when she calls me sir. But I told her no more sirs tonight.

I slap her ass, and she yelps. I slap it three more times, glancing between the bow and her face. Each time, her walls clench my erection. "What did I say about calling me sir right now?"

"You said not to."

"That's right. Why did you do it?" I rub the spot I just slapped.

"Oh!" she whimpers.

"Answer me."

"I don't know."

"You do," I insist, thrusting into her harder. My balls tighten, and my toes curl. "Now tell me."

"It stops me from calling you what I want," she blurts out.

"What do you want to call me, baby girl?"

"Master! I want you to be my Master so badly." Her eyes meet mine and that look she has whenever she says she wants to call me Master is in them.

Jesus. It goes against every ounce of morals I have left in me. Yet every time she says it, she unleashes a demon in me who wants it. Not in the way Jack had her, but in a way that allows her to be mine and tied to me forever, submitting while I control her. I growl, "Get it out of your head. Stop tempting me, baby girl."

"Obrecht... I'm going to...oh... I can't...please...oh...it's too...oh!" Her body convulses on me harder than anyone ever has before.

I lose any ability to control myself and violently pump into her, releasing my seed deep within her and holding myself over her on my elbows.

When I gain the ability to see straight again, she's still trembling, and her lids are fluttering. I kiss her neck and wait for her to come down.

A tear falls down her cheek. "I'm sorry. I didn't mean to disobey you. I couldn't..."

"Shh. You were perfect, baby girl." I have no idea how she's able to control herself as much as she did.

"You didn't permit me to come," she frets.

I roll off her and tug her into my arms. I tilt her chin and repeat, "You were perfect, baby girl. Nothing less than perfect."

She swallows hard. "I was?"

"Yes."

She smiles.

I kiss her. "Go to sleep, sweet angel."

She shimmies down my body with her head on my chest and obeys.

I don't sleep for the rest of the night. I shouldn't want her this much. She tempts me in too many ways. I'm not sure how to help her because I can't seem to control my dick around her.

I'm a sadist, and bringing her to tears, then making her tell me everything on her mind only added gasoline to an already lit fire.

12

Selena

EVERYTHING IS WARM AND SAFE. I SNUGGLE INTO OBRECHT'S chest, not wanting to wake up. I know it's him without opening my eyes. His intoxicating scent fills my nose. His lips flutter on my head. Tingles burst along the skin of my hip where he strokes it.

"Mmm."

"Are you awake, my dorogaya?" his delicious voice murmurs in my ear.

I slowly force myself to open my eyes and glance up at him. His lips are slightly curved up, but his gaze is serious.

"What's wrong?" I ask.

"Nothing. Are you feeling okay?"

"Yes. Why wouldn't I be?"

His blue orbs singe into mine, and more worry fills them.

Why is he looking at me like that?

The more he stares, the more uncomfortable I get. Then the events of the previous night assault me. I bury my head in his chest, embarrassed about my episode. I mumble, "I'm sorry. It hasn't happened in a long time. I'm not sure... I...please don't hold it against me."

"Shh. It's not your fault, baby girl. You haven't done anything wrong. But you're feeling okay today?"

I force myself to look at him. "Yes."

He smiles, but the worry lines around his eyes never disappear. I wish I could somehow force them to, but he continues studying me as if something is wrong.

My chest tightens, and I admit, "You're making me anxious."

His eyes widen. "How?"

I reach up and trace the lines around his eyes. "When these pop out, I know you're worried. I'm fine."

He smirks. "That's just from being old."

"You aren't that old."

He arches an eyebrow. "How do you know how old I am?"

I slide on top of him. "You handed me your driver's license, remember?"

He grunts. "Forgot about that. So you already know I'm an old man."

"Mmm... Is forty-five old?" *He's almost five years younger than Jack.*

"It is compared to you, Ms. Barely Thirty."

I freeze, trying to recall telling him my age, but I know I didn't.

"What?" he asks.

"How do you know I'm barely thirty? I never told you."

Guilt lights up his expression. He kisses my forehead and says, "I have my ways."

"Mind sharing your secrets with me?" I ask in a teasing tone.

He pins his gaze on me. "I told you I know lots of things about you, baby girl."

"But how?"

"I did my research." He winks, pecks me on the forehead, then flips me on my back. He cages his body over mine. My heart races, and he positions himself so we're face-to-face. "I have a friend coming over I want you to meet."

"Oh?" An excited flutter erupts in my belly. If he wants to introduce me to his friend, I must be special to him. I'm assuming he doesn't introduce his other bottoms to them. Maybe he realizes we can be more? Maybe he'll agree to being my Dom or Master?

He drags his finger over the curve of my waist. "Yes. She will be here in fifteen minutes."

"She? Do you hang out with a lot of women?" I ask, attempting to sound nonchalant.

"Hang out? No. I mostly only do things with my family," he says.

My suspicion rises. I have no right to feel envious of his friendship with her, but I do. "But you hang out with this woman?"

He shrugs. "She's a friend. I've known her for a long time, and she helped me with some things."

"Like what?" What could he possibly need help with from this woman? He's a real-life Superman as far as I'm concerned. Every inch of him is sexy perfection. He's successful and confident. I'm pretty sure he never needs help.

His face darkens. "How to deal with certain things." He pecks me on the lips, and the darkness fades. Amusement appears. "We should get dressed before she gets here. I mean, I could wrap you back up if you want. I wouldn't mind. She wouldn't, either, but she might get the urge to tell you to kneel and give you some commands."

My stomach flips. I attempt to sit up, but his dense frame doesn't allow it. "Are you trying to pawn me off on her?"

He chuckles. "No. Not at all. Sorry if I gave you that impression. She's another top at the club I belong to."

"She tops women?"

"Women. Men. Whichever bottom she wants to negotiate a session with. She's very popular," he says.

I bite on my lip, unsure why he invited this woman to his house to meet me, but something feels off about it. As much as I was initially excited about it, it's quickly deflating. Obrecht and I aren't in a relationship. He made it clear he doesn't get attached. I heard him say it. I try to push it out of my head when it pops up. As much as I want to be one of those cool women who are okay with open relationships or casual sex, I'm not. My pulse pounds in my neck. "Have you slept with her?"

His lips curl. He arches his eyebrows. "You heard me say she's a top, right?"

"Yes."

His expression is a mix of cocky and amused. "Is there any part of you under the impression I'd submit to anyone? If so, I'm going to have to show you more of what I got, baby girl."

I relax and laugh. "So you haven't knelt for her?"

"I don't kneel for anyone, my dorogaya."

"You knelt for me," I blurt out.

His face turns to surprise. "When?"

My cheeks heat. "In the shower."

Fire blazes in his orbs. He slides his hand between my thighs. "Not the same."

Tingles race right to my core. "No?"

He softly chuckles. "Who was determining what happened, baby girl?"

"You."

"There's your answer."

"So you haven't slept with her then?" I repeat.

He pushes my hair behind my ear. "No. I've not slept with her or done anything sexual with her. She's a friend. A very good one whom I trust, and I don't trust many people."

Relief fills me. "Okay. And you want her to meet me?"

"Yes."

Excitement pops up again. She's his good friend. If he wants me to meet her, I must mean something to him, right? "When did you say she's coming?"

"Mmm, my guess is we're in the ten-minute zone. She's pretty punctual."

I push his chest. "I need to shower then. She's going to think I'm your stinky bottom."

He sniffs hard. "You smell like sex. I'm down with your stinkiness."

"Obrecht!" I groan.

He rolls off me and rises. He holds his hand out. "Come on. I'll scrub you down."

"Yes, sir," I reply and take his hand. When I rise, the black ribbon falls around me.

"Spin," he commands.

I do as he says.

He pushes my hair off my neck and kisses me. "I never unwrapped your ass."

I laugh and stick my booty out to him.

He splays his hand on my spine and pushes my torso over the bed. Using his foot, he spreads my legs. He drags his other hand over the crack of my ass. "I haven't punished you yet," he murmurs.

My stomach fills with butterflies. "What did I do?"

He smacks my cheek.

I gasp and arch up, but his hand holds me down. He slaps me several times. Tingles erupt over the stings when he rubs his large hand over the spot where he smacked me. The few times he's spanked me weren't anything like when Jack used to do it. Before we were married, he did it a few times and I liked it. Once we were married, and he showed his true colors, the spankings became beatings with paddles. But I never forgot how I initially liked it, and Obrecht's slaps create delicious sensations in me.

"Don't ever ditch your bodyguard again, got it?" he barks.

"Yes, sir," I agree.

"Good, baby girl. Hand me my phone."

I reach for the cell and hand it to him. He keeps his palm on my back and calls someone. "We're jumping in the shower now. I'll text you the code. Come up and make yourself comfy." He circles my forbidden zone then presses against it but doesn't break the rigid barrier. "See you soon." He tosses the phone on the bed and smacks my other ass cheek.

I lurch up, but he still has me held down. "That's for assuming I'd submit to anyone."

I glance over my shoulder at him. He rubs the sting as his lust-filled gaze sends more heat through me. "Best gift ever, baby girl," he says as he pulls at the ribbon. When it's off, he tugs me off the bed and leads me into the shower.

I twist my hair into a knot so it doesn't get wet. "What's your friend's name?"

"Carla."

"Why is she coming over?" My chest tightens. I should be satisfied with him wanting to introduce me to his good friend, but I want him to admit I mean more to him than any other bottom he's topped.

His words rock me. "She's a therapist. I told her about you. She can help you."

I freeze. My skin begins to crawl. "Help me?"

He places his hands on my cheeks. "Yes. You've been through a lot, and she understands things other therapists don't."

My insides quiver. "Other therapists?"

"Yes. She's the best. A lot of people in the BDSM community who came out of abusive relationships work with her."

I glance down at his chest. Heat rises in my cheeks, and the air becomes harder to breathe. He talked to her about me. A stranger who I've never met. When I speak up, my voice shakes. "What did you do? Tell her I'm extremely fucked up?"

"No. Not anything like that."

"You told her about my marriage?"

"Yes, just that—"

I push out of his arms and step out of the shower. I grab a towel and don't even dry myself off. I wrap it around my body and keep going.

He follows me. "Selena!"

Anger, embarrassment, and betrayal surge through me. I don't trust easily, and I stupidly gave it all to Obrecht. He told whomever this woman is private details about me. Things no one knows, except him and me. Embarrassing parts of my life.

I can barely see straight while I try to find my purse. I leave the bedroom and see our plates from last night's dinner still on the table and the tray I cooked it in still on the oven, unwashed. I don't remember what happened between dinner and when I woke up in the middle of the night, but more shame fills me. It's not in me to leave a kitchen or table anything but spotless. Jack would have beaten me and made me go in my cage for a week. It's another reminder of how I majorly screwed up, since I'm so messed up. Tears prick my eyes as I look for my purse. I need to get out of here quickly.

"Selena!" Obrecht grabs my arm and spins me into him. "Why are you upset?"

I stare at his beautiful face and then at the snake tattoo wrapped around his neck. So many emotions hit me at once, I feel suffocated.

"Baby girl—"

"Don't," I whisper.

"I'm only trying to help you."

I see my purse out of the corner of my eye and shrug out of his grasp. I sling it over my shoulder and head toward the elevator.

"Selena, stop," he barks out.

I freeze and hate myself. He has power over me just from the tone of his voice, and I can't go against it if I tried. My insides quiver harder and I blink fast.

He steps in front of me. "What's happening here?"

"You honestly don't know?"

"No. I—"

The elevator opens. A gorgeous woman with an edgy bob steps inside. Her hair is brown with thick blonde streaks running through it. Her makeup is flawless, and she's beyond stunning. It's clear she has her life together. I don't, and both she and Obrecht know it. Her eyes dart between us. "Hi. Am I interrupting something?"

I wrap my towel tighter around me. "No, I was just leaving."

"Selena—"

"Am I free to make my own decision and go, or are you holding me hostage here?" I snap through tears.

Obrecht's eyes widen. "Of course you're free. I—"

I step away from him and jump in the elevator as the doors shut. I push the button for my floor and attempt to hold my tears in until I get inside my condo.

The elevator stops. I get in front of my door and dig into my purse for my key. I fumble with the lock but finally get it open. As soon as the door shuts, I sink against it and let the tears fall. It's one thing for Obrecht to know I'm screwed up and about my history. It's another for a complete stranger, and especially a therapist. I already went to the one Kora recommended. She said she was the best therapist in Chicago for women who had experienced domestic abuse. After two sessions, I couldn't go back. I felt like she was judging me. I don't need anyone else doing that. I'm hard enough on myself.

When I start to shake from my lack of clothing, I climb into bed and stay there for several days. I don't eat. I barely drink any water. I can't breathe.

I ignore the pounding on the door and calls and messages from Obrecht. I finally turn my phone off.

The first time my heart broke, Jack Christian was responsible. There was nothing I could do and nowhere to run. I thought he crushed my soul.

I was wrong. My soul survived him. As horrible as it was, it now seems overstated.

Nothing feels as bad as a betrayal from Obrecht Ivanov.

Obrecht

SELENA DISAPPEARS INTO THE ELEVATOR, AND CARLA CROSSES her arms. She glares at me and shakes her head. "You didn't ask her if it was okay before I came over, did you?"

I push the button for the elevator. "There wasn't a lot of time. I thought it was better if she got more rest. I'm not even sure why she's so upset. She's always open to me helping her."

Carla steps between me and the elevator. Anger fills her face. There aren't many times I've seen her upset, but she's definitely not happy with me right now. "Get dressed then sit down."

I glance at my towel then back at her. "I'm going to make sure Selena is okay," I claim as the elevator opens.

Carla points past me. "No, you aren't. Take a break, and let's talk."

"I need to make sure she's okay," I insist.

"You need to give her a break and realize what you've just done." Carla raises her eyebrows.

"I'm trying to help her."

Carla's eyes turn into darts. "Yes, but you didn't listen to me, did you? Now get dressed. If you don't, you're going to make this worse."

My heart stammers. I keep debating, and the elevator doors shut. There are so many things about Selena I don't understand. The last thing I wanted to do was hurt her.

Carla's voice turns gentler. "If you want to help her, you'll put on some clothes and then we'll discuss this."

I finally cave, put on clothes, and go into the family room. I plop on the black leather couch. Carla sits in the chair across from me. Silence fills the air. There are few women in the world who I think have the ability to intimidate a strong man. Carla is one of them. She can be sweet as sugar or hard as nails. I finally get tired of her piercing gaze. "You can tell me at any time where I screwed up so I can go fix it."

My comment doesn't help matters. She sarcastically laughs. "Your arrogance isn't going to help this situation."

"What are you talking about?"

She studies me a few more moments, tapping her fingers on the armrest.

"I'm not one of your subs you can intimidate," I bark.

She tilts her head, scowling. "You asked me to come here, remember?"

She's right. I take a few deep breaths to calm my raging nerves. "I'm sorry. Groveling isn't my forte. Can you tell me how to fix this, please?"

"Therapy is a personal decision. You can't push someone into it and not give them a choice. I told you to discuss it with her. To *ask* her. How would you like it if I showed up on your doorstep for therapy and you had no clue who I was or even if you wanted it?"

"Selena is very open with me. She's asked me to help her—"

"*You*, Obrecht. She asked *you.*"

"This is part of me helping her. I don't know what I'm doing. Most of the time, I'm worried I'm doing something to hurt her," I admit.

Carla leans forward. "Do you remember when you had a hard time having sex?"

My stomach twists. I turn and stare out the glass and at one of the buildings several blocks over. Shortly after Annika betrayed me, Natalia showed up on our doorstep dead. Everything felt wrong. I met Carla, and somehow, she got me to open up and deal with things. She introduced me into the BDSM world. Then she showed me I could still engage in sex while being dominant without any fear I was hurting a woman or having to be in a relationship. "Of course I do. It's why I wanted Selena to work with you."

"Do you remember how long it took you to trust me? To even talk to me about anything?"

The clawing in my gut grows. "Yeah."

"What if I told someone anything you disclosed to me without your permission? Even if I thought it was in your best interest?"

I groan. "I seriously messed up, didn't I?"

"Yep."

I turn back to Carla. "Do you always have to be right?"

She smirks. "You want me to answer that?"

"Funny." I scrub my hands over my face, then rise. "I need to go talk to Selena."

"She might need some time. If you push her, you could harm her."

"How would talking to her harm her?"

"I know you, Obrecht. You're going to go in there and push her to try and be okay with what you just did. You could do some serious damage if you do that." Carla rises and motions for me to follow her. She opens my balcony door, and we both step out. The sun is shining, but it's a windy Chicago day. She points to Lake Michigan. "See those white caps?"

"What about them?"

"They aren't always there, are they?"

This conversation only makes me more agitated. My doro-gaya is downstairs, upset, and Carla wants to give me a science lesson. I snap, "Can we discuss Selena and not the weather?"

"We are discussing Selena."

"How?"

"My guess is she's just like the lake. She has times she's calm and feels in control of where her life is going. Then there are times a storm comes, but no one can see it. In my experience, men or women who have lived as a slave in an abusive relationship are confused, scared, and trying to figure out what's normal. There's a storm going on under that water, and all you see are the white caps. You don't see the sand churning or feel the pull of the current. My guess is, she does. You just created a new storm within her."

My stomach pitches. I hate that I've caused Selena any pain.

Carla adds, "You've broken her trust. She's hurt. You can't go in there and force her to trust you again. If she needs time alone, give it to her. If you force yourself into her life, she'll start to put you in the same box she puts her ex."

Anger replaces my regret. "So I'm not supposed to talk to her about this?"

Carla shakes her head. "No. But I advise you to let her come to you when she's ready. Let her know you're here and sorry, but it has to be on her terms. She needs to regain a sense of control right now."

I stare at the water, and my own storm brews inside me. Disgust, self-loathing, and fear about what I did to Selena eats at me.

Carla pats me on the shoulder. "I'm going to go now. If you need anything, call."

"Thanks. Sorry I screwed up so bad."

"If you want a beating, let me know. I'll be at the club tonight and won't have any issues taking my new flogger to you," she chirps.

"Never happening."

"You might like it," she claims.

"Spoken from someone who would never be on the other end of the flogger."

She snorts. "That's the truth."

Carla leaves, and I pace my penthouse for a few minutes before hopping on the elevator and going to Selena's. She doesn't answer, and I pound harder. "Selena!" More time passes, but she never comes to the door. I resist the urge to break into her condo, trying to heed the warning Carla gave me. I finally give up and go back to my penthouse. I decide to focus on what I can control. There's unfinished business between Liam and me. I text him.

Me: *We need to meet. Today.*

Liam: *I don't think you're in the position to give me orders.*

Me: *Stop being a prick. Where are you?*

Liam: *None of your business. I'll meet you at the pub in an hour.*

I try Selena one more time, but she still won't open the door. She doesn't respond to my phone calls. I text her.

Me: *I'm sorry, baby girl. Can we talk? Please?*

After a few minutes pass, I knock again. She doesn't answer or reply to my text. I send another.

Me: *I'm going out to deal with a few work issues. I'll let you know when I'm back, but call or text me if you want.*

I finally go to the lobby. Matvey is there, and I say, "If Selena goes anywhere, make sure you text me." I address the security guard who monitors the building. "If she goes on the roof or my place, let me know that as well." I don't know if my dorogaya will attempt to talk to me at my place or not, but wherever she goes, I want a full report.

I step out of the building, and my driver is waiting. The entire way to Nora's pub, I attempt to switch over to the issues at hand. It doesn't work very well. I keep staring at my phone, waiting for Selena to return my text. A block from Nora's, I can't handle it anymore.

Me: *Can we have dinner tonight, baby girl?*

The message doesn't say delivered like the others, so I call her. It goes into her voicemail before it rings.

Great. She turned her phone off.

I bang my head against the back of the headrest as the car pulls in front of the pub.

Now I get to deal with Liam.

He better tell me what I want to know and not play games.

It's only ten in the morning. The pub opens at eleven, so I knock. Nora's brother, Killian, opens the door. He slaps my hand. "Obrecht."

"Hey, man. Liam here already?"

"Yeah. I just got here, but he's in the office talking to Nora. You here to talk about that cock sucker Gavriil?" He locks the door.

"Were you there?"

197

"Yeah."

"You should have let us handle him."

Killian sniffs hard. "Yeah, well, you don't always get a chance to stop and figure out who to send a memo to, do you?"

I cross my arms over my chest. "Don't act like you didn't know it was an Ivanov matter to deal with."

Killian shakes his head. "You seem to forget he was with Mack Bailey. You know damn well a Bailey is an O'Malley issue."

"He was my tracker. *My* guy. It was an Ivanov issue," I insist.

Killian's jaw clenches. "The Baileys killed our brother, which makes them ours to deal with. So we'll have to disagree. And since we have an alliance, you should be okay with it."

I step closer to him. The Baileys killed Sean. The Petrovs killed Natalia. He's partly right. "See, this is the problem with this alliance we've got. There doesn't seem to be any clear boundaries. Why don't we set them right now? I'm getting sick of—"

"You're getting sick of what, Obrecht? Us taking care of your traitors? Or protecting our families? What exactly are you sick of?" Liam's voice booms. I turn, and he has a scowl on his face.

I scoff. "An Ivanov traitor should be ours to take care of. If it were an O'Malley—"

"Sit down, both of you. The pissing matches between you two are getting old," Declan barks, walking into the main area of the pub with Nolan and Boris behind him.

We all take a seat. Liam and I continue scowling at each other.

"We're on the same team," Boris reminds me.

"Doesn't feel like it. Or did you know they were taking out Gavriil behind our backs?" I ask.

Boris clears his throat. "Of course I didn't. But the Baileys were involved. It's not clear-cut."

"We're wasting time squabbling over details. Do you want to know what we found out or not?" Liam asks.

I need to keep my mouth shut, find out whatever they got out of Gavriil, and get home to make things right with my dorogaya.

I don't respond. I stay quiet and wait, wanting to wipe Liam's cocky expression off his face.

"Cut the shit, Liam. Tell us," Boris demands.

"According to Gavriil, Ludis and Mack formed an alliance once Nora became an Ivanov and it was clear our families were aligned," Liam states.

Boris shifts in his seat next to mine. He snarls, "If they come anywhere near moya dusha, I'll cut their balls off and feed them to them."

"You'll have to do it before I do," Liam states. "But I think they are both getting nervous. Ludis told Gavriil he can't find Zamir or Wes. He has drug shipments, new women to place in their whorehouses, and other Petrov business he can't seem to get through the pipeline. It's all meant to be delivered west of the Michigan border. Without his father or brother, he doesn't have the contacts to deliver."

"He partnered with the Baileys to sell and move his goods past Michigan. And the Baileys are having issues with their suppliers since Crosby and Cullen are out of the picture," Declan adds.

"How do you know they're out of the picture?" I ask.

The O'Malleys all glance at each other. A tense silence fills the air.

"Whatever you know, you better tell us," Boris barks.

Killian taps his fingers on the table. "You remember when we were gone for a week, and we had Nora stay with you?"

"Yeah. Why?" Boris asks.

Killian's face turns hard. "We hunted Crosby and Cullen Bailey down and sliced them to pieces over several days."

Blood pounds between my ears. There's never been any love lost between the O'Malleys and Baileys, but Killian, Declan, and Nolan only recently got under Darragh's rule. They tried for years not to get involved in their family's criminal activities. I ask, "Why would you go after two head members of the Bailey clan?"

"Because they helped that piece of shit Cormac set up Sean with Lorenzo Rossi," Killian replies.

Every O'Malley's face hardens, but I don't miss the pain. I'm sure it's what Adrian and I look like whenever we discuss Natalia.

Silence fills the air for several moments. I finally ask, "So Gavriil was spying on us for Ludis and Mack?"

"Yeah. He was for the last three years," Killian confirms.

My gut flips. *How could I have missed it?*

"It doesn't make sense," I say.

"What doesn't?" Killian asks.

"The Baileys set up Sean so Lorenzo Rossi would kill him? Correct?"

"Yes," Killian confirms.

"And now Mack Bailey is hanging around and making deals with Ludis Petrov?"

"Yep. Scum seems to attract scum."

Don't dwell on it right now. Get the rest of what you came here for.

I focus on Liam. "Why do I have to wait until after Jack Christian's company goes public to kill him?"

Liam and the other O'Malleys exchange knowing looks.

"You better give me a good enough reason, Liam. If you don't, I'm picking Jack up tonight," I threaten.

"You can't do that," Boris says.

The frustration I feel about the Ivanov-O'Malley alliance only grows. I almost tell Boris he's an Ivanov, not an O'Malley, but decide against it. I sigh. "Why not?"

"You know how we get our money, right?" Liam asks.

My gut twists. How the O'Malleys make their money isn't something I agree with, either. I admit, "From what I know, drugs and gambling."

"Not for much longer," Liam claims.

I grunt. "Sure."

"It's true. My father's dying. We"—he motions around the table to his cousins—"want a different avenue for our family's future. One that doesn't involve addiction problems. He agrees it's the right move."

I glance at Boris to see if he's buying this or not.

"It's true," Killian claims.

I sit farther back in my seat. "Fine, I'll bite. How are the O'Malleys going to get out of the business they've been in for decades?"

"We need Jack's company to go public. It's our way out. Once it does, as I promised, I'll deliver him to you on a silver platter," Liam states.

"What does Jack's company have to do with your future? Tell me the missing piece."

Liam shakes his head. "No. It's O'Malley business. You know enough."

I glance at Boris. "You know?"

His jaw clenches.

I scowl at him, no longer able to hold my tongue. "Are you an Ivanov or O'Malley now?"

"Shut the fuck up," he growls.

"No. Since when do you keep your family out of the loop?"

"I'm not. I'm doing what's right for both families, which my child's blood is from. Don't touch Jack until his company goes public," Boris warns.

I slide out of my seat. "Have you talked to Maksim about this?"

Boris's face tells me he hasn't.

I shake my head. "You're playing with fire, Boris. Whatever you're doing here, tell Maksim."

"I will. When the time is right, I'll tell all of you," he claims.

"Why can't you tell us now?"

"Because I said he couldn't," Liam states.

The tension becomes thick. I shift my gaze between Liam and Boris. "Are you taking orders from Liam now?"

Boris snorts. "Hell no. Don't overreact, Obrecht."

Liam slams his hand on the table. "Jesus. When are you going to realize we're all on the same side and stop acting like I'm going to destroy everyone around me?"

I sarcastically laugh. "You sit here and don't give me full disclosure. What am I supposed to think?"

"You're supposed to trust all of us, including me."

"Yeah, well, trust needs to be earned, doesn't it?" I spout.

Liam's lip curls. "What did I ever do to you, Obrecht? Do you want to fill me in? I'd love to know."

"I'm not getting into this."

"Why not? Now's as good of a time as ever."

"Fine. You want to get into this, I'll tell you. I don't like all the shit you pulled Killian, Boris, and Adrian into when we were kids."

His eyes turn to slits. "Kids. The keyword being kids. I'm a forty-year-old man now."

I've hit my limit with Liam. I shouldn't say it, but it rolls out of me before I can stop it. "Yeah, well, I also remember you trying to pull all of them into the murder that got you thrown in the slammer for fifteen years. You haven't been out in this world like we have. You're all ready to lead the O'Malleys into whatever this big scheme is you have up your sleeve. All I know is your track record isn't too good. So excuse me if I don't give you my full faith."

Boris starts, "Obrecht—"

"No. Do you think for one minute if an Ivanov were in trouble, Liam would be sticking his neck out to help us? Unless there's something in it for him, I'm not betting my money on him."

"You're wrong," Boris claims.

"Liam's always been loyal," Killian growls.

I face Liam. "Are you going to sit here and tell me you'll put your life at risk for an Ivanov if there isn't something in it for you?"

His eyes turn to angry flames. "Yeah. I would."

"Bullshit." I slide my chair under the table. "Watch yourself, Boris. This alliance we all have, it feels a lot more like a one-way lane to me than a two-way street."

"You're out of line, Obrecht," he says.

"When the day comes where Liam does something for one of us with nothing in it for him to gain, I'll recant my statement.

Until then, I'm going to watch my back. Have a good day," I snarl and leave the pub.

I get in the car, seething, torn between ignoring their instructions not to touch Jack yet and tracking him down to rip his head off. I slide my phone out of my pocket in the hopes my dorogaya texted or called, but there's nothing and no updates from Matvey.

When I get back to our building, I go to her unit, determined to make things right, but she still won't answer the door. Suddenly, everything seems so messed up. Boris keeping information from us hits a nerve. I should trust him only to make that decision if it's necessary, but Liam's involvement makes it impossible. Gavriil's betrayal cuts me. The biggest thing making me feel entirely off-kilter is Selena.

I shouldn't be so affected by a woman. I don't get attached. For the first time in over fifteen years, I realize I'm developing feelings for a woman that go beyond friendship. When I try to go to sleep, I can't. I smell and see her everywhere, and it's like a knife slicing my heart.

14

Selena

WHAT DAY IS IT?

I need to get up. I can't stay in bed any longer.

Why does this still hurt so badly?

How many days has it been?

I slowly rise out of bed and open my blinds. It's an overcast day. The river is rougher than normal, which leads me to believe it's windy outside. Several pedestrians and runners pass my building.

What time is it?

I turn on my phone. It's before six in the morning. Dozens of text messages and missed calls pop up. They're only from one person. I scan through them with my heart beating harder and flutters in my stomach. The last message came only a few minutes ago. I read it, blinking back tears.

Obrecht: *I miss you so much, baby girl. Please let me know you're all right. I hate how much I hurt you. I'm really worried. If you don't show your beautiful face soon, I'm going to have to break into your place.*

I need to get out of here.

Shower and go for a walk.

Within fifteen minutes, I'm in the lobby. Matvey rises and smiles. "Good morning, Selena."

"Good morning, Matvey. I want to go for a walk."

He nods. "Very good. It'll be nice for me to get out of here."

I wince, realizing my hibernation probably meant he had to stay in the lobby for several days. "Sorry I've not gone anywhere and you've had to stay cooped up."

He chuckles. "No worries." He guides me to the front door, steps out before me and glances both ways, then motions for me to follow. "Where would you like to go?"

I shrug then gaze in both directions. "Let's go on the Riverwalk."

"Very well."

The fresh air feels nice. I take several deep breaths, already feeling better. It's a crisp morning. I only have on a T-shirt and shorts, and the cold air hits my skin, waking me up even more. I don't say anything to Matvey and get lost in my thoughts.

It isn't rational for me to think I can avoid Obrecht forever. I already know I don't want to never see him again, but I don't want to fall into my old situation.

Jack broke my trust.

Obrecht broke my trust.

Is it the same thing?

The debate goes on in my head, followed by more embarrassment over how screwed up I am. If I weren't, Obrecht wouldn't have had a therapist come to his house. A cloud of depression climbs back into my chest. I'm a thirty-year-old woman who doesn't even know who she is or what her purpose is anymore. At least with Jack, I knew my role. Good or bad, there were expectations on me, and I was someone to him. Wife, slave, whatever you want to call me, my life was clear. I was Jack's and there to serve and obey him. Everything I did was for him. Now the divorce is over, and I've escaped him, there's nothing to focus on.

I'm unsure how to act. The other night, I proved I can't even control my own body when I'm away from Jack. The events of the panic attack I had are still fuzzy. All I remember is waking up and wanting Obrecht. It all merges, making me hate myself. At least with Jack, I didn't have these confusing thoughts about what's wrong or right or how to act. For a split second, I wonder if going back to him would be easier. Is having my freedom and all these new problems better? The thought scares me more than anything because part of me considers it.

After I walk an hour, I veer off the Riverwalk and go into a cafe. The smell of coffee and freshly baked pastries flares in my nostrils. My stomach growls and I realize I haven't eaten much in the last few days. I order a vanilla latte and banana muffin then go to the waiting area. I'm still lost in my thoughts as I wait for my order.

"Selena?"

I glance over at the woman who said my name, and after a few seconds, a feeling of dread grows.

Did she follow me here?

No, she's waiting for her coffee and was here before me.

I relax and take a deep breath to calm my quivering insides as my cheeks burn.

She smiles and holds out her hand. "We didn't get to meet. I'm Carla."

I survey the room to see if Obrecht is with her, but he isn't.

"He's not with me," she says, as if she can read my mind.

"How did you know I was looking for him?" I ask and notice she's still holding out her hand, so I take it and shake it quickly.

"Carla," the barista calls out and sets her drink down.

She shrugs and picks it up then smiles. "He's freaking out. Never seen him this way. Surprised he didn't break down your door at this point."

My heart stammers. "How do you know this?"

"Selena," the barista shouts and puts my latte and pastry on the counter.

Carla's smile grows. "He's texting me every few hours. I keep telling him not to knock it down."

I chew on my lip, not sure how to respond to her comment. Should I feel upset she seems to know so much about Obrecht's and my problems? Part of me is irritated but only a small part. The rest of me wants to know what else she knows.

She hesitates. "I'm here by myself. Do you want to sit with me?"

I hesitate.

"Just two girls having coffee?" she chirps, and a hopeful expression fills her face.

I cave. "Okay."

She chooses a table in the corner. We sit, and my stomach clenches with nerves. I take a sip of coffee and stare out the window.

Why did I agree to sit with her?

"I want to apologize for how we met," she says.

I force myself to look at her.

She continues, "I told Obrecht to ask you before I came over."

"What did he tell you about me?" I blurt out, and my cheeks burn.

She puts her hand on mine. "Not a lot. But enough that I wanted to meet you. Have to admit, I was curious about you. Obrecht doesn't ever associate with his bottoms outside of the club."

I pull my hand away. "We live in the same building."

"So? He still had you in his bed."

My jealousy flares. "And you wanted to meet me because you wanted to be there instead of me?"

She snickers then takes a sip of coffee. "Sorry. I wasn't laughing at you, just the thought. I'm more like Obrecht, except I prefer to administer pain. Unless he wanted to suddenly become a submissive who needs a good paddling, what you're suggesting isn't possible."

I cringe. "Pain?"

She nods. "Only for those who want it. In a controlled situation."

"And you're a therapist?" I shouldn't judge her, but she's nothing like the strait-laced therapist I saw.

Amusement fills her expression. "Yeah. But I only work with those in the BDSM community."

My chest tightens. "Why?"

"I understand their needs, and there aren't a lot of therapists who do."

My knee bounces. "Will you please tell me what Obrecht told you about me?" I'm unsure why I want to know so badly, but I do.

Her face falls, and she glances behind us, then lowers her voice. "Sure. He said your ex-husband made you be his slave, and you never consented to that type of relationship. He also said your ex abused you, and you had a panic attack."

"What else?"

"He wanted to help you, was topping you, and you had gone to two sessions with Cascade but then stopped."

My gut drops. More embarrassment annihilates me. I'm unsure why I admit to her, "I never told Obrecht about Cascade."

She raises her eyebrows. "Yes. He told me. It made me want to meet you more."

Once again, like the majority of my life lately, I'm confused. "Why?"

She drinks more coffee and replies, "I've known Obrecht for a long time. He only digs if he's interested. Not sure if that makes it better for you or not."

"What do you mean?"

She taps her coffee cup. "Obrecht has a one-track mind. He's either interested or not. He keeps his circle tight, mostly his family. He goes to the club, gets what he needs, and leaves. He has a few bottoms he plays with and doesn't stray too far. None of them see him outside of their sessions. That makes you special."

My heart skips a beat.

Her brown eyes twinkle. "I'm glad you're making him pay for his actions."

My chest tightens. "Sorry...what? I'm not trying to hurt him."

She shakes her head. "No, I didn't mean for it to come across that way. I apologize. I meant it's good for him to see he needs to talk to you and not assume things before making decisions on your behalf. A little space for him to think hard about his actions isn't a bad thing. Plus, it reiterates you hold the power."

Again, I'm confused. Obrecht said it to me before, but I didn't understand what he meant then, and I don't understand what she means. I feel anything but like I'm in control where Obrecht is concerned or even in my life.

"Your expression tells me you don't believe me?" she asks.

I focus on my banana muffin and tear a small piece off. "No, I don't." I pop the food in my mouth and chew it slowly.

She leans closer. "You're a submissive?"

"I-I guess." More heat flies to my face, and I avoid looking at her. I'm not sure if I should be embarrassed or not, but something about wanting to submit when she knows Jack made me his slave makes me feel shame. With Obrecht, I could fall into my role, and it seemed okay, but I barely know this woman.

She smiles, as if I said something amazing. "In some ways, I wish I were a sub."

I glance up, surprised. "Why would you say that?"

She sits back in her seat. "Like I said, you hold all the power. You create all the boundaries. Us Doms are the ones who have to figure out how to give you what you need without going past your limit."

"Sounds tedious," I nervously tease.

She laughs. "It can be. But when you know your sub's needs and can give it to them, it's magical for both people."

I chew on my lip. She's so confident and knowledgeable about subs and Doms, and I barely know anything. "If you want to be a sub, why don't you just do it?"

She takes hand lotion out of her purse, adds a dab, and puts it on the table in front of me. She rubs her hands together. "Help yourself. And I'm not a sub because it's not who I am. You're either a sub, Dom, or a switch. I'm as Dom as they come."

"Switch?"

"Someone who can fall into both roles."

"More terms," I mutter under my breath then pick up the lotion and rub some into my hands.

"It can be confusing at first, especially since there is no right or wrong, and so much is subjective. The important thing is the two people coming together are clear on what they both need and want." She puts her oversized blue bag on the table and riffles through it. "Ah, here it is. You can keep this." She hands me a small booklet titled *BDSM Basics*. Her name is on it.

"You wrote this?"

"Yes. I got tired of my clients feeling ashamed and confused over the urges they felt."

I lock eyes with her and take a deep breath. "Urges?"

She gives me another kind smile and nods. "The world around us doesn't understand the BDSM lifestyle. There's a lot of misconceptions about it. We all have a desire to submit or dominate in most parts of life. Sexually, it can be confusing." She hesitates then adds, "Especially after someone submitted due to force but then finds themselves craving it."

Emotions overwhelm me, and I blink hard. I turn to the window to pull myself together.

She puts her hand on mine. "Can I make an assumption?"

I take a deep breath and nod but don't take my eyes off the building across the street.

"Based on the other women and men I've worked with who were in a Master-slave relationship that wasn't by consent and involved abuse, I'm assuming you experience a lot of confusion and maybe even shame and guilt around your urge to submit."

My lips tremble. Against my will, tears slide down my cheeks. I wipe my face and nod, still not looking at her.

"Nothing you feel is abnormal. I know this is hard to believe right now, but over time, if you embrace your urges in a healthy way and work through things, all those bad feelings will go away."

I finally turn back to her. "How?"

Her face doesn't display pity or judgment like the other therapist I went to. There's a confidence that makes me want to believe her without question. "Time. Education. Experimentation. And you should know, everyone in the BDSM community is on a journey. No one's path or experience is the same. There are no right or wrongs, except non-consent."

There's a shrill ring, and she groans, then pulls her phone out of her purse. She swipes the screen. "I'm sorry, Selena. That's my alarm to get my booty to the office. I need to go, but it was really nice having coffee with you."

"Umm, you, too."

She rises and points to the booklet she gave me. "If you ever want to talk or text, my cell is on there."

"Thanks. Ah..." My heart hammers harder.

"Please ask whatever you want."

"What do I do about Obrecht?"

Her face lights up. "Whatever you want. Remember, you hold the cards. I hope to see you soon." She winks, picks up her coffee, and leaves.

I stay for a long time, staring out the window, watching all the people pass by the cafe in their own worlds. They all make life look so easy. I wonder if I'll ever feel like I have it together. When I leave, I still don't know what to do about Obrecht, but I pull out my phone and text Carla when I get back to my condo.

Me: *It's Selena. Do you think I could schedule a session with you?*

Then I text Obrecht.

Me: *I'm okay. I'm trying to figure some things out. Can you give me some more time? I'm not ready to talk yet.*

Obrecht: *Whatever you need, baby girl. I really do miss you.*

Me: *I miss you, too.*

15

M

Obrecht

OUT OF ALL THE IVANOVS, I'M USUALLY THE ONE WHO'S THE most patient. Every day that passes without me talking to or seeing Selena is torture. I get full updates of everywhere she goes from Matvey and Vlad. Matvey told me she met Carla and is seeing her every morning for coffee. I called Carla to ask if Selena is okay, but Carla won't tell me anything. She even warned me to stay away from Selena and respect her wishes, so I've held myself back from going down to her condo or working out on the roof, since I know she goes there almost daily.

After a week, I can't take it anymore. Even my brother Adrian says I'm spinning out. He's the one in the family who normally does that, not me. I'm in the middle of going through my stock account, when I get a text.

Matvey: *Selena is on the roof.*

I go up to work out as an excuse in the hopes I can talk to her.

When I step outside, she's sitting on the lounger, facing the water. She has her earphones in and is on her laptop. I refrain from going over to her and start my exercises. I'm in the plank pose when Selena sits down on the turf in front of me.

My pulse flares. Her lavender scent surrounds me, and I fall out of the position to the ground.

"Don't let me stop you," she teases.

I sit up and face her. She looks beautiful. Her hair is in a messy bun. Her cheeks have a hint of pink in them. The green in her eyes swirls into the brown. She's smiling while biting on her lower lip.

"Hey, baby girl." I reach out for her and freeze. I pull my hand back to my side.

"Do you have a few minutes to talk?" she asks in a soft voice.

"Yeah. I'll confess, I broke down and didn't keep my promise to myself I'd stay off the roof when you're up here. The workout is a mirage. I came up here in the hopes you'd talk to me."

Her face falls. "You don't need to stay off the roof. You live here, too."

"I didn't want to disrespect your wishes, but I miss you. A lot," I admit.

Her lips twitch. "I miss you, too."

"You do?"

"Yeah."

Hope overpowers me. "Can we return to hanging out?"

She furrows her eyebrows. She opens her mouth to speak then shuts it. Her hands grip the AstroTurf.

My gut drops. "Sorry. I don't mean to push."

She shakes her head. "You aren't. Umm... I-I'm trying to understand some things...about myself and my time with Jack. I think right now, it's best if I keep to myself for a bit longer."

My heart feels like someone is squeezing it. I want to tell her to let me help her. That I'll do anything to have her back in my life again because it's driving me crazy, and some days, breathing feels difficult from not seeing her. Instead, I try to put on a good face. "Sure. I understand."

She looks toward the water, and several minutes pass. She finally turns back. "I've been seeing Carla, well, we have coffee in the morning. I'm assuming you already know this?"

I raise my hand. "Guilty. Always said you were smart."

She softly laughs. "Are Matvey and Vlad texting you when I go places?"

"Yes." I don't hesitate. I'm not going to lie to her. "How did you know?"

"They always text someone when we leave and when we get somewhere. Plus, I kind of thought it was something you'd do." She raises her eyebrows.

"I just want to make sure you're safe."

She smiles, and my heart aches further. "I know. It's okay. I kind of like the thought of you keeping tabs on me."

A moment of silence passes, and I can't take my eyes off hers. There are so many things I thought I would say when I got to talk to her again, but I can't decide what's the most important. I finally stroke her cheek. "You look good, my dorogaya."

She puts her hands on her lap and twists them together. "I wanted to thank you for introducing me to Carla."

I remove my hand. "Is she helping?"

"Yes."

I nod. "That's good. I'm sorry about how I went about things. I thought I was helping you and..." I swallow the big lump in my throat. "I should have talked to you first."

"It's okay. I don't think you did it to hurt me."

"I didn't. I would never intentionally hurt you," I assure her.

She brings her knees to her chest and hugs them. "I know." Something passes on her face.

"Is there something you want to ask me?"

"I've been wondering something. If you don't want to tell me, you don't have to."

"What is it?"

She hesitates.

"Go on, baby girl. You don't have to be scared to ask me whatever is on your mind."

"Okay. Carla told me you know I saw Cascade for two therapy sessions."

I squeeze my eyes shut. Blood pounds between my ears. I open my eyes and pin my gaze on her. "Yeah. I dug up everything on you I could find."

"Why?"

"The day Sergey came to talk to you up here, he texted me and asked me to watch out for you. Once I started digging, I couldn't stop. I knew you hired our guys for security, and my brother and I handle that part of the Ivanov business."

She straightens up and crisscrosses her legs. "And how did you know you were a Dom? Sorry, a top?"

My stomach clenches. There are only two options. I can tell her I don't want to talk about it, but it doesn't seem right after she's told me so much about her life. "Carla is the only person who knows."

She scrunches her face. "Okay. Sorry I asked."

"No. I'm going to tell you. I just wanted you to know no one else knows."

"Oh. Okay." She focuses on me and waits.

I choose my words carefully. It feels like someone is taking a nail gun and shooting it into my stomach. "When my sister died, I had just found out my fiancée was working for the Petrovs."

Horror fills her face. "The people who kidnapped and killed Natalia?"

I glance up at the sky. It's blue, with no clouds in sight, but I suddenly feel anything but sunny. "Yes. She was only with me to spy on me for them."

She scoots closer and grabs my hand. It's an electric shock wave of everything I miss about her. Her warmth and kindness and soft hands I can't get out of my mind. "That's horrible."

I force myself to look at her. I'm tempted to keep staring at the sky instead of facing her, but I don't. She's always open with me. She's never hidden anything. She deserves me to be the man who gives her the same amount of honest attention she always shows me. "After the Petrovs raped and murdered Natalia, I had a hard time having sex. I always was dominant. Not in the way I am now, nor did I even know what BDSM was, but I liked to make the woman I was with submit. After everything happened, I just..." I inhale a lungful of air. "I felt guilty. I didn't want to date anyone and ever feel the pain I felt when I found out about Annika's betrayal. I tried casual sex, and I couldn't do it. I keep thinking about men forcing themselves on my sister. When I met Carla, she saw how messed up I was and took me to the club we belong to. She helped me process things and find a way to get what I needed."

She stays quiet. Her eyes are full of sympathy, but it doesn't feel like pity. It's as if she somehow understands me and what I went through. "Thank you for telling me."

I shouldn't say it. She made it clear she needs space and to be by herself. She doesn't deserve a guilt trip or pressure, but I don't know what to do with this ache I can't get rid of. "I miss you. I spend my day checking my phone, hoping you'll call or text. I force myself not to come knock on your door."

A line forms between her eyes. "I won't lie. I've stopped myself from punching the code for your penthouse."

I reach for her waist and pull her over my body, so she's straddling me. "Then come up. Anytime. You don't even need to call or text. Just come up."

She blinks hard, and her lips quiver. "I umm..." She clears her throat. "I'm figuring some things out, but I'm not sure I fall into your parameters. I don't want to pretend I can do something I can't."

"What are you talking about? We don't have to do anything you don't want to."

She shakes her head. "I'm not talking about sexual acts. Well, not between us at least."

"I don't understand."

"It's what I'm trying to come to terms with, with Carla. I umm... I'm not sure I can be your bottom." A tear drips down her face.

My heart stutters. I wipe her cheek with my thumb. "What—"

"Obrecht! We've got an issue. You're needed now!" Matvey yells out.

She jumps off my lap and stands.

I rise. "Selena, if I did something—"

"You haven't done anything wrong. This is me. I'm trying to figure things out. It's why I've stayed away from you," she says.

"Obrecht!" Matvey barks.

She smiles. "I think you better go take care of whatever is going on before Matvey has a heart attack."

"When can we talk about this?" I ask.

"Just give me a little bit more time. Please? I don't want to say something I'm unsure about."

"Obrecht. This is important! The snake is slithering in the garage," Matvey's voice booms.

"Go," she says and nods toward him.

Sometimes, I hate my life. The snake is Adrian's ex-wife, Dasha. It's code that they have one of the Polish mob guys she's involved with at the garage, and I need to go spend who knows how many days, torturing the guy until he gives us the information we need.

"When you're ready, please let's finish this conversation," I say to Selena.

"Okay."

I slide my hands on her cheeks. I resist kissing her on the lips and peck her on the forehead instead. I begrudgingly leave her and take care of Ivanov issues. For several days, I'm at the garage. As soon as I get in my car, I turn on my phone.

No messages.

My heart sinks. When I get home, Matvey tells me Selena is on the roof. I put on my workout clothes, and déjà vu hits me. She's in the same lounger, listening to music and on her laptop. I don't say anything to her, trying to respect her boundary. I complete a full workout. When I turn to leave, Kora is talking with her.

I jog over to them. "Kora. I thought that was you. How are you?" I haven't seen her since her mother and sister's funeral.

She smiles. "Doing better. Thanks. And I never got to thank you properly."

"For what?" I ask.

She swallows hard. "Sergey told me you and Adrian kept DeAndre and Terrell away from me at the wake."

My heart goes out to her. The remaining family she has are grade-A assholes. "No need to thank me. You're family now."

She blinks hard and turns toward the lake. There's an uncomfortable silence.

I ask, "What are you doing here?"

She recovers. "I'd ask you the same thing, but it seems you live here?"

"Yeah. I moved in a little over a month ago. Maksim talked me into the penthouse and gave me a good deal."

"Aww. Maksim showed you his soft side, did he?" she teases.

I chuckle. "Something like that."

"Do you like it?"

"Yeah." I glance at Selena and try to keep my cool. "Hey, Selena."

She beams, and a small flush fills her cheeks. "Hi."

My dick hardens. With Kora here, there's no way I'm talking to Selena to find out what she meant the last time we spoke.

"Okay. I need to get ready for work. It was good seeing you, Kora. I'll see you later, Selena."

"Okay," Selena replies.

Kora waves. "Bye."

I shower then text Matvey.

Me: *Let me know when Kora leaves.*

Matvey: *She's already gone.*

Me: *Where is Selena?*

Matvey: *In her condo.*

I throw on clothes and go to Selena's unit. I knock on the door.

She opens it. "Obrecht."

"Can I come in?"

She opens the door wider and steps back. "Sure."

I resist pulling her into my arms and kissing her. She told me to give her time, and I did, but I can't continue not knowing why she thinks she can't be with me.

"Do you want something to drink?" she offers.

"No, thanks."

She motions to the couch. "Please sit. I'm glad you're here. I was going to see if you could talk today."

I release an anxious breath and sit. "Good. I don't want to push you, Selena, but I need to know what you meant the other day."

She nods. "Yes. I know." She sits down and turns to face me. "This is hard for me. I...umm..." She takes a deep breath and swallows hard.

My heart beats so fast, I think it might explode. "It's okay. Just tell me whatever you need to say."

I've not seen the expression on her face before, and it scares me. "Kora made some comments. I acted like we were nothing, and I barely knew you."

"We aren't nothing, and you do know me," I sternly say.

Nervousness appears on her face. "Yes. I know. It made me realize I need to stop hiding from you and get it over with."

I don't like the phrase, *get it over with*. It makes my skin crawl. "I'm listening."

"I really like you, Obrecht."

"I feel the same about you."

She bites on her lip and shuts her eyes.

My gut drops. "Baby girl—"

"I don't think you should call me that anymore."

My jaw clenches. A suffocating feeling overwhelms me. I sternly ask, "Why not?"

"I can't be your bottom."

"What did I do?"

She shakes her head. "Nothing. You haven't done anything wrong."

"Then why can't we be together? I know I made a mistake, but—"

"It's not that." She glances at the floor and twists her hands together.

"Then tell me why," I demand.

She pins her glistening orbs on mine. "I-I can't be anyone's bottom. It's not what I want. I might not know everything about myself, but I do know I can't stand the thought of you with anyone else. I don't want to go back to something where the man I'm with is screwing other women. I just... I can't do it again. And every time I try to convince myself I'm overreacting and can deal with it, I feel like I can't breathe."

I tug her onto my lap. "Listen to me, baby girl. I don't care about anyone else. I don't need to screw any other woman. And I don't want you to be a bottom for me or any other top."

She furrows her eyebrows. "But you said no attachments."

"Yeah. That's what I wanted before I met you."

She stares at me, her hot breath merging into mine, confusion all over her face. "What do you want then? I need to be clear on what you want so I don't have something else in my head."

"I want *you*. What do you want me to be? Your Dom? Your boyfriend? I hope to God you don't say Master, but if you do, I'm going to have to swallow my pride and somehow figure it out," I admit.

A tiny smile forms on her lips. "I don't want a Master. You were right about that. But I'm not sure beyond that."

I fist her hair. "But you want to be with me? In a committed relationship?"

"Yes."

"Good. Then the rest we'll decide together." I kiss her. Every second of suffering without her, I put in our kiss. My tongue parts the seam of her lips as I hungrily flick in and out of her mouth, taking every morsel of affection she'll give me. I pull back. "Go put something nice on."

"Why?" she pants.

"I'm taking you out, baby girl."

16

Selena

NERVOUS FLUTTERS FILL MY BELLY. I HAVEN'T BEEN ON A DATE since I was twenty. I study myself in my full-length mirror. Obrecht said to wear something nice, but I didn't think to ask for more details. I was too shocked he didn't care anymore about being a top with no commitment. It was unexpected and overwhelming, and I'm still trying to stop myself from questioning it.

The green dress I chose has little specks of navy in it. It's form-fitting and hugs my body so every curve is on display. It shows a hint of cleavage and is more than Jack would have ever allowed me to wear. Since I got divorced, I haven't had a reason to wear anything dressy, so I feel a tad self-conscious compared to my normal casual attire.

I attempt to push the thoughts of Jack and what he approves of out of my mind.

I'm dressing up for Obrecht, not Jack.

What if Obrecht doesn't like it?

I turn to glance at my ass, which is now round compared to the flatness I used to have.

Jack would have a fit if he saw me this big.

Why am I thinking of Jack?

I study my hair and makeup then finally decide I look nice and pace my condo. The thought to have a glass of wine enters my mind, but I assume we'll have something at dinner, and I don't want to go over my limit.

There's a knock on the door, and my butterflies take off. I reach for my door handle and freeze. My gut drops as I stare at my shaking hand, so I take a few deep breaths, trying to calm my nerves. There's another knock, and I jump, then open the door.

Holy...

My lower body pulses, and I cross my foot over my ankle. Obrecht has on a dark-blue suit. His white shirt has the top three buttons undone, displaying his chest and neck tattoos. His ice-blue eyes take in every inch of my skin as he slowly scans the length of my body.

"Turn," he commands.

I spin, and my flutters reawaken.

He steps behind me so his body is flush to mine, moves my hair to the side, and kisses the curve of my neck. "You're stunning, my dorogaya." He wraps his arm around me and holds out a bouquet of purple calla lilies. "These are for you."

I turn my head. "You got me Greek lilies?"

"Yeah."

"Did you know they're my favorite flower?"

"No, but I thought my Greek goddess needed something besides stereotypical roses."

"Thank you."

He gives me a chaste kiss on the lips then pats my ass. "You're welcome. Are you ready to go?"

"Let me put these in water." I take them, go into the kitchen, and pull the vase out from under the cabinet. I cut the stems, fill the vase with water and half the packet of the flower food, then stick them in it.

Obrecht leads me out of my condo, into the elevator, and through the lobby. We get in the car. Matvey gets in the front.

"Why is Matvey with us?" I ask.

He puts his arm around me. "Precaution. Forget he's here. He won't bug us."

"Okay. Where are we going?"

"Not to a buffet," he teases.

"Ha, ha!" My cheeks burn from embarrassment, thinking about the club I erroneously chose. "Are we going to your club?"

"No, baby girl. We're going to dinner. Then we're going back to my place," he says.

I squeeze my legs together. "Am I staying the night?"

He leans closer to my face. "You are. In the morning, I'll make you breakfast."

My lips twitch. "You sound like you have it all planned out."

He studies my face. "Not all. Some of it is yet to be determined." He winks, and my heart misses a beat.

"Carla said I need to be clear about what I want," I blurt out.

His face turns serious. "Always." He tugs me onto his lap. "Tell me what you want."

My pulse beats harder in my chest. Heat fills my cheeks. We haven't been in the car for five minutes, and I'm already thinking about sex with Obrecht. "I-I keep having a dream."

"Am I in it?"

"Yes.

He smiles. "Good answer. Tell me about your dream."

I stroke the side of his head, trying to find the courage to tell him what I can't seem to stop obsessing over. Every night for the last five days, I've had the dream. It's so vivid, I feel like it's really happening. "What did you do with the three items you had me buy?"

"They're in my closet." His thumb caresses my ass cheek. Tingles shoot up my spine, and I shiver. He asks, "Why do you ask?"

I drag my finger along his chest, outlining the handle of his sword tattoo. My stomach continues to have anxious sensations, but I take a deep breath. Carla said I need to be honest and transparent with any partner. I'm not even sure why I'm nervous, since it's Obrecht. I'm pretty sure he'll be open to whatever I want to try. "So..."

Amusement appears on his gorgeous face. "So..."

"Is there anything I got you want to use?" I inhale a large amount of air.

He doesn't hesitate. "All but that face hood."

Goose bumps break out on my skin, thinking about the face hood. I close my eyes, trying to get the memories of it out of my head.

Obrecht circles his arms around me. "You okay?"

I open my eyes. "Yeah. Can we still cut it up and burn it?"

He nods. "Tomorrow. Let's do it at breakfast."

"Okay."

He sweetly kisses me then says, "Tell me about your dream."

"It involved the neck-wrist restraints."

He licks his lips and leans to my ear. Wet heat flicks on my lobe, and I squirm on his lap. His hot breath hits my neck. He murmurs, "Were your hands in the front of your body or back?"

"Back. But they were in the air, attached to something else, and I was facing you."

He groans. "That's hot, baby girl."

"It is?"

"Did you think so in your dream?"

I nod. "Yes."

"There's your answer." He dips to the curve of my neck and lightly sucks, mumbling, "Were you begging me to come?"

My body hums against his. I close my eyes. My voice comes out raspy. "Yes. A lot."

A deep rumble fills his chest. His erection presses into my thigh. "What were you wearing?"

"Umm... I was topless but had on the white crotchless panties I'm wearing right now."

He puts his face in front of mine. "You're wearing white crotchless panties right now?"

"Yes."

"Jesus. Why are we going to dinner?" he asks, and the car stops in front of a restaurant. There's a line of people waiting outside. It snakes around the corner of the building.

"We can go home if you want?" I bite my lip.

He slides his hand through my hair and palms my head. "Don't tempt me." He fists my hair and kisses me, sliding his tongue in and out of my mouth with urgency until I can barely breathe. My body heats, and I moan into his mouth. "You're tempting me, baby girl," he mutters and returns to taking possession of my mouth.

"Let's go home, then."

Obrecht pulls back. "No. I'm taking you on a proper date first." He slides me off his lap, opens the door, and gets out. He reaches in to help me out and guides me to the front of the line and into the restaurant.

It's dark, and candles glow throughout the restaurant. A woman with spiky red hair, a nose ring, and a friendly smile greets us. "Obrecht. Your table is ready. Follow me." She picks up two menus and leads us through the restaurant. We're halfway through when a woman's voice in a Russian accent says, "Obrecht."

He freezes then turns.

A striking older woman, with blonde hair to her shoulders, the same icy-blue eyes as Obrecht's, and a bright smile, rises.

"Mom. What are you doing here?" Obrecht asks.

"Eating," she replies then softly laughs. Her grin widens, and she addresses me. "I'm Svetlana, Obrecht's mother."

My stomach flips with more nerves.

Obrecht tugs me tighter to his side. "Mom, this is Selena."

She steps forward and embraces me then kisses my cheek. "Selena, it's so nice to meet you."

"You, too."

Obrecht eyes the man at the table. "Sorry, I didn't catch your name."

The man at the table rises. He holds out his hand. "I'm Stefano."

Obrecht shakes his hand. "Obrecht. How long have you known my mother?"

Stefano glances at Svetlana and grins. "Few months."

Obrecht says something to his mother in Russian.

Stefano laughs. "I speak fluent Russian. I can't answer for your mother, but I'm serious about her."

Obrecht's jaw clenches.

Svetlana blushes and beams.

"We just arrived and haven't ordered yet. Do you want to join us?" Stefano asks.

"No, we're—"

"Yes! Please! I insist," Svetlana says. She takes my hand. "Sit down. Is that a Greek accent I hear?"

"Yes. I moved here when I was twenty."

"Mom, it's nice to see you, but we have a table—"

"Oh, shush! Selena, I never get to meet any of Obrecht's dates. You don't mind humoring an old woman, do you?" she asks.

"Ah...no, umm..." I break away from her hopeful face and glance at Obrecht.

He sighs then pulls out a chair and motions for me to sit. He says to the hostess, "I guess we're joining this table."

"Very well." She sets the menus on the table and leaves.

Obrecht sits next to me and slides his arm around my shoulders.

"You're very beautiful," Svetlana says to me.

"Thank you. So are you."

"Yes, she is," Stefano says and kisses her hand.

Obrecht shifts in his seat. "How did you two meet?"

"Stefano is a doctor at the home I volunteer at," Svetlana replies.

Obrecht raises his eyebrows. "The one Aspen's dad is at?"

"Yes. How do you know I'm friends with her father?"

"Maksim said you have some serious card games going on."

"Your mother is quite the card player. She doesn't show any mercy to my patients," Stefano states with pride in his eyes.

"Yes, she is," Obrecht flatly replies.

I put my hand on his thigh. I'm unsure if he's uncomfortable with his mom dating or if he doesn't like Stefano. He glances at me, and I smile, hoping he relaxes.

"Where did you two meet?" Svetlana asks.

"We live in the same building. Obrecht was kind enough to change my faucet out when the new one arrived," I tell her.

"He and Adrian have always been handy like that. Their father taught them. So how long have you been dating?" she asks.

At the same time, I say, "This is our first date," Obrecht says, "A few weeks." Heat rushes to my cheeks. I glance at Obrecht as the server comes over with a bottle of wine. He kisses my forehead.

The server hands Stefano a glass to taste the wine. He passes it to Svetlana, and she approves. The server fills all our glasses then rattles off a bunch of specials in Russian.

Obrecht turns to me. "Do you want me to explain each of those dishes or just order?"

"Just order, please."

He and Stefano begin to order things, and Svetlana takes my hand. "Do you have children?"

"No."

"Do you want them?"

"Umm—"

"Mom!" Obrecht reprimands.

Her eyes grow wide. "What? She's beautiful and young. I'm just asking."

I decide to answer honestly. "I used to think so. Then I was glad I didn't. I'm umm... I'm not sure anymore."

"You don't have to know, my dorogaya," Obrecht firmly states.

Svetlana beams. "It's okay not to know. But you two would make beautiful babies."

$$\mathcal{MC}$$

Obrecht

MY PLANS FOR A PRIVATE DINNER BETWEEN SELENA AND ME blew up. I wasn't aware my mother was dating anyone. I've never known her to have a boyfriend and didn't even know she went on dates. Stefano seems like a decent guy, but I'm digging into everything I can about him as soon as I get a chance.

My mother doesn't waste any time asking Selena about children. Her twenty questions start. I rotate between making sure Selena is okay and finding out what I can about Stefano.

At least she doesn't have any bridal magazines to throw at Selena.

"I've heard a lot about you and your brother. It's nice to meet you finally," Stefano says while rubbing his fingers on my mother's shoulder.

"I've not heard anything about you," I reply, glance at his fingers, then lock my eyes on his. Maybe it shouldn't bother me. I want my mom to be happy, but I don't know this guy. My mother sinks into him while gabbing with Selena, and my chest tightens more.

He doesn't seem fazed by my stare. "Yes, well, your mother probably wanted to be as sure about me as I am about her. Right, my tesoruccio?"

My mother blushes.

Jesus. When did she start blushing?

His what?

"What does tesoruccio mean?" Selena asks before I can.

"Little treasure trove," he replies, intensely gazing at my mother, so her cheeks heat up even more.

"Aww. That's sweet," Selena purrs.

Little treasure trove? My mother?

I force myself not to comment and ask, "How do you know Russian?"

His fingers stroke my mother's shoulder some more. I take several breaths, reminding myself she deserves to be happy.

She should have told Adrian and me that she was seeing someone.

We know nothing about this guy.

How did we not know this when they've been together for months?

I wonder if Maksim knows anything about this.

If he's anything but one hundred percent good, I'm going to take him to the garage and make him beg for his life.

"How do you know Russian?" I ask again.

He refocuses on me. "I study languages. I'm also fluent in Italian, Spanish, French, and German."

"Wow! That's impressive," Selena exclaims.

My mother nods as if proud of him. "Isn't it?"

I refrain from rolling my eyes and take a long sip of wine, wishing I had a vodka instead. "What kind of doctor are you?"

"I'm a neurologist. I specialize in the diagnosis and treatment of Alzheimer's and other dementias."

"Stefano is the doctor who's been caring for Aspen's father. He just got recognized in several senior citizen's magazines for his advanced techniques in dementia care," my mother boasts.

"That's amazing," Selena states.

He humbly shrugs. "I'm just doing my job."

"You're always so modest. Don't let him fool you. It's a huge deal, and he's made a real difference in a lot of people's lives." The look my mother gives him tells me she's serious about this guy.

Is she in love with him?

You better be on the up-and-up, buddy.

"I need to go to the restroom. Does anyone know where it is?" Selena asks.

My mother rises. "I'll go with you."

Oh no. The last thing I need is my mother cornering Selena by herself.

"I'll take her," I say, rising.

"No. I'll go with her since I need to go, too," my mother insists.

I groan inside. My mother is a loose cannon. Who knows what she'll say to Selena? Her dream is for Adrian and me to get married and pop out tons of grandbabies for her. Since Annika, I haven't introduced her to anyone, even when I attempted to date before I met Carla.

"Sit. I'll be back," Selena says.

I glance at Matvey, and he's already walking toward us. "Don't take too long." I kiss Selena's forehead. In Russian, I say to my mother, "Don't bring up weddings or babies."

She innocently smiles and chirps, "You aren't getting any younger."

"Mom," I warn.

She pats me on the shoulder. "Stop stressing, Obrecht." In English, she asks Selena, "Ready?"

"Yes."

They leave, and Matvey follows.

"Who's that man following them?" Stefano stares at Matvey.

"My guy."

He refocuses on me. "Is there a reason he's following them?"

243

"Yes, but it's not your business," I snap and motion for the server.

"If it has to do with your mother, it is."

His words slap me in the face. I don't dislike Stefano, but I'm not letting my guard down until I know for sure what kind of man he is. It's also apparent my mother and he are serious about each other. I cross my arms. "I think we should get something straight."

The server arrives. "Sir, can I get you something?"

I nod. "Double Beluga, neat."

"Very well, sir. And do you need anything else?" she asks Stefano.

"No, thank you."

She leaves.

Several moments of uncomfortable silence follows. Stefano never flinches, nor do I.

I finally break the tense air. "If you hurt my mother, it'll be the last thing you ever do."

His jaw clenches. "As it should be, but what about you?"

"Me?"

"You and your brother should spend a bit more time with her. If you did, you'd know about me, and we wouldn't be having this conversation, would we?" He raises his eyebrows.

"Excuse me? You don't know—"

"I know you're involved in your own lives, but one day, and I can say this from experience, you'll regret not carving more time out for her. She's a wonderful woman and loves you both. I see her with my resident-patients, so I know she's a great mother. Plus, she talks with so much pride about you two. Twice, I've been at her house for dinner when you and your brother both canceled on her at the last minute."

My gut flips. I clench my fists at my thighs. Adrian and I did cancel, but it was because we had to go to the garage. "Don't stick your nose where it doesn't belong. You don't know our reasons, and I guarantee you, our mother understands."

He takes a long sip of wine. "Yes. Things come up in life, but you didn't reschedule, did you?"

I hate that this stranger who's in a serious relationship with my mother is laying on the guilt. I can't rebuke him. Neither Adrian nor I made an effort, and we often do see it as a chore to get together with our mom.

He glances toward the direction Selena and my mother went then leans closer. His voice drops. "I'm glad we finally met. I hope to meet your brother soon. You should know I've bought your mother a ring. I'd like us to get along. This isn't an ideal way for you to discover your mother is in a relationship, so I'm going to forget about this little dose of hostility."

It feels as if a bomb hit me. "You're going to propose to my mother?"

His face lights up, and I want to smack it. "Yes. I'm unsure how she's never remarried, but I'm not a fool. I know a phenomenal woman when I see one."

The server returns with my vodka. "Anything else, sir?"

"No," I say in shock. Then I pick up the tumbler and drink half of it. The alcohol is smooth, but the amount I take causes it to burn my throat on the way down.

Will my mother say yes?

My instincts say she will. I don't want to deny her any happiness, nor do I enjoy the thought of her being alone. Both Adrian and I want her to find someone, but I still don't know this guy.

"When are you asking her?"

He scratches his chin. "I thought it was best if I met you and your brother first. Your mother already met my daughters."

"To ask our permission?"

He snorts. "No. I don't need your permission. Your blessing would be welcome, but I'm sixty-five and retiring next month. I assumed it would be better for us to know each other before asking your mother. I don't want her to have any reason to worry when she says yes."

"So you do need my permission," I arrogantly state then drink the remaining vodka.

He scoffs. "No. I want your mother to feel comfortable agreeing to marry me."

"You seem sure she'll say yes."

He studies me, and it takes everything I have not to blink. "She loves me. I love her. It's not a question of what she'll say."

She loves him.

How did Adrian and I miss this?

I motion for the server to bring me another drink. "How many daughters do you have?"

Pride lights up his expression. "Four. They've already become close to Svetlana. I'd love for you to meet them."

One big happy family.

"Any sons?"

"No."

"What happened between you and their mother? Or is it mothers?"

His face falls. "My wife passed in her forties. She had a rare form of early-onset Alzheimer's disease. It's what made me switch my focus."

My mouth turns dry. I realize I'm being a dick and need to relax a bit. "I'm sorry to hear that."

He drinks his wine. "It was a long time ago."

"Do you have any grandkids so my mom can get off my and Adrian's ass?" I ask. I was never opposed to kids, but my mom lays the guilt on thick. Adrian and I don't like disappointing her, but love hasn't really been on our side.

He chuckles. "Two and another one on the way."

"My mom's met them?"

"Oh, yes. She's a natural grandmother."

I can't help but smile. My mother is wonderful with children. She's always been a loving human being, and her family is everything to her. Natalia's death crushed her. Anything that brings her happiness, I need to be grateful for and support it.

If I only knew everything about this guy.

I need to cool it. I don't need to do something I'll regret and have to try and make up for later.

I pin my gaze on him. "If my mom is happy, and you're a stand-up guy, then both Adrian and I will be nothing but supportive."

The server sets another vodka down. "Anything else?"

"Not right now. Thank you," I reply.

Stefano puts his glass to mine. "We won't have any problems, then. Saluti."

I clink his glass. "If you're going to marry my mother, it's nostrovia."

He nods. "Nostrovia it is."

I'm in the middle of my drink when my phone buzzes. It's the ringtone for Matvey, so I grab it out of my pocket and rise, walking toward the direction of the restrooms.

Matvey: *Jack is in the building.*

My stomach clenches and my chest tightens. I scan the room then see Jack turn the corner of the hallway and continue to his table. I get to the corridor. My heart slams against my chest cavity. "Did he see her?"

"No. He just came out," Matvey replies, scowling.

The door opens, and Selena and my mom step out.

I point to the door. "Go back inside."

My mother scrunches her face. "Obrecht, what are you talking about?"

"Not now. Go back in the bathroom until we tell you to come out."

"Obrecht?" Selena asks.

"Jack's here. Go."

The color drains from her face. She spins and obeys. My mom gives me another quizzical look but follows.

"Where's the nearest exit?" I ask Matvey.

"What's going on?" Stefano asks behind me.

My stomach drops further. The last thing I want to do is explain myself, but my mother isn't staying in this restaurant anywhere near Jack, either. I turn. "I need you to pay the bill. Then come back here so we can get out of here safely."

He furrows his eyebrows. "Why? What's not safe?"

"This isn't the time for questions."

He pauses for a brief moment then nods. "Okay. I'll be back."

"Thank you," I say in relief.

I turn back to Matvey. "He doesn't know she's here?"

"Not right now. There's a door at the end of this hall. My guess is it leads into the alley. I'll text our driver." He types on his phone.

Several minutes pass, and Stefano returns. "All paid."

I point to the end of the hallway. "We're leaving out that door and quickly."

"All right," he agrees.

I open the door. "Ladies."

Selena steps out first. Matvey leads, and I motion for her, then my mother, to go. Stefano and I walk side by side behind them. We step out into the alley. My driver is waiting. The four of us get into the backseat, and Matvey gets into the passenger seat.

Selena's shaking, and I tug her into me and murmur, "It's okay, baby girl. He didn't see you."

Her eyes have so much fear in them, it pains me. Her voice cracks. "No?"

"No." I kiss her forehead and hold her tighter, trying to regulate my heartbeat.

"Obrecht, what's just happened?" my mother asks. Her expression is filled with worry.

I open and close my fist. "Selena's ex-husband was in the restaurant."

My mother's eyes meet mine. "He's trying to come after her?"

"We don't know, but we aren't taking any chances."

"I'm-I'm sorry I ruined your dinner," Selena chokes out.

"You didn't ruin it. Safety should always come first," Stefano says.

Good answer. You just scored a point.

"Yes. Don't think twice about it," my mother states. "Should we go to my place? I have leftovers I can heat up and several good bottles of wine."

I'm about to say no, but Selena blurts out, "Okay. If it's not too much trouble?"

My mother beams. "I'll never be troubled over spending time with my son and his girlfriend."

Selena

IT'S LATE WHEN WE LEAVE SVETLANA'S. WE ATE GREAT FOOD, drank more wine, and talked all night. "I love your mom," I tell Obrecht when we get into the car.

"That's good, my dorogaya. She loved you."

"Stefano is super nice, too."

Obrecht takes a deep breath. "Yeah. He seems decent."

I snicker. "Are you upset your mom's dating someone?"

His jaw clenches. "No. But I don't know enough about him."

I trace his jaw. "Your mom seems happy. I didn't get any bad vibes from him. Did you?"

He hesitates then admits, "No."

"Then shouldn't you give him the benefit of the doubt?" I ask.

Something passes in Obrecht's face. "I'm sure he'll pass my check. Let's change the subject. I'd rather talk about you."

I raise my eyebrows. "Pass your check?"

He pulls me onto his lap. "No offense, but Stefano isn't what I want to spend the rest of my night discussing."

"Okay, but what about Jack?" I blurt out. My pulse rises.

Obrecht stiffens. "I think it was a coincidence. My guys went in after, and he appeared to be there eating with friends, nothing more. Matvey insists he didn't see you."

I bite my lip.

Obrecht slides his hand through my hair. "He doesn't know where you are. We don't know for sure if he's even thinking about coming after you."

"But I still have the dreams," I admit.

He tilts his head. His eyes turn to slits. "What dreams?"

My chest tightens. "I'm back at his house. I'm in my cage, and he has the mask over my face. It doesn't go past that. I always wake up."

Obrecht's expression hardens. "Your cage?"

"Yes. He used to keep it in our bedroom to use as a punishment."

Obrecht's voice turns so cold, I get goose bumps. "He's going to pay."

Anxiety and fear choke me. "I just don't want to go back."

"It's a flashback. Nothing is happening to you. You have security on you at all times," he insists.

"It feels so real," I say.

"It's not."

I bite on my bottom lip. My dreams are often a prediction of the future. Not always, but the fact I've had it several times scares me.

Obrecht caresses my cheek with his thumb. "I thought you were dreaming of me?"

My cheeks heat. "I do. I wake up from our dream, and then it goes into the nightmare."

"I guess we need to change it then, huh?"

"How?"

His lips twitch. He fists my hair and tugs my head back. His mouth moves across my neck. He murmurs, "We're going to do everything in your dream then you're going to sleep in my bed, with me. You won't be with him or in any cage, baby girl."

"Is this our negotiations?" I ask.

He releases my hair, and his hand drops to my spine. "You want to negotiate?"

Flutters release in my stomach. "Yes. Before we get home." I let out a big breath and admit, "I've been dying to submit to you."

Blue heat flames in his icy orbs. "Okay. You told me about your dream. Tell me what you don't want. What are your hard limits?"

I recall the conversations I've had with Carla. The list I created is also in my mind. "Nothing over my face. Spanking with your hand is okay, but nothing painful beyond that. No paddles, floggers, or sharp objects. If you are going to use any toys on me, can you ask me first so I can say yes or no?"

He kisses me. "Yes, baby girl. I'm so proud of you. This is good. Anything else?"

"Umm, I'm not saying never, but right now, I don't want to do anything with ice or extreme heat." My stomach twists, remembering some of the things Jack did to me. I'm conflicted on this since Carla discussed some things that weren't abusive and piqued my curiosity, but I'm not ready for any of it and am unsure if I ever will be.

Obrecht traces my cheekbone. "Got it. What else?"

I shake my head. "That's it."

"Tell me your safe word."

"Faucet."

"And you're prepared to say it if you don't like something?"

I nod. "Yes."

He slips his hand up my dress and rests it between my thighs. His middle finger grazes my slit, and I shudder. He takes his other hand and holds my chin. "When we get home, you'll remove everything, except your panties. You'll kneel at the end of the bed and call me, sir. Understand?"

My heart beats faster. "Yes, sir." I swallow hard. "Umm, what about my other item?"

"We will destroy it tomorrow at breakfast as we discussed."

"No. Umm, I mean the other item, sir."

He inhales deeply. "You aren't ready for that. We need to do some things with smaller toys first." He teases my clit with his finger.

I squirm on his lap. "When?"

"I picked some things up. If you want, I can try it on you tonight." His face comes closer. "But I'm going in your ass before the toy you bought does."

A nervous excitement flares in my belly. I'm clueless why I want Obrecht to have me in that way. It was horrible with Jack. I discussed it with Carla. She said a good experience could help replace some of the bad memories. I also know I can say faucet at any time and Obrecht will stop. "Tonight?"

A deep rumble ignites in his chest. "Not tonight, baby girl. We'll try some smaller toys tonight and see how you do first."

I stare at him.

"What's on your mind?" he asks.

"What if I don't handle it well?"

"Then we won't do it."

"But you like it."

He strokes me faster, and I gasp. "I like your pussy, too, baby girl. I'll be fine. *We'll* be fine. And we don't have to even try if you don't want—"

"I do. I want to try."

He studies my face. It's dark, but his icy-blue eyes stand out against the darkness, like a wolf ready to eat its prey. The car stops. He pecks me on the lips and removes his hands from me. "Is there anything else you want to negotiate?"

"No. Did I do it correctly?"

He smiles. "Yes. And I'm hard as nails thinking about what I'm going to do with you tonight."

I slide off his lap and swallow the lump in my throat. "Should we go upstairs, then?"

He kisses my hand. "If you're ready, I am."

"I am," I assure him.

He gets out of the car, reaches in to help me out, then quickly maneuvers me into the building and through the lobby. I sink into his body, feeling safe and loved, wondering again how we're at this point when I woke up this morning thinking about how I needed to tell him I couldn't be his bottom. I thought I had to let him go, but he's proved me wrong in so many ways.

We step out of the elevator and into the penthouse. He stops walking and motions for me to go into the bedroom. I obey and remove my clothes. I fold them and put them on the chair then put my shoes next to it. I keep my white crotchless panties on and kneel at the end of the bed. I bow my head and wait.

I'm not sure how much time passes, but every second makes my anticipation grow. It also makes me wet thinking about what we've discussed. I finally hear his footsteps.

His finger moves down my spine, and tingles burst everywhere. "Who do you belong to?"

"You, sir."

"That's right. You're mine, baby girl. Lift your head."

I obey and focus on the dark bedspread in front of me.

He fists my hair and tugs my head back so it's against his cock. His face looks down upon mine. He says something in Russian then in English demands, "Get up and lean on the bed."

I oblige him. As soon as my torso is on the bed, he smacks my ass.

I jump.

"This is for making me think about you in these panties all night while hanging out with my mother. What do you say for yourself?"

"I'm sorry, sir."

He spanks me again. "I don't think you are. You wanted me hard all night, didn't you?" The sound of his hand hitting my bottom rings through the air.

"Yes, sir."

Another swift hand to my ass cheek echoes in my ears. "You withheld information from me. You said crotchless. These are also assless. Did you wear these in the hopes of having me take you there?"

"Yes, sir," I admit.

He sticks a finger in my pussy then spanks me several more times. I clench my walls around his digit, and he grunts, rubbing his hand over the sting. He removes his hands and demands, "Don't move."

I obey his orders. For several minutes, I lay over the bed, waiting and wondering what's next. He comes back and spreads my legs with his foot. He says nothing, and something cool, wet, and hard hits my forbidden zone in a circling pattern.

I gasp. I'm not familiar with whatever slippery thing he has. I clench up.

His hand strokes my spine. His voice softens. "Relax, baby girl. Take some deep breaths."

I take quite a few. He teases me with whatever he has and pushes it past my rigid ring. I inhale sharply, and his body hovers over mine. His lips flutter on my shoulder. He inches it in and out, and my breathing intensifies. "You okay?"

"Yes."

"Good. Don't move."

"Yes, sir."

He pushes it farther in me until I feel so full, I think I might explode. He leaves, and I hear the water running. He returns and says, "Stand up."

I push myself off the mattress and bow my head, awaiting his instructions.

"Head up."

I refocus my gaze on the headboard.

"Go into the closet. Don't bow your head for the rest of the night."

"Yes, sir." I make my way to the closet, aware of him watching me. Whatever is in my body creates an unfamiliar sensation when I walk. His wardrobe is enormous. Suits fill one wall. The other side has built-in drawers and shelves. I step to the middle of the space and wait for directions.

His hot breath hits the curve of my neck. "I'm going to tie you up, baby girl. Then I'm going to sink my dick in you so deep, you're going to beg me to come."

I shudder as goose bumps pop out on my skin.

He spins me then backs me up until I'm against the door. He puts the restraint around my neck and tightens it until there isn't any space between it and my skin, but it isn't too tight. It feels as if I'm wearing a turtleneck or choker.

"Are you doing okay, baby girl?"

"Yes."

He dips down and kisses me, licking my lips and tongue in a slow burn of everything that's to come.

"Clasp your hands together and put them in front of your body," he commands.

I weave my fingers together and hold them out. He restrains my wrists with the other end of the strap then moves my hands above my head and secures the restraint in the door hook. His warm palms slide down my arms. Tingles flare in their path. He steps back, strips, then fists his cock. "You look hot, baby girl."

"I'm happy I please you, sir."

He groans. "You do. So much." He reaches out and traces the fullness of my breasts with both hands then circles my areolas. My nipples harden, and my chest rises and falls faster. In a quick move, he does something to the strap so it's tight, and my head tilts up. My stomach quivers.

His face looks down upon mine. "Who do you belong to?"

"You, sir."

Fire and ice pool in his eyes. His jaw clenches as he studies me. "You left me for ten days, my dorogaya."

"I'm sorry," I whisper.

"Do you know what you did to me?" He arches his eyebrows, as if he's angry with me.

"I'm sorry," I repeat.

"Sorry doesn't answer my question, does it?"

I swallow hard.

He palms my sex. His body heat penetrates me. "From now on, you don't ignore my calls or texts or *me*. Am I making myself clear?"

"Yes, sir."

"I own you, baby girl. Do you know why?"

Every time he says I'm his, or he owns me, my insides throb. I've come to accept I want to submit, and it's okay. Carla helped me come to terms with it. We haven't discussed this issue. All the times Jack told me he owned me made my skin crawl. Obrecht says it, and it only makes me need him more. "No."

"You don't know?"

"No!"

His hot breath merges into mine. "But you like me owning you. I see it, my dorogaya. Don't you?"

"Yes," I admit.

He nods. "Good." He dips his head into the curve of my neck and slides his hands down my thighs then around my ass. "I own you because you own me, baby girl." He twists whatever he put in my ass. I had forgotten about it.

"Obrecht," I moan.

He kisses my neck until his mouth is next to my lips then picks up my legs and thrusts into me in one motion.

"Oh God!" I scream and squeeze my hands tightly above my head.

"I'm not God, baby girl!" he growls.

It's too much.

I'm so full. Whatever he put in me, combined with his cock, is pushing me to my limit. The restraints are keeping my neck raised toward the ceiling. His body entwines with mine, and he doesn't show me any mercy.

His thrusts are hard, then slow, then hard again. Every move ripples against my walls. I spasm, trying to clench any part of his shaft I can.

"Obrecht!" I whimper when I'm about to fly, and he slows back down.

His hand slides to my clit, tormenting me further. His lips cover mine, owning me, devouring me, solidifying the burning need I always feel for him.

"Please," I mumble into his lips.

His hand comes off my clit, and he shoves his finger in my mouth. "Suck."

I wrap my lips around his fingers and obey, tasting my arousal and closing my eyes. Sweat drips all over us. He speeds up his thrusts, pulls his fingers out of my mouth, and licks my mouth. He swipes his tongue on mine, grunting and sliding deeper in me.

My body trembles. I arch my back, but I can't go very far due to the restraints. "Please," I cry out.

"Please what?" he demands.

"Let me come, please."

"No. You'll come when I do, baby girl."

"Obrecht, please!"

His eyes pierce into mine. "Keep your eyes open. Don't you dare close them."

"Obrecht," I whisper, barely able to get it out. There's too much heat and adrenaline buzzing under my skin. I've never felt anything so intense.

He kisses my lip but pulls away when I open my mouth. "Who owns you, baby girl?"

"You do!"

His large palm holds my cheek. His thumb presses against my lip. "You thought I could walk away from you?"

"Yes. No. Yes. Oh...please!" I squeeze my eyes shut.

"Eyes open!"

"Please!" I plead, and he slams harder into me, growling for me to come.

My entire body collapses around him. My eyes roll, tremors course through me, and he detonates in me while pulling out whatever was in my ass.

He buries his face in my neck, saying something in Russian and breathing hard. I continue to tremble, hardly able to breathe from the intensity of his body merged with mine.

When several minutes pass, he unloops my restraints from the hook, and my tied hands fall behind his neck. He pushes my hair off my face. "I'm never walking away from you, baby girl. You understand?"

My heart hammers, and I nod. "Yes. Thank you, sir."

"No, not sir. Just me." He kisses me as if he didn't just have me and almost split me into two only to make me want to do it all over again.

He reaches for my neck and releases the restraint. It falls between us. He carries me to his bed and sets me down on my knees then unbinds my wrists. When I'm free, he studies me. "Are you okay?"

"Yes."

"Did you like it?"

My cheeks flare with heat. "Yes."

He strokes my cheek and smiles. His other hand palms my ass. "You liked all of it?"

I bite my lip and nod.

"You would tell me if you didn't?"

I put my arms around his shoulders. I drag my nails across his neck. "I loved every minute of it. If I didn't, I would have said faucet."

He pecks me on the lips and pats my ass. "Then get under the covers. And you better call me, sir."

Obrecht

SELENA'S ASLEEP IN MY ARMS. THE DARKNESS OF THE NIGHT IS breaking into the morning. I didn't shut my blackout shades. The faint glow lighting up the sky has a brilliant pink hue to it. There's a loud knock on my bedroom door. Selena stirs, and I jump.

The door opens. Matvey comes flying in. "We have an issue."

"You couldn't call me?" I ask and pull the blanket over my dorogaya's shoulders.

"It's going to voicemail."

I reach for my phone. My battery is dead. I forgot to put it on the charger last night. My gut twists. If Matvey is here, the issue can't be small. "Give me a minute and I'll be out."

He nods and closes the door.

Selena opens her eyes. "What's going on?"

"Something with work, baby girl. Close your eyes and go back to sleep. I'll be back in a few minutes." I kiss her forehead and slide out of bed then tuck the covers around her.

"Is everything okay?"

I smile so she doesn't worry. "I'm sure things are fine."

She doesn't look convinced.

"Go to sleep. It's an order," I tease.

She bites on her smile and turns on her side. "Yes, sir." She shuts her eyes.

I throw on a pair of shorts and a T-shirt then step into the main room. Matvey is staring out the window. I ask him, "What's going on?"

His face is solemn. He shakes his head in disgust. "Boyra Petrov kidnapped Sergey and Kora. Maksim, Liam, and Killian got there and took them to the hospital."

My stomach pitches. Earlier this morning, we found out about Boyra being in town and threatening Sergey and Kora. "Are they okay?"

"Yes. Kora shot Boyra and Igor. She was unconscious for a while but just woke up. Sergey has minimal damage from the incident. Maksim said you need to get to the hospital."

"Igor?" I ask in shock. He's been Sergey's trusted driver for as long as I can remember.

Matvey's face fills with red rage. His Russian accent comes out thicker. "He's a traitor, working for the Petrovs."

The blood drains down my body, and a chill takes its place. "For how long?"

"We don't know. He died too quickly."

Another one of our guys. How do we keep missing this?

"Tell Maksim I'm on my way. Have my driver ready when I get down to the lobby," I instruct.

"Obrecht, we need a clean sweep," Matvey states.

As much as I don't want it to be possible, we can't be naive and think we don't have more traitors among us. Whoever they are, we need to find them before something else happens. "Agreed."

He nods and leaves.

I scrub my hands over my face then go into the bathroom. I turn on the shower, undress, and wait for the water to warm.

How do we have these traitors among us?

Who else don't we know about?

Selena's arms slide around my waist. "Penny for your thoughts?"

I put my arms over hers, debating what to tell her.

She's going to find out sooner or later.

I spin. "There was an incident. Everyone is okay, but Kora and Sergey are at the hospital."

She gapes at me then composes herself. "What happened?"

"I don't know all the details. To be honest, I'm not sure if I can tell you once I find out. It might not be safe for you to know things," I reply.

She tilts her head. "Are you ever going to tell me what you're involved in?"

My mouth goes dry. I've been telling Adrian to disclose to Skylar what our situation is since it's been a huge issue between them. I don't want to hide things between Selena and me, but I also have never told anyone. Certain aspects of my work, I don't want to horrify her with. I choose my words carefully. "I don't want to keep things from you or give you any reason to think I don't trust you with my truth. Things in my life aren't..." I exhale, trying to find the words.

Selena reaches up and cups my cheeks. "I know you're capable of bad things, Obrecht."

My stomach flips. "Define bad things, baby girl."

She drags her thumb over my lips. "You want me to say it out loud?"

My chest tightens. I could say no, but unlike my brother, I don't want Selena not to understand who I am and the lengths I'll go to protect her or anyone I love. After everything she experienced, I don't think it's right to hide my truth from her. "Yes. Tell me exactly what you believe I won't hesitate to do."

The green in her eyes swirls against the brown. She calmly moves her hand down my neck and over my heart. "If someone hurts you in here, you'll show no mercy."

My heart pounds faster against her palm. It's the exact words I used when I told her I was a sadist. "What does that mean to you?"

She strokes my hair above my ear. "You'll kill them."

The water hitting the tile is the only sound as she keeps her gaze pinned on mine. She has no misconceptions about me. I'm unsure whether I should celebrate or be upset she can see my ruthlessness. I finally ask, "You're okay with what I'm capable of?"

She slowly nods.

I can't help myself and ask, "Why?"

She scrunches her forehead. "I vowed to love, cherish, and honor until death do us part a man who everyone sees as an upstanding citizen. For ten years, I lived in fear of that same man killing me. I'd rather know what the man I'm with is capable of than be left in the dark only to discover it down the road."

I weave my fingers through her hair until I'm firmly holding her head. "I would never hurt you."

She smiles. "I already know that."

"How?"

"When I first met you, I couldn't understand how you could have any of the traits Jack does."

My body tenses. "I'm not anything like him."

"You're both powerful men. I didn't understand how you could be so dominant yet kind. Then I realized you were nothing like him. He's sinister and twisted. Your violence comes from a place of protection. So I don't need to know every little detail or about things you deem unsafe for me. I've lived with someone who did anything they could to hurt, degrade, and weaken me. I know the difference. I'd rather be with a killer who avenges wrongdoing than one who creates evil for fun."

I stay silent, taking in her words and their meaning. She's so accepting of me and who I am. Any worries I had about how my truth may affect her view of me, she squashed in an instant. It adds calm and gratitude to the rage I always feel whenever I think about Jack abusing her for ten years. I attempt to contain it so I don't upset her.

She speaks first. "Can I go to the hospital with you?"

I don't debate long. In all reality, I'd rather she be within my eyesight. "Okay. But I may need to send you home without me. Matvey will come with us."

She scrunches her face. Her eyes glisten. "Will you promise me that you'll be careful? Whatever you have to do about this, will you take extra precautions?"

I kiss her and step back, taking her with me until we're in the shower. When I end our kiss, I state, "You don't ever need to worry about me, baby girl."

"Easier said than done, right?"

"I promise. You don't."

She smiles. "I'll try to remember that."

We take a quick shower, get dressed, and are soon at the hospital. Maksim, Boris, and Dmitri are in a corner talking.

"Where have you been?" Maksim asks.

"I forgot to put my phone on the charger." My cousins glance at Selena. "This is Selena." I point to the men. "These are my cousins, Maksim, Boris, and Dmitri."

They each kiss her cheek and say hello.

"How are they?" Selena asks.

"They're both doing fine. Kora is awake, too. They're resting right now," Maksim states.

Selena lets out a sigh of relief, and I tug her closer to me. I scan the waiting room. The seats are empty of anyone I recognize. I turn back to my cousins. "Are your wives here?"

"Anna and Aspen went to get a coffee. Nora's home with the baby," Boris confirms.

"I'll try to find them. I haven't met Anna, but I know Aspen," Selena states.

I nod. "Matvey will go with you."

"Okay."

I motion for Matvey, and he leads Selena away.

"What happened?" I ask as soon as I can't see her anymore.

Maksim's eyes turn to slits. "Igor was working for Boyra. He picked Sergey and Kora up from Adrian's and drove them to an abandoned warehouse. Sergey killed him. Boyra and his other thug strung him up and tortured him when Kora grabbed the gun from Boyra's pocket and shot both him and his goon. The thug fell on her when he went down."

"Matvey said you showed up with Liam and Killian?"

"Yeah. Sergey called and put it on speaker before he got out of the car. They were with me when I got the call."

I shake my head in disgust. "I can't believe Igor did this."

"Good thing the bastard is dead," Dmitri scowls.

"We need a clean sweep. This is too close to home. It's not one of our construction workers falling prey to the Petrovs or Zielinskis. If we have more traitors in our house, we need to take care of it now," I seethe.

"Talk to Finn," Liam says from behind us.

I spin and glare at him. "Finn? Why would we talk to your guy? Are you watching us?"

Liam crosses his arms. "Always thinking the worst of me, aren't you?"

I seethe, "What am I supposed to think?"

He raises his eyebrows at Maksim. "Do you think you could explain to Obrecht what the same side means?"

I step closer and point at him. "Don't waste my time, Liam. Either spit it out or shut up."

Maksim puts his hand on my chest, pushing me back. "Calm down."

I'm still reeling over my last meeting with Liam, and I don't need him playing the guessing game with me. Our family has once again been infiltrated by Petrovs. First Annika. Then all the workers. Now Igor. We need to get back to where Ivanovs didn't hold secrets from each other. I turn to Maksim. "Liam's pulled Boris into whatever shit he has going on with the O'Malleys. I think it's time we handle Ivanov matters on our own again."

A haughty expression lights up Liam's face. "He already knows. What do you think Killian and I were doing at his place when we got Sergey's call?"

My gut drops. I want to punch his arrogant face. I contain my anger and address Maksim. "Someone want to fill me in on what the fuck is happening? Especially since my woman's tied into whatever scenario you're all involved in?"

Maksim shakes his head. "We can't discuss it here."

I spin to Boris. "Maksim knows everything?"

"Yeah. But next time you want to rat me out, we're going to have issues," he warns.

"Next time you want to keep information from Ivanovs, we're going to have more than issues."

He sniffs hard and steps forward. "If—"

"Enough!" Dmitri barks so loud, the other people in the waiting area jump. His eyes turn to ice. "This isn't the time or place to have these conversations. Liam, whatever you're here to say, do it now."

Liam grinds his molars. He finally says, "Talk to Finn, Obrecht. If you want more intel on who he saw Igor with, then you talk to him."

"If you know—"

"I don't have all the details. My dad just called and said to tell you to talk to Finn. Jesus. Give me the benefit of the doubt for once. This shit is getting old," Liam sputters and turns to walk away.

I ignore Boris's scowl. "Where's Adrian?"

Maksim lowers his voice. "He left several hours ago with Killian and Darragh. The police chief needed to go through a few things at the crime scene."

"Like what?"

Maksim glances around us. "Keeping Kora and Sergey's name out of it."

I don't inquire anymore. Darragh has the police chief in his pocket. I don't know how or why, but every issue we have seems to suddenly disappear since our alliance with the O'Malleys. I'm not going to argue or dig further into it. The most pressing thing I need to find out is who else in our house is a traitor.

I turn to Boris. "Where can I find Finn?"

He shrugs. "Not sure. You'll have to ask Liam."

I groan.

Boris leans closer. "I get why you don't trust Liam, but you need to let go of old shit. He's doing the best he can. So far, he's making the right moves."

"Yeah? Well, it would help if you didn't leave us in the dark and if you remembered you're an Ivanov first."

Boris gives me a look of death. "I don't have any issues remembering I'm an Ivanov."

I say nothing and leave to find my dorogaya. Too much is happening. The only thing clear is I need to get a handle on it before things get worse.

Selena

OBRECHT'S QUIET WHEN WE GET IN THE CAR. I DON'T ASK A lot of questions. I'm still not sure what happened to Kora and Sergey besides the Petrovs were a part of it, but he assures me my friends are all right and resting. Whatever did happen, he says it's best if we don't talk about it right now.

I don't argue. I trust him. As long as they are safe and healthy, I don't need to know all the details if Obrecht thinks it can harm me.

"Are you seeing Carla this morning?" he asks.

"I'm supposed to. We usually meet in about an hour at the cafe."

He nods. "Let's go grab a coffee. I have things I need to take care of once she shows up. Matvey can take you home after."

I put my hand over his heart. It's racing. "You seem stressed."

He pins his icy-blue eyes on me. "I'm fine, my dorogaya. You don't need to worry."

"Did something happen between you and your cousins?"

"We're fine," he says, but it doesn't convince me.

I straddle him and slide my hands under the neck of his shirt and knead his shoulders. "You're tense." I dig my thumb into a knot.

He arches his eyebrows. "Have you been holding out on me? Do you have massage skills I'm unaware of?"

I wiggle my eyebrows. "Maybe tonight, I could put on one of the outfits I bought thinking of you. You could tell me to kneel. Then you could give me orders to show you my skills."

His lips twitch. He squeezes my ass. "Now I'm going to be distracted all day."

The car stops, and I glance out the window at the cafe, then back at Obrecht. "Will you be gone all day?"

He sighs. "Possibly. I'm not sure yet."

"Should I make us dinner tonight?"

He tucks a lock of my hair behind my ear. His face turns more serious. "You know what we discussed in the bathroom this morning?"

The hairs on my arms rise. I know what Obrecht is capable of, and although I'm not afraid of him, I don't like thinking about it. It worries me he'll be in a dangerous situation.

Whomever he's dealing with, I assume is a bad person to receive his wrath. "Yes."

He pauses, as if struggling to figure out his words. I patiently wait until he says, "There will be times when I need to be gone for several days. I won't have the ability to call or text you. It'll pop up, and there won't be a warning. When that happens, I want you to stay with Aspen, Anna, or Nora. Matvey and Vlad will still watch over you when it happens."

My stomach flips. "I've never met Nora."

"Yes, I know. In all reality, the three of them will probably be together during these times."

I ignore the anxiety forming in my chest. He wouldn't have me do something if it weren't in my best interest. There isn't a bone in my body that doesn't believe this. "Okay. Can you tell me why I would need to do this?"

He tugs me closer to him. "I'll feel better knowing you aren't on your own for several days in a row, wondering when I'm coming back. Aspen, Anna, and Nora have gone through it before. There will be additional security."

My chest tightens. "So you'll be in danger?"

He shakes his head. "No."

"I'll be in extra danger?"

"No, baby girl. But we take precautions when necessary."

There's no question about what I will do. If he wants me to stay somewhere else during these times, I won't question it. "Okay. Does that mean I shouldn't make dinner tonight?"

He smiles. "No, please make it if you wish. But if something comes up, I don't want you to be upset. I don't control these timelines."

I take a deep breath and put on my most cheerful face. I don't want Obrecht to worry about a missed dinner. If I make it and something comes up, it's not the end of the world. "Thank you for explaining to me what can happen. I understand. And you don't have to worry about me getting upset over a missed meal."

"I don't like the thought of you going through all the effort and me bailing on you."

I tilt my head. "Bailing?"

"Yeah."

"Are you leaving me for good or just a few days to do whatever it is you need to take care of?" I ask.

He blinks, and his head moves back. "No, baby girl. I'm not leaving you."

I shrug. "Then it's a missed dinner. As long as you come back in one piece, it isn't a big deal. They call it leftovers for a reason."

He gives me a chaste kiss. "Thank you. You're amazing. Let's go inside." We get out of the car, and Matvey follows us. Obrecht says, "Why don't you get a table, and I'll get the drinks. Do you want something to eat?"

"No, I'm okay. I'll take a double espresso hazelnut latte." I turn and walk toward the back corner, where I usually have my discussions with Carla. The table next to the window has a blonde lady and man at it, so I pull out the chair for the table across from it.

"Selena!"

I spin. Hailee is with a man I don't recognize. His hair is a brownish-red, and his eyes assess me. He has an aura of bad-boy danger about him, with tattoos all over his arms. If he weren't with Hailee, I might be afraid of him.

She rises, and we embrace.

"Hi! How are you?" I ask.

"I'm good. This is Liam. And this is Selena," she says to him.

He rises and holds out his hand, continuing to study me, as if he somehow knows me.

I take it. "Hi."

"Selena. It's nice to meet you," he says, and I can't shake the feeling he's aware of who I am.

I'm paranoid. How would he know anything about me?

"Are you here by yourself?" Hailee asks.

"No. I came with Obrecht. Do you know him?" I ask.

Her face lights up, and I can tell she wants all the details. She chirps, "I do. How do you know him?" She pulls the chair out next to her. "Please. Sit and join us."

I glance back at the line. Obrecht is ordering with his back to me. I take the seat. "We live in the same building. We just came from..."

Does she know about Kora and Sergey? Is it okay to say something?

She raises her eyebrows, waiting for me to finish.

Liam clears his throat. "You came from the hospital. So did we. Well, I had Hailee go home to get some sleep then I picked her up."

"How do you know where I was?" I ask.

Liam smiles. "I was there and spoke with the Ivanovs."

My face grows hot. I don't recall seeing him. "Sorry. I must have been distracted and not paid attention as well as I should have."

"No worries, lass. I came after you had already left to find the others." He picks up his cup of coffee. His tattoo catches my eye. It's Celtic with two hearts. One is upside down and one right side up. The middle has a Celtic H.

"Oh. That makes sense." I point to his ink. "I like your tattoo. Are you Irish?"

He chuckles. "One hundred percent purebred."

"Guess you can't get more Irish than that," I state.

"Do you know Nora? He's her cousin," Hailee informs me.

I shake my head. "I've not met her yet."

"Selena," Obrecht's voice rings out in a deadpan tone.

I turn in my seat. "Hey. Look who I ran into."

Obrecht's jaw clenches. "Hailee. How have you been?"

She smiles. "Good. Here. Take a seat." She motions next to Liam.

Obrecht and Liam pin their hardened gazes on each other. Neither moves.

Hailee and I exchange an uncomfortable glance, but I'm not sure what's wrong.

Liam pulls the chair next to him out. His voice is as flat as Obrecht's. "By all means. Sit."

Obrecht sets my latte on the table in front of me then his coffee. He finally takes the seat. I put my hand on his thigh, and he puts his palm on top of it. "Hailee, don't you have school today?"

"Yes, but we're delayed for a few hours due to the fog," she replies.

An uncomfortable silence occurs. Obrecht studies her then refocuses on Liam. Obrecht finally says, "I'll need Finn's number."

"I'm meeting him in an hour. You can come with me. He won't talk over the phone," Liam replies.

Obrecht rests his arm on the back of the chair. "Fine."

"Selena said you live in the same building?" Hailee asks.

Obrecht nods. "Yep."

More silence ensues. I attempt to think of something to say. Liam's tattoo catches my eye again. I ask, "What's the H stand for?"

"Hailee." He stares at her as if we aren't sitting next to him, and he's undressing her with his eyes or could screw her right on the table.

Her face turns beet red. She swallows hard. I turn to Obrecht, feeling like I'm invading their personal space or a private moment. It surprises me when I see him scowling at Liam.

I grip his thigh to divert his attention off Liam. He tugs me closer to him and sips on his coffee. He asks, "You teach kindergarten, Hailee?"

She tears her eyes off Liam. "Yes."

"In the inner-city, right?"

"Yes."

"But you've been offered positions by other schools?"

She furrows her eyebrows. "How do you know that?"

Obrecht shrugs. "I read the article last year in the paper about your award."

"What award?" Liam asks.

Hailee's face turns a deeper crimson. "It's not a big deal."

Obrecht snorts. "I thought it was when I read about it."

"Hales, what award?" Liam repeats.

"Just something the district gave me last year."

Obrecht shakes his head. "And the previous three. I think you're acting a bit modest."

"Hailee, what was the award?" I ask.

She sips her coffee. "Honestly, it's not a big deal. Those award banquets don't mean anything. It's just an excuse for the bigwigs to get together for free drinks and a meal. It's not like it helps the kids."

"Hales, what was the award?" Liam asks again in a stern voice.

"Teacher of the year," Obrecht informs us.

"Wow! Hailee, that's a big deal!" I exclaim.

"No, really. It's not. It's—"

"Of course it is," Liam insists.

"No, it's not. The district doesn't give me any more resources to help the kids or anything. I wish they would give me the money for the plaque to buy a few coats for the kids or something," she states.

Liam reaches for her hand. "When was this?"

"You were still inside," Obrecht says.

Inside? As in prison?

Liam freezes. His face hardens and he turns his head. He scowls at Obrecht.

Hailee shifts in her seat. She firmly says, "Spring. It's not a big deal though."

"It sounds like one. That's amazing, Hailee. Congratulations," I tell her, not sure why Obrecht put Liam on the spot.

"It's a huge accomplishment. You should be proud," Obrecht adds.

"Let's change the subject." She takes a long sip of her coffee.

Liam is about to say something when his phone rings. He removes his hand from hers and answers it. "Killian. What's the situation?"

Obrecht stiffens, staring at Liam.

"Tell my dad to meet me outside of Morning Java." Liam hangs up. "Sorry, Hales. I need to cut coffee short."

"It's okay."

"Obrecht, you should come with me," he says. "Can your driver drop Hailee off at her school?"

"Sure."

"I can take an Uber," she claims.

"No," Liam and Obrecht say at the same time, as if it's the worst idea they ever heard.

Hailee smirks. "I was only teasing."

Obrecht kisses me on the cheek. "Matvey will take you home when you and Carla finish talking. I'll text you when I know what time I'll be back."

"All right, but before you leave, can you give me your mom's phone number?"

He arches his eyebrows. "Sure, but why?"

"It's my secret." I want to get a list of dishes and recipes of Russian food Obrecht likes and learn to make them. I thought his mom might teach me.

He chuckles. "Okay. I'll text it to you when I get in the car."

"Thanks."

He pecks me on the lips, and he and Liam leave. Hailee asks, "So how long have you and Obrecht been together?"

My face heats. "Not long. What about you and Liam?"

"Same." She takes a sip of coffee. "Who are you meeting?"

"A woman named Carla. She's..." I contemplate whether to tell Hailee the truth or not but decide to trust her. "She's a therapist. My ex-husband did a lot of not-so-nice things to me, both physically and mentally. Obrecht knows Carla and introduced us."

Hailee's expression turns sympathetic. She hesitates for a moment. Her voice lowers. "I'm sure it's not the same thing, but..." She pauses, and a line forms between her eyes. "My father wasn't very nice to my mom. I don't remember every-thing, since she fled with my sisters and me when we were little, but what I remember is pretty violent. I'm sorry you experienced anything horrible."

I take in her words. Images of Hailee as a little girl with blonde hair and blue eyes, scared, pop into my mind. "I'm sorry, too. Is your mom okay?"

She smiles. "Yes. She's dating a nice man right now."

"That's great."

She nods. "She refused to see anyone until she met him. It's nice to see her happy and not by herself."

"Morning, Selena!" Carla's voice chirps behind me.

I spin in my seat. "Hi, Carla. Hey, this is my friend, Hailee."

Carla slides into the seat next to me and holds out her hand. "Carla Conway."

"Hailee O'Hare. Nice to meet you."

"You, too." She leans forward. "So, what are we talking about, ladies?"

Hailee rises. "Nothing too exciting. I should go to work and use my extra time wisely. It was nice meeting you."

"You, too," Carla says.

I rise and hug Hailee. "It was great seeing you. Will you be at yoga Saturday?"

"Yes. I'll see you then."

"Okay. Bye."

She leaves, and I sit down across from Carla.

"How's it going today?" she asks.

"Good. I have some things to tell you."

She leans forward. "Oh?"

My stomach flutters thinking about last night. "I told Obrecht I can't be his bottom."

Her smile falls. She slowly nods. "I see. What did he say?"

"He said we could be whatever I wanted."

Her lips twitch. "Well, I'll be. Obrecht Ivanov finally commits. And what did you tell him you wanted him to be?"

I tap my fingers on my coffee mug. "We haven't labeled it. But I think he's my boyfriend and my Dom? Is that possible?"

"Sure." She drinks her coffee. "There aren't any rules. You two can create whatever type of relationship you want."

I take a deep breath. "We also used the neck-wrist restraints last night."

She tilts her head. Her eyebrows raise. There's concern in her expression. "How did it go?"

More heat floods my cheeks. "I liked it. A lot."

Her lips twitch. "That's great. Did you negotiate before you started?"

"Yes. Obrecht told me I did a good job."

"It doesn't surprise me. He's very good at keeping boundaries and making sure he's clear on them," she says.

My jealousy ignites. "You've seen him negotiate?"

"Yes. I was his mentor, but you already know this."

I glance out the window and stare through the fog that has barely lifted off the ground. Pedestrians move through it, and I can barely make out the building across the street.

Carla taps my hand. "It was before you."

I meet her gaze. "Yes, I'm aware."

"But you're jealous?" She arches an eyebrow.

I bite on my lip for several moments. She drinks her coffee, allowing me to gather my thoughts. I finally reply, "Should I be okay with the thought of him being with other women?"

She huffs. "I didn't say that. I'm sure if you asked him how he feels when he thinks about you with Jack, he'll tell you he's got a lot of emotions as well."

"So I'm not irrational?"

She puts her hand on her chin. "Lots of people are territorial when it comes to their partner."

"You aren't?"

She sits back in her chair. "I'm different from a lot of people, and especially women."

"How?"

She smiles. "I don't see male or female. When I look at someone, I try to figure out what they need, like what gets them off mentally and physically. It's about an exchange of power for me and making my sub or subs happy."

"Subs? You have two subs at a time?" Jack made me watch him take part in orgies with multiple women, but he wasn't a Dom the way Obrecht or what I imagine Carla would be. He just did what he wanted to them, and I had to kneel the entire time and view it all.

She softly laughs. "Yeah. It usually is more of a sub and service sub."

"Service sub?"

She glances behind her. She lowers her voice. "Sure. All submissives want to be controlled and please their dominant partner. Some subs, their desire to please is deeper. They enter a session, knowing they are there to please their top, Dom, or Master and the other sub involved."

The other sub? "Why?"

"It's what they want."

"Sounds like a big orgy."

She shakes her head. "No. It can be extremely intimate between a couple."

"How?"

Something passes in her expression, as if she knows secrets others don't. "The Dom does it for his sub. Everything is about her or him. The service sub is there to comply, and it feeds everyone involved."

I attempt to wrap my mind around what she's saying, but it's challenging.

"Anyway, I don't get territorial, but I've also never found the person I want to commit to, either. So maybe it would change if I did. But this isn't about me. It's about you. So let's move on to my next question."

I take a drink of the latte and it slides down my throat. "Okay. What is it?"

Her eyes drill into mine. "You told me you're having dreams about Jack and being back in the cage. Are you still having them?"

My insides quiver. "Yes. And he was in the restaurant we were at last night. Obrecht saw him and whisked me out the alley door."

Her eyes widen. "He knew you were there?"

"Obrecht said he thought it was a coincidence."

She studies me. "You don't appear convinced."

A chill moves down my spine. "How can I be? Nothing with Jack is ever by mistake."

MC

Obrecht

LIAM AND I STEP OUTSIDE THE CAFE. DARRAGH'S CAR PULLS UP, and we get inside. Maksim is there, and I look at him in question. Darragh goes into a coughing fit, and the vehicle is several blocks down the road by the time he catches his breath. His handkerchief has specks of blood. Liam tries to get him to drink some water, but he waves it off. He rolls down the window and takes a drag of his pipe. "Maksim, I keep telling you to get your house in order."

I clench my jaw. It isn't something we can deny. There are severe issues we need to solve. Darragh pointing out Ivanov problems doesn't make Maksim or me happy. But I'm not in the mood to deal with his *I told you so* lecture. "What do you know, Darragh?"

He scratches his beard. "Did you ever learn the reason why Lorenzo Rossi had the mayor sell him the plot of land you needed for your development right under your nose?"

Maksim taps his fingers on his thigh. "Darragh, whatever you know, spit it out. You know damn well we still don't know why he targeted us."

For months we've tried to figure it out. We understand why the Petrovs and Zielinskis want to take us down. We employ Russians and Poles and give them above-average wages. When men work, they don't need the assistance of either mob family. We made it harder for them to recruit men. It makes sense why they want to destroy us. The Rossis coming after us is still a mystery. They are Italian and we don't employ a lot of men in their community.

Darragh takes another puff of his tobacco. He slowly exhales, and the cloud of smoke streams out the small crack of the window. "Maria Rossi."

"Lorenzo's twin sister? What about her?" Maksim asks.

"Seems that ex-wife of your brother's gets around."

"I told Adrian she was trouble," Liam mutters.

My hands curl into fists. "What did that snake Dasha do?"

"She's kept tabs on your activities. She and Maria seem to be very close," Darragh states.

My gut drops, and Maksim and I glance at each other. Anything to do with Dasha is bad news. We've been looking for her and can't find her. It's bad enough she got involved with Zielinski. Did she really insert herself into the Rossi family, too?

Maksim scowls. "Get to the point, Darragh."

"They met in Italy. Dasha made a deal with Maria. She sold her information on all the properties you own and what you were buying."

"You kept this from us?" I accuse.

"No. I just found out," Darragh replies.

"Why would the Rossi's want to take us down? What's the motive?" Maksim asks.

"Giovanni was going to put his brother in charge when he went to prison. He didn't think Lorenzo was capable of leading or earning money. Maria convinced Giovanni to let him earn it. She saw your properties as the avenue. Lorenzo's plan was to take millions from you so he could show his father he was capable of stepping into his shoes," Darragh informs us.

Silence fills the car. I try to process that our war with the Rossis is due to Dasha. If she hadn't put us on their radar, we wouldn't have started this conflict between the Rossis and Petrovs.

Darragh's next words send a chill down my spine. "It's not all."

Maksim's fingers dig into his thigh. "What else?"

Darragh leans forward. "When Bruno Zielinski visited Giovanni Rossi in prison to create an alliance, Maria formed it. Dasha helped her. She introduced Bruno's son to Maria."

Jesus. This just keeps getting worse.

"Dasha knows no limits," Liam states. "She's playing with two crime families. And now that we pinned the Zielinski prison murders on Rossi, her head is going to be on a platter."

"Good. Let them take care of her," I state. I'm tired of having my hands tied where Dasha is concerned. She's a woman, so it limits our ability to deal with her in our normal ways. The Ivanovs don't torture or kill women or children.

"Wishful thinking," Maksim mumbles.

"You need to take care of her. She's a liability and problem," Darragh orders.

"We're dealing with her," Maksim states.

"Not hard enough."

Maksim speaks before I can. "Trust me. No one wants her taken care of more than we do."

"Why isn't she already taken care of? She has come into town, made deals with Zielinskis in your name, and almost killed your tracker. Loose ends aren't something you should feel sympathy for," Darragh warns.

"What are you suggesting, Darragh? You want us to take her to the garage and spend days doing to her what we do to men?" I bark.

He sits back in his seat. He lights his pipe and takes another drag. "When your house is at risk of catching fire, you put it out."

Tension fills the air. Even Liam can't cover the horror that flicks across his expression. We haven't come to any conclusions about what to do with Dasha, but she's still a woman. We've never killed or hurt a woman.

Maksim shakes his head. "Ivanovs have boundaries. There are lines we don't cross, and this is one of them."

"Sometimes, there are exceptions to rules." Darragh blows another mouthful of smoke out the window. "We have people who can handle this if you don't have the balls."

My skin crawls with the thought of hurting any woman, even someone like Dasha.

The car stops. "No one puts our family at risk. This problem you have, it's not going away. A threat to the Ivanovs is a threat to the O'Malleys. Decide what you're going to do about it and let me know. If you don't take action, I will." Darragh opens the door, and we all watch him get out.

The door shuts, the driver continues, and Maksim and I scowl at Liam.

"This is why we should never have created an alliance. Our values don't align. I'm a lot of things, but I'm not a killer of women. I won't torture and kill her like she's a man. Count me out on crossing that line. I didn't sign up for that, and I sure as hell didn't sign up to take orders from Darragh," I angrily bark out to Maksim.

He stares at Liam. He quietly asks, "Is this how you want to run your empire?"

Liam's face hardens. "I didn't say I agree with my father."

"No? You sure as hell didn't interject," I accuse. "You going to be the one who kills her?"

He glares at me. "No. I'm not killing a woman, either."

"No? You going to call upon your thug in your clan?"

Liam sniffs hard. "Don't discuss my clan and thugs in the same breath."

"What would you call it?"

"I'm losing my patience with you, Obrecht," Liam threatens.

I scoff. "What are you going to do, Liam? Fight me? Kill me? Bring what you got. I won't hold back."

"Enough!" Maksim orders. "Jesus. You two need to figure out this shit between you. It's getting old."

No one speaks for several moments. I stare out the window, fuming once more we're tied to the O'Malleys. The landscape changes from the city to abandoned buildings. I ask, "Where are we going?"

"To see Finn," Liam claims.

"Why out here?"

"We need to pick him up."

I heavily sigh. I'm used to being in charge, and this little field trip to wherever we're going reminds me I'm not. It also doesn't solve my other issue with Liam. I order, "Tell me why I have to wait until Jack's company goes public."

Liam grinds his molars before answering. "I told you. I'm getting the O'Malleys out of the drug and gambling trade."

I scoff. "You think your family is magically going to stop all the things they've done to get ahead their entire life?"

Liam shakes his head. "You don't get it, Obrecht."

"Fill me in," I sarcastically reply.

In a firm and arrogant voice, he says, "They'll do what I say. I'm the head—"

"Did you forget about dear old dad?"

Liam blinks hard. "My dad's dying. Did you not see the blood on his handkerchief? Do you think we've made it up? I can assure you, he's already past his due date."

And I'm an asshole.

It's Liam. Proceed with caution.

"The power is shifting. The clan will be taking orders from me. And what I'm making happen for my family isn't going to leave anyone in need of anything."

I snort. The O'Malleys, minus Liam, Nora, and her brothers, reproduce like rabbits. Most of them have a minimum of four kids. There's a ton of them. It would take a large fortune to financially take care of them so they don't have to resort to drugs and gambling anymore.

The car stops outside of a dingy hotel. It's the type that rents rooms by the hour. I'm sure you'd find STDs and other germs all over every inch of each room. Finn shoves off the brick wall he's leaning on and walks over to us. He gets in the car, and the driver takes off.

"This is where you hang out?" Maksim asks.

"Haven't seen you for twenty years, and this is the welcome I get?" Finn smirks.

Maksim nods and smiles. He holds his hand out. "How've you been?"

Finn holds his hand out with the tattoo that first made me take notice of him. Adrian was trying to find dirt on Jack. He was in the photos, and the snake slithered between bones inked on his hand is the first thing I noticed in the multiple pictures Adrian had of Jack.

"You've aged," he says to Maksim.

"Prison wasn't the fountain of youth for you, either," Maksim teases.

Finn shrugs. "Women still love me."

Maksim chuckles. "I bet."

"You two know each other?" I point between them.

The two men stare at each other. Maksim nods. "Yeah. We used to spend a lot of time together. You were still in Russia. Finn, this is my cousin, Obrecht."

Finn pins his green eyes on me. "The tracker."

I stare at him, not sure if I like him or not. Until I can trust him, I'm erring on the not side. And I don't like him knowing information about me when I don't know anything about him, except his jail record and that his last name is O'Malley. "You have information for us?"

He scoffs and turns to Liam. "He gets right down to it, huh?"

Liam replies, "His mother is a lovely woman. She taught him manners, but he must have forgotten them."

"Don't talk about my mom," I warn Liam.

He holds his hands in the air. "Your mom loves me. I saw her the other day, and we had a nice chat over coffee."

The blood boils in my veins. "You did what?"

His eyebrows furrow. "I ran into her. She was on her own at the cafe, so we had coffee. Is there a problem with me talking to your mom?"

"Stay away from my mother," I snap.

Shock and hurt fill Liam's face. "You think I would hurt your mom?"

Do I?

No.

She's my mom, and I don't trust Liam as far as I can throw him.

"Fuck you, Obrecht," he snarls.

"Enough!" Maksim repeats.

"No. I helped his mom learn English. I used to eat dinner at their house at least three times a week. She's like a second mother to me, and if I want to buy her a cup of coffee and talk to her, I will," he insists.

I scowl at him. Liam would never do anything to hurt my mom, but I still don't like it. The O'Malleys are in our lives enough. He doesn't need to be hanging out with my mom.

"Finn, can you tell us what you know before these two kill each other?" Maksim asks.

He nods. "Sure. Is there a reason Aleksei would be meeting with Igor and Gavriil?"

The blood drains from Maksim's face. "Aleksei? Boris's trainer?"

Finn nods. "Yeah. I had to double-check it was him. He didn't have gray hair before I went inside. But it was him."

"When?"

"A month ago, they were at an underground nightclub. Two nights before Boyra Petrov showed up at Sergey's house, Aleksei and Igor met again. This time it was at a strip club on the Indiana-Michigan line. Zamir Petrov's son, Ludis, showed up. They were together all night."

"Aleksei was best friends with my father," Maksim states.

Finn's face falls. "I know. I'm sorry, but unless he can give you a hell of a reason why he was with both Gavriil and Igor, then with Ludis as well, he's involved with the Petrovs."

My stomach twists. Aleksei has been a father figure to my cousins and Adrian and me. He's Boris's trainer. The rest of us work out with him, too. I swallow down the bile rising in my throat. Maksim's pale face tells me he's having a similar reaction.

"I'll kill him if he betrayed us," Maksim seethes.

"There's one other thing," Finn adds.

"What?" I ask.

"Aleksei seems to be running the show. And he and Ludis, they seemed rather close."

I study Finn's face. "What do you mean?"

"Did Aleksei ever get married, or does he have a long-time girlfriend?"

"Not that I'm aware of," Maksim says.

Finn leans closer. "Ludis swings both ways. He keeps it under wraps, but I'm pretty sure Aleksei doesn't."

My chest tightens. "What are you talking about?"

Finn's face hardens. His next words are a bomb hitting Maksim and me. "Ludis is his boy toy."

Silence fills the air. It feels as if a bear is clawing my gut. I don't care what way Aleksei swings, but if he's involved with Ludis, there's no way he's not betrayed us.

Maksim clears his throat. "Thank you for telling us."

"Sure. I'm sorry to break it to you. I know he's like family," Finn states.

"You want me to pick him up?" I ask Maksim.

Maksim's eyes turn to slits. "No. I will. Get the others, except Sergey. Let him rest with Kora. Meet me at the garage."

"Is Aspen at work?" I ask.

"Yes."

"I don't want Selena waiting on her own. We don't know who else is compromised."

Maksim nods. "I'll direct Aspen to Boris's. Tell Dmitri to send Anna. Nora will be home with the baby." I knock on the window and give the driver Adrian's address. It's the first stop, and he can round up the others while I get Selena.

"You want us to do anything?" Liam asks.

"No. This is an Ivanov issue. Thanks for letting us know, but we'll handle it," Maksim replies.

"Okay. I'll talk to Killian and we'll keep an eye on the women while you handle it."

As much as I distrust Liam's ability to lead the O'Malleys, I do feel better knowing he and Killian will be another layer of security. Maksim and I both reply, "Thanks," at the same time.

Within a few minutes, I'm standing in Adrian's lobby. I get in the elevator, and when I step into his penthouse, I call Selena.

"Hi," she answers.

"Hey. Do you remember our conversation about staying with the girls?"

Her voice turns to worry. "Yes. Did something happen?"

"Yes, but nothing you need to worry about. Can you pack a bag? I'll pick you up in the next half hour or so," I tell her.

"Okay."

I sigh, relieved she isn't pushing me for more details and agrees without further conversation. "Thanks, baby girl. I'll be home to pick you up soon."

"No worries."

I hang up and yell, "Adrian!"

He doesn't respond, so I go into the bedroom. The sound of the shower hits my ears. I approach the bathroom door but stop before entering in case Skylar is with him. "Adrian."

"Jesus! You scared the shit out of me," he replies.

"Is Skylar with you, or are you alone?"

He turns off the water then comes to the door in a towel. "Skylar's not here. She left me."

I freeze. Adrian pushes past me and goes into his closet. I turn and ask, "What happened?"

"She won't let it go."

I shake my head. "Adrian, just tell her."

"I'm not—" His phone rings. He groans then answers. "Hey, Mom." He stares at the ceiling. "Tonight?"

"No. Nothing tonight," I tell him. He looks at me in question, and I mouth *garage*.

"Mom, Obrecht and I are going to be tied up for a few days. We'll set up dinner when we're back." He listens for a few minutes then says, "I need to go. I'll call you in a few days. Bye."

"There's a reason she wants us to come to dinner," I inform him.

"What's that?"

I snort. "We should take her bridal magazines when we go."

He furrows his eyebrows. "Are you trying to encourage her?"

"Not for us."

"No? Then, who?" He puts a T-shirt on.

"Mom's dating a doctor named Stefano."

Adrian freezes. "Mom's dating?"

I cross my arms and lean against the doorframe. "Yep. Selena and I ran into them last night at dinner. She met him at the home where Aspen's dad lives. But that's not all."

Adrian raises his eyebrows.

"He told me he's going to propose."

He jerks his head back. "Propose?"

"Yep. Pretty sure Mom will say yes. And she's already met his daughters and grandkids," I add.

Adrian grabs his boxers and slides them on. "Did you run a check on this guy?"

"No. I just found out last night. He seems legit."

Adrian grunts. "We all know the mistake of assumptions."

"Yeah. Well, as soon as we get done with the garage, I'll start digging."

He slides a pair of black sweatpants on. "Who's at the garage?"

My pulse creeps up again. "Aleksei."

22

Selena

OBRECHT COMES INTO MY CONDO. I ALREADY PACKED MY BAG, and it's near the door. He wraps his arms around me. "I'm taking you to Nora's. Aspen and Anna will stay there, too. If you go anywhere, Matvey or Vlad will take you, but I'll feel better if you don't venture too far. Aspen and Anna will go to work and then return to Nora's."

My insides quiver. "Should I be worried?"

"No, my dorogaya. This is more for my reassurance that you're okay while I'm gone."

I nod and force myself to smile. "All right."

He picks up my bag and leads me out of the building and into the car. Boris and Nora's place isn't far. When we pull up to the curb, my stomach flips with nerves. "What's Nora like?"

Obrecht smiles. "She's a feisty O'Malley. You'll get along fine."

I softly laugh. "Feisty makes her sound a bit scary."

He shakes his head. "No, she's not. Don't worry." He opens the door, and I put my hand on his arm.

"How many days do you believe you'll be gone?"

He turns. "I'm not sure. The longest we've needed to be gone in the past has been eight days."

"Eight?" I swallow the lump in my throat.

"It's normally two to three. This is why I don't want you on your own." He puts his hand on my cheek. "Please don't worry. We're in a controlled environment and not in any danger, okay?"

I release a nervous breath. "Okay. Should I cancel my sessions with Carla?"

He hesitates. "Ask Carla to come to Nora's. Their penthouse is huge, and you can talk in private."

"Okay."

He gives me a peck on the lips. "Come on." He gets out, reaches in to help me out, then leads me into Boris and Nora's. We step out of their corridor and into the main room.

A red-haired woman is sitting on the couch with a baby sleeping on her chest. Surprise fills her face. She smiles and nods at me. "Obrecht. What's going on?"

"We have a situation. I'm having everyone stay here. Where is Boris?"

Nora's face falls. "Garage or something else?"

"Garage."

Relief replaces her worry. "He lost a bet and is doing laundry. Go on back." She refocuses on me. "I'm Nora. Please come in."

Obrecht tugs me closer to him. "Sorry. This is Selena."

Nora pats the seat next to her. "It's nice to meet you. Please make yourself at home."

"Thank you. Sorry to barge in," I reply.

She laughs. "No worries. It'll be nice to have company."

Obrecht kisses my forehead and leaves the room.

I take the seat next to Nora and stare at the baby. "Congratulations. She's gorgeous. What did you name her?"

"Shannon."

"Very Irish," I tease.

Her face lights up. "It was my nana's name."

"Were you close?"

"Very. Do you want to hold her?"

I hold my hands out. "Yes, please."

She gently hands the baby to me. Shannon never stirs and cuddles right into my chest.

"She's precious."

"Thanks. We think so. Is that a Greek accent I detect?" she asks.

"Yes. I moved when I was twenty." I stroke the baby's red hair. "I can't believe how much hair she has!"

"I know. Crazy, huh?"

"Yes. So Liam is your cousin?"

Nora puts her knee on the couch and turns toward me. "Yes. Do you know him?"

"I met him this morning. He was at the coffee shop with Hailee," I reply.

Her green eyes bore into mine. "How do you know Hailee?"

I open my mouth to speak, and a man's voice booms, "That traitor."

"Shh. The baby is sleeping," Nora reprimands.

Boris comes into the room with Obrecht. His face is red, and he sniffs hard. "Sorry. I need to go. Nora, I don't want you or Shannon going anywhere while I'm gone." He glances at me. "Hi, Selena."

My insides quiver. He and Obrecht both look angry. "Hi."

"Boris! Nora!" another man's voice booms.

"Shh. The baby!" a woman's voice says.

Nora shakes her head. "I think I need to give you Ivanovs lessons on how to be quiet around infants."

Dmitri and Anna come into the room. He sets an overnight bag next to mine, along with a laptop bag. "Sorry, Nora."

Anna pushes her blonde hair behind her ear and sits on the couch next to me. She kisses Shannon on the head and softly murmurs, "Hey, sweet girl."

"Where's Aspen?" Dmitri asks.

"Maksim went to pick Aleksei up. Maksim said Aspen would come after work," Obrecht states.

"Aleksei?" The color drains from Nora's face and she looks at Boris. He snarls.

Dmitri shakes his head. "Aspen isn't staying at work. Until we know the entire situation, the women stay here." He takes his phone out of his pocket, swipes the screen, then says, "Bogden, go pick up Aspen at City Hall. Take her home to pack a bag and bring her immediately to Boris's." He hangs up. "Sorry, ladies, but no one leaves the penthouse."

Nora and Anna exchange a glance, which makes me nervous. I look at Obrecht.

"This is precautionary," he reiterates. "You don't need to worry. We're at the garage. It's more for our assurance you're safe."

"He's right. They control the garage," Nora states.

I don't know what the garage is, but something tells me now isn't the time to ask.

"Time to go," Dmitri states.

The three of us rise. I hand the baby to Nora. Obrecht pulls me aside and firmly holds my head. His icy-blue eyes drill into mine. "There's nothing to stress about. Just stay here so I don't have to worry where you are."

My stomach flips with nerves. "You'll be safe?"

"Yes." He kisses then hugs me. "I'll see you in a few days."

I don't want to let him go, but he releases me. I reluctantly step back, and the three men leave. When they're gone, Nora and Anna turn. Nora says, "Make yourself comfortable. Help yourselves to anything in the house." She hands the baby to Anna. "Here, get some practice before yours comes. I'm going to finish the laundry Boris started."

"Are you pregnant?" I ask Anna.

She beams. "Yes. We found out last week."

"Congratulations. Do you have other children?"

She shakes her head. "This is our first."

"How far along are you?"

She shrugs. "I'm not sure but not very far. I only peed on the stick. Well, I should say sticks, since I kept confirming it. My doctor's appointment is next week."

The baby wakes up. Shannon's face scrunches and turns red. A shrill cry fills the air.

"Oh, sweet girl. Let's go change your diaper." Anna repositions her in her arms and walks to the corner of the room where there are diapers and wipes.

I follow her. "Obrecht said you designed our building?"

She unsnaps Shannon's onesie. "Yes. It was the first project I did for the Ivanovs."

"I love all of it, but the roof is my favorite part."

Her face lights up. "I'm happy to hear that. It was fun to design. Dmitri was open to it when I suggested we utilize the space."

"Well, I've spent more hours there than I can count. It kind of saved my sanity," I add before thinking.

She pauses and tilts her head. "What do you mean?"

My heart races. I'm not around many people, but I also don't normally blurt out things about my private life. Now that I said that, I'm not sure how to get around it. "I went through a difficult divorce. Kora was my attorney. Sergey found out about my situation and moved me into the condo. I couldn't go anywhere for a while. The roof was my way of not going stir crazy."

Anna's expression turns sympathetic. "You were scared your ex would come after you?"

My heart beats harder. "Yes."

"And he would hurt you?"

My mouth turns dry. "Yes. I don't doubt he still would."

She opens her mouth to speak then shuts it. Her brows furrow. I wait, and she carefully says, "Before I met Dmitri, my boyfriend hurt me."

"He did?" I'm surprised. Anna seems to have it all. She's married, about to have a baby, and has a successful career. She's also beautiful and kind. I can't imagine her in any situation that isn't perfect.

"Yes."

"Are-are you still scared he'll come after you?" I ask.

Her expression turns confident. She shakes her head. "No. Dmitri took care of him."

Her words hang in the air. Obrecht's voice enters my mind, telling me he won't show Jack mercy and will have his day with him.

"If you're with Obrecht, my guess is he'll deal with your ex-husband, accordingly," Anna adds.

My chest tightens. I admit, "My ex was at the restaurant we were at last night."

Anna puts a fresh diaper under Shannon. "What happened?"

"Nothing. Obrecht thinks he didn't see me. He ushered me out the back alley."

She snaps the onesie back in place. "Did that stir up things for you?"

I bite on my lip. I don't like admitting it, but it did.

She puts her hand on my arm. "I went through a lot of counseling. If you ever want to talk, I'm here. But I also can give you the name of who I worked with if you want."

"Thanks, but I'm already seeing a therapist."

She nods in approval. "I'm glad. Is it helping?"

"Yeah. She's great. Obrecht told me to have her come here while he's gone." I glance toward the direction Nora went. "It's okay, right?"

"Absolutely." She picks Shannon up. "There you are, precious girl. All dry."

Aspen arrives as Nora brings a basket of clothes into the main room. Bogden sets her suitcase next to ours and leaves.

Aspen twists her fingers. "What did I miss? Maksim isn't answering his phone. Please tell me they're at the garage."

"Yep. All good," Anna chirps.

This is confusing. "I have a question. Well, several."

Shannon starts whimpering, and Nora takes her from Anna. "Shoot. If we can answer it, we will."

"What is the garage?"

The room goes silent. The three women exchange a knowing glance. Aspen finally says, "Obrecht didn't tell you?"

My anxiety grows. I don't want to make assumptions about what they know or don't, or even if their husbands' wrath means the same as Obrecht's. "He's told me things. But I never heard of the garage until now."

Aspen sits next to me. "What did he tell you?"

I hesitate. I don't want to break Obrecht's confidence. Several minutes pass. I struggle about how to discuss things without saying something I shouldn't.

"If I tell you that there isn't anything Obrecht does that our husbands don't also do, does that help this conversation move forward?" Anna asks.

I breathe a sigh of relief. "Yes. Thank you."

She nods. "Sure. So the garage is where they take men who have harmed the family and will continue to if they don't stop them."

A chill runs down my spine. I ignore it and straighten up. If someone is a threat to the Ivanovs, I don't feel bad for them. Maybe it's all my years of having Jack hurt me, but I don't care to sympathize with anyone who could potentially hurt Obrecht. "And they are in control, so we don't have to worry?"

"Yes. If they weren't going to the garage and had to take care of things somewhere else, we would be nervous. But the safest place they can handle things is at the garage," Nora assures me.

"Okay. So what do we do while they're gone?" I ask.

She shrugs. "Hang out. Relax. Try to avoid wondering when they're coming home."

For the next few days, that's what we do. We make meals together, watch movies, and play games. Liam, Killian, Nolan, and Declan all visit at different times. Carla arrives each morning, and we have a session. At night, I put my head on the pillow and deal with the ache I have to see Obrecht. My dreams vary from the same nightmare I've had about Jack and a new one, where I'm in a hotel with Obrecht and a girl with blue hair. We're standing in the room and she keeps saying, "Happy birthday," but it never goes past that point, so I don't understand what the dream is about.

When the third day arrives, I feel like I'm going stir crazy. I've bonded with the girls and had a good time, but I miss Obrecht. As much as they've told me not to worry, I'm starting to. They keep assuring me this is typical, but I also see the anxiety growing on their faces. I begin to pace, wondering where he is and when he's coming back to get me.

My phone rings and the screen displays the word private. I answer it, hoping it's Obrecht and he's on another phone. "Hello."

"You think you can hide, but you can't. You're mine. I own you. Once a slave, always a slave," Jack's voice echoes in my ear.

I drop the phone.

"Selena, what's wrong?" Anna asks and picks up the phone.

I grab it from her and hang up. My hands shake and my lungs feel like they can't hold any air. I stare at her and can't help the tears that drip down my face. I barely manage to get out, "He found me."

Anna's eyes widen. She yanks the phone out of my hand, takes out the SIM card, and goes into the kitchen. In seconds, the card is cut in half. She goes into the corridor to get her bodyguard, Victor, and tells him about the phone call.

Liam walks in. He studies Anna and Victor. "What's going on?"

"Selena's crazy ex-husband somehow found her number and called her," Nora blurts out.

Liam's eyes turn to slits. "What did he say?"

My cheeks heat with embarrassment, but I find my voice and tell him. I avoid the gazes from the other girls.

I just admitted I was Jack's slave.

"I destroyed the SIM card," Anna says.

Liam nods. "Good." He pulls his phone out of his pocket and puts it to his ear. "Finn, are you still in the vicinity?"

I watch him, not sure who Finn is or why he's calling him.

"Get his phone. Do whatever you need to and get it fast. Call me when you're done." Liam hangs up. "Do you know how he would have gotten your number?"

I open my mouth to answer then stop.

Liam raises his eyebrows.

I finally ask, "Do you have someone watching my ex-husband?"

He doesn't confirm nor deny it.

"Why?" I ask.

"Sorry, lass, but I can't discuss things with you."

"Obrecht told you to follow him?"

He shakes his head. "No. But he knows."

When I don't reply, Nora steps next to me and puts her arm around my shoulder. "Liam, what's going on? If this involves Selena—"

"It doesn't."

"You knew who I was, didn't you? Before Hailee introduced us at the cafe?" I ask.

Guilt passes into his expression. "Yes."

"Are you watching me, too?" Maybe I should feel scared at that thought, but I'm not. I'm just super confused.

"No. But I have eyes and ears on your ex at all times. He's not going to make a move without me knowing," he claims.

"Why?" I ask again.

"It doesn't involve you, but he also isn't going to come near you."

"He was at the restaurant the other night."

"Yes. We didn't know you were there. It was a coincidence," Liam claims.

"How do you know?"

"I just do." His phone rings again. "Finn."

The baby cries through the monitor. Nora releases my shoulder to attend to her.

Anna steps next to me. She puts her arm around me where Nora's was. "That's good if Liam is watching him."

Liam hangs up. "We have his phone. It doesn't look like he had a tracker on it."

"How can you know that?"

"Declan is with Finn. He's going through it again, but he is ninety-nine percent sure he didn't track the call."

"And Declan knows about these things?" I ask.

"Yeah. He's a tech guru. He got through his passcode in no time and doesn't see anything that could have traced the call."

I sigh in relief. "Okay. Thank you."

Liam hesitates then says, "Can I talk to you privately?"

A knot forms in my throat. I swallow it and nod. Liam leads me into the den and shuts the door. "There's something I hope you can help me with."

"What?" I nervously ask him.

Liam's green eyes assess me. "Can you tell me about Jack's family?"

"He doesn't have family. He was an only child and his parents died in a car crash. Why do you ask?"

Something passes in Liam's expression. I'm not sure what it is. "Did you ever meet his parents?"

"No. He was ten when the accident occurred."

Liam's jaw clenches.

"Why are you asking about his family?"

He smiles, but it seems forced. "No reason. I must have gotten my information mixed up." He takes out his phone and shows me a photo. "There's one more question. Do you know this man?"

A chill digs its way into my bones. I've seen the evil eyes staring back at me too many times. I can still hear his voice, telling me he's going to get his chance with me one day. I grab Liam's arm to steady myself. "Why do you have his picture?"

"So, you have seen him?"

I try to catch my breath. "Yes. It's Mack."

Liam lowers his voice. "Did he hurt you, Selena?"

I meet his gaze. "No. But he wants to."

23

Obrecht

IT'S BEEN THREE DAYS. I ONLY KNOW BECAUSE SERGEY JUST pulled me out of the interrogation room. He came into the garage and said he dropped Kora off at Boris and Nora's.

I pull my bloody gloves off and crack my neck. "What's going on?"

Aleksei screams, and Sergey and I glance through the door. His shoulder just tore out of its socket. We stretched his limbs out as far as they could go. Boris, who's spent more time with Aleksei than anyone, pulled on the ropes and yanked his limbs another inch, knowing what would happen.

Sergey scowls, watching the scene unfold. "Fucking traitor."

"You come to take a shot?"

He turns to me and shuts the door. It instantly goes silent since our walls are soundproof. "Liam was going to come. I told him not to."

"Liam has no right to be here. We already told him Aleksei was ours to handle."

Sergey shifts on his feet then crosses his arms. "Jack called Selena on her cell."

The hairs on my arms stand up. "What?"

Fresh hatred fills Sergey's face. "Liam got to Nora's right after it happened. Anna destroyed Selena's SIM card. Finn somehow retrieved Jack's phone almost immediately. Declan was with him. He doesn't think Jack traced the call."

I strip off my shirt. What's going on in the garage is important, but I need to get to Selena. She must be petrified. "How did he get her number?"

"We don't know."

I toss my shirt in the burn barrel and release my pants. Anger fills me. "What's the point of Liam's guys tracking him if they don't know these things?"

Sergey holds his hands in the air. "Easy. You know as well as I do, nothing is foolproof. They can't monitor what Jack has going on behind the scenes."

"Not good enough," I bark. I kick my shoes off, remove my socks, and put everything in the bin on top of my shirt. "Did your driver leave?"

"No. I'm not dealing with Aleksei. Kora's at Nora's, but after what she went through, I'm not leaving her for days on end to worry."

"Wait for me, then." I step into the bathroom and scrub my skin. So far, Aleksei admitted to falling into a relationship with Ludis Petrov. He said it's been going on for five years. Besides Igor and Gavriil, he named two other of our men. Adrian and Maksim went to pick them up. For years, they've been feeding information on all the Ivanov dealings to Ludis. Aleksei fell into Ludis's web and then recruited our guys at Ludis's direction. I don't need to know if he's telling the truth since it's been consistent for the last two days.

I'm reeling over these traitors, but right now, I'm more worried about my dorogaya. I know how scared she is of Jack finding her. This should never have happened. It adds salt to my wounds with Liam, which may not be fair, but it doesn't add confidence he knows how to deal with this issue. If I'm holding back on destroying Jack, Liam better step up his game while monitoring him.

I finish my shower, dry off, then step out of the bathroom and put on the new clothes we keep at the garage. Sergey is standing in the doorway, his hands clenched into fists.

"You can stay and go in for a few hours. Kora will be okay if you're back before dark," I tell him, knowing he's itching to take his turn with Aleksei.

He spins. Hurt and vengeance are on his face. I've seen it too many times. Like always, it pains me to see Sergey struggle with his past and current demons. He wears his emotions more than the rest of us. He shuts the door. "No. If I go in, you know I'm unable to come out."

I nod. "Yeah. You have a joint on you, or do I need to take my stash?" I only smoke when I finish torturing and killing men. My bag of weed is in the desk drawer. I need it to reduce the vibrating nerves I always have after these events.

"I've got my pipe."

"Good. Did you tell the others I'm going?" I ask.

"Yeah."

We leave the garage and get in the car. Sergey hands me his bowl. I light it up, inhaling the smoke into my lungs and holding it for several seconds before releasing it. I hand it back to him, and he does the same.

"Liam isn't capable of guaranteeing Selena's safety. I should never have agreed to it," I seethe.

"You and I are the only two who haven't come full circle on Liam's abilities yet. I get where you're coming from, but this isn't his fault, and you know it. He took care of it right away," Sergey states.

I take another hit. "Did you know Jack was at the same restaurant Selena and I were at?"

Sergey raises his eyebrows. "No. Did he see her?"

"No. I don't think so. But where were Liam's guys then?" The more I stew over the close calls the last few days, the more irritated I become. I'm having a harder and harder time obeying Liam's instructions not to touch Jack until his company goes public. I add, "We need our own guys on Jack."

Sergey's jaw twitches. "Talk to Liam. But, Obrecht, who would we put on him? Our guys are quickly going down. We can't take our trackers off monitoring the war. Our women need to have protection at all times with this shit going on. We've got to figure out who else is in the Petrov's grasp. Then we need to rebuild quickly."

I don't reply, wishing I could refute his statement. I can't. It takes years to train a tracker properly. We don't know who else in our house is against us. Every time we think we've found all the traitors, another blow smacks us in the face. Aleksei, Igor, and Gavriil are hard knocks. If they could be against us, who else is?

Sergey hands me the pipe. I shouldn't take another hit. His stuff is as potent as possible, but I can't seem to stop the quivering in my gut. It's a rage so deep, I'm not sure how I'll ever make it dissipate. By the time we get to Nora's, I've taken two more. My buzz seems to intensify the anxiety I'm feeling about protecting my dorogaya.

We go up to Boris's. As soon as I step into the penthouse, Selena sees me. She is quickly in my arms. I say, "Sergey told me what happened. Are you okay?"

She puts on a brave face. "Yes."

"Where're the others?" Nora asks.

"Still at the garage. Everything is fine," I assure her.

She releases a big breath of air and nods. "Okay. Thanks."

"Nora, I think Shannon—" Liam freezes. "Everyone done?"

I kiss Selena on the forehead then release her. "No, but we need to talk." I tell Selena, "Stay here. It won't take long. Then we'll go home."

Liam motions for us to go into the other room. Sergey and I follow him. I shut the door behind me. "Is this how you protect my woman?"

He scowls. "We contained the situation. He doesn't know where she's at."

"Not good enough. How did he get her number?"

"Declan's going through Jack's phone now. He also hacked into his email server. From now on, any email communication he has, we'll be able to see."

"You should have already done that," I accuse.

"How? We just got his phone so Declan could tap into it," Liam insists.

"Jesus. Do you need a step-by-step guide on how to dig into someone and continue to monitor them?" I snap.

Liam steps closer to me. "This shit's getting old, Obrecht. If you have ideas on what we should do to watch Jack better, then by all means, let me know."

I jab my finger in his chest. "They aren't ideas. It's called the proper way to do things. Not the half-assed way."

Liam sniffs hard. "Touch me one more time. Go on."

"Enough!" Sergey cries out and steps between us. "Liam, you've got shit you need to learn."

Liam's eyes burn with fire. "Never said I didn't. I don't see either of you trying to help me though. You want to accuse me of shit, but you do nothing to assist me. So much for the same team."

I scoff. "I never asked to be on your team. And I'm not holding off on Jack. Whatever you have up your sleeve, it's got nothing to do with me."

More anger rages on Liam's face. "You've made it clear how you feel. But let me tell you what will happen if you touch Jack before the deal goes through. I will have every O'Malley hunt you down until you're nothing but ashes in Lake Michigan with all of the men you've tortured and killed. The war the Ivanovs will need to worry about won't be the current one. It'll be one against the O'Malleys. So if that's what you want, make your move."

"Fuck's sake, Liam! Do you hear yourself right now?" Sergey barks.

Liam shakes his head. He lowers his voice. "I didn't ask to run the clan. I didn't ask for my father to be dying. I certainly wasn't around when your family came to mine asking for an alliance. In a perfect world, this should work. We've known each other forever. But this isn't a perfect world. I know my weaknesses. I've asked for help. I've been open to suggestions. I've even stood up to my father. All you two want to do is create a rift. Well, hear me and don't forget this. If you go against my wishes and lay a finger on Jack before his company goes public, I will not be forgiving. This is the O'Malley clan's future. If you want to destroy it, I will use every weapon in my power to create ten times the damage for the Ivanovs. Do I make myself clear?"

"And true colors shine," I seethe.

He shakes his head. "No. I'm doing exactly what an Ivanov would do. Now, if you have methods you want to discuss on monitoring that bastard, I'm all ears." He turns to Sergey.

"Excuse me. I'm going to say goodbye to our niece and hope you two don't do something stupid to put her in a situation where she doesn't know one side of her family." He brushes past us and slams the door shut.

"That mother—"

"Stop!" Sergey shouts and holds up his hands.

Blood violently slams between my ears. "You're taking his side?"

Sergey crosses his arms. "Did you listen to what he said?"

"His threat?"

He shakes his head. "No. Everything else."

I stare at the ceiling.

Sergey continues, "We need to make this work. I'm not going to have my niece in a war between her families. He's right. He has asked for help. If we're on the same side, which we are, then we need to work together. You're the best tracker we have. Work with Finn and Nora's brothers. Teach them what you know. Right now, we can't be sure about how deep the Petrovs have infiltrated our family. We can trust Finn and Nora's brothers. And it's a much better bet than determining who else is on our side and getting it wrong."

I close my eyes, trying to think of another way. There isn't one. I finally look at Sergey. "Fine. I'll work with Finn and Nora's brothers. But so help me God, if Jack attempts anything else with Selena, I don't care what Liam threatens."

Sergey nods. "Okay. I'll talk with Liam, but we both need to cool it with him. No matter what, we need to remember we're on the same side."

I concede. "Fine. I'm taking Selena home. Tell Liam I'll contact his guys tomorrow."

"One more thing," Sergey adds.

"What?"

"I'm looking forward to taking Jack out, too. No one, including Liam, wants him alive any longer than he needs to be."

I release a stress-filled breath. It's true. I don't believe Liam cares about Jack's life, but I still hate the reality I'm in. He should be off this Earth by now.

We go out to the main room. I don't waste time getting Selena out of the penthouse. When we get in the car, she straddles me and sweetly kisses my lips. She pulls back and raises her eyebrows. "Have you been smoking weed?"

My nerves rile up again. I'm not sure what Selena's stance is on a lot of things. Recreational drugs are one of them. "Yeah."

She tilts her head and strokes the hair behind my ear. "I didn't know you smoked."

I stare at her intently. "I don't usually. After I finish at the garage, I need it."

"Why? What does it do?" she asks.

I try to compile the right words. "When I'm at the garage, or anytime I need to do what I do there, I have a hard time mentally escaping it after."

She scoots her knees so they're on the backseat. A line forms between her eyes. "It stays with you?"

"Yes."

"For how long?"

I shrug. "It used to be weeks. Now I can typically forget it in a day or so, depending on what the circumstances were."

"You mean who it was?"

"Yeah," I admit.

She opens her mouth then shuts it. I wait, and she finally says, "The girls told me who Aleksei was and how close you were with him. I don't know what he did, but I assume this one is harder for you?"

My heart races. So much about Selena has taken me by surprise. Her intuition about this situation when she barely knows any details catches me off guard. "Yes."

She bites on her lower lip.

I trace her jaw with my thumb. "Are you okay, baby girl?"

Her eyes glisten. She swallows hard. "What if he finds me?"

"He won't. You're safe," I firmly insist, but as I say it, my fear and annoyance that he's still breathing pops up again.

Her lips tremble. "I keep having dreams. He's in one of them."

"It doesn't mean it's going to come true."

She doesn't appear convinced.

"You said dreams. What else are you dreaming about?"

"I don't know. I think I'm in a hotel room. You're there and this girl with blue hair. She keeps saying, 'Happy birthday,' but then I wake up."

"Do you know any women with blue hair?" I ask.

She shakes her head. "No. So I don't know what it's about."

"Are you scared in that dream?"

She pauses then replies, "No. I think I'm nervous and... maybe excited?"

"Hmmm. Well, I'm glad you weren't only terrorized in your sleep."

Compassion fills her expression. She slides her hands around my neck. "Are we doing anything the rest of the night?"

"Not unless you have something planned?"

She smiles. "No. But I don't want to think about Jack anymore, and I don't want you to dwell on the garage, either. I-I know what I want to do."

I drag my fingers down her spine. "What's that, baby girl?"

Her expression turns to a mix of mischief, love, and hope. The corners of her mouth curl up higher. "Things we haven't before."

Selena

"DOES WEED MAKE YOU RELAX?" I ASK OBRECHT WHEN WE GET inside his penthouse.

He arches an eyebrow. "Have you never tried it before?"

Heat fills my cheeks. I shouldn't be embarrassed, but it's a reminder that Jack controlled everything in my life, including my choices to engage or not engage in things. It included alcohol and all the drugs he did. I'm not interested in trying anything else, but pot doesn't seem like a big deal. I know Sergey smokes it, since I've smelled it on him. Now that I'm aware Obrecht does, I want to experience it. "No."

"But you want to?"

I nod. "Yes. If nothing bad is going to happen."

His lips twitch. "It won't. Have you ever smoked a cigarette before?"

"Once, when I was sixteen. My girlfriend stole a pack from her grandfather. It made me cough so much, I never did it again. I'm not a fan of smoke," I admit.

He studies me. "Let's avoid the smoke, then."

"What do you mean?"

He picks up my hand and leads me into the kitchen. He opens the cabinet and takes out a small, white container. It resembles a pill bottle. He opens it and hands me something that looks like a yellow gumdrop.

I naively ask, "What is this?"

"It's a gummy. Chew it well. Then you don't need to smoke anything."

I pop it in my mouth and follow his orders. "It tastes like candy."

His expression turns to amusement. "Yep." He puts one in his mouth, too.

"Now what?"

He chuckles. "Give it a bit to kick in. It might take an hour or so."

"All right."

He leads me to the couch, sits, and tugs me onto his lap. His hand slides through my hair. "Did you have fun with the girls?"

"Yes. They're all really nice. Nora's family is, too. We played cards and other games. I hadn't ever played any of them before. Nolan and I ended up winning the euchre tournament."

Obrecht's expression hardens. I'm not sure what to make of it.

"Did I say something wrong?"

He sighs. "No. I'm glad you kicked their asses. What else did you do?"

The flutters in my chest I felt whenever I held Shannon erupt. I'm not sure what it means or what to do with it. "I spent a lot of time playing with Shannon when she wasn't sleeping. Actually, I'm not sure if I can call it playing, since she's only a few days old and can't do much."

Obrecht's face lights up. "She is adorable. Thank God she looks like Nora and not Boris."

I slap his shoulder with the back of my hand. "Boris is good looking."

"Nora's much better looking."

"Mmm...is she?"

"Yeah."

"I'd ask you what you did, but I'm assuming you won't say?"

He nods. "You've assumed right. Except, there is one thing."

"What's that?"

"I told Adrian about my mom and Stefano. You should have seen his face."

"I still haven't met your brother."

He pulls his phone out. "That reminds me. I need to schedule dinner with my mom. She called Adrian before we left. You'll come with me, right?"

My heart skips a beat. I loved meeting Svetlana. I like her. It makes me happy Obrecht wants me part of their family event. I've not had a family since I left Greece. One of the things I can see with Obrecht is how close he is to his family. I don't know them very well, but it's hard not to want to be a part of it. "Yes. Of course."

He pecks me on the lips and says into the phone, "Hi, Mom." He tucks a lock of hair behind my ear. "Let's plan on Friday for dinner. I'll let Adrian know."

I can hear his mom's muffled voice but can't make out what she's saying.

"Yes, Selena already said she'll join us." He winks at me then his face falls. "You're going to need to talk with Adrian, Mom. Skylar broke it off with him. He's not back yet, but my guess is he will be in a day or so."

I've met Skylar a few times and like her. I didn't know she was with Adrian. My heart hurts for them. I can't imagine breaking up with Obrecht and how hard that would be.

"I don't know the details, Mom." He puts his hand under my shirt and strokes my back. Tingles erupt on my skin under his palm. "She's right here. Hold on." He holds the phone out. "My mom wants to ask you something."

I take the phone. "Hi, Svetlana."

333

Her thick Russian accent comes through the line. "Selena. How are you?"

"I'm good. And you?"

"Great. I'm not sure if you're interested in this or not, but Stefano's daughters want to plan a spa day. I mentioned I met you, and they said to invite you as well. Would you like to come with me?" she asks.

I can't contain my grin. "Sure. I'd love to."

"Perfect. Have Obrecht send me your phone number, and I'll call you when I have the details," she chirps.

"Actually, Obrecht gave me your number. I had some things I wanted to ask you. Is it okay if I text you?" I ask.

"Sure, darling. I have to go now. Stefano just got here and is taking me to dinner and a new jazz club he just discovered."

"Okay. Tell him we said hi."

"I will. Bye now."

"Bye." I hang up and hand the phone back to Obrecht. "Your mom invited me to a spa day with her and Stefano's daughters."

Another expression I can't figure out crosses his face.

I lightly knead his shoulders. I asked him the night we went to dinner, but I repeat, "Do you not like your mom dating?"

He sighs. "It's strange."

"She's not dated before?" I ask. It surprises me. Svetlana is gorgeous. She doesn't look her age, and she has the confidence I wish I had. Kindness also seems to be at the core of everything she does.

He grunts. "Not that I'm aware of, but what do I know? She's been dating Stefano for months."

"Aren't you happy for her?"

His face turns serious. "I am, but I need to get used to it." He moves his fingers up my spine until he's firmly palming my head. "Let's get off the subject of my mom. I think we should negotiate before you get buzzed."

"Yeah, I don't feel anything," I reply.

He smirks. "Don't worry, baby girl. It'll kick in."

I tease, "Maybe we should negotiate when it does and see if anything changes in what I let you do to me."

His face falls. "No. Let's do it now."

"Okay." I straighten my back, reach around, and cup his balls. "What would you like to do, sir."

He sniffs hard. "If you're going to sample the goodies during the negotiations, I'm going to have to punish you."

I squeeze him a few times and lean as close to his face as possible. "Are you going to spank me?"

His lips twitch. "I think I need a new punishment. You seem to like it too much."

"I do, sir."

His icy-blue eyes erupt in flames. They study my lips then hold my gaze. His hand slides in my pants until it covers my ass. "What's off-limits, baby girl?"

MAGGIE COLE

My heart beats faster. I swallow. "Nothing."

He wags a finger between us. "Wrong answer. You have hard limits. Tell me."

"But you know them."

"Humor me. Tell me again."

I take a deep breath. I suddenly feel like laughing but manage to keep it together. Our breaths merge, and I steal a quick kiss. "Don't put anything over my face. You get to look at me the entire time."

He squeezes my ass cheek. "I like looking at you. Go on."

"No ice or extreme heat. No paddles, floggers, or sharp objects. Your bare hand is required."

"Required. All right, baby girl. What else?"

I can't help myself. I'm generally not a giggler, but I suddenly feel super happy and it comes out. "Toys are at your discretion."

"Mmm..." His eyes turn to slits. "I think you forgot I'm supposed to ask you."

I shake my head. "No. Go ahead and surprise me."

He freezes and studies me. "Are you high already?"

Maybe. I'm giggling. "No. I trust you."

He continues assessing me.

"What?" I attempt to get rid of the perma-grin forming on my face but can't.

He orders, "Tell me your safe word."

"Faucet."

He runs his thumb over my lips. "What do I want, baby girl?"

"To control when I can and can't come. Some mind games. Bondage. Toys." I lean into his ear and flick my tongue on his lobe. "You also want to penetrate me anywhere in my body you want." I pull back and attempt to study him the way he does me without smiling.

I bet I look super goofy right now.

Why can't I stop smiling?

He takes a few controlled breaths and slides his fingers over the slit of my ass. I squirm in his lap, and his cocky expression appears. "Go into the bedroom. Take off all your clothes and kneel in front of the bed."

"Yes, sir." I giggle and rise. I spin and wiggle my booty in his face.

He slaps my ass. "On second thought, strip here and kneel facing the window." He leaves the room.

I strip, fold my clothes, and put them on the side table. I drop to my knees in front of the glass. All of Chicago seems to be in front of my eyes. The lake, buildings, and streets are alive. The sun has set, and darkness will soon fill the sky.

Obrecht turns the lights out. The room glows from the fireplace on the wall. Soft music fills my ears. I wait, feeling his stare on me, wondering when he'll give me orders. I sit on my knees, back straight, head bowed. A slight humming vibrates in my body, and I feel more relaxed than usual. I have to fight to keep my body in the position it is.

"Head up. Crawl to me with that sexy ass in the air," Obrecht commands.

I obey, feeling sexier than usual, taking my time and slinking across the room to the armchair he's sitting in, naked. When I get to him, I position myself between his knees and wait.

He sniffs hard then pats his chest. "Straddle me, my little dorogaya."

I obey. A feeling of relief fills me when my skin touches his. Not being with him the last few days was torture. I close my eyes then quickly open them, remembering he didn't tell me I could.

His hand cups my cheek. "Did you miss me, baby girl?"

"So much."

"Kiss me, then. Show me how much."

I don't hesitate. Our lips mold and tongues slide against each other. I rise on my knees to get closer to him, thrusting my tongue in and out of his mouth.

His one hand palms my head. The other moves around me. Something wet hits my forbidden zone. He inches his finger in, and I gasp into his mouth but don't clench up for very long. I'm not sure if it's the weed or the fact it's him, but I want everything with him. I relax quickly and return to kissing him with fervor, grinding my ass into his hand.

He tugs my hair and ends our kiss. His icy-blue flames drill into me. "You seem to want me everywhere inside you."

"I do," I breathe. "Please. Take me however you want."

He smirks. "I'm not taking you, baby girl."

Shoot. I forgot the rules.

"Please, sir. I'm sorry I forgot to use your name."

His expression hardens. "I'm not taking you, baby girl. If you want it, you take it."

"What?"

He tilts his head and removes his hand. He wipes it on a towel on the side table and grabs my hip. "One way or another, you're riding me, my dorogaya. What's it going to be? Your pussy or ass?"

All the times Jack took me in the ass were from behind. It was rough and hurt. There's no rationale as to why I'm okay with the thought of doing it with Obrecht. Now that he's given me an option, I'm feeling like a fish out of water.

He tugs my head back until I'm looking at the ceiling. His lips trail down the middle of my neck. He mumbles, "Pick, baby girl."

The tip of his cock hits my forbidden zone. I take a deep breath and sink on it. It can't be much, but it feels like a lot.

Obrecht puts my mouth next to his. "You want more, baby girl?"

"Yes."

"Take it," he demands.

I inch more of him in me. Short breaths compete with my racing pulse. His hand squeezes my hip, and I rise back up, then take more of him.

A rumble fills his chest. He keeps my face in front of his, kissing me, studying me, taunting me to take all of him. When I finally do, he groans. "You feel so good."

"Yeah," I agree, wondering how things can be so different with him, and hungrily kiss him some more.

His hand on my hip begins to guide me. He moves his other one from my hair to between us. A soft hum fills the air and his finger vibrates on my clit. It surprises me. I never saw anything. Whatever he has isn't very big, yet the sensations sweep through me and instantly fill me with heat.

I dig my nails into his shoulders, rocking on his cock, with adrenaline sitting on the edge of all my cells. "Obrecht," I shakily cry out.

"I love you like this, baby girl."

"Please," I beg him, wanting to come, not sure how I'm going to stop myself. Every part of my body is so relaxed. I didn't anticipate how this would feel. Or how the drugs would interfere with my ability to control myself. Or how every part of me would feel like it's on the edge of a cliff, desperate to dive off so soon.

"You're gorgeous. You know that? Every piece of you. And you messed me up these last few days. I had a job to do that shouldn't have anything to do with you. You didn't belong in my mind then. Yet, all I could think about was getting it over with so I could come home to you. I had to stop myself too many times not to make a mistake and end it earlier than I should have. Then you tease me with this hot, juicy ass and sweet, tight pussy of yours. So no, you can't come right now." He returns to my mouth and sticks his tongue inside.

Like always, I submit. I return his kiss, as if it's the last one I'll ever get. Every move of my body is sweet friction against his. Each second that passes creates an atmosphere of delicious tension. It's sex, and love, and two people uniting in the darkening of the night.

My whimpers get louder. Sweat, the smell of our arousal, and pulsing flesh intensify.

He's merciless in his expertise, thrusting into my body with fluidity as he firmly controls my hip. Unlike in the past with Jack, bursts of sensations tease and torture me until I can't hold on anymore.

My body betrays me. Tremors ignite with such potency they could be rupturing my soul. Everything spasms, and Obrecht mumbles Russian against my lips, detonating inside me and stretching me farther than I thought possible.

I collapse against him. Our chests push into the other's, trying to find air. He circles his arms around me, holding me as we both come down. When I pull away and lift my body off him, he rises with me in his arms.

I say nothing as he carries me into the bathroom. A warm bath is already waiting. He sets me in it then gets in behind me and pretzels his limbs around mine.

I glance up, and he kisses me. I turn to him more and fully embrace every ounce of affection he offers me.

"You okay, baby girl?" he asks.

"Yeah." I lay my head on his chest and slide my finger through his chest hair. I absentmindedly say, "I'm sorry I came. I couldn't stop it. Was it the weed?"

He chuckles. "Probably." He tilts my chin so I'm looking at him. "And don't ever apologize again for anything we do together. You're perfect, baby girl. Every single part of you is perfect for me."

Obrecht

Several Months Later

TINY WHIMPERS FILL THE AIR. I LIFT MY HEAD. IT'S DARK INSIDE the room, but I see the glow of my dorogaya's beautiful porcelain cheeks and closed eyes. Her lilac scent and little moans make my cock harden. Her lush red lips are slightly open, and her chest starts rising and falling faster.

"Oh," she whispers so quietly, I strain to hear it again. Her fingers twitch against our legs then slide onto her sex.

Is she having a sexy dream?

Fuck me. My dorogaya's going to keep me young.

I slowly remove the covers off her body. I scan every inch of her gorgeous silhouette. I debate my three options.

MAGGIE COLE

I could wake her up and remind her I didn't give her permission to play with herself or come. After I do that, I could edge her for a few hours. Or, I could put my body on top of hers and thrust my aching dick into her. I could...

"Please suck me. Oh God!" she cries out louder.

Amused, aroused, and intrigued, I glance at her face. Her eyes are closed. When I drag my eyes down her torso, I see her hand lightly stroking herself. Her legs part.

I decide to give her what she wants. I move between her legs, put my hands on the back of her knees. Slowly, I move them over her soft skin toward her wet heat.

"Mmm," she moans then thrusts her hips up while gliding her fingers inside her body.

The scent of her arousal mixes with the lilacs, and my adrenaline pumps harder. If I had a list of what a woman should smell, feel, and look like, she would be it. Whatever this dirty little dream is she's having, it only makes me appreciate her more.

I slide my finger through her juices then add my finger into her hole next to hers.

"Obrecht," she whispers.

I gaze up, but she seems to still be asleep.

Jesus. She's my fucking dream girl, calling my name out in her sleep.

I keep my finger moving with hers and, with the flat end of my tongue, lick her pulsing sex. I put my other hand on her

344

nipple, pinching and playing with it as her free hand laces through my hair.

"So good."

I slowly eat her out and finger her at the same pace. She circles her hips on my face harder, but I control her in her sleep, too. I sternly command, "Slow down, my dorogaya."

She draws a deep breath and slows. "Obrecht...oh God!" Her hot skin turns dewy. "So hard...please let me go faster, Obrecht...oh God! Please!" Her body quivers, and she tugs at my hair.

She's never begged this early on. It riles my ego and hormones to the point of overdrive.

"No. Slow," I demand.

Her lips tremble in sexy terror. Terror for my dick, which is dying to slam into her tight little pussy that our two fingers are slowly widening so I can slip in a third.

Her voice shakes in a whisper. "But it's my birthday. Please."

Her birthday? It's not for a few more months.

It better not be her birthday and the information I dug up on her was wrong.

"You want to come hard on my cock, don't you, my dorogaya?"

"Yes," she barely gets out and trembles harder.

"Is it my mouth or cock you want?" I dip back to her clit and start sucking on it while shoving another finger in her.

"Oh God!" she cries out.

"Which one? Mouth or cock?" I flick my tongue on her clit like a cat lapping up water.

"Both, please! Just like this. You and her. Oh God!" she cries out.

Her? Did she say her, or did I misunderstand that?

My erection strains. "What do you like about her?" I ask and slow everything down.

Her hands massage the side of my head. She strokes the top of my ear. "Her mouth. It's so good like this." Sweat rolls down her thighs.

"Tell me what it feels like, Selena."

"You know," she whispers and thrusts her hips faster into our fingers.

"Slow down. I didn't give you permission to come," I remind her. She obeys, and I continue, "Now tell me what it feels like." I put my mouth back on her body.

"So good. Oh God! Your cock feels like it's going to split me and...mmm," she moans.

"And what?" I demand against her pussy then continue feasting on her.

"Her lips and tongue. When she hits your cock, I can feel you pulse in me. It's always when she's back on my clit. Oh God!"

Fuuuuck.

I study her face while twisting my fingers in her. "What about her hand on your breasts, twisting those sexy nipples of yours?"

"No! Don't remove your hands. I love your hands on me. Just...oh God...please let her keep...oh!"

"Keep what?"

"Her mouth on us. Please. Her mouth is so good. So good with your big dick in me."

Jesus. I didn't picture Selena to be into some girl-on-girl action, but I'm down if she wants to play.

"Like now?" I ask and return to eating her out a bit more intensely than before.

Her body writhes. "Yes! Obrecht! Oh God! Let me come, please!"

"No!" I tell her and slow down. She's going to beg me more. Plus, I want to know more about this girl she's dreaming about, so I ask, "What color is her hair?"

"Blue."

I almost freeze. The first time she told me about this blue-haired girl, I didn't think anything of it. Now I'm extra curious. "Is she white? Black? Asian?" I run my tongue around her clit but don't touch it.

She groans. "Please, Obrecht. I need it."

"Answer me first."

"I think she's biracial? She's so hot, isn't she?"

"Yes, but no one's as sexy as you, my sinful dorogaya." I nibble on her clit, and she gasps.

"Obrecht," she breathes.

347

"Don't yell my name until I'm coming. You can say her name. Give her credit for devouring your sweet pussy so well." I rotate sucking, licking, and biting from the outside of her sex to the middle of her sensitive nerves.

"Giuliana!" she cries out. "Please! Obrecht!" Her plea is desperate, and if I don't slip my cock in her soon, I'm going to die from an aching cock.

I move my hand to her other breast and say, "You can come, my dorogaya." I move our fingers faster, intensify my mouth on her clit, and give her an orgasm so powerful, her juices soak the bed. I immediately lurch over her, caging my frame around hers and gliding my arms under her. My cock thrusts into her spasming walls. She cries out. Her eyes fly open, and her mouth forms an O.

"That was so hot," I admit to her.

Confusion fills her face then she moans.

I say against her lips, "So fucking hot." I slip my tongue in her mouth, and she matches the speed of my kiss. I pull back and slow our thrusts. "Is that what you want, my dorogaya? A woman to lick us while we fuck?"

Her flush deepens. "What?"

I lick her neck and gently bite the curve of her neck. "No lying to me. Tell me yes or no. Did you dream of letting a woman eat your pussy?" I firmly ask.

I put my face in front of hers. Her hot breath is a flame merging into mine.

"Tell me. Was that your dream?"

"Yes," she whispers.

"But who does your pussy belong to?"

"You."

"That's right." I slide my hand down her back and over her ass cheek and push her harder against me when I thrust into her.

"Oh!" she yells.

I growl in her ear, "I own this pussy. You're such a naughty, greedy girl. You want my cock and Giuliana's mouth all over you, don't you?"

"No."

Surprised, I put my face next to hers. "Don't lie to me."

"I'm not. I only want it on us when you're in me."

Jesus, I love this woman.

"But your body belongs to me. Only me."

"It's just a silly fantasy."

"Do you want your own bottom for a night?" I ask, feeling the grip of her walls tighten on me more rapidly. Heat burns through my veins.

"Wh-oh.. oh please! Please!"

I slow. "Be honest. Do you want a blue-haired, biracial girl named Giuliana to eat you out while you're full of me?"

"Please! I can't—"

"Answer. No lying. Yes or no?" I demand.

"Yes! Now please, Obrecht! I... I... I can't...oh!" She digs her nails into my back, and tears roll down her cheeks. Her body quivers against mine.

"Come, baby," I say, licking her tears off her cheek as she arches her back into me and her eyes roll while she moans. Her walls convulse against my cock, and I explode into her harder than ever.

She screams as I come, stretching her farther, her heat once again erupting on me like lava. A deep groan rumbles through my chest, and in Russian, I mumble into the curve of her neck, "How are you so perfect?"

We stay silent aside from our labored breaths. Our hearts pound into each other. She turns her face and kisses my neck.

I lift my head off her and put my lips on hers. "You filthy, naughty, delicious girl." I slide my tongue in her mouth, and she hungrily returns my affection. I end our kiss and roll on my back, pulling her with me. "What else do you want to do with a woman? And remember, you can't lie to me."

Her cheeks heat against my chest. I push her chin up so she can't hide from me. She furrows her eyebrows. "I wouldn't ever want to do anything without you."

"Good. You aren't allowed."

She smiles and bites on her swollen lips.

I drag my finger down her cheek. "Have you been with a woman?"

"No!" The heat on her face burns hotter.

"Why are you embarrassed, my dorogaya?"

"I'm... I wouldn't be a good lesbian."

I stifle a laugh. I ask her a teasing but also curious question. "What makes you a bad lesbian candidate?"

She groans and puts her hand over her face. "Can you ask me other things?"

"Nope. I want to know what your good and bad lesbian tendencies would be. You've been holding out on me." I remove her hands so I can see her expression.

She winces. "I'd only be a taker."

"A taker?"

"Yeah. You know."

And because this is amusing me, and she's giving me another hard-on, telling me what she's curious about, I play dumb. "No. I don't know. Explain."

She groans. "Obrecht."

"Selena," I mock her in a teasing tone. "Tell me."

She stares at me and sighs. "Okay. But I only have one fantasy. I...well, I've had it for a long time, but everyone has always been faceless until now."

"I thought you were having dreams about a blue-haired girl," I state.

"I did, but I've always had this dream but no faces or hair color. The dream I told you about only popped up when you were gone and it wasn't this."

I stroke her back and kiss her on the forehead. "Okay. Go ahead and tell me why you'd be a bad lesbian. I'm listening." I pull her on top of me.

She puts her elbows on my chest and rests her chin on her hands. I palm her ass and keep tracing her spine. She takes a deep breath. "You and Giuliana—like how I made up some random chick—were so vivid in my dream tonight."

I don't tell her Giuliana is real. There's a woman who fits her detailed description in Atlanta, right down to her name. She enjoys being a service submissive. The only place I've ever seen or talked to her is at the club.

"And why does that make you a taker?"

She grimaces. "I don't want to do anything to her."

"Well, well, well..." I sing and stick my fingers that still have the residual of her orgasm in my mouth. I pull them out and say, "Greedy girl you are."

Her face turns tomato red. "I know. I'm so bad, aren't I? It's like, hey, I'm here. Please suck my pussy while I ride my man. Oh, and make sure you lick his cock every now and again, too, please. We'll take all the pleasure, and you just service us." She hides her face in my chest.

I refrain from laughing. "Who said she doesn't get anything out of it?"

She lifts her head. "Umm...did you miss the part where she's licking me, and I'm doing nothing to her?"

"Why is that?" I innocently ask.

She runs her nails over my semi-hard shaft, perking it up. "I love this too much to switch sides. And you know I'm territorial. So she's not doing anything else with you, that's for sure. Not unless I have some other dream."

"One, I love this conversation for so many reasons."

"You're a dirty old man?" she teases.

"Do you want to call me Daddy?"

She bursts out laughing. Then her face gets serious, and she says, in a breathy tone, "Oh, Daddy!"

I'm officially a pervert. That was hot.

I continue, "Behave, or I'm popping a blue pill and showing you what Daddy can do all night, rotating between your ass and your tight, wet pussy."

She leans into my ear and strokes my balls. "Don't tease me, Daddy."

Jesus. I slap her ass playfully. "Back to your giver-taker worries. Two, if a submissive doesn't see gender, and they are a service sub, they aim to please. It would turn her on."

"Yeah, but it doesn't seem right she would have to get herself off."

Nope. You send her to another Dom, all hot and bothered.

"I mean, you're not touching her unless you want to die from my hand," Selena states.

"How exactly would you kill me, my dorogaya?"

"Ha, ha! Not funny!"

I stroke Selena's long hair. "So tell me more about your girl-on-girl action."

She palms my shoulder. "Stop it. Ugh. This is so embarrassing. I can't believe I was sex talking while sleeping! And I would never do it. I would totally chicken out."

I flip her on her back and hover over her. "It was sexy as hell. And Daddy's down with your fantasy, baby girl. But no one, man or woman, touches you without my permission. You're mine, and don't forget it."

26

Selena

"DON'T LOOK NOW, BUT HE'S CHECKING YOU OUT," I TELL Skylar, referring to the bartender who's getting ready for the reception. It's Kora and Sergey's wedding. There wasn't any water in the room Kora's getting ready in, so Skylar and I volunteered to go ask for it.

Skylar mumbles, "No more dating for a while. It's not working. I'm wasting people's time and my own."

"Is it that bad?" I ask. In all reality, I've dated very little. Nothing about Obrecht's and my situation was typical.

She sighs. "It's not the guys' fault. It's mine. I need to figure out how to get past Adrian."

I put my arm around her shoulder. Adrian wouldn't tell her anything about where he goes or what he's involved in. I don't know every detail about Obrecht, but I know enough.

Obrecht said Adrian is afraid she won't be able to handle the truth since his ex-wife couldn't. I wish he'd come clean so she could have the choice, but it isn't my decision. I offer, "At least the bartender is cute."

She softly laughs. "Guess there's always points for eye candy."

We walk a few more feet. The bartender smiles, displaying his straight white teeth. His brown orbs eye both of us over but mainly Skylar. "Ladies. What can I do for you?"

Skylar clears her throat. "There isn't any water in the bridal room. Could we get a few pitchers and glasses?"

"Sure. I'll have it sent right over. Anything else?" He checks her out again.

"No. Thank you."

"No problem." He winks.

Skylar ignores his gesture, and we turn and leave. Adrian walks in. She freezes then says, "I need to go to the restroom. I'll meet you in a few moments."

"Okay." I continue toward the bridal room.

Adrian pecks my cheek and says, "Selena. You look beautiful."

"Thanks. You look nice, too."

Svetlana and Stefano turn the corner with Obrecht. Svetlana's face lights up. "Selena, that dress is stunning on you!"

I glance down at my chocolate-brown, off-the-shoulder cocktail dress. "Thanks. The same goes for you."

Svetlana's in a blue evening gown, which makes her eyes pop more. Her blonde hair is in a sleek French twist. Happiness radiates off her. The engagement ring Stefano gave her a month ago shines brightly.

Stefano kisses my cheek.

Obrecht puts his arm around my waist. "What are you doing out here? I thought you'd be engrossed in bridal duties."

"I am. There wasn't any water."

"I can't wait to see Kora in her dress," Svetlana says.

Adrian sarcastically says, "All of your bridal magazine dreams coming to life."

Svetlana smacks his arm with the back of her hand. "Watch it. Those magazines are full of beauty, happiness, and love. If you weren't so stubborn—"

"Don't start," Adrian warns.

Svetlana sighs and shakes her head. She pats him on the cheek. "Selena, can you show me where Kora is?"

"Sure." I lead her to the room.

"Jesus, Mary, and Joseph!" Nora exclaims when we walk in. "I need to go home and change."

"What happened?" Svetlana asks.

Nora spins. A wet spot covers her chest. "I can't stop leaking. Every time I go anywhere, I'm the poster mom for a hot mess. I knew I should have worn the pads."

"Can you use a hairdryer? Your dress is so nice," I say.

"No. It stains until it's washed. This dress is dry clean only, too."

"There's a rush dry cleaning service around the corner. One of the guys can take it," Svetlana offers.

Hailee steps in front of her and studies her chest. She smirks. "If you want, we could call your auntie and have her bring you a jacket. I'm sure she would disapprove of your sleeveless dress."

Kora groans. "Please keep your auntie's opinion about our dresses out of here."

"She's not coming in here. This is my break zone," Hailee says.

Nora raises her eyebrows. "Break zone?"

Hailee's face turns the color of a tomato. She winces. "Sorry. I know she's your aunt."

Nora scoffs. "Doubt you're going to say anything I haven't. What's going on?"

"Yeah, Hailee. Give us the details. Did she see your furry pussy and disprove?" Aspen chirps.

Svetlana's eyes go wide. The rest of the room breaks out in laughter. Hailee crosses her arms. "I do not have a furry pussy."

Kora slides her arm around Hailee. "We know. You wax."

"Probably several times a week now that Liam is down there a lot," Skylar adds, walking into the room.

Nora scrunches her face. "Eww. Still my cousin. Don't want to imagine Liam going—"

"Can everyone stop talking about this? Please," Hailee begs.

"Stop talking about what?" Dmitri asks, stepping into the room behind Anna.

"Hailee's furry pussy," Kora says.

Dmitri raises his eyebrows. "Still having issues, Hailee?"

"How do you know about it?" she blurts out, turning almost purple. "And I'm never telling any of you what men say to me online ever again!"

Dmitri chuckles. He kisses Anna. "You need anything before I leave you with these wild women?" He glances around then stares at Nora. "Did you spill something?"

She groans. "Nope! Good old breast milk leakage. Can you tell Boris to come get me?"

"Sure." He turns back to Anna. "Need anything?"

She smiles. "Can you see if they have any ginger?"

"On it." He pecks her on the cheek and leaves.

Hailee groans. "You all need to stop with that joke!"

"Who are these men you're talking to?" Svetlana asks.

"No one anymore. It was before Liam."

"Which goes back to the question, what did my auntie do?" Nora asks.

"Yeah, Hailee. Spill it. Inquiring minds want to know," Skylar says.

She shakes her head then plops down on the couch. "She heard I was making Liam his favorite potato soup. So what did she do? She brought a huge pot over on the same night I made mine. Then she taste-tested mine and told me all the things she thought I needed to do to make it better."

"She didn't offer to show you how to make it?" I ask.

Disapproval crosses Hailee's face. "I don't need her to show me. I can follow a recipe."

I glance at Svetlana. Over the last few months, I've spent tons of time with her, learning how to cook a lot of different dishes Obrecht enjoys. Every moment I spend with Svetlana, I love. I can't imagine not wanting her to show me or have her critiquing what I made.

"Sounds like my auntie," Nora admits.

"Yeah, well, she doesn't like anything Liam put in his house that I suggested. And the woman needs to learn to knock."

Kora sits on the couch next to her. "I feel like we're about to get something good here. Keep going, Hailee."

Hailee tilts her head. "Gee. Don't look so excited."

"Oh, come on. It's my wedding day. You can't deny me my fun."

Hailee rolls her eyes. "Fine. She came over and rang the doorbell. A normal person would leave when no one answers the door. Not Liam's mom. She walked around the back and came into the kitchen."

Kora leans forward. "And?"

Hailee's face is as red as Nora's hair. "Liam and I were...umm...well, we were on the kitchen floor."

"Naked?" Kora asks, her eyes light up.

Hailee puts her hands over her face. "Liam wasn't. I kind of was."

"Kind of doesn't work in court, so that won't work here. Keep spilling, Hailee," Kora says.

"Use your imagination."

"Raise your hand if you want Hailee to give more deets," Skylar says, holding her arm in the air.

Everyone raises their hands, except Svetlana, who has an amused expression on her face.

"Outnumbered," Kora says.

Hailee groans. "All I'm saying is, I was in the middle of O town when she walked in. I'm pretty sure she heard it from outside but still came in."

"Are you a screamer, Hailee?" Aspen asks.

Hailee points at us. "You all are missing the point."

Nora pats her back. "I'm not. My auntie means well, but she's a bit crazy when it comes to Liam. What does he say about it?"

"He wants us to get along. He said she's acting crazier since Darragh is dying, but I'm worried she's going to get worse when something happens." Hailee picks up her mimosa and takes a sip. She snaps her fingers. "Oh, and get this. I had my dress hanging in Liam's closet. She bought a matching shawl and wrapped it around the dress when we weren't there."

"Why does she have a key to Liam's house?" Kora asks.

Hailee finishes her drink. "Liam gave her the code. She claimed she forgot her glasses, but I think she just wanted access to snoop."

I'm suddenly even more grateful for how awesome Svetlana is. She's kind and respectful. She seems to be aware of her son's boundaries and always has made me feel welcome and special. I put my arm around her. "I guess not every mother can be as awesome as Svetlana."

She smiles. "You make it easy, dear." She turns toward Kora and Hailee. "I'm sure she means well. Kora, stand up and let me see you in your dress, darling."

Kora rises. Svetlana has her spin and says, "Breathtaking. I love the pink. Very unique and quite the fashion statement."

Kora beams. "Thank you."

Boris comes into the room, and Nora leaves with him. The pitchers of water arrive, and we keep chattering. When Liam's mom comes into the room, Hailee stiffens.

Svetlana embraces her. "Ruth, you look beautiful. How have you been?"

Ruth smiles but blinks hard. "Hanging in there. It's nice to have something to celebrate."

"We should grab coffee sometime," Svetlana says.

"Sure. I'd love to." Ruth turns toward Kora. "You look lovely, dear."

Kora nods. "Thank you. So do you."

Ruth takes the seat next to Hailee. She quietly says, "You look nice, Hailee."

Hailee puts on what I've come to learn is her tolerant face. I imagine she uses it a lot with the kids she teaches. "Thank you. You, too."

"Did you get the shawl I left in the closet? I know it's cold out and—"

"Can we talk outside, please?" Hailee rises.

The room goes silent. Tension fills the air.

Ruth nods. "Sure." She leaves with Hailee. I'm unsure whether I feel sorry for Hailee or Ruth right now. Ruth seems a bit fragile, as if something is upsetting her.

Obrecht comes into the room as they're leaving. My heart skips a beat. I'm too busy appreciating how sexy he is in his tux to notice the line between his eyes. "Selena, I need you for a minute, please."

My stomach flips from the seriousness of his tone. When we step outside, he guides me past Hailee and Ruth. I ask, "What's wrong?"

He holds his phone out. "Everything is fine, but can you tell me how you know this man?"

A chill digs into my spine. I grab Obrecht's arm to steady myself. "He used to meet Jack at the clubs we went to. I told Liam I knew him when he showed me a photo."

Obrecht takes a deep breath, as if to calm himself down. "Yes. He just told me. Why do you appear frightened right now?"

My insides quiver. I push the phone down so he isn't staring at me anymore. "He..." I swallow the lump in my throat.

Obrecht tilts my head. "It's okay, baby girl. Just tell me what-ever it is."

I take a few moments to gather my thoughts. "Sometimes, Jack would make me kneel for hours in front of him when he had sex with other women. Then there were times he made me kneel in a cage. If I was out in the open, no one was allowed to come within ten feet of me. If I was in the cage, men could come as close as they wanted without touching the cage. He wanted to buy me from Jack. He would tell me all the things he wanted to do to hurt me."

Obrecht's face fills with rage.

"I'm sorry. I—"

"Why are you sorry, my dorogaya? You've done nothing wrong," he insists.

"I don't know. Why are you asking me about him?"

"Something just came to my attention. It has nothing to do with you, but Liam said you knew him."

I release a breath. "He isn't coming after me, then?"

Obrecht snarls, "No. But I'll make sure he doesn't have the choice."

My chest tightens. I usually don't worry about Obrecht. He can handle a lot of things. Over the last few months, I've never felt safer or more loved. A few times, he's been at the garage, but they are few and far between. He always has me stay at Nora's with Aspen, Anna, and Kora. I never know who the bad men at the garage are, except for Aleksei. Some-thing about him going after Mack makes me nervous.

He dips down and kisses me. "I see you're worried, baby girl. Don't be. Today is not a worrying day."

"I don't want anything to happen to you."

"It won't." He drags his finger down my neck and over the top of my shoulder. "The wedding is starting soon. Let's go take our seats, okay?"

"Sure."

We sit with Adrian, Svetlana, and Stefano. By the time the ceremony is over, I've forgotten about anything bad. Obrecht and I spend the night dancing and having a good time with the Ivanovs and O'Malleys.

When Sergey and Kora leave, we all trickle out of the building. Obrecht tugs me close to him. The car pulls up to the curb, and he leads me to it. The driver opens the door, and bullets ring through the air.

"Get down!" Obrecht pushes me into the car. "Adrian!" he screams and shuts the door while ordering the driver to keep me inside and leave the vehicle running.

So much chaos erupts. Aspen gets shoved in our car. Neither of us speak as we peek out the window, watching the Ivanovs try to keep Adrian alive. Skylar is screaming. Sirens soon fill the air. It feels like forever before Obrecht and Maksim get in the car and we go to the hospital.

"Is he..." I can't finish the statement.

Obrecht tugs me into him and says nothing. His chest shakes, and his breath is heavy. He and Maksim are both covered in blood.

Right when we pull up to the hospital, Obrecht looks at Maksim. "As soon as we know he's okay, we need to take care of this. Darragh was right. She wanted a war. Now she's got one."

I've never seen Maksim's eyes so cold. They pierce into Obrecht's. When he nods in agreement, a new chill moves through me.

27

Obrecht

"Obrecht?" Skylar whispers, gazing at me for some answers.

She and Adrian somehow made up at the wedding. All night, they were happy again. Now my brother is lying on a cold metal table and losing too much blood.

His ex-wife is responsible for this. I don't need confirmation it was Dasha and those Polish thugs she's involved with. Even last night, she threatened Adrian.

How could we have not been more careful about leaving the wedding?

Adrian could die.

My dorogaya wasn't protected any more than Skylar and Adrian.

I can't answer Skylar. The pain and confusion on her face are too much. Every bone in my body wants to find Dasha and tear her to pieces. I no longer care if she's a woman. She tried to take out my brother. Until she's dealt with, no one is safe. As soon as I know what's going on with Adrian, I'm going after her.

I blink hard, attempting to control my emotions, and walk away. I'm unsure where I'm going, but I need to breathe. My lungs constrict, making it hard to take in oxygen. The doctors and nurses passing me in the hallway barely come into focus. My skin crawls with the need to go find Dasha and make her pay. She went too far when she used the Ivanov name and tried to hurt us. This act is the point of no return. I suddenly understand what Darragh meant when he said loose ends don't get sympathy.

The stale air suffocates me, and I step outside. I walk to the end of the building, away from the smokers. "Fuck!" I bellow out and slap the wall.

"Obrecht." Selena's voice fills the air. Her hand touches my back.

Several moments pass. I stay frozen, unable to turn, trying to pull it together. She steps closer and circles her arms around me.

Selena could have gotten hurt.

Dasha even threatened it one time, mentioning she knew about my relationship with her. How could we have not secured the exit better?

I finally spin toward my angel. She scrunches her face. Tears are in her eyes. She reaches for my cheeks, and I close my eyes. She quietly but firmly asks, "Did Jack do this?"

I tug her into me. "No, baby girl. Adrian's ex-wife is to blame."

Selena tilts her head. Her eyes widen. "Why would she do that?"

I glance around us and realize I'm outside, and anything can happen. "We need to go inside. It may not be safe out here."

Selena doesn't argue.

We move into the hospital, and I guide her to a private area. I gather my thoughts about what is safe to tell her. "Dasha is involved with the Polish mob. She threatened us multiple times, but she saw Adrian last night and warned him again."

Selena gapes.

I sniff hard. "I'm sorry. I don't want you anywhere near this. You could have—"

She puts her fingers over my lips. "Don't do that. Let's focus on Adrian right now. I'm fine. Nothing happened to me."

"Obrecht," Killian calls out.

I put my arm around Selena and turn. Liam, Killian, Nolan, and Declan still have their wedding attire on. Hailee and her sister Gemma are with them, also still dressed up.

"How is he?" Liam's eyes are in slits. He clenches his jaw.

"In surgery. They said he's losing a lot of blood," I state, swallowing the emotional lump growing in my throat.

"Where are the others?" Nolan asks.

"Down the hall in the waiting room."

Nolan glances at the women then me. "Let me take Hailee, Gemma, and Selena to the others."

Selena glances at me, and I kiss her forehead. "Go with Nolan. I'll be there soon."

Hailee squeezes my arm as she passes me, and when they're out of earshot, I turn back to the O'Malleys. "Did you find out where Dasha is?"

Declan shakes his head. "No. Your trackers lost her at some point tonight. But we know where the shooters are."

My pulse increases. "Where?"

"At one of Zielinski's safe houses. I know you prefer your method of a long, drawn-out death, but we've got other issues. Dasha is behind this. They aren't anyone important in the organization. Give us the all-clear so we can take care of this while you're here," Liam says.

"You'll do no such thing," Darragh's voice booms behind me.

"Adrian's in surgery. There's no choice in this matter. Those motherfuckers need to pay," Liam insists.

Darragh moves into a coughing fit. We all wait until he manages to breathe again, exchanging glances. His face is red like the blood on his handkerchief. He drills his watery eyes on Liam. "We'll take a few days and decide whether to pin this on the Rossis or Petrovs."

Rage fills me. Those bastards don't deserve to live for another moment. Adrian's fighting for his life. Darragh's determination to use it to balance out the war only infuriates me. I step closer to him. "Those thugs tried to kill my brother. He's not out of the woods and may still die. Don't tell me we're using this for the war or waiting days. Their lives need to end now."

"Agreed," Killian says.

"Second," Declan replies.

"It's not even a question," Liam states.

Darragh takes off his tweed cap. He addresses the O'Malleys. "You seem to have forgotten who's in charge. *I* make the decisions. This isn't a democracy. You take orders from me. Every action has a reaction. O'Malleys don't react without taking advantage of every possible angle."

Intense anger almost destroys me. I bark, "My brother's situation isn't for you to use as a pawn in this fucked-up war."

Darragh turns to me. "Every move has consequences. Remember that, son."

"Don't call me son. I'm not your son. And if this is your stance, then count me out of this alliance. I'm not standing down on this one. I guarantee you the other Ivanovs won't, either. So you're either on our side or against us. Take your pick, Darragh," I seethe, my insides fuming with rage and all the hatred I feel toward this alliance. All I've seen is how the O'Malleys benefit from this agreement. If they can't take care of a situation when an Ivanov is harmed, then we aren't on the same side as far as I'm concerned.

Darragh steps closer to me. "The O'Malleys will take care of this my way. It is best for both families."

"Screw you and all the O'Malleys." I scowl at them all and leave. When I get to the waiting room, my mom is in a chair. Skylar and Selena are on each side of her. She rises, and I hug her. I ask, "Any more news?"

She pulls back. Her eyes are glassy. She's always been so strong, and I can see her fighting not to cry. "Stefano is trying to find out if there's any other information he can get. Adrian is still in surgery. Did you give blood?"

"No. Why?"

"They asked us to." My mom blinks hard, but several tears fall. I tighten my arms around her. The O'Malleys come into the room, and I tense. Darragh pulls Maksim aside.

Hailee rises. "Liam, we need to go donate blood."

"Go with him. I'm not sure if they'll let you since you've been drinking, but go see," my mom orders, and I hold back my groan. If it's in Adrian's best interest, I remind myself to deal with the O'Malleys. At least we get their blood if possible.

Selena rises and takes my hand. "I need to donate and I only had a few sips of wine at dinner."

I tug her close to me and we go to the onsite blood bank. I send Hailee and Selena in first. I try to ignore the O'Malleys. The rage bubbles so fiercely inside me, I have to hold myself back from taking out my pocketknife and slicing through each one of them.

"I need Hailee to stay here with everyone, under the Ivanov's protection," Liam says.

I glare at him. I'd never let anything happen to Hailee, but he's got a lot of nerve asking me to do anything for him.

"Why?"

Liam's face hardens. "My dad isn't calling the shots anymore. At least not in this situation. As soon as we give blood, we're leaving. I need to know Hailee is protected while I'm gone."

My stomach drops. I'm not sure if I'm hearing things correctly. "You're going to go against your father's orders?"

Liam sniffs hard. He glances around, and the O'Malley brothers step closer to him. "Alliance or no alliance, those bastards are paying for what they did to Adrian tonight. Promise me you'll watch over Hailee."

"You have my word," I agree then focus on Nora's brothers. "You're going to defy Darragh?"

Declan scratches his chin. "It's not an option. A hit on an Ivanov is a hit on an O'Malley. We don't just say it. We mean it. Darragh means well, but this supersedes the war. You take care of things here. When we finish, we'll let you know, but no more talk about breaking our alliance. From now on, we all work together."

I study the O'Malleys. For the first time, I see the rage on their faces. If they are willing to go against Darragh on this issue, then I have more respect for them than I ever could.

"Next," a woman calls out.

Liam takes off his jacket and rolls up his sleeve. Bogden comes out from behind the curtain. He was at the wedding but part of security, focusing on the inside reception so he could still partake in some of the wedding functions. It gives me a little comfort to know at least some Ivanov blood is being donated. I doubt they will let me after all I drank. Liam takes his place behind the curtain and I stare at it.

Killian speaks quietly and I turn toward him. "Darragh's going to be pissed. He may even try to send the other O'Malleys to stop us. It's best if you go back with the girls and state there's a long line."

I don't argue and do as directed. For hours we wait. I pace the hallways. From time to time, Bogden comes in and out to give us updates on the search for Dasha. The doctor finally comes appears and tells us they finished surgery. The bullet lodged in Adrian's back was safely removed.

My relief is short lived. Killian and Liam come back into the room. Darragh tries to rise and goes into another coughing fit, but we ignore him and move to the corner. Killian has an expression I've never seen before. I don't know what to make of it. Liam's eyes look a bit crazed.

"Is it done?" I ask.

"Partly. Anyone at the safe house, we took out. The man who drove the vehicle and the one who shot Adrian are on their way to our garage," Killian says.

I raise my eyebrows. "I thought—"

"They deserve worse than a quick death," Liam insists.

"They don't go to your garage. They go to ours," Boris seethes.

Liam doesn't hesitate. He takes out his phone and puts it to his ear. "Nolan. Change of plans. Take them to Boris's."

"Am I hearing this right?" Darragh barks behind us.

We spin.

"I gave you strict orders—"

"Your judgment is off," Liam says.

Darragh glares at him.

"It was the right thing to do," Maksim insists.

Darragh turns to him. He snarls, "I've told you numerous times to get your house in order. You let that woman run wild instead of taking care of her. Now, you support these bad decisions."

"You're the only one who seems to think that," I point out.

Darragh scowls then says to Liam, "They go to our garage. We still have time to salvage this and help balance things out."

"No. They go to our place. We take it from here," Boris insists.

Darragh's face turns red with anger. "Son, you're messing with the wrong person."

"No, Dad. We're making a call you should be making," Liam growls. "You want me to lead, well, let me lead."

"If you're making these types of decisions, you aren't ready," Darragh states.

Liam sarcastically laughs. He looks at the ceiling, shifts on his feet, then refocuses on Darragh. "Guess I'm going to have to figure it out then, aren't I? You're not leaving me much of a choice, now are you?"

Everything goes quiet. Darragh's face hardens further. Liam turns to Killian. "Time to go."

M C

Selena

Several Months Later

I WAKE UP. OBRECHT'S BODY IS CAGED OVER MINE. SWEAT coats my skin, and I'm breathing hard. He cocks his eyebrow. "You had your dream again."

My cheeks burn. "So embarrassing." I don't know why I keep having this threesome dream. It's the third night in a row.

He kisses me, and I taste my orgasm on his tongue. No doubt, he went down on me. He mumbles, "No way. Super-hot."

I kiss him back and lift my hips, but he rolls off me. "We need to get ready. You've got your session with Carla and then we need to get to Dmitri and Anna's."

I moan, "Noooo. Come back."

He holds his hand out. "Come on. If you're a good girl, I'll play some shower games with you."

I jump up on my knees and lean on my ankles, bow my head, and reply, "Yes, sir."

Obrecht laughs. "No time for that."

I whine some more and follow him into the shower. We have a quickie and get dressed. Obrecht takes me to my session with Carla.

Over the last few months, we've reduced my sessions to weekly. It was shortly after Adrian got out of the hospital. His ex-wife broke into his penthouse and almost killed Skylar. Carla suggested that after this session, we move to bimonthly ones.

Obrecht stays and makes phone calls at a table nearby while I talk with Carla. When my session is over, we go to Dmitri and Anna's.

She's looking for an assistant for her interior design business. Her reputation is growing quickly, but she also wants help since she's pregnant. I've not worked since I waitressed tables in Greece. I don't need to get a job, but I think it sounds fun. Plus, I'm ready to get out of the house more.

We get in their elevator. My palms turn clammy. "I'm nervous."

Obrecht glances at me. "Don't be. It's Anna. She wouldn't have asked you if you were interested if she didn't think you would be great."

All the insecurities I feel come rushing to the surface. "What if I mess up? I don't want to let her down. Or what if she hires me because she feels like she has to?"

Obrecht's lips twitch. He picks up my hand and kisses it. "She wouldn't. And you won't. Just talk to her and see what she's looking for then make a decision."

I take a deep breath. "Okay."

The elevator opens, and we go into the main room. Dmitri meets us near the entryway. "Come in. Anna's just freshening up. She got sick again."

"Is she okay?"

Dmitri nods. "Morning sickness. Everything is normal, the doctor said."

We talk for a while, and Anna comes out. "Sorry for making you wait."

"It's okay. Are you feeling better?"

She smiles. "Yep. It never lasts long. It just hits me at odd times. I hopefully won't get it for much longer." She points down the hall. "Do you want to go talk in my studio?"

"Sure." Obrecht squeezes my hand. I nervously follow Anna down the hall. We sit on the couch in her office.

She goes through the different things she needs help with. Some things I already know how to do and others I would need to learn.

Her eyes shine bright. "So? What do you think?"

"It sounds fun."

"I think it is."

"What about the things I haven't done before? I don't want to hurt your business," I admit.

She waves her hand in the air. "I'll train you, and you'll catch on in no time. What do you say? Want to work with me?"

"Are you offering me the job?"

She laughs. "Yes! Of course! It'll be great."

My insides do a happy dance. I realize how much I want this job. "Thank you. I'd love to work with you."

Anna claps. "Yay. Okay, so should we start Monday? That will give me some time to organize things. Dmitri is going to add another desk in here, too. You can do some stuff from home, but I'll also need you here, maybe half of the time."

"Sounds good."

She rises. "Great. Should we see what the guys are doing? I'm hungry. Do you want to stay for lunch?"

"I'm free if Obrecht is. I'm not sure of his schedule."

We walk out to the main room. Dmitri and Obrecht are in a heated conversation in Russian. Anna and I glance at each other. The color drains in her face, and I remember she learned Russian. She clears her throat.

They turn.

"Everything okay?" she asks and holds her belly.

Dmitri gets up. "All good. Taking care of some loose ends." He kisses her. "Are you feeling okay?"

She beams. "I'm great. Selena accepted the position."

Obrecht and Dmitri congratulate me. We stay for lunch then go home.

We go back to our building, and Obrecht leads me to his elevator.

"I need to go to my place and switch some things out. My clothes are all dirty. My plants are probably thirsty, too." I haven't been in my condo in several days.

He pushes the button for my elevator, we go to my unit, and I hand him the watering can. "Here. You water while I'm gathering my things."

"So bossy," he mutters and slaps my ass.

"Ha!" I go into my bedroom and stare at my closet, debating what to take upstairs.

He comes into the bedroom, pulls me to the bed, and positions me on his lap. The intense gaze he always pins on me makes me nervous. He says, "Why are we doing this?"

My chest tightens. "Doing what?"

"This. Moving your stuff back and forth all the time."

My stomach flips. My voice shakes. "Are you trying to break up with me?"

His eyes widen. "No. The opposite."

"I don't understand."

He tucks my hair behind my ear. His icy-blue eyes bore into mine. "I know you love your condo, but my penthouse is bigger."

I stay silent, not sure where he's going with this.

"Why don't we have movers come and move all your things into my place?"

My heart skips a beat. "Really?"

He nods and studies me. "Yes. You shouldn't have to move your things back and forth. We're together every night. Move in."

I want to yell yes but also want to be smart. "All right. Say I move in. What do I do with this place?"

"Sell it. Rent it. Whatever you want."

The thought of selling my condo when it saved me doesn't sit well. It was the only place in America I lived where I felt safe. I feel the same in the penthouse, but this place is all mine and has special meaning. "I don't think I can sell it."

"Okay. Don't. Rent it out," he says.

I tilt my head. "You're serious about me moving in?"

He strokes my cheek. "Would I ask you if I weren't?"

"Probably not."

"There's no probably about it. Tell me yes, and I'll schedule the movers."

I laugh. "I don't know if I need movers. Besides my clothes, plants, and some personal items, I don't have anything else I would want to take."

"However you want to do it, baby girl. As long as you have whatever you need and are in my bed every night, I don't care how we move your stuff," he says.

I reposition myself so I'm straddling him. "What about laundry soap?"

"I have laundry soap. I'll buy you as much as you want," he claims.

"Yeah, but yours doesn't smell like mine."

"We can switch the laundry soap." He sniffs near my collarbone. "Is that why you smell like lavender?"

"No. Well, maybe. My perfume and soap are, too," I admit.

He kisses the curve of my neck. "What else do you want?"

"Hmmm. What about dish soap?"

He arches his eyebrows. "You don't like my dish soap?"

I can't keep my face straight and laugh. "I'm teasing. The laundry soap is my only requirement."

"You drive a hard bargain. But there's a more important thing I need to tell you."

"What?"

He flips me onto my back. His body hangs over mine. He pushes the hair off my face and stares at me intently.

My heart races. "What's wrong?"

"Nothing's wrong. I want to tell you I love you."

My heart soars. I smile. I don't ever remember feeling so protected or happy. If I lost him, I don't know what I would do. He's become my life. "I love you, too."

He kisses me then says, "Pack a bag for the weekend."

"Are you trapping me in the penthouse?" I tease.

He grins. "No, baby girl. I'm taking you on a trip for your birthday."

Obrecht

"I've never been to Jamaica," Selena says as we pull up to the tarmac. Excitement lights up her face, which only makes me happier.

The car stops, and my phone rings. I glance at the screen. "I have to take this."

"No worries."

The past few weeks, Jack's been working harder to find Selena. Now that Declan tapped into his emails and text messages, everything he writes, we see. We also are recording his phone calls. His desperation to find Selena is growing, along with his stress over taking his company public. The Ivanovs and O'Malleys know I'm taking Selena on a trip for her birthday, so they would only call if something is important.

I answer in Russian, "Dmitri, what's going on?"

"We have another one."

My skin crawls. It's code that our intel discovered another thug Jack hired to find Selena. I do the best I can to stay calm. "Secured?"

"Yes."

Good. He's at the garage.

"How close?" I ask.

"He's better than the others, but we don't believe he found or reported anything of significance," Dmitri replies.

A small amount of relief fills me. However, it's short-lived. As soon as this guy doesn't get in contact with Jack, he'll find another. Each man he hires is more aggressive, smarter, and another level of dangerous compared to the last. "Let me know what you find out."

"Will do. Enjoy your weekend. Tell Selena happy birthday for me."

"Thanks." I hang up and force myself to smile. "Dmitri said to tell you, 'Happy birthday.'"

No matter how calm I stay, Selena always seems to know something is going on. It's as if she has a sixth sense. She tilts her head. "Is everything okay?"

I slide my hands onto her cheeks. "Yeah, baby girl. Everything is great." I kiss her, putting everything in it I have, trying to squash any worries she may have. I don't want her experiencing anything but fun this weekend.

"Are you going to kiss me like that the entire trip?" she teases.

"I'd give you another, but our plane awaits." I nod at the private jet sitting on the runway.

She beams. "I can't believe you're taking me somewhere for my birthday."

I push down more rage and disgust that she was married to such a vile man who didn't worship her every day as she should be. He should have made her birthday special every year but did nothing for her. I open the door, get out, then reach in to help her out.

She steps out and glances at Matvey, Vlad, and Bogden. Her lips twitch. "Are we under attack?"

I laugh. "What?"

"Three bodyguards? Is something going on?"

"Nope. Bogden's catching a ride for a weekend off." In all reality, we're probably safer from Jack in Jamaica than Chicago. But I'm not taking any chances and leaving her security team at home.

She turns back to them. "So you do get a life outside of your Ivanov duties?"

"Yes, Ms. Christian," Bogden replies.

Ms. Christian. My stomach flips in disdain. Every time I hear her called that, I feel ill.

"Please, call me Selena."

"Yes, ma'am," he replies.

I put my arm around her. "Time to board." I lead her to the plane. When we get inside, Carla, Adrian and Skylar, Sergey and Kora, and Maksim and Aspen are already in the aircraft.

"What are you doing here?" Selena asks and hugs them all.

"Helping you celebrate your birthday," Kora says.

"Couldn't let our girl turn thirty-one without an entourage," Skylar adds.

Selena beams and gives me a quick kiss. "Thank you!"

The air hostess approaches us. "Happy birthday! Can I get you a glass of champagne?"

"Sure. Thank you."

"Happy birthday!" Hailee sings as she and Liam enter the plane. Since Liam stepped up and took care of Adrian's shooters, we've come to a new understanding. I'm trying to put the past behind us and concentrate on the future. Hailee and Selena have also grown close, so it wouldn't be right for me not to ask her to go. Nora and Boris both wanted to come, but the baby is only a few months old, and they didn't want to leave her. Dmitri didn't want Anna to leave the country since she's pregnant, even though the doctors said she could travel for a few more months.

Selena's grin widens. "You're coming, too?"

Hailee hugs her. "Yep!"

"Did you wax your furry pussy, Hailee?" Sergey belts out.

Hailee's face grows red. "Again?"

"Don't talk about my woman's pussy," Liam growls.

"Easy. It's just a joke," Sergey says.

"Some people are into that," Carla says.

"That's true," I state, knowing some of the club members' fetishes I've heard about over the years.

"Not funny. No more talk about Hailee or her body parts unless you're discussing how hot she is," Liam claims. He hugs Selena. "Happy birthday."

"Thanks."

The plane is perfect for groups. Only four chairs face forward. The rest is seating designed for entertainment. We spend the plane ride playing cards, pulling up pictures on the resort, and drinking. The four-hour trip goes quickly. We land, and the party bus I hired to take us to the resort is waiting on the tarmac. After a quick check with immigration, Selena and I get on first and go to the back of the bus.

"Wow! This is gorgeous," Selena says, staring out the window at the turquoise water.

"Yes. It never gets old." Carla focuses on the landscape.

"You've been here before?"

Carla turns. "Yes. I'm a bit addicted. I visit about once a month."

"Really? Do you stay at the same resort?" Selena asks.

She softly laughs. "Nope. I don't have the money for where we're going. I stay in different places but always near the club."

Selena raises her eyebrows. "The club?"

"Yeah. I'm sure Obrecht would have visited, but he met you around the time it opened."

Selena leans into my ear. She lowers her voice. "Is that why we're here? Are you taking me to your club?"

I shake my head. "No. I found the resort."

"So you aren't going to take me?"

I study her. "I wasn't planning on it. Is that something you want to do?"

She shrugs. "I don't know. Maybe."

The club doesn't interest me. Now that I have Selena, I don't have the use for it. I can understand her curiosity though. "If you want to go, I'll take you."

"Okay. I'll think about it." She turns to Carla. "Do you go every day?"

Carla nods. "Yep. At night. I get as much use out of it as possible while I'm here."

Sergey turns in his seat. "Where do you go?"

"There's a club I'm a part of in Chicago. It has locations throughout the world. The newest is here in Jamaica."

Sergey smirks. "Are we talking about a dance club or a sex club?"

Carla doesn't miss a beat. She's probably more open about sex than anyone I know. "Sex."

Sergey eyes Kora. "Send me the link, will you?"

I shake my head. "You won't get in. You have to be tested. The membership requirements are strict. Unless you go with a guest, and members can't bring couples."

"They added a fast-test application. It's a twenty-four-hour turnaround," Carla informs us.

Sergey exchanges a glance with Kora. "Send me the link."

"What are you researching?" Adrian asks.

"You won't be interested," Sergey replies.

"Why?"

"It's a sex club."

Adrian rolls his eyes. "Yep. You're right."

"Oh. He discriminates," Carla teases.

He shrugs and tugs Skylar closer. "Not my thing. I've got my woman. Don't need anything else."

"What if she wanted to go?" Kora asks.

Skylar laughs. "I don't. I'm taking advantage of the luxury bungalow and this stud." She pats Adrian on the thigh.

He arrogantly smirks at Sergey. "See?"

"Whatever. Send me the link," Sergey repeats to Carla.

"Hailee! They have waxing services at the spa!" Aspen calls out.

She groans. "For real?"

"What did I say?" Liam barks.

"I didn't mention her...you know," Aspen teases.

The bus stops, and Liam jumps out of his seat. "I'm not joking. No more discussion on Hailee's body parts. No more talk about waxing, shaving, or anything remotely referencing this little joke you have going on. Got it?"

"Jeez. A bit uptight, don't you think?" Sergey replies.

Liam crosses his arms. "Do you want me to start talking about Kora?"

Sergey laughs. "Kora's my piranha. Try it." He winks at Kora.

"No more. I mean it," Liam warns again.

"Fine. Chill out and get off the bus," Maksim demands.

We all file out and check into the resort. Then we hop on golf carts and are taken to our bungalows.

"Holy..." Selena grabs my arm, staring at the overwater structure. Gorgeous blue water sparkles all around it. Each one has its own pool, deck with loungers, and butler. You can dive right off the deck into the ocean.

"Looks like the pictures," I happily state. I grab her hand. "Let's go inside and tour the place."

The butler is waiting for us when we step inside. He shows us the bedroom, living area, and kitchenette. Every room has a view of the water.

After he leaves, Selena throws her arms around me. It might be the happiest I've ever seen her. "This is amazing. Thank you!"

"I'm glad you like it. Happy birthday, baby girl. Do you want your present?" I ask.

Her eyes widen. "Isn't this my present?"

"This is your birthday trip. It's not your present."

"No?"

"Nope. Hold on." I dig into my bag and pull out a white square jewelry box with a sea-green bow. I hand it to her.

"My birthday isn't until tomorrow."

"Do you want to wait?"

She bites on her lip, staring at it.

I laugh. "Are you going to open it? Or wait?"

"It's beautiful." She runs her fingers over the ribbon.

"The gift is inside, my dorogaya," I tease. She's like a child at Christmas, staring at presents under the tree.

She slowly pulls the bow apart. She lifts the lid and picks up the assortment of Greek bangle bracelets while gaping at them. Each one is a different metal. One has her birthstone— a tourmaline gem. It's a mix of green and brown and reminds me of her eyes. The other bracelets have intricate designs with flowers, hearts, and stars. She traces her finger over each one then glances at me. Her eyes glisten. "These are beautiful."

"I'm glad you like them."

"I love them." She blinks, and a tear falls.

I slide my hand on her cheek and wipe the tear with my thumb. "Why are you crying?"

"These are Greek?"

"Yes. I had them flown in from a jeweler I contacted," I admit.

"They are from Gallanis," she states.

"Yes."

"How did you know?" she asks.

"Know what?"

Her lips tremble. She traces the gemstone. "My great-great-grandfather started Gallanis. He sold it during World War II. My mother had these types of bracelets. I used to get in trouble when I was little. I would wear them, and she would reprimand me for going into her jewelry box. I've always wanted a set." She rises on her tippy-toes and kisses me. "Thank you."

"You're welcome. I have something else for you to go with the bracelets," I tell her.

"You're overwhelming me," she blurts out.

I chuckle. "It's more for me." I release her, dig into my bag, and pull out another package.

She slides her wrist through the bracelets and takes the package. It's wrapped the same but is larger than the jewelry box. She opens it and pulls out a white string bikini and softly laughs.

"Told you it was for me," I state.

"Should I put it on?"

"Yep."

Amusement fills her face. "Are you wearing a speedo?"

"Nope."

"Not fair then, is it?"

"Wouldn't want the other guys jealous," I claim.

She laughs.

I playfully spank her ass. "Get changed. I'm ready to rub sunscreen all over you."

Selena

"OH GOD!" ADRENALINE BURSTS THROUGH ALL MY CELLS.

"I'm not God, baby girl," Obrecht booms.

I sit up in bed, trembling. The sun peeks through the windows. Sparkling water surrounds us.

His head's between my legs. He wipes his mouth on his forearm. The smirk on his face is sexy as always. "You had your dream again."

Heat fills my cheeks. No matter how many times I have the dream, it always embarrasses me. It also comes directly after I dream I'm back in the cage with Jack heckling me.

Obrecht lunges over me. "Happy birthday, my dorogaya." He kisses me, parting my lips with his tongue and hungrily rolling it in my mouth, as if he can consume every particle of my existence.

I return his kiss with a matched fervor. I'll never get enough of him. No matter how much time passes, there's nothing that could reduce my craving for him. Within seconds, he's inside me. He grumbles Russian in my ear. Our sweat merges, and I cling to him.

"I love you so much," I whisper.

He puts his face in front of mine. "I love you, too, baby girl."

I kiss him and hold him tighter as endorphins crash through my body. In my aftermath, I move my face out of the curve of his neck. "Obrecht?"

He strokes my hair. His icy-blue eyes drill into me. "Hmm?"

"Sometimes, I wonder if this is all a dream."

The corners of his mouth curve. He shakes his head. "It's not."

"I don't want it to end," I admit.

He sits up and pulls me onto his lap. "Do you mean vacation or us?"

"Us."

He drags his finger over my lips. "There's no end to us, my dorogaya."

I don't say anything. There's no reason to think anything will happen to us besides the reoccurring nightmare I have about the cage. But I can't shake the feeling.

Obrecht tilts his head. In a commanding voice, he says, "Tell me to kneel."

I laugh. "What?"

"It's your birthday. Tell me to go somewhere and kneel."

"I'm a bit confused here. Aren't I the one that kneels?"

"Humor me. Tell me to kneel and where then wait a few minutes before you come out," he directs.

"Why?"

"Do I need to spank you on your birthday for not obeying?" he teases.

I turn my body and throw my ass in the air.

He chuckles. "Forgot you like it. If you want your birthday spankings, do what I ask."

Intrigued, I say in a stern voice, "Obrecht, kneel." I crack up laughing. I put my hand over my face. "I can't. It's not right."

He raises his eyebrows. "Try again. Don't forget where."

I take a deep breath. "Fine. Kneel in the sitting room in front of the window. And make sure you bow your head. Hands folded on your lap."

"Ooh. Sassy girl. Yes, ma'am."

"You'll call me madam."

He stifles a laugh. "Yes, madam."

I admire the back of his body as he leaves the room. I slide into the robe provided by the resort. Obrecht kneeling in a submissive position isn't anything I ever thought I'd see. I'm not sure why he's even doing this. When a few minutes pass, I saunter out to the main area.

Obrecht is facing the window. His muscular ass is sitting on his ankles. His hands are in front of his body, and his head bowed.

I stand in front of him, not sure what to do next. Anything I think of saying seems odd. I finally say, "You may look up."

He obeys and intently gazes at me. He reaches around my waist and pulls me closer. "The only thing I've ever been sure about is you. There is no end to us. No matter what, this is only our beginning. I submit my heart and soul to you, not just now but forever. Will you marry me?" He opens his hand and holds up the most breathtaking ring I've ever seen. A brilliant round diamond glistens on platinum. Metal twists together with more diamonds set where the strands meet.

I gape between him and the ring. Tears stream down my face. My voice shakes. "You want to marry me?"

"More than anything."

I can't answer. Too many emotions flood me. He's already given me more than I could ever imagine. I nod through my blurry vision.

"Is that a yes?" he asks.

I swallow hard. "Yes."

He slides the ring on my finger. I don't even look at it. I can't. I dip down and press my lips to his, trying to show him how much I love him. He stole my heart from the first day we met. Officially being his is more than I could ever ask for.

I pull back. "I should let you get off the floor."

He wiggles his eyebrows. "You don't want me to become your sub?"

I laugh. "Is that even possible?"

"Probably not." He kisses me one last time and rises then tugs me into his arms. "You just made me the happiest man on earth, baby girl."

So much joy fills me. I don't ever remember feeling so utterly happy. But I also feel cherished. Every day, that's how Obrecht makes me feel. I chirp, "I guess we'll be the annoying, super-happy couple all day, then."

He laughs. "Speaking of which, we need to meet everyone for your birthday brunch."

"Oh?"

"Come on. It's shower time. I've got a full day planned."

"You do?"

He grins. "Yeah. It's your birthday."

We spend the day with our friends. They shower me with gifts. We explore the bay on wave runners, utilize the Hobie Cat sailboats, and snorkel in front of our bungalows.

After a late-afternoon nap, we gather with our friends and go to dinner. We order, and I rise. "I need to use the restroom."

Carla stands. "Me, too. I'll go with you."

Obrecht puts his napkin on the table. "I'll show you where it is."

"We can find it," Carla says.

"Yep. I know. Still coming."

I smile. I love how protective he is of me.

My future husband. I'm going to be Mrs. Obrecht Ivanov.

More happy flutters erupt in my stomach. It hasn't just been the best birthday ever. It's been the best day of my life.

Carla and I go into the restroom and are washing our hands when I freeze.

A woman with blue hair, a beautiful biracial complexion, and a face exactly like in my dream steps next to me. Her floral scent is the same, too.

"Giuliana! I didn't know you were in Jamaica," Carla blurts out.

Her name is Giuliana.

My heart beats faster. Heat scorches my cheeks. I've had dreams come to fruition in the past, but meeting the woman in my naughty dream has me speechless.

The woman's face lights up. My heart hammers harder against my chest cavity when she speaks. I've heard her voice too many times to count while I'm sleeping, and it's the same in real life. "I've been here a week."

"Are you going to the club tonight? I'll be there," Carla says.

Giuliana nods. She glances at me with approval. "That's the plan."

"Giuliana, this is my friend, Selena. She's Obrecht Ivanov's fiancée." Carla motions to me.

Giuliana's expression changes, and I'm not sure how to interpret it. "It's nice to meet you. Umm... are you and Obrecht here on your own or did umm..."

"He's here," Carla says.

Giuliana releases a breath and washes her hands. "Is he going to the club tonight?"

Who is he?

Carla turns the water off and tears off a towel. "I don't know, but he was there last night."

Giuliana dries her hands and smiles. "It was nice meeting you, Selena. I'll look for you tonight, Carla."

"Okay. See you later, then," Carla replies.

Giuliana leaves, and I stare at the door.

"You okay?" Carla asks.

I turn back to her. She has a concerned expression on her face, and my stomach flips again. "Why didn't you tell me you knew a girl that fit the description of my dream?"

Carla tilts her head. A line forms between her eyes. "She lives in Atlanta. I didn't think you'd ever meet her. Plus, if I told you that, would you have felt comfortable talking to me about it?"

I consider her question. No matter how much I want to tell her she's wrong, she isn't. "No, I wouldn't have discussed it with you."

"Okay. Now that you know she exists, what do you want to happen?"

"What do you mean?"

Carla's face stays neutral. "If you want to make it happen, now's your chance. Obrecht knows her. She's a service sub. I'm pretty sure he'd be open to whatever you want."

Jealousy flares in my belly. "Has he been with her?"

"I don't believe so, but you'll have to ask him."

"Who was she referring to? The man she asked about."

"Obrecht's cousin."

My pulse creeps up. "Which cousin?"

"Bogden."

Relief fills me that it isn't Sergey or Maksim.

Carla puts on fresh lip gloss. She finishes and says, "I think you need to speak to Obrecht. Tell him what you want and don't worry about it. He's going to be your husband. If there's one person you should be able to talk honestly to, it should be him."

"What if I don't know what I want?" I ask. But deep down, I already know.

Carla smirks. "I'm pretty sure you know what you want. Don't do anything you'll regret, whether it's doing it or not." She pats my shoulder and passes me.

I follow her. When I step outside, Obrecht is leaning against the wall and texting someone. He looks up and tugs me into him. "There's the birthday girl." He studies me, and my cheeks flush hotter.

He drags his finger over my cheekbone. "What's going on, baby girl?"

I take a deep breath. "You saw her, didn't you?"

His expression doesn't change. "Yeah."

"Why didn't you tell me you knew someone who fit her description?" I ask.

He slowly inhales then releases it. "You were already embarrassed by it, and I didn't want to add to it. And I didn't want you not feeling safe talking to me about it."

His explanation makes sense. In some ways, he knows me better than I know myself at times. I can't fault him for his decision. It makes me love him more that he once again thought about how I would feel.

"Are you mad at me?" he asks.

"No. Umm..." I glance behind us then turn back to him. "Did you ever sleep with her?"

"No. I've never done anything with her."

"You haven't?"

"No."

"Why? She's beautiful and seems nice."

He shrugs. "She is, but it wasn't my thing."

"What do you mean?"

Obrecht brushes a lock of hair off my forehead. "Remember I said we all have our limits?"

"Yes."

"I'm not into pain during sex."

Confusion fills me. "I'm lost. Carla said she's a service sub."

"Yes. She likes to play that role and then move into pain before her aftercare. I can't fulfill that need for her, so I stayed away. Some tops have a session with her and then send her to a different top, but I usually feel too responsible for my bottoms. I would have felt too guilty to send her off to someone else to take care of her after," he admits.

"And Bogden is into pain?" I ask.

Surprise fills his face. "Why did you bring up Bogden?"

"She asked about him. She seemed almost desperate to see him."

Obrecht pauses then says, "They've gotten close over the years. He knows how to give her what she needs."

"Even after she is a service sub with someone else?" I ask.

"Yes." His piercing gaze makes me shift nervously on my feet. He hesitates then says, "Selena, is this something you want to do?"

My cheeks once again scorch, as if on fire. I struggle not to avoid him, but I stay fixated on his eyes. "I-I'm not unhappy with anything we have. I love you and us."

"I know that, baby girl."

"I don't understand why I keep dreaming about it. Nothing has changed. I'm still a total taker and don't want to do anything to her. And if you weren't there, I wouldn't want it," I blurt out.

"But you want it?"

Blood pounds between my ears. I contemplate lying due to my embarrassment, but I stop myself. Obrecht never lies to me. He deserves my honesty. "I think I'm curious. And that damn dream won't go away."

His lips twitch. "Your dream is pretty hot, baby girl."

My internal struggle to say no to this weakens. "Yeah, but it isn't real. And I'm super jealous. Like if you told me you did anything with her, my skin would be crawling right now. But if we're together... I don't know. It seems like it wouldn't bug me if it were like my dream where you were only focused on me."

He steps closer and holds my cheeks in his hands. All I see on his face is love. There's no judgment. He's not trying to convince me. The only thing I see is my future husband trying to help me. "The only woman in the entire world I'm focused on is you. It won't ever change. If you want this, or need this, tell me. I've had my share of everything. So if you want to experience this tonight, tell me. I'll make it happen."

My chest tightens, and my heart beats harder. "I want *you*."

"That isn't the question. I already know that. Answer me, Selena," he orders in a stern voice.

I swallow the lump in my throat. "What if I say yes, then don't want to go through with it once it starts?"

"You use your safe word and it stops. At any time, you say faucet, and it ends. There's nothing different than before. You still hold the cards," he claims.

A group of voices interrupts us. Obrecht moves me closer to the wall. They pass us and go into the restroom.

"Tell me what you want, baby girl. Say yes, and I'll set it up. Say no, and we'll still have a fun night." His eyes never leave mine. There's so much love and care for me in them. That's the thing with Obrecht. It's always all about me where I'm concerned.

His thumb grazes my jawline. "I need you to be honest with me right now. Yes or no?"

"Yes," I whisper.

His lips crash onto mine. He grips my head and circles his tongue in my mouth until my knees go weak. "For the record, I didn't kiss you since you said yes. I kissed you because you were honest with me, and I know it was hard for you." He kisses my forehead and spins me. "Let's go eat dinner."

I spend the rest of the meal attempting to engage in conversation, but I'm full of nervous energy. Obrecht is on his phone texting a few times, but other than that, he has his arm around me, and nothing is different. It's like he's unfazed by it all.

Everyone splits up after dinner. I barely hear where anyone is going, but Obrecht and I end up back in our bungalow.

I ask, "Are we going to the club?"

"No." The doorbell rings. My stomach flips, and Obrecht puts his fingers to my lips. "Don't forget, you're in control. If you want to stop, use your safe word. Now go into the bedroom and wait on the bed for me."

I do as he says. I twist my fingers in my lap, waiting. It feels like forever passes until Obrecht comes in. I jump off the bed.

He kisses me. "Did you change your mind?"

"No."

"Okay, baby girl. Pull your dress to your hips and bend over the bed."

I don't know why he's telling me to do this. It wasn't in my dream, but I do as he says. The sound of a drawer sliding open hits my ears. A moment later, his hands are sliding my panties off. Lube hits my ass, and his finger slips past the hard ridge. He works more fingers inside me and leans over my back. His hot breath hits my ear. "If we're doing this, you're getting everything, my dorogaya."

In my dream, we aren't having anal sex. But I trust he knows what's best for me.

His fingers come out, but he stays leaned over me. His lips hit my neck, and he kisses me as something goes back inside me.

I'm so relaxed, I hardly gasp. Obrecht and I have done every-thing together. I've learned he knows my body like it's his.

"Okay, baby girl. Stand up." He goes into the bathroom, and I hear water running. He returns and slides my panties up my body then pulls my dress over them.

I gaze up at him.

He holds my chin. "Don't forget you're always mine. No matter what, it's you and me."

"We don't have to do this is if—"

He covers my lips with his fingers. "I'm okay with this situation. But no other guys. And service sub only. I don't want you touching anyone else. She's here to add to your pleasure for your birthday, and that's it. I know she's safe, so that's why I agreed to this. You're going to enjoy it. I'm going to enjoy it. Then she's leaving. As soon as we step out there, I'm in charge."

"You aren't now?" I smirk.

"I'll give you the birthday spankings I owe you, later." He winks then pecks me on the lips. "Are you ready?"

"Yes."

"Good. Go kneel next to Giuliana."

"She's been kneeling this entire time?"

"Yes."

"We aren't doing it here?"

"No. This is our room. No one comes in here. Now don't get sassy since it's your birthday. Go," he orders.

I smile and obey. Fresh nerves hit me when I step into the other room. The lights are dim. Giuliana is kneeling in nothing but a black bra and underwear. Her head is bowed and she sits in a perfect sub position. The pink dress she wore is folded on the table. Matching stilettos are under it.

I kneel next to her. Several moments pass. The longer I kneel next to her, smelling her floral scent, the more nervous I become.

Obrecht finally stands in front of us. He crouches down. "Look at me."

We both raise our heads. He addresses Giuliana. "Look at my fiancée."

She turns toward me. I continue focusing on Obrecht. He says, "She's sexy as hell, isn't she?"

"Yes," she breathes.

"What did you think when you met my soon-to-be wife in the bathroom?" he asks.

"I thought she was beautiful. When I heard you were engaged, I imagined you controlling her," she says.

"And why did you imagine that?"

"I-I've always wanted you to control me, but you never have," she admits.

My jealousy high-fives my ego. I have Obrecht. She wants him but can't have him. It adds something even more taboo and exciting to what we're about to do.

"And why haven't I?" he asks.

"You can't give me what I need."

"That's right. What else did you think when you saw my dorogaya?"

She firmly says, "I wondered if you would ever allow me to service her."

My heart races faster.

"And what would you do if I permit you?" he asks.

"Whatever you allow me, sir."

My lower body pulses. I struggle not to look at her. Obrecht finally holds my chin and stares at me. "What are your hard limits, baby girl? Tell Giuliana."

I open my mouth to speak but stop. "You mean for her?"

"Yes."

I don't need to say the other things. Obrecht is in charge of those. "No kissing me above my belly button. She can't touch you, except when you're in me, and she's also touching me."

"What else?"

"That's it, sir."

"You don't call me sir. She calls me sir. I'm Obrecht to you," he says.

"Yes, Obrecht."

He leans forward and pecks me on the lips. "Good girl." He takes my hand and helps me stand. "Rise, Giuliana."

She obeys.

He steps back. "Take Selena's dress off."

She steps behind me, moves my hair to the side, then unzips my dress. My chest rises and falls faster as I stare at Obrecht's icy-blue flames. The dress hits the floor.

"Remove her bra," he commands.

She unlatches my clasps. Her hands slowly push the straps down my arms. Tingles break out across my body.

Obrecht demands, "Now her panties."

She does the same, but she kisses my spine where my belly button would be as she releases them.

"What do you think of my dorogaya's ass?" he asks her.

"It's perfect."

"Yes. It is. Step in front of her."

Giuliana stands in front of me, and I can no longer avoid her. Her eyes are bright blue; so much, I wonder if she wears colored contacts. Her electric blue hair hangs past her breasts. She licks her plump lips, and my body pulses again.

It's just like my dream but real. I swallow hard as she stares at every part of my body as if she's desperate to have me.

"She has beautiful breasts, doesn't she?" Obrecht moves behind me and slides his hands on my ass. He kisses the curve of my neck, and I shudder.

Giuliana steps closer. "Yes. They're perfect. Are they real?"

"Yes. Everything about my baby girl is real."

I turn to look at him, and he slides his tongue in my mouth. His arm glides around my waist, and he slips his finger through my wet heat, circling my clit slowly. He withdraws from the kiss. "Say happy birthday to my future wife."

"Happy birthday," Giuliana says.

"Do you want to show Giuliana how well you crawl to me?"

"Please," I respond, desperate to do something normal to balance my nervous flutters.

He crosses the room and sits in the chair. He pats his thigh. I drop to my knees and crawl with my ass in the air, feeling the girth of the plug with every inch I take toward him. When I get to Obrecht, I kneel between his legs.

He leans forward, fists my hair, and aggressively kisses me. "You get sexier, baby girl. You did such a good job, I'm going to allow you to sit on my cock now."

"Thank you."

He pats his thigh again, and I rise. "Undress me."

I unbutton his shirt then slide it over him. I release his pants, and he lifts his hips. When he's naked, he commands, "Spin."

I turn.

He straddles me on him so I'm facing away from him. The tip of his erection slips an inch inside me. He holds me so I can't go any farther then leans into my ear. "Look at Giuliana."

I gaze in her direction. Her chest is rising and falling faster. Her lips are trembling.

"Tell her to crawl over to us," he mumbles and sucks on my lobe.

"Crawl to us, Giuliana," I squeak out.

Obrecht softly chuckles. As we watch Giuliana come toward us with her ass in the air, he pushes me over him and murmurs, "Since it's your birthday, you get to come as much as you want tonight."

"Oh God," I cry out, his length and girth filling and stretching me more than ever before. I briefly forgot about the plug. It has to be bigger than anything we've used before. He might just split me in two.

"I'm not God, baby girl. Don't call for him," Obrecht growls in my ear then grips my hips and starts moving me.

"Obrecht," I whimper.

"We're just starting." He turns my head and looks me in the eye. "Do you want to tell her what to do? Or should I?"

"You. Please!"

Satisfaction fills his face. He keeps looking at me. "Giuliana, what do you think of my future wife's pussy?" He gives me tiny kisses, pulling back every time I try to extend them and assessing me.

"It's perfect. She's perfect," Giuliana replies.

"Do you want a taste?" he asks and licks my tongue, keeping the speed I'm riding him slowly, teasing my walls with his hard shaft.

"Please, sir."

"Oh...oh...f... Obrecht!" I cry out the moment her warm tongue swipes me.

A deep rumble fills his chest. His jaw clenches and dick pulses in me just like in my dream. He never looks at Giuliana, only me. He commands, "Suck her clit." His demands only turn me on more. He's so powerful and confident. He always knows what to do, but he's mine. She wants him, yet she's only here because I allowed her to be. She only

413

gets a taste of him with me on him, and it sends me on a power trip I didn't know I had in me.

Giuliana latches on to me so hard, I instantly come.

Sweat pops out on my skin. A soft hum fills the air, barely audible through Giuliana's moans. The plug thrusts up in my ass as Obrecht's cock slides in the opposite direction.

It's a perfect storm of sensory overload. Adrenaline, heat, and dizziness consume me. Obrecht's finger plays with my breasts. His other hand stays on my hip, controlling the speed I'm riding him, stopping me from going as fast as my body is begging me to.

I put my hands on the side of his thighs, digging my nails into them.

"Grip her hair. You can touch her like that," he allows.

Sweet relief fills me. I do as he instructs, placing both palms on her head. She moans louder and returns to licking me. When Obrecht's cock comes out of my body, she licks that, too, then nibbles on my clit.

"Oh!" I cry out.

"Feel good?" Obrecht's tongue slides across my jaw.

I can't answer. Every part of my body spasms in delight. I've never felt so deliciously full or assaulted with so many orgasms. It's a Ferris wheel of orgasms that never stops. When I get to the top, I go down, only to go right back up.

Obrecht groans and he thrusts faster into me. "Look at me!" he barks when I close my eyes.

"I'm so...oh... I..."

"I love you, baby girl. Understand?"

"Yes. I lo... I... Obrecht!"

"Eat her faster," Obrecht demands, and she intensifies everything.

"Squeeze his balls!" I yell out.

"Fucking love you, baby girl," he growls then shouts out in Russian while continuing to stare at me. His erection pumps hard in me, stretching me farther, hitting me somewhere so deep inside me, I ejaculate my juice all over them. I collapse against him, no longer able to hold myself up.

The thrusting in my ass and humming sound stops. He tightens his arms around me. He lifts his face to mine and kisses me. Our kiss is broken momentarily for him to mumble, "Giuliana, clean us up."

I don't look at her. I can't. All I can do is stare into Obrecht's eyes as he watches me intently then continues to devour my mouth.

Giuliana begins licking us clean, and I lose the ability to kiss him. It's unlike anything I've ever felt. I'm so sensitive everywhere, and it's like soothing a sore muscle with a massage.

"Feel good, my angel?"

My raspy voice is barely audible. "So good."

Several minutes pass. Obrecht continues to kiss me, holding my head firmly. He finally says, "That's enough, Giuliana. Thank you." He releases my head and says, "Tell Giuliana, thank you."

I look at her. She's kneeling between our legs with her head bowed. Her body is shaking slightly.

"Thank you, Giuliana."

"Look at me, Giuliana," Obrecht says.

She looks up, smiling.

"Did you enjoy that?" he asks.

"Yes, sir. Very much."

"Would you like to see Bogden now?"

Her eyes glisten, and she blinks hard. "He's here?"

"Yes. Would you like to spend the rest of the night with him?"

"Yes, sir. Please," she says in a desperate voice.

"Very well. Get dressed. The bathroom is through that door if you wish to freshen up. He's waiting outside for you."

She rises, picks up her clothes, and goes into the bathroom.

"Stand and bend over," he commands.

I obey, and he pulls the plug out of my ass and sets it on a towel. It's the third item I got from the sex store that we still hadn't used. I straddle him but suddenly feel shy. "Hi."

"Hi." Like always, he studies me, assessing me in ways I don't even understand. "You okay?"

I nod.

"Intense, wasn't it?" he asks.

"Yes."

"But good?"

I agree again. "Yes. Did you like it?"

His lips twitch. "Yeah. I was with you."

Giuliana comes out of the bathroom. "Happy birthday, Selena."

I turn. "Thank you. It has been."

"Have a great night." She leaves.

Obrecht stands with me wrapped around him. He locks the door and takes me into the bedroom then starts the jacuzzi. When it's full, we get in the tub.

I lie against him and glance up. "I told you I was a taker."

He breaks out laughing so hard, his eyes tear up. "No plans to become a giver?"

"I'll stick to only being a giver with you."

"I'm good with that." He kisses my head. "Did you have a good birthday?"

I turn so I'm lying on top of him. "I had the best birthday ever. Thank you." My engagement ring hits the light. "When can we get married?"

His face lights up. I once again feel the ego trip that this man is mine. This man who does anything he can to give me what I want or need. This man who's fully devoted to me and only me. He claims, "As soon as you want."

"I'd say tomorrow, but your mom would kill us if she weren't here," I reply.

He groans. "Plus, you'd miss the barrage of bridal magazines."

I trace the snake tattoo on his neck. "Are you serious though? We can get married sooner rather than later?"

"Yeah, baby girl. Name the date and place, and I'll make it happen."

Obrecht

Several Months Later

"Is this too much?" Selena bites her lip. She glances at the quote and pulls on her hair.

"Baby girl, we have more money between us than we'll ever spend. Whatever you want, we'll do," I reply.

She sets the papers down and taps her fingers on the table. Lines form on her forehead. She opens her mouth then closes it.

I lean closer to her. "Want to tell me what's causing you this much stress?"

She takes a moment to gather her thoughts. "The day you proposed to me, I would have married you then, with no one around. Now we have a hundred people invited. To get the venues we wanted, we had to set our date a few months from now. I wanted to be married by now, and it just seems to get more complicated."

I rise, take her hand and pull her up, and go to the couch. I sit and tug her onto my lap. "Do you want to cancel everything?"

"What?"

"If this isn't what you want, we'll cancel it all. We can elope anywhere in the world. Just say the word, and we'll go today," I tell her.

She shakes her head. "I want your family there."

"Do you want to change the venue? We can find somewhere else."

"We already have deposits down."

"So what? I'll marry you any day, anywhere. If this isn't what you want, we need to change it."

She releases an anxious breath. Stress is all over her face. Her distress is avoidable, but she needs to be honest with me. "Selena, is what we're planning what you want?"

Tears fill her eyes.

Blood pounds between my ears. The last thing on earth I want is her not having the day she wants, especially after hearing how she married Jack in a room full of strangers and had no control over anything. I tighten my arms around her. "What's going on?"

She squeezes her eyes shut. Her chest shakes. "The night-mares keep getting worse. Whenever someone calls me Ms. Christian or I see it on the wedding quotes, I feel like I can't breathe. I want what we're planning, but it seems so far away."

"We've got two months, my dorogaya. It'll go fast," I try to reassure her.

"I should have changed my name after I divorced, but every-thing was overwhelming. There was so much paperwork. I still don't understand it all. But every time someone calls me Ms. Christian, I want to scream, "'I'm Obrecht's, not Jack's,'" she admits and wipes her face.

I kiss her head and cradle her close to my chest. "Who's the most important person you want at the wedding?"

She looks up. There's no hesitation. "Your mom."

Since they met, my mom and Selena are together a lot. They formed a bond right away. In some ways, my mom is like a second mother to Selena. I know how much it hurts her that her family cut her off. I secretly reached out to them, but they still want nothing to do with her even though Jack is out of the picture. Her father and brothers claim once you're out, you're out. I give her a quick kiss then pull my phone out. I dial my mother and put it on speaker.

"Who are you calling?" Selena asks.

"My mom."

"Why?"

"You'll see."

It rings twice. My mother chirps, "Good morning, Obrecht."

"Good morning. You're on speaker with Selena and me," I disclose.

"Hi, Selena."

"Hi, Svetlana."

I stroke Selena's hair. "Mom, do you know where we can get a wedding dress today?"

Selena scrunches her face in confusion.

"What's wrong with Selena's dress?" my mother asks.

"It's not ready. We need one today. And can you and Stefano clear your schedules tomorrow?" I ask.

"Obrecht, are you eloping?" my mother asks.

Selena gapes at me.

"Yep. We're still going to have the wedding we're planning, but we're getting married tomorrow."

"Where?" my mother asks.

Selena sits up straighter. She stares at me in question.

I admit, "I'm not sure yet. I need to figure it out. Can you take Selena to get a wedding dress today?"

"Of course. Selena, what time do you want to go?"

Selena recovers. She clears her throat. "Umm... I can be ready in an hour. Does that work?"

Excitement fills my mother's voice. "Sure."

"Thanks, Mom. I'll have my driver pick you up and then swing by and get Selena," I tell her.

"Okay. See you soon."

"Bye," Selena replies, and I hang up. She tilts her head. "We're going to get married twice?"

I nod. "Yep. I don't have a problem professing my lifelong devotion to you twice, do you?"

She smiles. "No."

"Good. Problem solved. Tomorrow you'll be Mrs. Ivanov. We'll still have everything we've planned and celebrate with the people we love."

She wraps her arms around my shoulders. Relief, love, and happiness swirl in her expression. "Did I tell you how much I love you?"

I put my hand to my ear. "You can tell me again."

She laughs. Her face turns serious. "I love you. More than I ever thought possible."

"That's good, baby girl. Now, do you want somewhere cold or tropical?"

She shakes her head. "I don't care. I just want to be yours."

I tuck a lock of her hair behind her ear. "You are mine. You've been mine since I laid eyes on you. And I'm yours."

She kisses me. It's sweet and loving and everything I craved for so long but didn't know I needed. She's my everything. When she ends the kiss, she says, "Do you want your brother there?"

I don't need to think about it. "Yeah. I'll ask him and Skylar to come. But no one else. We have our other day for everyone else."

She strokes the side of my head. "Good. That feels right to me."

I pat her ass. "You better get ready. Enjoy your day dress shopping. I think you're making my mom's dreams come true, picking out two dresses."

She laughs. "Your mom has good taste."

"She should. She's studied those magazines for years."

Selena playfully slaps my shoulder. Whenever I make comments about my mom and her wedding obsession, Selena sticks up for her. "Hey now!"

I chuckle. "Go get ready. I have planning to do."

She pecks me on the lips again. My girl is happy once again. Her joy is my mission. I hate these nightmares she has, and I cringe every time I hear or see Ms. Christian, too. She bounces off my lap and goes into our bedroom.

I call Adrian and invite him and Skylar and ask him to clear their schedules. I turn on my laptop and start researching where we can get married tomorrow. Vegas is an obvious choice, but I also research other places. Selena has a green card, but I'm unsure how weddings out of the country work.

Best if I limit it to the United States.

I need no residency or waiting period requirement.

Before Selena is done getting ready, I've applied for our marriage license, arranged for a private jet, and booked rooms at a resort for our party. I text my mom and Adrian.

Me: *Can you clear several days from your schedules?*

Adrian: *Sure. How long?*

Me: *It depends on how long you want to stay.*

Mom: *Now that Stefano retired, we can do anything.*

Adrian: *Where are we going?*

Me: *Hawaii.*

Adrian: *Nice! I'm ready for the sun. Who else is coming?*

Me: *Just the six of us. Don't tell anyone else.*

Adrian: *Wow. Okay, Hawaii it is.*

Mom: *Good choice. Oh, the driver's here. I'm so excited!*

I send them the travel plans.

Me: *If you need to come back earlier, I can arrange the plane.*

Adrian: *Skylar and I are down for more time in the sun.*

Mom: *Us, too.*

I take care of a few more logistical issues and shut my laptop.

Selena comes out of the room. She's wearing leggings, an oversized green sweater, and boots.

"You look hot," I tell her and steal a quick kiss.

She bats her eyes. "Glad you approve, future hubby."

I smirk. "Get a dress for the tropics."

She raises her eyebrows. "Where are we going?"

"Hawaii."

She gapes. "Really?"

"Yep. All set. We just need to show up."

She throws her arms around me. "You're the best! Thank you!"

The doorbell rings, signaling my mom is coming up. We meet her in the corridor. Her face is as bright as Selena's. I chuckle inside, thinking about my mom and how much she loves anything to do with a wedding. I hug her.

"Obrecht, what are you wearing?" she asks.

With all the planning, I forgot about my wedding attire. I turn to Selena. "What do you want me to wear?"

She beams. "Ohh. Something beachy!"

"Do you want us to handle it?" my mom asks.

"Please. Have at it. As long as we're married by sunset tomorrow night, I don't care what I wear." It's the truth. I'm secretly relieved we're doing this. Every day that goes by where Selena isn't my wife nags at me. I want her to have everything she wants and deserves, so I went along with all the other wedding plans. This lets us have our cake and eat it, too. "Plane leaves after dinner tonight, baby girl. Be back by five, okay?"

She rises on her tippy-toes and kisses me. "Got it!"

They leave, and I call Liam. The interference we're running on Jack finding out anything about Selena is complicated. He's got a lot of money. In some ways, I'm surprised he hasn't found her yet. Chicago is a big city but also small. We're cautious, but we aren't exactly hiding out. I'm trying to keep Selena living an everyday life not in fear but still protect her. However, it's getting harder.

Jack's company goes public in six weeks. The itch to finish him off makes my skin crawl. My dorogaya wakes up from night terrors almost daily and sometimes several times the same night. I don't think changing her name is the only thing that will stop them. Until he takes his last breath, I don't believe she'll have the peace she deserves. Since he's still looking for her, he's sending a clear signal he won't stop until he finds her, either. A few nights ago, the O'Malleys picked up another one of the men Jack hired to search for Selena.

"Obrecht," Liam answers.

"Did you find out anything?" I ask.

"Nothing new. Same as the others." The others were all instructed to pick Selena up and take her to Jack's.

I clench and unclench my fist. "I want more men on this."

Liam sighs. "We're already stretched unless you have new guys?"

My gut flips. He's right. With all the security we have on the Ivanov women, monitoring the war, and this situation with Jack, both our families are low on men. I'm in the middle of training two new trackers, but they aren't ready yet. I admit, "No. We don't."

"Six weeks. It's right around the corner," Liam says.

"Not soon enough."

"Same conversation as always. It's not going to change." He lowers his voice. "We're close to the goal. Stay focused. I promise, the moment the bell rings on the Exchange, I'll have him picked up and brought to you."

I hate every part of this agreement. I've got two guards on Selena at all times, but whenever she's not with me, I worry. "He better not get any closer, or I'm ending this."

"We're all on it. No one wants anything to happen. I need you to stay the course," Liam reiterates.

"Yeah, I know. I need to go." I hang up. It's pointless arguing.

I spend the rest of the day packing and making other arrangements for Hawaii. I start dinner and sit at the island. I review the new statements for Selena's accounts. We always go through them together, since I think it's important she understands what she owns. She doesn't like it, though, and has pretty much designated me her financial manager.

Selena comes back into the penthouse right before five. An excited expression fills her face. She's glowing, and nothing makes me happier.

"Cutting it close?" I tease.

She beams. "Sorry. There was a lot to figure out and do. What are you making? It smells good."

"I threw in one of the trays of lasagna you froze. I packed your suitcase, but it's open on the bed if you want to look it over and make sure I didn't miss anything."

She leans over the counter next to me. "You packed my bag?"

"Yep."

She ruffles my hair. "You're a keeper."

"I hope so since by this time tomorrow, you're stuck with me."

She pecks me on the cheek. "Wish granted, then."

We eat dinner, leave for the airport, and after the initial excitement dies down, all of us sleep until we arrive in Hawaii.

We get to the resort. After a quick check-in, the women separate from us. Matvey and Vlad stay close to them. Adrian, Stefano, and I spend a few hours at the pool. We have drinks and lunch. The wedding is at sunset. As it nears, I've never felt so calm.

My dorogaya, the sexiest woman in the world, the only person who truly gets me, is going to be mine forever.

I change into my linen slacks and white shirt. The wedding staff person puts a purple lei around my neck. I stand on the beach, with the ocean crashing around me, wondering how I ever lived before her.

Music starts. It's a traditional Hawaiian wedding song. My mom and Skylar appear and then I finally get to see her. My bride. My heart. My life.

She's breathtaking as always. A large white orchid is tucked in her long hair. Her white dress flutters in the breeze. The smile on her face makes my heart soar.

As we say our vows, no words have ever meant more to me. I made sure my vows were the same as hers. To love, honor, protect, and obey.

When the officiant says, "Please congratulate Mr. and Mrs. Obrecht Ivanov," I've never seen my dorogaya's face shine brighter.

Selena

Four Weeks Later

"YOU'RE UP EARLY," OBRECHT SAYS. SWEAT COVERS HIS BODY. He leans down, and I tilt my head up. He gives me a quick kiss on the lips.

I put my makeup brush down and spin on the vanity stool. "Anna isn't feeling well. She called and asked if I could check on the flooring install. They screwed it up the first time, and she made them redo it."

"Which project?"

"That Sasha guy."

He strips his wet clothes off and tosses them on the floor. "Sasha must be going nuts. That's going to cost him an arm and a leg."

"Yep. He wasn't too happy." I point. "I'm buying a laundry hamper for that corner today."

He glances at his pile of workout gear. "I always put it in the basket after I shower." He sticks his hand under the water to test the temperature.

"It makes sense to have one in the bathroom and one in the closet." I rise and walk toward him, checking out every inch of his hard body, from the snake face on his neck and his Natalia tattoo to his rock-hard calves. I bend over, pick up his dirty clothes, and pat his ass.

My husband.

He glances at me. "Whatever you want but careful what you're slapping, Mrs. Ivanov. I'll drag you into the shower, and you'll miss your appointment."

"Hmmm." I tilt my head and trail my finger down his spine. "That sounds tempting."

He chuckles and steps into the shower. "What time are you done today? Should I meet you here or at Skylar's office?"

Skylar started her own fashion line and her office is finished. She's having a small party. "I'm not sure. Can we play it by ear? I'm meeting your mom for lunch with the wedding planner to solidify loose ends."

He smirks. "Have fun with that. Text me when you know if I'm picking you up or meeting you."

"Okay, I will!" Ever since we got married in Hawaii, I only feel excitement about the wedding. My night terrors have gotten a bit better, but they seemed to have sprung up again the last few nights. I'm trying not to let them ruin any of the joy I feel. I'm Mrs. Obrecht Ivanov. My husband loves and adores me. And I get to repeat my vow to him, in front of all the people we care about, that I dedicate myself to him forever.

He kisses the top of my head and slaps my ass. "Have a good day, baby girl."

"You, too."

He winks and returns to his shower. I leave the penthouse and go through my day. I work on several projects for Anna, meet Svetlana and the wedding planner for lunch, and go to the showroom to pick up a few samples the manager called to say arrived. On my way back to the penthouse, I remember the laundry hamper.

I redirect my driver and go into the store and text Obrecht.

Me: *Meet me at Skylar's office. I forgot about the hamper.*

Obrecht: *Okay, baby girl. Don't take too long. I'll wait in my car. I've got a present for you to open before you go inside.*

Me: *What is it?*

Obrecht: *You'll find out later.*

Me: *Okay, sir.*

Obrecht: *Get moving, madam.*

I smile and send him a photo of me with my cleavage showing.

He returns a photo of his fingers in a V and his tongue sticking through them.

The car stops and Matvey opens the door. He and Gleb follow me inside. Matvey stays near the front of the store, and Gleb trails me. He's a new bodyguard. Obrecht has a rule. The two new guys are never with me alone. One is always with Matvey or Vlad.

The hampers are in the back of the store. I spend a few minutes looking them over and finally decide on a gray wicker one with a cloth interior. I pick it up and turn, expecting to see Gleb. Normally, I can't carry anything without someone taking it from me. I used to feel guilty having them lug all my stuff everywhere, but I realized it's just the Ivanov men or anyone under their employment. They see it as a sign of respect for women. It no longer bothers me.

My chest tightens as I look for Gleb but then I hear something crash and his voice several aisles over. "Sorry. Let me help you pick that up."

I relax, and a mirror in the next row catches my eye. I'm on my way to view it when a black-gloved hand goes over my mouth. The smell of tobacco flares in my nostrils. An Irish accent says in my ear, "Move, and I slice your spine."

I freeze, unsure what to do. I try to see Gleb or Matvey in my peripheral vision, but they are nowhere. I'm dragged through the employee door and down a white hallway. The exit door is at the end of the hall. I'm swiftly taken outside and thrown into the backseat of a black sedan.

The car takes off the moment the door shuts. A hood with only a hole in the mouth gets pulled over my head, and I begin to scream.

"Shut up!" a man barks, holding me tight on his lap. "If you don't, I'm tying an anchor to your legs and dropping you over the bridge."

My screams turn to whimpers. The spandex fabric suctions against my skin. It's a feeling I know too well. It's the same as when I was with Jack and in my dreams. The tightening in my chest sends pain through my heart.

The car ride doesn't last very long. When it stops, the door opens. The man yanks me out of the car, and I count the steps I walk.

One. Two. Three. Four. Five. Six. Seven.

No. Please. No.

The door opens. The scent of musk consumes me.

Jack's scent.

My heart squeezes tighter. Tears soak the cloak over my head. I'm in the place I never again wanted to be. Jack's home. My prison for a decade. Hell on earth.

I try to fight, but the man takes my wrists and pins them behind my back. He pushes me forward, and I almost trip. The counting begins again. This time, there are twenty-three steps, including the landing I have to make a ninety-degree turn on.

My chest seizes so badly, I hyperventilate. I try to scream but nothing comes out. The sliding of metal screeches in my ears. A knife slits my shirt, pants, bra, and underwear so they fall off me. He shoves me until I'm on all fours on a cold, metallic floor. The clanging of metal fills the room.

No amount of crying or fighting will save me. I've spent too many hours in this cage. It's dug into my very core how there is no escaping it. I am once again, Jack's prisoner. His slave.

The heavy oak door slams shut. I stay on my hands and knees, not able to move, knowing cameras are filming me. If I attempt to get into another position, there will be consequences. I try not to think about them, but they consume me, making me tremble harder.

More reality hits me. I defied Jack and left him. I broke our vow by divorcing him. If he could hunt me down and kidnap me, he has to know I married Obrecht. The fear gripping me is stronger than ever.

He's going to make me pay.

Time passes, and my body aches. The position I'm in and the lack of movement creates more pain than I remember. The ticking of the clock is the only thing echoing in the room. I shiver from the cold and my anxious fear.

The door creaks open. The smell of Jack's musk becomes overpowering. I shake harder, and the heat from Jack's body penetrates through the cage.

The voice I hear sends a deeper chill down my spine. The Irish accent is thick. I've heard it too many times in the past. "Do you want to have some fun with her before you sell her to me?"

Obrecht

THE VIBRATING PANTIES I BOUGHT FOR SELENA SIT IN A GIFT bag next to me. I'm going to make her put them on in the car and wear them during this little event of Skylar's. Then I'm going to tie her up and edge her when we get home until she loses her voice from begging me.

I stare at the picture she sent me. *My naughty little wife.*

Matvey's image pops up on the screen. I answer, "Matvey, are you on your way?"

"They took her," he barks out.

My gut sinks. Bile rises in my throat. I bark, "What do you mean they took her?"

"We were in the store. Someone dropped something. Gleb was picking it up—"

"His job is to not take his eyes off her! Where the fuck were you?" I demand opening the car door and practically sprinting inside Skylar's office.

"At the front, I—"

"Call Maksim. Call Liam." I hang up and Skylar's assistant Bradley, who has the hots for Adrian, but isn't opposed to checking me out as well, approaches me with a big smile.

"Obrecht! It's so—"

"Where is my brother?" I seethe.

His eyes widen. He points behind him. "They went into the office."

I brush past him and see Maksim across the room. He hangs up his phone, and his face is pale. He motions to Dmitri, Sergey, and Boris.

I bang on the office door as hard as I can. Rage fills me in a way I've never experienced it before. My dorogaya is in the hands of the devil. "Adrian! Open up, now!"

The door opens. Adrian and Skylar are behind it. He asks, "What's wrong?"

"You need to come with me now!"

"Obrecht, what's wrong?" Skylar repeats.

I can barely say it. My insides are shaking. "He took her."

"Who?" Adrian asks, the hairs on my neck standing up.

Who? Why the fuck is he asking me who?

"Selena. Her bastard ex took her."

His eyes turn to slits. I barely hear Maksim say, "Skylar, can you leave the room?"

She goes, and the Ivanovs gather in her office and shut the door.

"Do we know where he took her?" Maksim asks.

"My guess is his house. The bastard always orders his guys to take her to his house," I claim.

"Arrogant prick," Sergey mutters.

"We need to go now," I claim.

"Hold on. We need to find out what Liam knows," Dmitri says.

"I don't give a fuck what Liam knows. I'm going to get my wife, and he's dying tonight by my hands," I claim.

"He was tracking Jack. If we know where Jack is, we'll know for sure where she is," Dmitri claims.

"Fine. You call him. I'm leaving."

Adrian steps in front of the door.

"Move!" I yell.

"Wait. You can't go by yourself. Chill out a minute."

"He has my wife," I grit through my teeth.

Adrian nods. "I know. We'll get her back. If you don't do this right, she could get hurt."

"He could be hurting her right now. Either come with me, and we plan in the car, or I'll do it myself." I shove him aside.

"Hold on. Obrecht! I'm with you. We all are." Adrian follows me through the office. My cousins are in tow. Liam and Hailee step inside right as I get to the front.

I throw Darragh's words in his face. "Do you see what not taking care of loose ends does?"

Hailee moves out of the way, and Liam holds his hands in the air. He claims, "She's at his house."

I step outside and ask, "How many men are there?"

"Only one and the driver. They're waiting for Jack to arrive."

"Fine, I'll take them out, too."

"It's Mack Bailey."

I freeze. A new horror fills me. Selena told me what he wanted to do to her. Over the last few months, everything has come out. As much as I deplore Jack, in many ways, Mack might be worse. I turn and jab Liam's chest. "You're to blame for this."

"Obrecht, this isn't the time. Let's go," Maksim says and opens the car door.

I scowl at Liam and get in with Maksim. Boris follows, and Liam jumps in. The door shuts, and the car takes off. Liam's phone rings.

He answers, "Finn. What's the situation?" His jaw clenches, and my gut spins. "Keep your eyes tight. We're on our way." He hangs up.

"What?" I bark.

"Jack's home. He and Mack just went into the house."

439

I shake my head. "You and your deal. I should have never listened to you."

"We're two weeks away. Let's take out Mack and his driver. Jack goes with me to the garage. As soon as—"

"Enough! It's over, Liam. I don't care how the O'Malleys make their money going forward. Sell your souls to the devil for all I care. He goes to our garage," I seethe.

"Obrecht, you don't understand—"

"Everyone, calm down. We need to be on the same page so Selena doesn't get hurt," Maksim says.

I continue to glare at Liam. *Why did I ever agree to this?*

Liam's phone rings. He answers, "Killian."

"He's going to our garage," I reiterate to Maksim.

Maksim nods. "Yeah. I need you to calm down, though, or Selena could get harmed."

I take a deep breath. He's right.

"We're five minutes away. Stay put." Liam hangs up. "Killian took out Mack's driver."

"How?" Boris asks.

"I'm not sure until we get there."

"The house is large. Where do you think he'd have her?" Maksim asks.

More disgust and fear fill me. Selena's dreams were too frequent and intense to be wrong. My wife has a sixth sense. I should have known we couldn't escape this from happening with Jack still alive. I feel ill as I say it. "He'll have her in the bedroom in the cage."

I ignore the horror-filled expressions and pull my gun out of my pants. While I prefer tearing into these men with my knife, I'll shoot them with no hesitation if it comes down to it. I double-check the chamber is full of bullets.

"You're positive he'll have her in his bedroom?" Maksim asks.

"Yes."

Liam scrolls on his phone. "I've got the layout of Jack's house. Up the stairs, then turn right. Only door on the right. Finn said they went in through the garage. His house locks through his app. Declan has the code and said all doors are unlocked. The security system is off as well."

We turn into a wealthy subdivision. Extensive lawns and mature trees surround each estate. The sun has set, and the streetlamps are on. The driver turns the lights off and veers onto Jack's street.

Liam puts his phone to his ear and knocks on the divider window. The driver rolls it down. Liam speaks into his phone. "Finn, are we clear?" A few seconds pass. "Okay, coming up now." He hangs up the phone and says to the driver, "Go slow. It's thick foliage the entire driveway and clear to the garage. The bedroom is on the backside of the house."

It feels like forever before we get to the mansion. I don't wait. I storm out of the car, putting my black gloves on as I move toward the entrance. My heart's racing. Images of what they may be doing to my dorogaya fill my head. I push past nausea and remind myself to be smart so Selena doesn't get hurt.

The others are behind me. I pull out my gun, flip the safety, and creep into the house. I move toward the dual staircase and quietly go up, grateful there is carpet. At the top, I turn right. I hear their voices before I get to the room. Selena's scared whimpers break my heart.

A thick Irish accent says, "Are you sure you don't want one last go before I pay you? I don't mind giving you a final round. I'll even take part."

More bile rises in my throat.

Jack's voice makes the hairs on my arms rise. "Tell you what, you pay me, then I'll let you have your first go here. I want to watch and listen to her pay for disobeying me."

Selena's sobs get louder.

In a mocking tone, he says, "What's wrong, dear wife? Rethinking how good you had it with me?"

I stop at the edge of the door. I glance back at Maksim, Boris, and Liam. With my gun aimed straight, I peek into the room.

Both men huddle over the cage. It's barely big enough to fit a Labrador retriever, much less a woman. Selena is naked and on all fours. She's shaking. They have the same black hood over her face she bought from the store as the thing that scared her the most.

Jack sticks his fingers through the cage and drags them over her ass. "She got fat. You're going to need to starve her a bit."

Selena shakes harder.

Mack reaches in and grabs her chin. "She'll learn how to behave with me."

I aim my gun and shoot Mack in the head. He topples over the cage with blood pouring out of him. Selena screams, and Jack spins. "Get on the ground," I shout at him. I want to shoot him, too, but he's going to pay. I'm going to string out every last moment he has with pure pain and fear.

He gapes at us and raises his hands in the air.

"Get on the ground," I order again.

He does as he's told. Boris stands over him, pointing his gun.

I race to the cage and pull Mack off. Selena is screaming. Blood covers her. I attempt to open the cage, but there's a padlock on it.

"Where are the keys?" I growl.

Jack laughs. Maksim kicks him then crouches down and threatens him, but I don't hear what he's saying. All I can focus on is Selena and getting her out of this cage.

I reach in and pull the face mask off her. I get on my knees and bend until I'm eye level with her. "It's okay, baby girl. I'm going to get you out of here."

Her eyes will haunt me for the rest of my life. There's so much fear in them, it pains me to look at her, but I force myself to keep my gaze on her. I reach through the cage and push her hair off her face. "Can you get into a different position, my dorogaya?"

She stares at me. Tears fall everywhere. Her breathing is erratic, and I worry she may have a panic attack or an actual heart attack.

"Someone get me the keys," I say, attempting to stay calm for her but doing a poor job. I want to rip Jack's head off. If Selena weren't in this cage, I would. I keep repeating, "It's okay. You're safe. I'm getting you out of here."

A lifetime passes before someone hands me the keys. I don't know who, since I won't tear my eyes away from her. I finally get the cage open and attempt to move her out, but she screams in pain.

"She's been in there too long," Liam says. "I've seen it in prison. Go slow."

I'm unsure what he means by that comment, but I don't care at this point. He brings a blanket over, and we slowly help her out. When she's free, she breaks down in my arms.

"Shhh. It's okay. He won't ever harm you again. I promise."

Her cries sound like a wounded animal. I've never felt so much agony. I wrap her in the blanket and pick her up.

Jack's on the floor, surrounded by Boris and Maksim. I warn Liam one last time, "He goes to our garage. Take that cage and put him in it." I don't wait for an answer. If he doesn't comply, there's going to be a war between our families. Liam will be the first O'Malley I take out.

I cover every part of Selena except her face and carry her down the stairs and out of the house. Another car is waiting. Sergey is in it. When the door shuts, we pull out. He says nothing for several moments but finally speaks. "Do we need to go to the hospital?"

"No! Please. I don't want anyone touching me," Selena cries out.

I stroke her hair. "Okay, baby girl. I'll take you home if you let Stefano examine you."

"Don't leave me. Please," she cries.

I tighten my arms around her. "I'm not leaving you." I kiss her on the head, and she starts crying again.

Sergey's eyes meet mine. "The others are waiting. Do we need them for cleanup? Are they dead?"

"Mack is. Send them in."

Selena shakes harder. "Jack is still alive?"

"Not for long, baby girl. I promise you, his death is going to be drawn out and painful."

3 4

Selena

OBRECHT GETS IN THE SHOWER WITH ME. BLOOD MIXES WITH the water and runs down my body and into the drain. I'm so cold. I can't get warm. It feels like I've been shaking forever.

When there's no more blood, Obrecht moves us into the tub. I curl into him. He pretzels his arms and legs around my body. A long time passes. In a gentle voice, he asks, "How are you doing, baby girl?"

I close my eyes. I don't want to think about what Mack would have done to me. "Why does my face still feel like the spandex is on it?"

Obrecht's chest rises, filling with air. He strokes his thumb on my hip. "It's not, baby girl. It never will be again."

I swallow hard. My mouth is dry. My muscles are sore. I admit, "I'm tired. So tired."

The doorbell rings, and I jump.

"Shh. It's okay. It's my mom and Stefano."

Panic fills me. I glance up. "Don't leave me. Please."

He gives me a chaste kiss. "I'm not. But I want a doctor to examine you, Selena. You're okay if Stefano does, instead of a doctor at the hospital, right?"

I slowly nod.

He kisses my forehead. "Let's get out and put some warm clothes on, okay?"

I agree. He diligently dries then dresses me in pajama bottoms and a long-sleeve top. He sets me on the bed and puts socks on me. "Do you want me to call Carla?"

I ponder the question then shake my head. "Not tonight."

"Do you want to get under the covers or go out into the other room?"

All I want to do is dive under the blankets and have him hold me. But I know if I don't let Stefano examine me, Obrecht will take me to the hospital. "I'll go to the couch."

He smiles. "Okay, baby girl." He takes my hand and leads me into the family room. Svetlana and Stefano are on the couch and rise when we enter the room. Svetlana's eyes tear up. She pulls me into a hug, and I cry again.

"Shh. It's okay, sweetheart," she coos.

I wish I weren't crying. I used to have no one and dealt with much worse than what happened today. Why can't I stop the tears from falling?

She rubs my back. "Let's have Stefano give you a quick exam to make sure you don't need any further medical attention. And when did you eat last? Are you hungry?"

My day spins in my head. "At lunch with you."

She pulls back and strokes my hair. "Why don't I make some dinner?"

"I don't know if I can eat."

She smiles. "I'll make it, and you can decide later, okay?"

"Sure."

She gives me another hug then releases me and goes into the kitchen.

I sit on the couch. I glance at Obrecht, and he takes the seat next to me.

Stefano smiles kindly at me. Over the next fifteen minutes, he asks questions and gives me an exam. "I don't think there is any long-term physical damage. You've got some bruising. You might feel a little worse in a few days from the lactic acid buildup in your muscles from holding that position for so long. Epsom salt baths will help with muscle stiffness. Overall, I think you got lucky."

Obrecht releases a breath as if he's been holding it in for a long time. He tugs me closer to him. His body is so safe and warm. I wish he could wrap it around me and I never had to leave it. He says, "This is good."

Stefano tilts his head. "Selena, I think it would be wise to see a therapist. This is a lot of trauma."

"I have one."

He smiles. "Great. I would feel better if you discussed this with him or her."

"I will," I promise him.

Svetlana comes over with a tray. She sets it on my lap. One of my favorite meals, avocado toast with a poached egg, is on it. A mug of hot tea is next to the food.

"I'm suddenly hungry," I tell her, grateful for her and all she does for me.

She puts her hand on my cheek. "Good." She turns to Obrecht. "You should eat, too. I'll go make you a plate."

"Thanks."

The doorbell rings. I question Obrecht, "Who would that be?"

"I'm not sure. Let me go see." He rises and leaves the room. Within minutes, Obrecht and Liam talk loud enough to know they are both upset but not enough for me to decipher what they are saying.

Their argument gets louder. Svetlana, Stefano, and I exchange a nervous glance. I set the tray to the side and walk out of the corridor right as Liam says, "Two weeks. He has to live for two weeks. Once his company goes public, then you can do whatever you want to him. I'll watch and hand you whatever instrument you want to torture him. The entire time, we'll keep him at the garage, in the cage, just like he did to Selena. But you have to give me two weeks."

Obrecht steps closer to Liam. "I don't give a damn what you have going on. He dies as soon as I get to the garage tonight."

"You're leaving me tonight?" I cry out. New tremors take hold of my quivering insides. I can't handle Obrecht being away from me right now and especially not for days on end.

Obrecht spins. "If not tonight, tomorrow. Jack needs to pay."

"And you want him alive?" I ask Liam.

"You shouldn't hear this. Jack is going to pay. We aren't waiting two weeks," Obrecht seethes.

"Why do you want him to live for two weeks?" I blurt out.

"For nothing important," Obrecht states.

Liam's eyes widen. "You think I'd let that monster live all these months, and now for another second, after what he put Selena through if it wasn't important?"

Obrecht sniffs hard. He turns to me. "I failed you, my doro-gaya. I shouldn't have listened to anyone and killed him when I learned what he did to you. For that, I'm always going to be sorry. I'm not making the same mistake again."

Liam squeezes his eyes shut. He breathes deeply a few times. His hands clenched into fists, similar to Obrecht's. It's clear they both want to get their way.

"Where is Jack?" I ask.

"I told you. At the garage," Obrecht says.

I cross my arms. All the months I've known about the garage, I've never asked questions. I suddenly want answers. "Where is the garage?"

"It isn't anything you should know about."

"Why?"

"It could put you in danger."

"How?"

Obrecht shifts on his feet. "If anyone ever finds out where the garage is, legally, you could be in trouble."

"No, I can't."

"Yes, you could."

"No. We're married. Isn't there some rule in America where whatever a spouse tells another spouse is protected?" I ask.

Obrecht shakes his head. "I don't know. I'm not an attorney. But I'm not putting you at risk."

I step closer. I ask Liam again, "Why do you want Jack to live?"

He scoffs. "I don't want him to live. I only want to keep him breathing until he signs for his company to go public."

"Why?"

"I can't tell you."

It's rare for me to feel strong, or act like I have any power over decisions men make, especially ones as strong as Liam and Obrecht. Usually, I would never interfere in whatever they're involved in. All the years of suffering Jack caused me suddenly make me feel as if it's my decision what happens to him. In a firm voice, I demand, "If you want my help, you need to tell me why."

Obrecht blurts, "Selena, this isn't—"

"I'm not talking to you right now. I'm talking to Liam. Don't try to sugarcoat whatever is going on. I don't believe Liam would make this decision if it weren't important," I snap, and Obrecht's eyes widen.

"Thank you. It is," Liam states and glares at Obrecht.

"Don't scowl at my husband," I reprimand.

Liam's face turns red. "Sorry."

Obrecht gives him an arrogant look.

"Don't be an ass to Liam," I scold Obrecht.

He arches an eyebrow. Confusion isn't something I see in Obrecht a lot. I also don't usually tell him what to do. Something within me has shifted. It's like all the broken pieces within me are jagged glass and I want to utilize them appropriately. Jack always had all the control. For the first time ever, I hold some sort of power over his fate. I want him dead. I'm not sure what to do with this decision, but something within me tells me there's a crucial choice to make.

I assess both men. One is my husband, whom I love more than life. Without him, my life would be empty. The other is a friend who seems desperate for Obrecht to wait to unleash his wrath on Jack. This is why Obrecht didn't take care of Jack all these months, so it must hold some importance.

"If Jack's company goes public, will it be destroyed, or will it survive?" I ask Liam.

His face hardens. "It'll go up in flames until it's nothing but ashes."

"And you can keep him alive, suffering for these next two weeks? You guarantee he won't be able to escape or harm me ever again?" I ask.

"Selena—"

"Obrecht, please let me speak and don't interrupt me."

He clenches his jaw and sighs.

I step toward him. He puts his arm around me and tugs me closer. I focus on Liam and repeat, "Can you guarantee those things?"

"Yes. I one hundred percent guarantee you he will suffer and will never harm you again. There is no escaping his fate at this point," Liam claims.

"How quickly will his company go down?"

Liam tilts his head and squints. "Two to four weeks once it goes public is the estimate."

I nod and pace the corridor. It's so quiet you can hear a pin drop. Jack may have abused, broken, and disrespected me, but I know everything about him. His company is his lifeblood. Part of me wants him to be alive when it falls apart. Another side of me wants him to die as soon as possible.

I speak to Liam. "You have two weeks. At that point, you will ask me what I want. You will tell him that I'm in charge of his life at this point. I want a photo of him in the cage—every day. I want an untraceable picture, and you're going to deliver it to me." I turn to Obrecht. "You aren't allowed at the garage until I'm ready for him to die."

His eyes widen. "Selena!"

I cup his cheeks. His jaw clenches under my fingers. "I don't care about having input in a lot of decisions you make. I trust everything you do. If this weren't important, you would have gone against Liam."

"I was wrong." His jaw clenches under my fingers.

"No, you weren't. And I want him to suffer," I admit.

Obrecht fiercely states, "He is going to suffer. I will make sure he suffers."

Tears fill my eyes. My voice shakes. "Yes. And until that day comes, I want him to know what it's like not to be free. I want him to crouch in his cage and go crazy, learning what it's like to be powerless, feeling like an animal. I want him to think of me and all the ways he tortured me. Then, when he thinks he can't take it anymore, I want you to unleash whatever it is you want to do to finish him off."

Obrecht studies me. For months, he's spent countless minutes watching me, staring into my eyes, trying to figure out what I'm feeling or thinking. No moment has ever been this intense.

A tear drips down my cheek. I manage to summon all the courage I have inside me not to crumble and back down. "I need this. I need to know everything Jack valued is gone. It includes his business. He spent his life building it. All the shady things he did that he bragged about to his friends to get ahead, I know about. He thought I was too brainless to understand things. His belief that he's untouchable, and I could never take him down, was ingrained in him. Every moment, from here on out, I want him to know that I'm pulling the strings."

Obrecht continues to pin his icy-blue eyes on mine. He finally nods and quietly says, "Okay, baby girl. If this is what you need, I'll agree to it."

I lean into him. "Thank you." I spin back to Liam. "Are you clear on what I want?"

"Yes. I will deliver your photos each day."

"Thank you."

"Thank you, Selena." He nods and steps into the elevator.

Obrecht circles his arms around me. I embrace him as tight as he holds me. What we have is precious. It's unbreakable, but we as individuals aren't. Since I left Greece, I've never had a family or friends. Now, I have everything. Jack is going to get what's coming to him. My husband, the man who has shown me nothing but love, loyalty, and compassion, will always protect me. He'll always have my trust and heart. There's no doubt he'll always do what he believes is the right thing for me.

But he also taught me there are times I need to stand up and do what I feel is best for us or just me. I may not exercise it a lot; I usually don't need to. The few times I have, he's always put me first. Unlike Jack, he made it clear, relationships need balance. There are times each person has to submit to the other. If you don't, you risk tearing the other person apart and destroying everything you hold dearest to your heart.

I reach up and hold his cheeks. "I love you."

"I love you, too, baby girl."

"I'm not letting Jack steal any more of our life."

He palms my ass. "I'm sorry—"

"Shh! This was not your fault."

He closes his eyes briefly and stares at the ceiling. I already know I can tell him until I'm blue in the face there was nothing he could do to prevent what happened, but he's always going to feel guilty. I wish I could change it. Some things, no matter how hard you want the reality to be different, just aren't. All I can do is show him every day how much I love, adore, and am grateful for how much he loves me.

"Hey," I softly say.

He glances down at me.

I smile and trace his jawline. "You're going to love what I want us to do for the rest of the night."

He arches his eyebrow. "What's that?"

"Sit down with your mom and go through all the loose ends for our wedding."

He chuckles. "Bring out the bridal magazines."

EPILOGUE

Obrecht

Two Weeks Later

"I'm glad we did this twice," I murmur in Selena's ear. We're in the elevator, heading to the bridal suite. The day has been perfect, just like our other wedding day. My stunning wife is glowing. Her smile lit up the room all night, and I once again wonder how I ever lived without her by my side.

She glances up. "Me, too."

I steal a kiss, something I didn't get enough of all night. Then again, I'll never get enough. "You've made an old man happy."

A smile plays on her lips. "You aren't that old."

I snort. "Says the barely thirty-year-old."

"Hey, I'm thirty-one now."

"So old," I tease.

The elevator opens. I lead her to our suite and lock the door behind us. I admit, "I never thought someone would make me so happy."

Her sweet expression gazes up at me. She opens her mouth then shuts it. She bites on her bottom lip and strokes the side of my head.

"What are you thinking, baby girl?"

"Do you want kids?"

My pulse increases. I tug her closer to me. "Are you pregnant?"

"No. But I have to decide whether to get the shot again or not." The green in her eyes swirls with the brown.

"Since I'm forty-five, if I'm not shooting blanks, I'd be happy with little Selena's running around," I admit.

She laughs. "Highly doubt you're shooting blanks."

I shrug. "You never know. We probably should have talked about this before we got married though."

She tilts her head. "It wouldn't have changed my mind. I'd still have married you."

"You would have?"

"With no hesitation."

"I assume since you're asking me about this, it means you want kids?" I ask.

She stares at me, putting her thoughts together. I can always see her wheels turning when she does this. I wait until she says, "If we don't have kids, I'm okay with it. When I was with Jack, I was grateful he didn't want them. Now that I found you..." She smiles and traces my snake tattoo. "I'd like to try. If it happens, it happens. And if it doesn't, well, I'm still the luckiest, most loved woman in the world. And I'm okay with either scenario."

My heart swells. I couldn't have put it into better words. But I also have to push aside the rage I feel whenever Jack's name comes up. His company went public Friday. Selena said she isn't ready yet and wants to watch it burn to the ground first. She also claimed she didn't want anything taking our focus off the wedding, which I couldn't argue with. When I do end his life, I'm going to be there for days. Right now, I don't want to be away from her for a second.

I dip down and kiss her. "Guess we're going to have to practice a lot, then."

She wiggles her eyebrows. "Will it involve me kneeling?"

"Definitely."

"Will I get spanked if I'm naughty?"

I chuckle. "I can make that happen."

She rises on her tippy-toes and murmurs in my ear, "If you unzip my dress, I might have on something you like, sir."

Oh, my sexy, naughty wife.

"Spin," I command.

She obeys, and my phone rings. We both freeze. It's the tone I have for Adrian. He wouldn't call me if something weren't wrong.

I pull the phone out of my pocket. "Adrian, this better be important."

His voice sends a chill down my spine. "Darragh is dead."

My mouth goes dry. Goose bumps pop out on my skin.

"You know what this means," Adrian says.

I swallow the lump in my throat, unsure how I feel about my next statement. "Liam is now head of the O'Malleys."

READ UNCHOSEN RULER - FREE ON KINDLE UNLIMITED

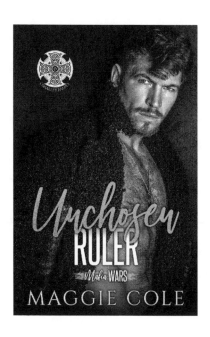

He's the future unchosen ruler of the O'Malleys.

Locked away for too many years.

Underestimated and pissed off.

Protective beyond all rationale.

Possessive unlike any man I've ever known.

I should run. Except Liam O'Malley isn't a choice. He's the air I breathe.

Still, I wonder if I can really be queen of the O'Malleys—especially when I discover the truth about who I am.

Anyone else in our shoes would make a different choice, but nothing with Liam is predictable.

In our world, anything but strength gets you killed.

It's what makes him the perfect unchosen ruler.

**READ UNCHOSEN RULER - FREE ON KINDLE
UNLIMITED**

Hailee O'Hare

IN MY WORLD, BAD BOYS HAVE ALWAYS BEEN OFF-LIMITS. IT never mattered how attracted I was to them. Every man I felt drawn to who fit the definition, I avoided like the plague. It didn't matter how many times they asked me out or how much pressure my friends put on me to stop dating the safe, boring guys. I had my rule for a reason, and I wasn't about to break it.

The guidelines I set for dating were all due to my childhood. Stability wasn't something I experienced early in life. My mother fled with my sisters and me to Chicago. She did it to get away from my father, who was an abusive criminal. No matter how much time passed, my mother never stopped worrying about him finding us.

The year I turned twelve, everything changed. That's when my father went to prison for murder. My mother morphed into a new person after she told us. Her stress lifted, and it's like she could finally breathe again. However, that didn't mean any of us forgot.

There are times I still have flashbacks of the violence that reigned over our house. Those moments serve as reminders to never let anything I can't control into my life. Also, to always choose the safe route because nothing in life comes free. Everything has risk. Managing it is the only way not to get hurt. Dating a bad boy was a surefire way to go directly into the danger zone, and that wasn't an option.

Then Liam O'Malley set his sights on me. The moment our eyes met, it was like an earthquake ripping through my core. No matter how much I tried to stay away or told him we couldn't be together, I always found myself running toward him. Once our worlds collided, there was no way to escape each other.

Everything about Liam is one hundred percent bad boy. Unbelievably sexy. Fearless. Protective beyond all rationale. Possessive, unlike any man I've ever known. And a hard-core convicted criminal. But that isn't all. He's the only son of the head of the O'Malley crime family. And the Irish clan's successor. The O'Malleys rule all of Chicago and are enemies with too many other crime families to count.

That one fact should have been dangerous enough to keep me away, but it didn't. And my mother never told me everything about my lineage. She never disclosed to my sisters or me who we were or what our bloodlines made us a part of. To this day, I wonder if I would have stayed away from Liam or he from me had either of us known. There's no way to tell for sure. My head says we would have. The honest side of me says if Romeo and Juliet couldn't, we didn't stand a chance. There would have been no way to stop us from being together.

Then there's the question about what would be different in my life had I known.

Would anything?

Would everything?

The truth unleashed makes me a hypocrite. *Do unto others as you would have them do unto you* is spelled out on my classroom wall. It's in front of me all day, every day. Each morning, my class recites it, and we discuss it. I always tried to live by it. And it always felt easy.

That is, until now.

The thing about secrets is they don't always stay buried. Sometimes they come to life. It doesn't matter if you want them to or not. The moment it hits you who you really are and what your birthright bears, you're at a fork in the road. You have to choose the direction to take, even when both have risks more significant than anything you could ever fathom.

They say good triumphs evil. I used to believe it, but I'm no longer sure. How can it when to get what you want, you have to go against everything you've ever preached and destroy anything that stands in front of you? Do you morph from good to evil? If that's the case, does it give you the ability to overlook things in the future you always thought in the past were wrong?

There isn't a lot I'm sure about anymore, except one thing: Liam O'Malley isn't a choice. He's the air I breathe. Staying an innocent, good girl is no longer an option.

465

READ UNCHOSEN RULER - FREE ON KINDLE UNLIMITED

ALL IN BOXSET

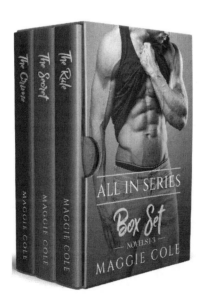

Three page-turning, interconnected stand-alone romance novels with HEA's!! Get ready to fall in love with the characters. Billionaires. Professional athletes. New York City. Twist, turns, and danger lurking everywhere. The only option for these couples is to go ALL IN...with a little help from their friends. EXTRA STEAM INCLUDED!

Grab it now! READ FREE IN KINDLE UNLIMITED!

CAN I ASK YOU A HUGE FAVOR?

Would you be willing to leave me a review?

I would be forever grateful as one positive review on Amazon is like buying the book a hundred times! Reader support is the lifeblood for Indie authors and provides us the feedback we need to give readers what they want in future stories!

Your positive review means the world to me! So thank you from the bottom of my heart!

CLICK TO REVIEW

MORE BY MAGGIE COLE

***Mafia Wars - A Dark Mafia Series** (Series Five)*

Ruthless Stranger (Maksim's Story) - Book One

Broken Fighter (Boris's Story) - Book Two

Cruel Enforcer (Sergey's Story) - Book Three

Vicious Protector (Adrian's Story) - Book Four

Savage Tracker (Obrecht's Story) - Book Five

Unchosen Ruler (Liam's Story) - Book Six

Perfect Sinner (Nolan's Story) - Book Seven

Brutal Defender (Killian's Story) - Book Eight

Deviant Hacker (Declan's Story) - Book Nine

Relentless Hunter (Finn's Story) - Book Ten

Behind Closed Doors (Series Four - Former Military Now International Rescue Alpha Studs)

Depths of Destruction - Book One

Marks of Rebellion - Book Two

Haze of Obedience - Book Three

Cavern of Silence - Book Four

Stains of Desire - Book Five

Risks of Temptation - Book Six

Together We Stand Series (Series Three - Family Saga)

Kiss of Redemption- Book One

Sins of Justice - Book Two

Acts of Manipulation - Book Three

Web of Betrayal - Book Four

Masks of Devotion - Book Five

Roots of Vengeance - Book Six

It's Complicated Series (Series Two - Chicago Billionaires)

Crossing the Line - Book One

Don't Forget Me - Book Two

Committed to You - Book Three

More Than Paper - Book Four

Sins of the Father - Book Five

Wrapped In Perfection - Book Six

All In Series (Series One - New York Billionaires)

The Rule - Book One

The Secret - Book Two

The Crime - Book Three

The Lie - Book Four

The Trap - Book Five

The Gamble - Book Six

STAND ALONE NOVELLA

JUDGE ME NOT - A Billionaire Single Mom Christmas Novella

ABOUT THE AUTHOR

Amazon Bestselling Author

Maggie Cole is committed to bringing her readers alphalicious book boyfriends. She's been called the "literary master of steamy romance." Her books are full of raw emotion, suspense, and will always keep you wanting more. She is a masterful storyteller of contemporary romance and loves writing about broken people who rise above the ashes.

She lives in Florida near the Gulf of Mexico with her husband, son, and dog. She loves sunshine, wine, and hanging out with friends.

Her current series were written in the order below:

- All In (Stand alones with entwined characters)
- It's Complicated (Stand alones with entwined characters)
- Together We Stand (Brooks Family Saga - read in order)
- Behind Closed Doors (Read in order)
- Mafia Wars (Coming April 1st 2021)

Maggie Cole's Newsletter
Sign up here!

Hang Out with Maggie in Her Reader Group
Maggie Cole's Romance Addicts

Follow for Giveaways
Facebook Maggie Cole

Instagram
@maggiecoleauthor

Complete Works on Amazon
Follow Maggie's Amazon Author Page

Book Trailers
Follow Maggie on YouTube

Are you a Blogger and want to join my ARC team?
Signup now!

Feedback or suggestions?
Email: authormaggiecole@gmail.com

Made in the USA
Middletown, DE
09 August 2022